LEAVING

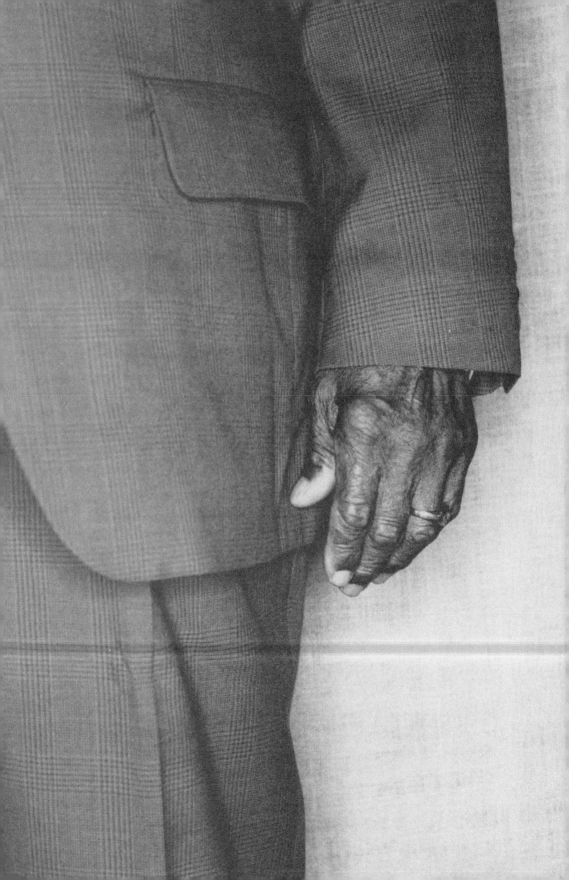

LEAVING

A NOVEL

RICHARD DRY

ST. MARTIN'S PRESS ❧ NEW YORK

www.stmartins.com

Acknowledgment is given for permission to quote from the following sources:

Fawcett Books: *Black Protest: History, Documents, and Analyses 1619 to the Present,* by Joanne Grant, editor. Copyright © 1968 by Joanne Grant. Used by permission of Fawcett Books, a division of Random House, Inc.

Harcourt Inc.: *Black Metropolis: A Study of Negro Life in a Northern City,* by St. Clair Drake and Horace R. Cayton. Copyright © 1945 by St. Clair Drake and Horace R. Cayton and renewed © 1973 by St. Clair Drake and Susan Woodson. Reprinted by permission of Harcourt Inc.

Hill and Wang: *From Plantation to Ghetto: An Interpretive History of American Negroes,* by August Meier and Elliott M. Rudwick. Copyright © 1966 by August Meier and Elliott M. Rudwick and renewed © 1994 by August Meier. Reprinted by permission of Hill and Wang, a division of Farrar, Straus & Giroux, LLC.

Scribner: *Manchild in the Promised Land,* by Claude Brown. Copyright © 1990 by Claude Brown. Reprinted by permission of Scribner, a division of Simon & Schuster.

University of Chicago Press: "Hagar and Her Children" from *The Negro Family in the U.S.* Copyright © 1948 by Edward Franklin Frazier. Used by permission of the University of Chicago Press.

Library of Congress Cataloging-in-Publication Data

Dry, Richard.
 Leaving / Richard Dry.—1st ed.
  p. cm.
 ISBN 0-312-28331-8
  1. African American families—Fiction. 2. Oakland (Calif.)—Fiction.

PS3604.R9 L43 2002
813'.6—dc21   2001041959

First Edition: March 2002

10 9 8 7 6 5 4 3 2 1

TO MY PAST, PRESENT, AND FUTURE:
MY MOTHER, FATHER, WIFE, AND FRIENDS

TO RUBY

AND TO THE KIDS:
MAY YOU KNOW THE RIVER

SOMETIMES I FEEL LIKE A MOTHERLESS
CHILD, A LONG WAY FROM MY HOME.

—Traditional, author unknown

THE END IS IN THE BEGINNING AND LIES
FAR AHEAD.

—Ralph Ellison, *Invisible Man*

FAMILY TREE

COMPILED BY P. LeROY

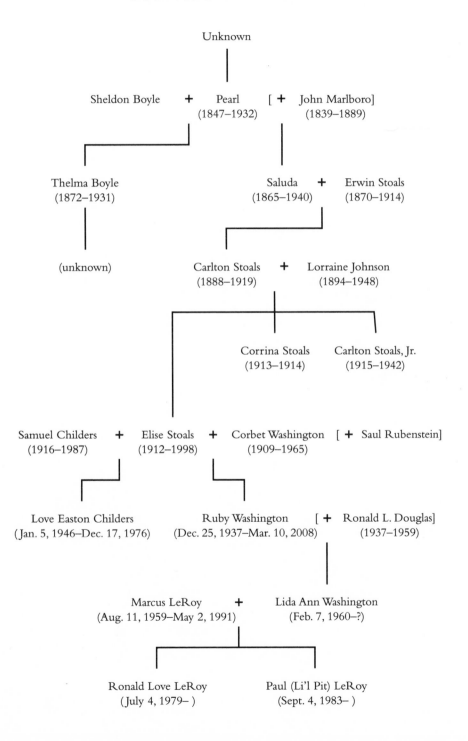

Unknown

Sheldon Boyle **+** Pearl **[+** John Marlboro]
(1847–1932) (1839–1889)

Thelma Boyle Saluda **+** Erwin Stoals
(1872–1931) (1865–1940) (1870–1914)

(unknown) Carlton Stoals **+** Lorraine Johnson
(1888–1919) (1894–1948)

Corrina Stoals Carlton Stoals, Jr.
(1913–1914) (1915–1942)

Samuel Childers **+** Elise Stoals **+** Corbet Washington **[+** Saul Rubenstein]
(1916–1987) (1912–1998) (1909–1965)

Love Easton Childers Ruby Washington **[+** Ronald L. Douglas]
(Jan. 5, 1946–Dec. 17, 1976) (Dec. 25, 1937–Mar. 10, 2008) (1937–1959)

Marcus LeRoy **+** Lida Ann Washington
(Aug. 11, 1959–May 2, 1991) (Feb. 7, 1960–?)

Ronald Love LeRoy Paul (Li'l Pit) LeRoy
(July 4, 1979–) (Sept. 4, 1983–)

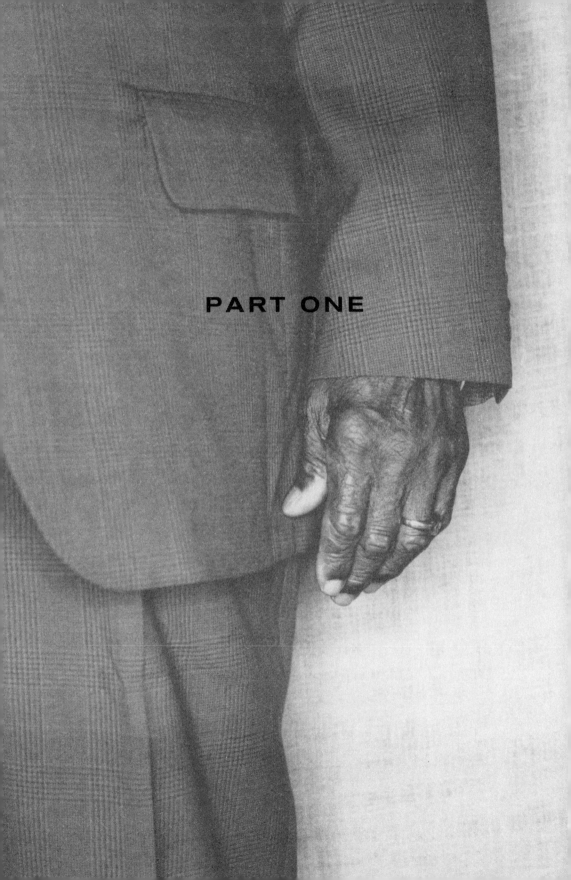

PART ONE

CHAPTER 1A

ON JUNE 19, 1959, Ruby Washington traveled through Texas on a bus from Norma, South Carolina, to Oakland, California, with her thirteen-year-old half brother, Love Easton Childers. They sat across from the toilet, the septic fumes souring the air. Ruby's forehead rested against the hot window, and Easton, or Love E as Ruby alone could call him—which she pronounced "Lovey," like an adoring wife—slept on her loose shoulder, his mouth open, bouncing with the bus over the highway. Even in sleep, he brushed at his cheek with his fingertips as if shooing away a persistent fly.

Ruby pulled her brother's hand from his face and held it down in her lap. At twenty-one, she was a large woman. She'd always been big-boned with meaty hips and shoulders, a body shaped like an acoustic guitar. She watched a stretch of fence alongside the highway, small purple and yellow flowers growing against the lower rung of wire. A red-tailed hawk lifted itself from one of the posts and flew over the farmland, then circled smoothly above the houses and gentle hills. She followed the hawk with her eyes, tilting her head and feeling every turn of its wings as it sailed across all that luxurious space.

The bus hit a pothole and Ruby held both hands on her stomach. She waited, holding her breath. She'd never heard of a baby being shaken loose from a bumpy ride, but already her life had been filled with things she'd never heard of happening to anyone else. It wasn't even a baby yet, just a kidney bean inside her, but Ruby felt her as much as a full-grown baby girl. She imagined her with Ronald's dark eyes and his long, beautiful lashes. The sadness started to grip her again in her belly. Then the tightness of anger spread through her chest. There are certain things people never imagine living without, and faced with their loss, their minds make up ways to circumnavigate the truth of their senses, inventing conspiracies or forgotten clues. It had been so dark when they'd taken him away; she'd had to leave town before the funeral; the paper had talked about sending him to Charleston. She preferred to believe in false hope rather than despair. She had decided it was her God-given duty.

She looked out the window and searched for the hawk again. It was climbing higher into the clouds, and as she watched, it swooped out of sight. When it was gone, she realized how tightly her teeth were clamped together, and she forced herself to breathe out a steady, circular stream of air. She had to forget. For she feared that the tightness and pain of memory would suffocate her child right there inside her.

So she told a story. She put her hand on Easton's hair and spoke to him softly:

"Love E, didn I ever tell you 'bout dat boy who gon chasin de angels?"

Easton shook his head and kept his eyes closed. He spoke English only as Ronald had taught him, what he called "News English," but Ruby's stories in her own voice were like her soft lap to rest his mind into.

"Well he wasn no fool, dis boy. He foun hisself a fishin net an a fishin hook an he was waitin up in de tree for de angels to pass on by. He knew dem angels has to come by soon fo his mama who jus pass on dat night. Well de firs angel dat come on by fell right into his trap an he scoop him up wit his net. You listnin to me?"

"Mmm-hmm."

"Well de angel had to give him wishes. 'I know what you want,' say de angel. 'You want fo me to bring yo mama back to life.'

" 'No,' say de boy. 'I want a great big castle.' An wit a clap a lightnin he had a big ole castle. Den he aks for all de money in de worl, an wit a clap a lightnin a whole hill a money an gole rise up.

" 'Now dis is yo las wish,' say de angel. 'I know you got to want fo me to bring yo mama back to life.'

" 'No,' say de boy.

" 'Well what you want den? Tell me quick, so I can go on 'bout my regular business.'

4

" 'Well,' say de boy. 'I want you to make me White.'

" 'Make you White?'

" 'Yes.'

" 'You sure dat's what you want, more den bring yo mama back to life?'

" 'Yes,' say de boy. 'Now make me White.'

" 'Alright,' say de angel.

"De boy hold his arm up to his face to watch his skin turn. A clap a lightnin wen off, an he watch his arm fo his color to change. He waited, but nothin happen. De boy look up at de angel and yell, 'You got to keep yo promise, you an angel.' But den he see somethin movin round de corner of de house. Out from a bush step his mama, standin tall and mean as a mountain lion, walkin at de boy like she gonna et him up. Well de boy gone jus 'bout out a his mine.

" 'But you promised to make me White,' yell de boy. He jump out the tree and start to run away.

" 'I sure did,' say de angel. 'An jus look at yo'self, you as white as a sheet.' " Ruby shook her head and laughed, but Easton had fallen asleep again.

She looked at her half brother drooling a little on her sleeve. He was now her responsibility. And she was glad for it, for that distraction, and for someone who could remind her, even in his sleepy silence, that she was not alone with her memories.

She'd never left South Carolina before, never gone farther than fifty-three miles to Charleston—and there only once, when she was seven, to see a parade for her real papa, who supposedly hadn't come home from the war in Europe. Just as she was getting to understand how there could be a parade for someone who didn't show up to the parade, she found out that he had come back after all, just not back to them. There was no telling what kind of man her real papa, Papa Corbet, would be, but if he beat Love E like Papa Samuel had, she promised herself that she'd take him away. They could always try to live on their own in California.

THEY PULLED INTO the Oakland Greyhound station at ten in the morning. As Ruby sat on a bench and waited for the driver to fetch baggage, she unfolded a black bandanna in her lap, shielded her eyes from the sun with one hand, and counted it again: forty-seven dollars. All the money they'd earned from the last batch of dresses. Among the bills was a slip of paper with her father's address and a phone number for the West Oakland Army Base.

Easton played cards with a boy from the bus. Ignoring all the colored children, Easton had chosen to play with this White boy on the ride over, even though he hadn't known crazy eights and Easton hadn't known gin. They'd settled on hearts, which Easton hadn't known either, but the boy taught him well enough to win two out of five hands.

The boy's mother came over and picked her son up by the wrist.

"All right, that's plenty." She brushed off his pants, licked two of her fingers, wet back his hair, and pulled him away to stand among the adults. Easton wandered back to Ruby, who was watching for the trunk they'd brought.

"I thought your father was killed in the war," he said to his half-sister. He brushed his right cheek with his fingertips.

"I guess he ain't dead no more." She scooted over on the carved wooden bench and patted it for Easton to come sit next to her.

"Is your father big?" he asked.

"I don't recollect."

"Does he scold with a switch?"

"You find out soon enough."

Easton watched his friend leave with his mother and father.

"They ours," Ruby said, pointing to a dark green trunk. "Help me carry it." Inside the trunk were all the belongings they could fit for both of them, including the sewing machine. They carried the trunk out front and convinced a cabby to take them for a dollar.

On the drive, they passed through the heart of West Oakland. Seventh Street was alive with people—colored people. Ruby had never seen so many finely dressed men, bustling along the street in their double-breasted jackets, and women with flowered hats (and some in fur coats!) standing in the doorways of shops just as if they owned them. Bright red trolley cars ran down the middle of the street in both directions. On either side were stores packed shoulder to shoulder in the brick buildings. Every shop had a striped awning. Long vertical signs jutted out from their facades with bold names announcing their services and proprietors: Borden's Candy and Ice Cream, Adeline Station Hotel, GLOW, Dine and Dance at Slim Jenkins' Supper Club. There were furniture stores and barbershops, beauty salons and soda fountains, all patronized by Negroes and, as far as she could tell, all run by Negroes too. There were Negro shoe-shine boys shining Negroes' shoes, white-jacketed Negro pharmacists in the pharmacy, and Negro lawyers sitting behind their desks in the window-front law offices; it was like the movies, but everybody had turned colored.

"Tremendous," Easton said, his favorite of Ronald's words. He pressed his finger up against the window. The produce bins on the sidewalk were piled high with oranges, striped watermelons, apples, grapes, plums, and peaches. "I bet those peaches came from South Carolina. Johnston is the peach capital of the world, you know?"

"That fruit might have come from China," said the cabby. "You're in a port town, man. You think it's fancy now, you should have seen it before the bridge. The ferries used to cross to the city from here, so everyone came on through town. The trains were running and we were still building ships over at Moore's. Roast beef *and* pork chops every night, man." He stretched his arm across the top of the seat as if relaxing after a good meal. "Then come the airplanes and there's no need for the Pullman porters either. Trust me, man, people don't spend the way they used to. Some of the shops already moved out."

He turned the cab off Seventh Street and headed away from the Southern Pacific train yards. "Then they went and built this monster-ugly contraption." He pointed up toward a freeway overpass. "Who can blame them wealthier folk for leaving, the way things are getting."

They turned one block north of the freeway. "This here is your street, man, Cranston Avenue—still a nice street. Lots of these blocks were wiped out for the housing project. I know a woman who, to this day, still comes back and stares through the fence to where her house used to be." The cabby stopped and helped them unload. "They didn't touch certain streets, but even the ones spared can't never be the same. Lost that sense of security."

The cabby left Ruby and Easton staring at the house from the side-walk, their green trunk in front of them. It was a Victorian, two stories high, with a cellar level below the stairs and a dark red coat of paint, like the Palmers' barn in Norma. Burgundy lace curtains hung in all the windows, and an American flag stuck out from the side of the black mailbox. Ruby looked down at the address on the paper and then up and down the block. The rest of the houses on the street were just as pretty and brilliant, each one painted its own colorful personality—bright pink, yellow, turquoise.

An older White man dressed in all black with a black hat and long curly black hair streaming down his cheeks nodded to them, then walked up the steps to the house. He ate fleshy purple grapes and spit the seeds out onto the lawn as he opened the door and went inside.

"It looks like your father doesn't live here anymore," Easton said.

"Maybe he be de lanlord."

"Maybe we should go over to the army base."

"How we gonna get a cab here?"

"You can stay with the trunk and I'll run to that main street."

"Maybe dis ain't de right block."

The front door opened again and out stepped a thin, middle-aged man with mahogany-brown skin. He wore black horn-rimmed glasses and a brown derby cap and smoked a pipe.

"May I help you?"

"We jus lookin at your pretty house," said Ruby. Her heart pounded so fast that she rested her hand on her brother's shoulder to steady herself.

The man turned and looked up at his home. "Yep. This here's a GI Bill."

Easton considered the house carefully, as if he were going to draw it:

the front two windows of the second story looked like square eyes facing the street and the bottom bay window like a mouth with the stairs as a tongue hanging out of the left side.

"How come you named your house Bill?" he asked.

"Well that's a good question. You hear that, Saul?" He turned and looked back into the house. "He asks why I named this house GI Bill."

"Well," a voice came from inside, "it's because the government gives you the house and then they send you a bill for it." The man with the pipe laughed.

"Well, he is a pretty house, sir," Ruby said. "Thank you for lettin us look at him."

"He's even prettier on the inside," the man said. "You come take a look."

Ruby and Easton didn't move. The man took off his cap and wiped his forehead with his arm.

"*Entrez vous, mes enfants,*" he said. He turned and walked back into the house, leaving the door open. "And bring your trunk on in with you. We can't have your mama's trunk gettin all left out in the weather."

CHAPTER 1B

LIDA DIDN'T USE an alarm clock on the first day of seventh grade. Too loud. She woke up on her own, from a little pocket of fear that kept something alert in her at all times.

"Rabbit, rabbit, rabbit," she whispered, as she did every morning before moving a muscle, then crawled under her sheets and came out at the bottom end. She sat up and saw the new dress that Ruby, her mother, had sewn for her—canary yellow with a white lace collar, lying across the dark green trunk at the foot of her bed. She stayed in her nightgown, folded the dress over her arm, and tiptoed down the hall-way. Ruby had already gone to work and Lida crept past her uncle Easton's door.

"Rabbit, rabbit, rabbit," she prayed silently. There were days when he woke up at the sound of a cough and days he slept through a car crash. The uncertainty kept her perpetually on edge.

So as not to wake him, she had everything she needed in the first-floor bathroom. For weeks now she'd transferred her toiletries down-stairs one by one—toothbrush, hairbrush, Vaseline—pretending to have just absentmindedly left them there.

She walked gently down the stairs, pausing after each step. At the bottom of the staircase, she turned to the wooden ball atop the handrail. She bent down and, taking the deep mahogany sphere in both hands as if it were a baby's head, licked the wood twice, from middle to top. It tasted waxy and bitter, but the more bitter and tormenting, the better. She let out her breath, and although she'd made it downstairs, she held her arms close to her body. She went into the bathroom, closed the door, and washed her face with lavender soap, beginning in a circular motion on her forehead and then moving counterclockwise. She showered only in the evenings, when her mother was home and Easton was out. She finished soaping, then rinsed and looked in the mirror at all the ways her face had failed her: hundreds of little bumps on her stone-black forehead, her nose too wide, her lashes too long. He was right—she was too dark and ugly. She pulled the kerchief off her head and applied a coat of Vaseline to her hair.

When she was done fixing up, Lida poured herself a bowl of corn-flakes and ate alone at the dining room table, taking special care to lay out the red cloth place mat so the dish wouldn't knock loudly against the table. She let the flakes soak in the milk until they were soggy and didn't crunch; then she ate slowly—listening.

As she chewed, she looked at the sepia photographs on the living room wall: Grandma Elise, whom she'd never met, and Grandpa Corbet, whom she couldn't remember meeting, in his army uniform, half smiling, half looking at something in the background. He'd died when Lida was only five, and he was young in that picture, so when Lida imagined her father, Ronald, she mostly imagined that picture of Corbet.

She cleared her dish, washed it, and put the place mat back in the drawer; she erased all signs of herself, nothing to make him think of her, nothing to make it her fault if he did.

She took the quarter for the bus off the shiny oak vanity and hopped to the doormat on one socked foot as quietly as possible, though she couldn't help but make a hollow thudding. This last test was obligatory now that she was nearly out, to prove that she deserved to make it.

Her shoes sat by the front door. She had come to putting them there so she didn't have to make any more noise upstairs, but she told Ruby it was out of respect for the wooden floors. Ruby liked the idea so much that she insisted everyone do it. But if Lida saw Easton's hard, scuffed black loafers touching her shoes, she picked hers up and moved them to the other side of the entrance.

It was not yet six-thirty in the morning when she stepped outside. Cranston Avenue was still silent and dark. She walked with her head down, careful to step over the cracks in the sidewalk. Other children came out of their houses now. So loud—slamming their doors, running across the street, calling to each other. The recklessness of it made her heart freeze. She didn't talk to anyone, and no one talked to her. Except for Marcus LeRoy.

She recognized Marcus from behind by the sky-blue pick in his hair. In elementary school they used to play kickball together on the street. Then he started to come over after school, and sometimes they danced to Easton's James Brown records in the living room if nobody was home. But over the last summer, Marcus's father had made him help out at the health food store, so she hadn't hardly seen him at all.

Marcus sat on the bus bench at San Pablo and turned around to wave to her as she approached. He smiled. He looked different. His shoulders were just starting to fill out and he seemed taller. She hugged her purple notebook to her chest, held the sides of her bare arms, and whispered without moving her lips, "Rabbit, rabbit, rabbit."

CHAPTER 1C

"FUCK YOUR MAMA!"

Love, Lida's eldest child, clenched his long fingers into fists; his bony knuckles sharpened, and his manicured nails cut into the palms of his hands. His arms stiffened at the sides of his thin body, and he glared at the White attendant, his eyes squinting and venomous.

The attendant didn't challenge Love by looking directly back at him, which he feared would just escalate the child's behavior. Instead, he looked away, at the floor, at the ceiling, out toward the courtyard of the school. But Love had an acute sense of fear; on the streets, fear in others was not only a sign of their inability to defend themselves, it was a sign that they could not control a situation, could not keep *you* safe. It was the same with the attendants here, on the inside, at Los Aspirantes. The fearful attendants were the ones who didn't keep the other kids from kicking you under the table, from punching you in line, from sneaking into your room with a nail.

Los Aspirantes School for Severely Emotionally Disturbed Children had two blocks of classrooms. The lower block served day-treatment children, those who still lived with their parents, grandparents, aunts, or in foster care but had been kicked out of the public schools, or assessed under AB 3632 as needing more intensive mental health provisions. The upper block schooled kids from the residential program, the group homes, each of which housed six children, staffed 24-7 in three shifts. Some of these kids had been removed from their homes under the Child Welfare Protection Act, then failed in their foster placement due to violent or destructive behavior. Others had been released to Los Aspirantes after serving time in Juvi and had become 601s, criminal wards of the court. In cases like Love's, they were released from Langley Porter Psychiatric Hospital after a 5150, a forty-eight-hour hold for being a danger to self or others, then placed in the group home with the agreement of their legal guardians. For Love, this was his grandmother, Ruby.

"Take your time-out in the quiet-room to refocus, Love." The attendant pointed out the back door to a small carpeted room, a padded cell with a rope attached to the outside door handle. Each upper-block classroom had a quiet-room outside to contain the children when they blew up.

"Fuck you, dog! You better stand back!" Love walked into the courtyard and the attendant followed closely. At thirteen, Love was tall enough to reach up and smack the top of the door frame. He kicked the plastic chair in front of the guinea-pig cage, stopped, and turned back.

"Take your time-out in the quiet-room, Love." They stood facing each other, the boy rigid, his jaw clenched and bulging below his high, sculptured cheekbones. The attendant continued to look away; he pointed to the corner of the darkened cell where he expected Love to walk.

Love swung, twisting his body from his hips. His fist struck the left lens of the man's glasses, cutting his cheek in a semicircle and breaking the bridge of his nose. The glasses skidded across the courtyard, and the attendant covered his face with both hands.

Love ran back into the classroom. Tom, a tall Irish man with a shaved head, grabbed him in the doorway. Love hit him in the forehead, but Tom looked straight at Love and caught the boy's flailing arms. He held his wrist and reeled him in, turned him around, and bear-hugged him from behind. He wrapped Love's arms across his chest, locking one elbow under the other like a straitjacket, then turned to his side and pushed the boy into the quiet-room with his hip and held him face forward in the corner.

When Tom was sure that Love was completely immobilized, his arms trapped between his own body and the wall, he let go of the boy's wrists and pushed with one hand on the center of his back. With the other hand, Tom reached down and picked up the tail end of the rope to the door, then ran out of the room, pulling the door behind him. Love had only enough time to turn and yell before the door shut flush with the inside wall.

"White-Ass Nigger Mother Fucker!" He kicked the handleless door. "Bitch, Mother Fucker, Faggot-Ass Bitch. I'll cap your fucking punk ass." He kicked the door again. He couldn't do damage from inside the quiet-room, yet he struck out even more recklessly, hitting all the walls in a helicopter-like torrent. "Fuck your mother, dog! I'll bust her face and stuff her in a garbage can." He punched the small, square, reinforced-plastic window in the upper center of the door. "Your mama sucks dick for a baggy. Your mama's a crack-ho fiend!"

He walked to the back wall and kicked it with his red Air Jordan sneakers, a Christmas present from the residential house manager. He hit the wall again, listlessly this time, his fingers in a loose fist, half grazing the carpet. He then walked to the far corner where he had been instructed to stand.

"I'm taking my t-i-m-e-o-u-t." He spelled "time-out," as if he couldn't bring himself to say the word. He stood unmoving, arms at his sides, his face five inches from the wall. There was no response from Tom, and he didn't expect any. Love stayed that way, frozen, for three minutes.

As he waited, he watched a line of ants crawl up to the ceiling. He chose one black ant and blew on it with a quick, solid burst. The ant changed direction and ran back toward the bottom of the wall, antennae flapping in panic. He blew at it again and let it run for a while. With each blow, the ant changed direction, frantically running from the invisible force attacking him.

There was no real time inside the quiet-room, only one long extended series of moments. A minute never ended or began until the attendant on the outside said that it did, so there was no way to measure how close or far you were from getting out, and this complete lack of control and the sense that you'd been forgotten was what tested you the most, more than being trapped inside. He'd swear it had been an hour, that the veins in his neck were about to burst from frustration, that he couldn't stop himself from yelling even if it meant getting more time in the room; only the ants moving in their determined trails kept him distracted enough to stay calm.

At the end of the three minutes, the door to the quiet-room slowly cracked open.

"Have a seat, Love. Your sit-time will start now." Love sat in the corner with his knees up to his chest. Dark tracks of dried tears streaked his face. He could not see Tom through the open door, only the rope held taut across the space and a leg of the plastic chair.

Love sat silently for twenty minutes. His breathing slowed. He knew the inside of the quiet-room intimately but examined it again, every scratch mark on the walls, every stain in the carpet from some kid urinating or defecating. There was a Plexiglas ceiling over the lightbulb and a vent for letting in air. Behind the vent, a fan turned with a slight hum and ticking, light cutting through it as it spun. He counted the ticks, trying to beat his own personal best, but repeatedly lost count before three hundred. He heard Tom turn the page of a magazine and tap his foot.

"Did I b-l-i-n-d him?" Love spelled softly. The rope went slack and Tom nudged the door open wider. Tom had worked with Love since the boy had arrived at Los Aspirantes four years earlier. They could see each other completely now. Tom had a red splotch on his forehead.

"Are ya worried ya mighta hurt Rick?" Tom asked.

Love shrugged his pointy shoulders.

"So ya think ya blinded him?"

"I cut his eye."

"How does that make ya feel?"

Love shrugged again. They both watched a spider walk across the wooden strip in the doorway.

"Can ya tell me how ya feel about cuttin his eye?"

"T-r-e-m-e-n-d-o-u-s," Love spelled.

"Ya don't look tremendous."

"You can't tell me how I feel, dog!"

"I didn't tell ya how ya feel; I told ya how ya look. Don't ya think your anger has anything ta do with ya havin ta leave?"

Love puckered his lips and sucked in through his nose. Tom yanked the rope taut, but before the door slammed shut, Love spat a wad of saliva that hit Tom in the knee.

"No, Bitch!"

SANTA RITA JAIL

HE CAME TO the front of the recreation room, stood on the table, and spoke to the men:

We were not the first people to be slaves, and we won't be the last. But all the knowledge about slavery—about how to break a man down, how to keep us in check, how to make us forget we ever had the power or right to be free—all the experience with slave-making, from the time the Jews were slaves in Egypt and before that, went into our enslavement. If you want to know how to make a slave the right way, you can learn from the past. And if you want to learn how to be a free man, you've got to learn from the past too. The most dangerous part of having been a slave is not knowing what it means to be free. You've got to know how you were robbed, know what was taken, before you can get it back.

What's slavery got to do with me? you ask. That foolishness ended a hundred and fifty years ago; what's that got to do with me sitting in jail right now, over a decade into the new millennium? Didn't we leave all that behind us?

I know what you're thinking: what's that got to do with me lightin up, or bustin a cap into some punk's head, or my father taking a switch to my ass? You say, not all Black men are in jail, in fact most are not, so it must be my own damn fault that I'm here and not CEO of Ford Motor Company, or a congressman, or a lawyer, or a teacher, or a busboy.

And it is.

You heard me: it is.

And it ain't.

It is and it ain't.

You are an individual, but you are on a raft. The limits of that raft are the limits of who you think you are and how you think you have to be. That's true if you're Black, White, Red, Brown, or Yellow. Right now you don't even see that you're on a raft. You don't know that your raft is floating down a river, the River of History, and that the events of the past have surrounded you and brought you to this place, and that unless you get off of this raft, you are going to stay in the course the River has been pushing you. But first you've got to recognize that you're on a raft, and to see how the River has surrounded you to make you believe in your limitations. You must know rivers.

I'm calling you from the shore.

I'm telling you to dive into your history. It's your job to learn about that River, how wide it is, how strong the current is. Without the knowledge of the past, you're likely to drown in it by making the same mistakes as those who came before you, or jump right back onto that raft, and worse yet, pace back and forth on that raft forever, like a beast in this jail-cage, until it takes you right over the edge.

CHAPTER 2A

TO RUBY, THE inside of GI Bill on Cranston Avenue was like a church. Not a church she had been in, but the way she believed a church should be, beautiful and frightening, with polished wood floors and high ceilings. The front windows arched across most of the living room wall facing the street, and the burgundy lace curtains blossomed in an intricate pattern of roses and thorny stems.

"I told your mother she should come on out with you," Corbet said, as he took them on a tour of their new home. "If you were in so much danger, why was she so safe? I asked her. But she said she wouldn't be herself if she left the South. I said, 'Elise, I don't think that would be such a bad thing,' but she didn't take to that." Behind the living room was a large kitchen with wooden cabinets and a fancy refrigerator that made its own ice cubes.

"I sure hope your mother taught you to cook," he said to Ruby. "I miss pork chops with mustard and onions, and fried chitlins. All Saul knows how to fix is spaghetti and soup." He stood up straight and looked directly at her. "Besides, there are a lot of people who'll hire a woman who can cook and clean."

"She's not a maid," Easton spat out. "She's a seamstress."

"Hush," Ruby whispered. "I do all the cookin an cleanin you want. An I serve up some fancy corn fritters when I put my mine to it."

"Très bien, car je suis affamé."

Easton raised his eyebrows and laughed, not a sincere laugh but forced, like he was trying to insult Corbet and make something happen. He covered his mouth and waited. Ruby watched Corbet to see what he would do. There was no question what Papa Samuel would have done if Easton had laughed at him: he would have picked up the iron that sat on the counter and thrashed him across the face with the cord.

Corbet walked to Easton slowly. He raised his hand in the air and Easton closed his eyes.

"Est-ce que j'ai l'air stupide?"

Easton opened his eyes.

"Repeat after me," Corbet said. "Raise your hand and repeat."

Easton raised his hand.

"Je suis un nègre et j'en suis fier."

Easton laughed again, then tried it.

"Well, listen to you, a regular man of the underground. A man of the Resistance."

THE UPSTAIRS HAD three bedrooms. Corbet told them to drop their trunk in the front room to the left and said that Easton could have the room across the hall. They were not to go into the back room because that was Saul's. But he knew better than to tempt curiosity, so he opened the door and showed them. In the corner was a rolltop desk next to a bookcase and, on the far side, a dresser with black slacks folded on it. The room had all the fixings of a bedroom, without a bed.

"Where's he sleep?" Easton asked.

"He stays with me when he's here." Corbet closed the door firmly and didn't offer any more explanation. He took them back to Ruby's new room to get them set up.

Within a week of their arrival, Ruby had her sewing machine running all day while Corbet went to his job at the docks. They'd enrolled Easton at McClymonds. The school was integrated, which he had never experienced, but still there were very few White children. Out of thirty-five students in his class, five were White, two were Chinese, and one Japanese.

He quickly found his favorite class. His math teacher, Miss Claudia Grossbalm, was young and serious. She paced across the front of the room with her head down, her dress pressed against her body by the force of her movement, deep into her explanation of an algebraic equation as though she were rediscovering her own religious conviction; at times she would even raise the math book in the air like a Bible, revealing small stains of sweat under her arms. She was strict with the boys in the back and didn't take any of their lip, strong and curt, the way Easton had never seen a White woman act before.

"Quiet, Mr. Waters," she chastised a boy whom most teachers ignored out of fear. But she continued with her lesson, and he had no opening to respond, for she was not confronting him, simply pushing aside an obstacle in the way of her mathematical quest.

"Now!" She turned to the class suddenly, breathing hard through her nose and looking out over the faces with passionate and hopeful eyes. "Who can tell me how to find twenty-five percent of XY when X equals five and Y equals one-half X?" There was a silence so strong it sucked at the marrow of every student. Easton could not bear to see the slow transformation from rapture to despair on Miss Grossbalm's face. He could not help but raise his hand.

"Yes, Mr. Childers." He stood, as he had been taught to do in Norma, and a few kids chuckled. He felt the eyes from the back row upon him, yet the smile of anticipation on Miss Grossbalm's lips drew him on.

"Point two five times five times two point five."

"Yes, and then?" She practically ran to the board to write out his equation.

"Uppity nigger," he heard from the back of the room. "Whitey." He was lighter-skinned than most of his family, but he'd always seen that as a source of pride.

Miss Grossbalm turned. "Mr. Waters, stand up."

"But it wasn't me," Charles Waters said without conviction. She never involved herself in a tug-of-war. If it wasn't him, it was one of his lackeys.

"Stand up and come here to the board to finish this equation."

At this challenge, Charles stood, pulled his shirt out of his pants, and swaggered up the aisle toward the front of the room where Miss Grossbalm held out the chalk. It took him a long time to make it to the front row. He forced a confident smile, but everyone knew he could not possibly solve the equation. As he passed Easton, he covered his mouth and coughed into his hand: "Daddy's a homo." The rest of the class laughed. Charles sneezed, "Up the ass."

Easton knew the time would come when he'd have to settle into the pecking order with the back-row boys, and the sooner he got that over with, the better. He grabbed Charles by the hair and brought his face down onto his knee with the solid force that ensured he and Charles would become close friends in the future. At that time, kids in Oakland didn't carry knives like everyone did in Norma, so the whole class screamed when Easton pulled a blade out of his back pocket and brandished it toward the rest of the back row. Charles was still on the ground when Miss Grossbalm walked directly to Easton and took the knife from his hand. That's when he knew he was in love. She led him by the wrist and walked him to the principal's office.

He was suspended for a day. It would have been much longer had Miss Grossbalm not explained that Mr. Waters had antagonized him, which was no surprise to the principal. But he did punish Easton for bringing a knife to school, and he did call Corbet.

For this act of self-defense, Papa Samuel would have been proud of him, not for being suspended—for that, he still would have gotten a whipping—but for having fought back and won. However, Corbet was different in every way from Papa Samuel, and Easton didn't know what to expect.

WHEN EASTON RETURNED home, Corbet sat him down on the couch in the living room and then went to his rocking chair. Ruby came up behind Easton and put her hands on his shoulders, watching her father carefully. He pinched tobacco between his thumb and forefinger and ground it into his pipe very slowly, as if he were squeezing the life out of it. He lit the pipe and leaned back in his chair. Easton wiped his cheek repeatedly as he looked around the room for a switch or any long piece of wire. The only thing he saw was a thick leather belt, and that was still firmly wrapped around Corbet's waist.

It was a long time before anyone spoke. Ruby shifted her weight a few times in the silence. Finally she said, "Sometimes I think we should jus tie all de boys to dey desks at school." Corbet nodded his head slowly and took another drag from his pipe. The tobacco glowed orange for a moment. It wouldn't be the first time he'd been burned, Easton thought. Ruby continued: "But dat jus remine me of de racehorse dat all de folks love in Greenwood. Dis horse beat all de udder horses in town and beat all de horses out to Orangeburg County, an all de people love dis horse 'cause it be fast and beautiful, wid his shiny muscles on his legs. But when dis horse ain't racin, it still had a whole lotta mischief. He always jumpin out de fence and runnin into someone's field. He run 'round an et all de carrots and de turnips and run through de rice patties, an jus do a general stompin all over. It was jus in his nature to be wile. But de people got real mad 'cause dey losin dey crop. So de owner, he tie him up to de barn. Well de horse start neighin and kickin and makin all kind of a racket all night long. So de owner start to whip him to make him stop. But de horse jus get madder and madder. He stop while de man whip him, but when de man come out again, he see dat de barn door done been kicked down. So he made de horse lay down and he tied de animal's legs to de stable. But dat nex night, de horse pull de ropes so hard, he break his own leg, and de nex day de man had to take him out an shoot him. Lose hisself a mighty fine racehorse."

Easton looked at his sister in bewilderment.

"Tell me this," Corbet said. "Who started it?"

Easton stood straight up in front of the couch, as though he were answering a question in the classroom. "I'll tell you I sure enough finished it. He didn't get a chance to hit me. Not one boy could take me in that whole school."

"You sound awfully proud of yourself."

"Yes sir."

"What did he do to start the fight?"

"He said something to me."

"Something? Just spoke to you, so you hit him."

"He called me a name."

"What did he say?"

Easton looked straight at Corbet but didn't answer. He measured his new father's eyes, his ability to catch a lie. There was a white glaze over their color, like a dog who was going blind.

"What did he say," Corbet repeated, "that made you risk getting kicked out of school and ruining your future?"

"He called me a nigger," Easton said.

"He didn't call you no nigger!" Corbet yelled. He stood up and came at him. "I'll call you nigger, nigger. You get called nigger ten times a day. Now you tell me what that boy said to you or you'll wish you were back in Carolina."

"He called me a faggot."

"A what?"

"A faggot! And he called you a faggot too. He said you take it up the ass."

"Stop that nastiness, Love E," Ruby yelled.

"He said you make him sick. He said you're unnatural as a tree growing into the ground!" Easton wiped his mouth and waited.

Corbet stared at him. Easton's nostrils flared and he clenched his fists. The cavernous space of the living room held Easton's epithets like the chiming of a clock. Corbet shook his head, turned, and sat back down in his rocking chair.

Ruby pulled Easton back by the shirt.

"Why are you sayin all this?" Ruby begged. But Easton ignored her and went on.

"So I took his face and I slammed it into my knee. He didn't get up even by the time I was walking out the door."

"And you think that makes me happy?" Corbet said. "You think that makes me proud of you?"

"I don't care."

Corbet lowered his pipe and looked into its ashes.

"Dat's just de kind of foolishness dat's gonna keep you from making somethin of yo'self," Ruby yelled. "What do you think Ronal would have said to you 'bout acting like some street nigger with no brains in yo head. Ronal was never suspended for fighting even once."

"And look where that got him: six feet under."

Ruby slapped him and looked as if she might slap him again, but Corbet stood and came between them.

"Come on. Come on. That's just the lesson he's got to unlearn. Why don't you go on in the kitchen. Let's have some dinner."

Ruby didn't move, but Corbet stared her down. She gave Easton one last hard look, turned, and went into the kitchen.

Easton and Corbert stood side by side and watched her go, mostly to avoid looking at each other. When the door closed behind her, Easton went back to the couch and Corbet went back to his chair. They sat and listened as pans crashed onto the stove.

"She's just trying to look out for you," Corbet said.

Easton nodded. They could picture Ruby's movements by the sounds she made, the opening of the refrigerator, the washing of the vegetables, the swish of the trash bag.

"Is it true?" Easton asked, looking down.

Corbet rocked back and forth. "What's that?"

Easton didn't reply. From the kitchen came the sound of fat sizzling in the hot frying pan.

"Oh," Corbet said. "You mean am I a faggot."

Easton looked at him and then away.

"I can't answer that, not in the way they mean it," Corbet said.

"Never mind." Easton shook his head and stood to go.

"No, I mind. Sit down." Corbert reloaded his pipe and lit it. "Does it bother you if I am?"

Easton shrugged.

"It's okay if it does. It still bothers me sometimes. That kind of talk gets into your blood. If people tell you that you're bad long enough, for whatever reason, you start to believing it. It takes a lot of strength to like yourself."

Easton did not look at him. In some ways he would have preferred a beating to this talk. At least in a beating there wasn't anything expected of him; it happened and it was over. But with this . . . Corbet seemed to be waiting for something. Easton stood again and brushed his palms against his slacks.

"I'm going to help her with supper," he said.

"Okay." Corbet watched him walk into the kitchen and disappear. He listened carefully, listened for what they might say about him, but they didn't speak. He turned to his phonograph, put the needle down, and sat back in his chair.

CHAPTER 2B

IN HIGH SCHOOL, Lida and Marcus often hung out in the back of his father's health food store. This night Lida scooted between the boxes and waited for him, her naked ankles showing between her tapered red pant legs and red pumps. Marcus tiptoed back into the storage room. He had a purple cloth band tied around his hair, which was fully grown out into a Hendrix Afro. He held a joint in one hand and sang into a jar of honey: " 'Have you ever been experienced?' "

Lida bent forward laughing, and Marcus sat down next to her. He pulled off the headband and wrapped it around her.

"It don't look right on my skinny face," he said. "You got your face already. It takes a man's face a long time to show, but a girl got her face when she start high school. That's how I know you'll be pretty for sure. Now!" He took a hit from the joint.

While he closed his eyes and inhaled, she scratched herself once on the arm for the one compliment, hard enough that a white line appeared. He held the joint out to her, and she pinched the end but didn't smoke it.

"Have a hit," he said.

"Say I'm bad," she said.

"You're bad, girl. You're so bad."

She took a drag off the joint.

"That's why I love you," he said.

"You lie."

"I'm not lyin."

"You don't love me. There ain't nothin about me to love."

"Sure there is. I love your big ole nose and your big ole dark eyes and your big ole big oles." He bent forward laughing and she slapped the back of his neck.

"Stop it," she said.

"Honest, though." He sat up, looked at her, his thick eyebrows raised. "If I was on my own, I'd marry you. We'd live in our own big ole house, and I'd take you with the band on tour all around the country."

This time Lida laughed, but Marcus's face was serious.

"That ain't right," he said. "Now! You gotta say you'd marry me."

Lida looked at her feet and put the toes of her pumps together, which meant it was going to be a wish she wanted to have come true. But before she made the wish, she tested him.

"You'd still marry me if I got a ugly ole mustache?"

Marcus looked at her face closely to make sure she didn't. "Sure. Yeah."

"What if I got no big ole big oles?"

"But you got 'em. Can't do nothin 'bout that." She had to move away from him, go somewhere so she could see him better. She stood up and crossed the concrete aisle, sat on a box and looked down at him in his white tee and bell-bottom jeans. He had wide shoulders and a hard chest from swimming at school.

"What'd you do if I got another man?" she asked.

"I see you most every night and every day at school and every morning 'fore school, and you're only with me."

"But if I did?"

"I'd kill him."

"How you gonna kill him?"

"I'd shoot his head off with a bullet."

"How you gonna shoot no one's head off?"

"We gotta gun right behind the register since the BART tracks went up."

"You a liar."

He scrambled to his feet and disappeared into the front of the shop. Lida waited without moving. There weren't any windows in the stockroom, and she stared at the ceiling where the smoke had settled around the hanging yellow lights. It was easy to forget in this room, forget that there was an outside.

"All right. Who is he?" Marcus returned with a black .38 revolver hanging by his leg. Lida looked at his big hand, his long fingers, the same ones that strummed his guitar, now gripping the handle of a gun with a firmness she'd never seen in him.

She turned away and walked slowly toward the back of the room; she tried to picture the confrontation—the shooting, the body—but she couldn't get herself to willingly conjure Easton's face. She turned and looked at Marcus instead.

"You're crazy," she said. "I ain't got no other man. Get yourself up outta here with that."

CHAPTER 2C

LOVE WAS IN the quiet-room almost every day that month, including the morning of his last day at the house. A residential staff member sat in the office holding the rope to the quiet-room door, only Love's shiny knees visible.

They'd carried him in an hour earlier during breakfast, all three staff on duty, one holding each arm and one wrapped around his legs. They carried him from his room, where he'd broken his window with the Sega, through the living room with the Rocket-ship Behavior-Level Board pasted to the wall, past the dining room table where the other five children sat on Silence, eating their Frosted Flakes.

"Wheeeeeeee. I'm a hornet!" he yelled, trying to kick the books off the cubbies as he went by.

"One thousand Bonus Points to everyone who's ignoring," said the staff holding Love's legs. The other kids turned back to the table and took slow sips of sugary milk off their spoons.

An hour later, Love was doing his sit-time against the back wall.

"Here's your buddy, Love." The staff guarding the quiet-room stood up and handed the rope to Tom. "You guys can talk, and then we'll process."

Tom still had a red splotch on his head where Love had hit him earlier that week. He wore beige drawstring pants and an orange and black West African dashiki.

"Hey there, Love." Tom took a seat in the plastic chair. "I'm sorry ta see ya havin a hard time." Love looked away at the ceiling and sucked his bottom teeth. "I wanted ta come say good-bye. I'm still angry about ya hittin me and Rick, but I didn't want ya ta leave and think that I'd always be angry." Love looked at a scar on his own leg. Tom leaned forward, put his elbows on his knees, and rested his chin in his hands. Right behind Love's head was the tiny hole in the wall that, four years earlier, Love had dug with a nail he'd managed to sneak in. Tom had held him in his lap and pried the nail from his fingers.

"I really hope things go well for ya at your grandmother's. I heard her house is very nice. I think you're capable of succeeding." That was the line the therapist had said wouldn't put too much pressure on him. Love let out a long, aggravated breath; he'd heard the rhetoric so often that he used it at the talent show as his imitation of White people.

The other children in the house were transitioning for school. They looked into the office one by one on their way to the bathroom to brush their teeth. Tom rubbed his forehead. "Anyway, I didn't come here ta lecture ya about things you've heard a million times."

The staff turned off the TV in the den, and the house went silent. The other children were sitting on the couch, and then they were called to line up at the door.

"Chris, you may line up," said a staff member. Chris walked to the door in an exaggerated gangsta swagger. "No. Go back to the couch and try it again, without the dramatics. No. Now take a time-out at the blue wall for not following directions." There was a possibility during a time like this that every kid in the house would go off and have to be restrained, just to let off some steam. They knew from the other kids who had left that it was likely they wouldn't see Love again, and there was no telling what kind of maniac would move into the house in his place. But Chris went to his time-out corner, hit the wall once, and then remained calm.

Love could hear every sound in the living room and imagine every move, down to the nervous smiles on the kids' faces.

"At least ya don't have ta put up with this anymore," Tom said.

Love didn't answer.

"Just try and keep outta trouble."

"Whatever."

"Listen. Rick could have pressed charges against ya for breaking his nose and ya'd be in juvenile hall again, right now."

"So?"

"Oh yeah, I forgot, ya don't care about that crybaby shit. Come on, man. I'm not telling ya this as a staff. I can't tell ya what ta do anymore. I'm tryin ta give ya the best honest advice I can. Ya can't go around doin that kind of shit if ya want ta have a chance in life. No college is gonna look at ya if ya've been in jail. I'd like ta see ya in the newspapers sometime: 'Dr. Love LeRoy talks ta bugs.' The Nobel Prize in bug studies, or whatever it is you call it." Tom waited for Love to respond.

"E-n-t-o-m-o-l-o-g-y," Love spelled.

"Right, entomology."

Another staff came in from the den. "Okay, man, the kids are in the van. We're taking off. Karl's gonna stay back with you." Tom nodded his head.

Love stared at the carpeted floor between his feet, picturing the kids leaving outside. He heard the front door slam and the van door slide open and shut. There was a moment before the van started, and Love knew Peter, or whichever staff was driving, had turned around to lecture Alfred about keeping his hands to himself during the ride. Then the van started, beeping as it reversed out of the driveway, and drove off.

The house fell silent except for the faint clanking of Karl doing dishes in the kitchen. Tom looked through a small locked window at the lush green leaves moving silently on a tree outside in a neighbor's yard. Now that Love was leaving, Tom couldn't wait to quit this job.

"How come nobody wants me?" Love asked. He didn't betray any emotion at all, as if he'd asked why flies have four thousand eyes. He stretched the edge of his Warriors shirt over his bare knees.

Tom shook his head and continued to stare out the window into the open space of the neighbor's backyard, at the sunlit rooftops beyond it, and the windblown, light blue sky. He remembered when Ronald Love LeRoy first came to Los Aspirantes and Jenn, his teacher, affectionately called him by his middle name one day. Love was outraged and felt teased until he noticed how much the girls liked it.

"I know ya've been here a long time," Tom said. "But your grandmother wants ya now. Everyone has ta leave here by fourteen. It has nothing ta do with you."

Love punched the back wall and Tom squeezed the rope more firmly. Karl came in to check out the sound.

"All right, Love." Tom stood up to go, thinking he might be aggravating the situation further. "All right," he said again. He slid his hand over his shaved head. "I hope that I see ya again, but I don't want ta promise that I will, because sometimes people just don't get around ta doing what they intend ta do. I want ya ta know that I care about ya. All right?" Love didn't look. Instead, he turned around and faced the wall.

"Well. Good luck ta ya in life, anyway. Just remember that we care about ya." Tom cleared his throat and waited a moment, but Love was silent, facing the wall in a self-imposed time-out. Tom considered how much Love had grown in four years, from someone more like a baby than a boy to a young man with a hard, set jaw. He wondered if Love was any better for being at Los Aspirantes, or if it had left him less prepared to return to the streets.

"Bye," Tom said. Love didn't say anything.

Tom left the office and walked slowly through the den to the front of the house. He opened the door and waited again, just in case. But there was nothing.

SANTA RITA JAIL

HE CAME TO the front of the recreation room, stood on the table and read from a book in his hand, *The Slave Narrative of Clay's John:*

They put all the men in the hold and lay us chained to the bare floor, up to six hundred in one ship. When the bottom was covered with bodies, they put in another shelf of us, two feet above our faces, so we couldn't sit up on the whole journey to the West Indies—three thousand miles, weeks bound to the floor. At night the rats would crawl over us, sniffing our faces, biting our infected sores. On the decks above, they raped our wives, our mothers, our sisters, our daughters, for their pleasure, but also so we would multiply their profits: every pregnant woman was a slave-and-a-half.

After long nights in the rolling sea, we'd wake up in our own vomit. Sometimes we'd wake up and the man chained to us would be dead from sickness, starvation, or beating. And sometimes that man was our brother or best friend or father.

They didn't want us to die—we were only valuable to them alive—but they wanted to maximize their profits, spend the least possible for transport and food, keep us weak and submissive, which meant they would at times incur the "affordable loss." Some of us who were too sick to take care of were thrown into the ocean to the sharks.

Eleven to fifteen million of us came across the Atlantic this way, to work in the "New World," not just North America, but Central America, the Caribbean, and South America, our families split up and torn apart, leaving behind everything that we knew, everything that made us who we were.

CHAPTER 3A

RUBY AND EASTON rode the 72 up San Pablo and then transferred to the 51 on University. Ruby wore an olive-green dress that was purposefully wrinkled, a dry-leaf-textured cotton with straps and a high V-neckline. She'd sponge-oiled her skin with vanilla, and it shone red on her meaty shoulders. She carried Lida wrapped in a yellow blanket of the same material, like a loose, wrinkled cocoon. Ruby had been in California only one year, but she was already going around to restock the department stores with her dresses.

Easton carried a multicolored stack of these dresses, his chin buried into the center and his eyes peering over the top. He wore Corbet's suit jacket, brown slacks, Corbet's dark brown loafers, a blue-collared dress shirt, and a dark brown tie. Corbet had even let him use his cologne for good luck; when Easton smelled himself, which he did often on the bus ride, he thought he smelled like a man.

They got off the 51 on Shattuck by the theater. Ruby kept her eyes down on the brick sidewalk as they weaved among people toward Woolcrest's Department Store.

"Love E, you ask her this time," Ruby said to him as they walked through the main lobby where women stood around large glass cases of perfume and scarves. The mirrors and counters reflected the lights from the chandeliers.

Ruby walked down the middle aisle toward the back of the store to a carpeted area filled with rows of dresses and ladies' undergarments. Easton could already feel his face heating up. Mrs. Usher met them at the back counter behind Women's Wear. She had a lazy left eye that drifted to the side. She came out from behind the counter, walked directly up to Ruby, and lifted the baby from her arms.

"Oh, this baby. This sweet child." She brushed her age-spotted White hands against Lida's cheeks. On her arm was a shiny gold bracelet, and on her left middle finger, a ring with a large diamond cut in a rectangle. Ruby stood silently watching Mrs. Usher rock Lida, watching as Lida crinkled her face and then began to wail.

"Oh. Oh. Don't cry." Mrs. Usher shook her head. "What a big, beautiful girl you have, Ruby. She looks just like you. Are you going to be a brilliant dressmaker like your mama?"

"I brought the new dresses," Ruby said.

"Oh good. Yes. Yes. Here." She handed the baby back to Ruby and directed Easton: "Set them on the counter, son. Oh, they're just beautiful. All the others sold like hot dogs. You have such an eye for color. Of course, it goes with your skin so beautifully. I've always believed coloreds have such beautiful skin. Look at these ugly, old yellow hands of mine."

Easton looked at her hands as she turned them above the glass counter, ugly and old, as she had said, yet somehow desirable, like the gaudy diamond on her finger.

"Thank God my husband can't see anymore. It's a blessing in disguise, I tell him."

Easton smiled at her joke, and she looked up at him and smiled too. Ruby nodded to him, but he looked at the carpet.

"You look very swell today, young man," Mrs. Usher said.

"Thank you, ma'am."

"Love E turn fourteen las month," Ruby said.

"Oh, that is marvelous. What a glorious age. What I wouldn't give to be fourteen again. I had a big crush on Joe Rolands. Oh my." Her eyes glazed and she touched her chest. "I can feel it still, right here. We had to audition for *Romeo and Juliet*, and I was so nervous. Well, don't tell Mr. Usher." She laughed again. Easton smiled.

"You said maybe you might have a place for him when he turn fourteen," Ruby said.

"Oh." Mrs. Usher looked straight at Easton as if she'd never seen him before. He brushed his cheek with his fingers and wished he still had the stack of dresses to hide behind. He looked down, unable to watch her left eye lazily drift around. But he felt her other eye stare at his shiny, kinky hair, his long forehead, and wide, flat nose. He felt his brown skin burning on him like hot mud and wished he could wash it off. He swallowed hard.

"Well actually, I just don't know what he could do," Mrs. Usher said.

"He's real good at math in school. He gets real good grades. He even teach me some."

"I could work the register," Easton said quietly. He lifted his eyes to see her reaction.

"Oh no." Mrs. Usher shook her head. "You couldn't handle the money." She looked up the aisle toward the front counter where a man in a tie and gold watch was setting a perfume advertisement straight. "No, you couldn't do that. You'd have to have experience with money to do that."

"He helps me at home with the dresses," Ruby said. "Maybe he could work in this department. He can tailor the clothing already. He's good with pins."

"Well." Mrs. Usher picked up one of the new dresses and unfolded it. She shook it out and hung it on a rack behind her. With her back to them she said, "You probably wouldn't feel very comfortable here." She turned back and shook out another dress. "You understand." She stretched the shoulder strap over a hanger and turned away again. "Aren't there any positions nearer where you live?"

"This ain't so far from us," Ruby said. "Here, let me help you." She handed Lida to Easton and went around the counter to help with the dresses. "He could come after school and help with de evenin customers. The shoe department always seem so busy."

Lida began to cry. Easton shook her, but she continued. Mrs. Usher stopped what she was doing and looked at him. He shook harder, but Lida wailed louder. Other customers stared and whispered. He could feel them pointing, hear their accusations. He squeezed Lida's warm body as tightly as he could and she stopped.

"He's very good with your baby," Mrs. Usher said. "Why don't you have him take care of all your children while you sell your dresses."

"She is all my chilren; and besides, he would really like to work at dis store."

"That's all right," Easton said. The lights seemed brighter now, blinding almost, reflecting from the metal rack, the glass counter, and dress mirrors. He stepped back toward the aisle.

"I'm sorry," Mrs. Usher said, as she twisted her ring. "I just don't see our customers feeling very comfortable. They're very old-fashioned, many of them. You'd be the only colored employee. It's not that I wouldn't hire you because of that. We fully support—my husband and I both voted for Rumford and we're glad those laws were made—it's just I wouldn't want you to feel uncomfortable, and we can't afford to lose customers. And really, I don't know where we'd put him." She licked her lips quickly and went back to the rack of dresses. She took a green one off and put it with the other green ones and arranged the yellow with the yellow.

"What about de stockroom," Ruby said. "Or he could run de elevator."

"I've told you." She stopped sorting and looked right at them, her voice louder now. "We just don't have a proper place for him. If I knew you were going to push your whole family on us, we would have never taken these dresses. It was a favor to you, really. We have many other suppliers. I hope you understand that."

Ruby stepped away from the counter and backed up to Easton.

"I'm sorry. We done mean nothin by it."

Mrs. Usher continued to talk, her face to the counter. "We never take dresses right off the street like that, and I personally asked Mr. Caulfield to do it this one time. And he didn't think twice about it, you understand."

"Yes ma'am."

The lights made Easton feel as if the floor were moving and the walls collapsing. He closed his eyes and Lida started crying again. Ruby took her from his arms.

"I didn't think twice about you being colored, Ruby. I don't think you could say that we're prejudiced here. We simply can't lose customers. I would hate to feel that we couldn't sell your dresses anymore because of some sort of accusation or misunderstanding."

"No ma'am. That's not what I meant. If you don't have a spot for him, we'll jus look nearer where we live." Ruby rocked Lida gently in her arms, but the baby did not stop crying.

"Yes. Yes. I'm glad you understand. I'm sure he'd be much happier there."

"Yes ma'am."

Easton turned and walked up the aisle quickly, as if he were underwater and dying for breath. Ruby thanked Mrs. Usher for taking the dresses and apologized again for disturbing her.

When she finally emerged through the glass doors, she found Easton leaning his head against the telephone pole. Ruby shifted Lida into one arm and put her hand on Easton's shoulder.

"Come on, now. You got to get yourself used to it. I jus put it out a my mine and say de Lawd has his reason for everything."

"Leave me alone." Easton shrugged her hand off him and shook his head.

"Don't be angry at her, Love E. She doin us a favor."

"I'm not angry at her." He turned and yelled, "I'm angry at you. I knew I shouldn't have tried. I shouldn't have listened to you and your countryfied ways."

"Why you angry at me?"

"You sound like some field nigger in a henhouse: 'Oh, yes ma'am. He jus turn fourteen.' 'No ma'am, we don mean nothin by it.' 'You jus gots to listen to de Almighty.' 'Oh, yes ma'am. Hallelujah.' Why don't you learn to speak proper now that we're out of Carolina."

He turned away again and walked to the bus stop. On the bus, he sat in a separate seat behind her, and they rode in silence the entire trip home.

CHAPTER 3B

LIDA SHOWERED IN the evenings before going to work at Lucky's, her first job ever. She raised her arms in the air and held on to the curtain rod, breathing the thick steam into her nostrils, the water running down her back and thighs.

Through the half-open rectangular window by her face, she listened to the evening sounds of the street: the scraping of metal roller-skate wheels; Telli, their Jamaican neighbor, laughing from her stoop; and on this night, a car honking and a man calling out, "Come on, come on."

She picked up the orange clamshell soap and scrubbed her arms from her shoulders down in a counterclockwise direction, then put her nose against her arm and smelled the peach scent on her skin. The warm soapy water gathered around her feet over the partially clogged drain and she put her big toe on the holes of the mesh, pressed down, then lifted up, and the water drained more quickly. She turned her foot over and looked at the geometric imprints on her skin.

The door to the bathroom opened, and as if a sudden breeze had blown through the stall, she put her foot down for balance and pulled her arms to her sides. The curtain, normally transparent between the flower pattern, was all steamed up.

"Mama?" she asked. The bathroom door closed and then the medicine cabinet squeaked. Lida pictured her towel hanging on the door hook. "Mama? That you?"

"Naw. Just me," Easton said.

"I'm taking a shower. Can't I get privacy?"

"Can't never wash all that ugly off a you," he said, without a trace of his old News English.

"Where's Mama?"

"She fixin supper."

"What you want in here?"

"I'm just gonna shave." He tapped the razor on the sink and turned on the water.

Lida faced the shower nozzle and put her forearms together in front of her chest, as if she could make herself narrow enough to hide in the stream of water. She heard the spray of the shaving cream and his hands slapping together, then another tapping on the sink.

She closed her eyes and let the water run over the top of her head and over her mouth. She pressed her elbows into the sour spot in her stomach and burped softly. Any transmission of fear might provoke him. She knew this. To show anger was fine, an act of embarrassment reflecting only on herself, but fear was an invitation. She heard the razor scrape against his face, swish in the water, and then scrape again.

She stood on her tiptoes and peered out the rectangular window. She could see only the side of the house next door and a cat in the garbage below.

"Mmmm-hmmm! You sure turned into a full-grown woman." She spun around and saw him looking in at her from the back of the curtain, licking his tongue over his gold-capped tooth. "You out all night shakin that all over town, lettin those little boys stick they thangs up into you?" His eyes traveled up her body, stopping at the small stream of water running off her pubic hair..

She stared at the razor clenched in his hand. "Mama." The word stuck in her throat.

"She ain't never gonna believe you."

"Mama!" she yelled.

"Shut your mouth." He stuck the razor out at her, its straightedge covered with small hairs. She raised the shell of orange soap to throw at him and he laughed.

"Look at that." He pointed his chin at her hard nipples. "You can't hide how you really feel."

She covered herself with her elbows.

He let go of the curtain, perhaps to come in from the other side and grab her, perhaps to take off his clothes. She heard the toilet seat lift, then the spatter of urine. She backed against the window and waited, the sour smell flooding her nose and sickening her. She breathed out for as long as she could. It wasn't the smell of urine that most disgusted her, but that it was his urine, like his hand reaching out and touching her, getting inside her. When she couldn't breathe out any longer, she faced the open window and sucked in the cold air.

He flushed the toilet, and for a moment she couldn't hear anything else. She couldn't tell what he was doing. The shower got cold, but she didn't complain. Then she heard the cabinet close and the bathroom door open again. The hiss of the toilet died away slowly. The pipes rumbled. She stood in the back of the tub, listening, frozen in the silence. Finally she peeked around the corner of the curtain, crouching down low, where he wouldn't expect to see her. The bathroom was empty, his razor and shaving cream gone from the sink, but he had left the door wide open.

CHAPTER 3C

"YOU CAN STAY in Love E's ole room." Ruby led Love up the same shiny wooden stairs she and her brother had first mounted more than thirty-four years ago. "You wasn't never loud in here when you was a chile, but that time's all over now. This here's the biggest room. That's his drawing pad and charcoals on the table. Jus done touch nothin what ain't yours. My brother was fond of his pictures."

Ruby went to a sketch on the wall beside the closet. "This here is John and Bobby Seale. Huey shot jus 'round the corner on Seventh. And that there John Coltrane. Your great-grandpa Corbet fond a Charlie Parker, but Love E always say he ole school." Ruby laughed and looked down at the long wooden floorboards a moment.

Love tossed the garbage bag full of his belongings from Los Aspirantes onto the bed.

"I'll let you alone to get yourself the feeling for a bit." Ruby closed the door behind her.

Love looked around his new room, the single bed in the middle of the floor, the rolltop desk. Then he went to the window and looked onto Cranston Avenue. Many of the wooden Victorians were still standing, but the colorful paint had curled off, and every third house was boarded up. The houses that were still inhabitable looked as Ruby's did—tall fences around the yards, black bars on the lower windows, and pieces of tar paper ripped off their roofs. The homes were each tilted in some way, collapsing in on themselves as if they'd been punched in their stomachs.

In a burnt-out house across the street, two young men in black shirts and blue jeans hit the charred pilings with crowbars. One of them was in a wheelchair and had a snake over his shoulders, a thick brown snake like a muscular arm. The other one, with a long braid of hair down his back and a black bandanna in his back pocket, looked up and saw Love in the window.

Love almost stepped back but caught himself. He looked down and squinted at the young man with the braid, who was maybe eighteen and had dark, swollen triceps. They stared at each other like two cats before a fight. Then the man turned and hit the charred stairs of the house again, breaking the top step right in the middle.

Love walked back to his bed and dumped his clothes on the home-patched quilt. Sifting through his white shirts, he grabbed a faded black bandanna his mother had given him before he was taken to Juvi. He knew what to expect: they'd know the black rag, know that he was claiming to be down with them; they'd jump him in, beat him up, and then it would be over. He tried not to picture them hitting him or using the metal crowbars. He tucked the bandanna into his jeans and stuffed the rest of his clothes back in the bag.

The stairs thumped and creaked loudly as he jogged down to the front door. Ruby came in from the kitchen. "Where you off to already?"

"I got some business, dog."

"Don't you call me dog. I'm not your pet. What sort of business you have already? You just got here. Why don't you wash up and I'll fix you somethin. I got some burger I could heat up."

"I got to go." Love opened the front door and stepped out onto the porch. He looked down the street toward the corner liquor store where the two young men had headed. Ruby followed him to the porch.

"I got these here insects I was gonna give you, but if you just 'got to go' to your business, you go on ahead. I can give 'em to someone else."

Love looked back over his shoulder. Ruby walked inside and opened a drawer in the vanity. She pulled out a blue denim binder and took it into the living room.

"What you mean, insects?"

"Close the door and come sit here on the couch." An orange-striped cat ran past him and into the kitchen. "That cat's name's Lion. You remember Lion?"

Ruby sat on the couch, opened the book on her lap, and thumbed slowly through the first pages. "You probly never heard a these special names." She put her finger under the name of a big orange butterfly and tried sounding it out slowly. "Dannaus . . ."

"Dannaus plexippus," Love said. "P-l-e-x-i-p-p-u-s. That's just a monarch, but they have a heart poison in them so the birds don't eat them."

"What's that ugly creature?"

Love came inside to see. He stood behind the couch and looked over her shoulder. Ruby pointed to a cricketlike bug pinned on its side.

"They only ugly 'cause you're not used to looking at them up close, and you ignorant about them. That's a cicada. They the ones that make that high-pitch weeeeeee all night from this drum they got in their stomachs." Love picked the binder out of Ruby's lap. He turned the page to a beetle almost four inches long with a nose like an elephant. "That's a Hercules. Where'd you get this from? They don't even live around here."

"Keep them in that plastic. That man from your old school say to never take them out of that plastic." Love looked into Ruby's hazel eyes, swimming and red from years at the sewing machine.

"No he didn't. You went out and got these."

"He say to give these to you when I went in for a meeting. He say you been like a little brother."

Love looked back at the Hercules beetle. It was the longest beetle known to mankind, hidden in shiny black layers of armor.

"But now you here with your real family to stay," said Ruby. "You remember these folks, don't you?" She got up and went to the photographs on the wall above the stacks of records: on the bottom, Lida with Marcus and Easton; Elise and Corbet on top.

"I hope you don't never put my picture up on that wall," he said to his grandmother.

"Why not?"

"It's like the Hall of Shame up there."

"Don't you talk that way. Maybe we ain't the Huxtables—"

"No, we more like *America's Most Wanted*."

"I know you talkin out of anger when you say that, but that kind of disrespect ain't gonna be tolerated in here, you understand?"

Love shrugged and went back to turning through the pages of pinned insects.

"You understand?"

"You gonna kick me out and I ain't barely got here yet. I can see this ain't gonna last long."

"It's gonna last as long as you respect me and your family. So it's up to you. Don't blame it on anybody else, 'cause it's all up to you. You can stay here as long as you please. You hear? As long as you please."

TWO MONTHS LATER, Love ventured into East Oakland for the first time. It was four-thirty in the evening on East 14th near Fruitvale BART. The broad street was heavy with traffic, littered with French-fry containers, crushed golden malt-beer cans, cigarette butts, and yellowed newspapers. A black soot coated the sidewalk and the air was thick with bus exhaust.

Love walked past a motorcycle shop, a lamp store, a check-cashing corner mart with lightbulbs around its blue sign. He pulled his white jeans halfway down around his boxers, drooped his eyelids, and stared straight ahead.

There were a lot of Mexican families and shops in this area, but gang sets were not divided by race, not in Oakland; there were Blacks, Mexicans, Filipinos, Salvadorans, Chinese, and White kids on both sides of Lake Merritt. Sets were divided by territory, and ESO, East Side Oakland, was rival turf. If he was spotted by Ace Trey, 13th Street, they'd surely think he was slippin, coming across the lines from West Side to earn his props or to cap someone for revenge.

At a bus stop, three young Latino men in black slacks and ties kicked an empty pack of cigarettes back and forth. On the bus bench sat an older woman wearing a scarf on her head and a beige overcoat. One of the young soccer players kicked the cigarette pack hard, and it went sailing past the woman's shoulder toward Love. The man who went and fetched it clasped his hands in front of him as he passed the woman.

"*Lo siento,*" he said. "They're just learning." The pack landed by Love. The young man in slacks picked it up without looking at him and went back to his game.

Love read the white graffiti tag on the back of the bus bench as he passed. His heart beat quickly, but he swaggered his step with a slow rocking from side to side. He glanced left to the parking lot across the street. Two kids, younger teens in flannel shirts buttoned only at the top, sat on dirt bikes leaning against a silver catering truck. One ate something in a yellow wrapper and motioned toward Love with his chin. The other turned to look, but Love walked straight ahead. He did not slow down. He did not swallow. He heard the bikes swivel in the dirt lot, but he didn't look.

Thirty seconds later the bikes were riding alongside him, one behind the other in the gutter by the sidewalk.

"Whas up?" said the first boy. He wore dark, curved sunglasses that wrapped around the sides of his light brown face. These situations were hopeless: to ignore meant a beating and to challenge meant a beating. The second boy was a pimply faced, pale kid with orange foam earphones hanging half off his head. Love saw a black knife handle in the first one's waistband.

They both jumped the curb and skidded to a stop in front of him. Love stared at them as the cars rushed by, the gawking passengers locked inside.

"East Side," the first boy yelled, calling his affiliation. He held up one hand and made an "E" with three fingers pointing horizontally, curling his ring finger down and holding it with his thumb. He looked at his own hand to see that he had gotten it right. When he was satisfied, he patted the sign against his chest like a hungry gorilla. "Give us your shoes, muthahfuckah, or we'll cap your ass." Love didn't say anything.

"Hey, you Pit, huh?" the one with the headphones yelled to him. "You used to go to Prescott. You killed that kid Snapple, huh?" The first kid looked at his friend and then at Love again, now with less challenge in his eyes than fascination.

"Where you claim now?"

Love still didn't move or speak. He just stared straight ahead.

"Give us your shoes and we'll let you go this time," said the pale kid. "Your little brother'll kick your ass anyway."

"Yeah. A free pass to Go. Don't collect your two hundred *dólares.*" Both kids laughed and waited, as if they thought Love would laugh with them, or at least thank them in some way. But he didn't. Love took off his shoes, the Air Jordans from Los Aspirantes. The pimply boy picked them up, tied the laces together, and slung them over his shoulder. The other one flashed his sign one more time, then they rode their bikes away into traffic, back toward the lot.

Love walked in his socks without looking down at the pavement. He turned on High Street by Lucky's market, and even though he saw his mother in the lot, he walked a block up and stopped at the pay phone on the corner.

He watched through the tagged glass as Lida sat on one of the parking blocks. She wore a blue wool cap over her head, and her long breasts sagged into a black nylon shirt under her black and silver Raiders jacket. She glanced up and down the parking aisle and then along the sidewalk to the telephone booth. Love turned away quickly and then looked again. Lida was staring at him and smiling. He smiled back.

She stood up, her hands in her jacket pockets, her thick thighs strangled into stretch pants. She walked toward Love, stumbled to the left on her heels, and then regained her balance. She smiled at him again.

Love was not smiling now. He looked to both sides of the lot. A man with a six-pack glanced at him. Love glared back and the man got into his brown Honda Civic. Lida stood at the edge of the lot near the phone booth, one pointed heel up on the curb.

"Hi darling." His mother's eyes blinked and darted around his face. "Long time no see."

"Hi." Love stepped out from behind the glass. He looked toward East 14th, then up toward the freeway, then back at her. Her cheeks were sunken, her dark skin chapped and flaky. Her bangs spread out from under the front of her cap. He stuck his hands in his pockets as she came closer.

"You lookin good," she said. He could smell the beer on her breath.

"Thanks."

She reached out and caressed his cheek with the back of her hand. He flinched. It had been four years.

"Don't be shy," she said.

"I ain't shy."

She unzipped the bottom of her jacket completely and let it swing open, revealing dark crescents of sweat under her breasts.

"What you like, then?" She smiled; her teeth were yellow with pieces of sunflower-seed shell caught between them.

"What you mean?"

"You know what I mean. What's your pleasure?"

Love backed away from her. "You know who I am?" he asked.

"Sure, baby."

"Who am I?" he demanded.

She looked away toward East 14th. "Listen, honey. Don't play no games with me. You too young to be a cop. What you want? Or you got something for me?"

Love looked at a rust streak that ran down her jacket along the zipper to where she nervously picked at her nails with her thin, burnt fingers. Her eyes darted around the street for danger.

"Look at me," Love said.

"I am."

He fixed his eyes on hers. They were a dark hepatitis yellow. An airplane passed overhead and dampened all other sounds for a few seconds, as if they were standing in a private room. Neither of them spoke or moved. He begged her silently for recognition, but she continued to stare back at him vacantly. A car honked and drove past. Lida turned, then looked back to Love.

"Now tell me what you want?" she asked.

"I don't want nothing," Love said.

"Well, you missin out." She turned and walked away, a pear-shaped stain on the butt of her pants.

She sat down on a parking block again. The brown Honda pulled out of its space and stopped in front of her. She stood and bent down to the window. The man inside cleared some papers from his passenger seat, and Lida went around and got in. The brake lights flickered and the car turned slowly onto East 14th.

Just as the car began to accelerate, a young kid in a silver and blue Dallas Cowboys jacket stood up from behind the stacked shopping carts and tossed a large brown beer bottle at the car. The bottle broke by the back tire and the car stopped short. The kid did not run. Instead he began walking toward the car with another bottle in his hand, barking like a wild dog: "Rah, rahr, rah."

The car pulled off again.

Love stepped over the curb into the parking lot toward his brother. He approached him quickly with his hands at his sides. The boy did not see Love until he was a car length away.

"Li'l Pit," Love yelled to him. His brother turned and raised the bottle. He barked at Love and bared his teeth: "Rah rahr rah, rah rahr rah."

"Damn, bro, you still slobbering all up on yourself."

"East Side Ace Trey!" Li'l Pit yelled.

"Drop that shit. You ain't all that."

Li'l Pit hurled the bottle in Love's direction, missing by a foot.

"Shit, dog." Love stayed in his place, careful not to step on any of the shards in his socks.

Now the little boy's fists were clenched at his sides.

"Take him down, blood," came a yell from the street. At the edge of the lot were the two kids on their bikes.

"East Side Ace Trey!" Li'l Pit yelled again, and glanced at his crew.

"They ain't your blood, dog," Love said. "You got your props with me."

Love took a step toward him, and Li'l Pit didn't step back. He stared him in the eye. He had a part shaved in his hair like a sickle.

"Shit, I raised you hard," Love said.

"Go on, kick his ass, Li'l Pit," the kid in the dark glasses yelled. Li'l Pit didn't move. There was no breeze, and for a minute no one came or went from the market. Love watched Li'l Pit stare at the boys on the bikes as if hypnotized. And then the wind blew gently and the sun hit the windshield of a car entering the lot.

"Why don't you come kick my ass yourself, dog?" Love yelled back. The kid threw down his bike and it bounced off the pavement. He pulled his blade from his belt and walked quickly toward Love. His partner with the orange headphones followed. Love flashed the West Side sign even though he wasn't affiliated with them—middle and ring fingers crossed, thumb down—a bluff for protection.

As the East Side kids came across the lot, Li'l Pit also turned and faced them. They shed their flannels and strutted in their white tank tops. The boy with the sunglasses wore Love's shoes. Love bent down and picked up the neck of the broken bottle beside him. He stepped toward the kid with the knife, looking him straight in the eye. The kid stopped, as if surprised this guy hadn't run away yet.

"I'm gonna fuck you up," the boy said.

Love took a step forward.

"You gonna wish you stayed up wherever you been hiding," said the kid with the headphones.

"I'm gonna—" the first boy started to say, but Love ran at him, the bottle in his hand. The boy stepped aside and slashed at him with the knife, but Love didn't slow down. He kept running past him, across the lot. The boy with the knife laughed, and his friend laughed with him.

"That's right, punk," the boy yelled, and they laughed harder until they saw Love grab one of the dirt bikes. Then they ran after him, all three of them.

Love threw his bottle and sped up High Street past the telephone booth. He rode standing in his socks. The air felt good on his face. He heard the pedaling of the other bike behind him, but he didn't waste time to see how far back it was. He would keep riding until he saw the 580 and then turn; then they would be far enough away that it would only be one person to fight. He tried to remember what it was like to be in a full-on brawl without staff to break it up. How did you know when to stop? How did you keep from killing each other? He would go for the throat, choke him until he passed out so he didn't have to keep fighting.

Love got to the overpass, stopped, and turned. Li'l Pit came right at him, howling at the top of his lungs like a young coyote. But he didn't slow down. He sped past Love, jumping the curb onto the sidewalk. Love mounted his bike again and followed, catching up to him just as they turned on to MacArthur, and they headed west together.

SANTA RITA JAIL

AND HE CAME to the front of the recreation room and stood on the table with a book in his hand:

So we are brought ashore and we don't know where our wives and sisters are. We have been unloaded separately, and when we call out to them, we are flogged. It is forbidden to speak in our languages. And even when we find a secret moment, the Africans around us are from different tribes and do not speak our language. That's right, we have a tribe, we have a history and place of origin. That is why some of us are tall and thin, some of us are round and thick, and some in-between.

Do you know your tribe, brothers? Have you ever thought of yourself as anything but the children of slaves, with no history but that of an inferior and victimized race? Are you Baul, the great musicians of Africa; Zulu, the master iron-smelting spear-makers whose soldiers could not marry until they were forty; Mandingo, Wolof, Serer, Fula, Fanti, or Ashanti. Are you from Dahomey with their awesome female warriors, or of their enemy, the Yoruba of Oyo, artisans secured behind the village walls, whose king had to commit suicide if he had a vote of no confidence—now that's Power to the People!

When we get off this ship, we still have our history within us, but we will not be allowed to tell it to our children. They will never know the accomplishments of our people. We will not be allowed to pass down the songs that teach of our tribes' battles, the dances that tell of how the world began, or the sciences our ancestors discovered: how to make powder from the dried leaves of the baobab tree to cure dysentery; how to use the pyrethrum plant as an insecticide that doesn't hurt animals and to which insects cannot develop immunity; how to use the leaves of the shea-butter for headaches. The Europeans would not have even been able to colonize Africa if they hadn't learned from us that quinine from the cinchona bark could cure malaria. By losing the language, we lost the religion, the food, the crafts of building and farming, the art of our tribes' baskets and healing.

We once held a position in our village: we were the scientist, the reader of the sky, who knew if there would be rain or drought this season by the smell of the wind and the cloud formations; or the zoologist, a Pygmy animal tracker, who knew the difference between a deer and an antelope dropping, between the paw print of a jaguar and the paw print of a lion. Or we were the slaves of another tribe; yes we might have been slaves of Black people, but we had respect, we had dignity, and we kept our culture to pass down to our children. In America, all will be wiped out, our children are given a new set of rules. Everything wise and powerful will seem to have been created by the White man.

CHAPTER 4

EASTON SAT ON the brick steps of the university's West Lawn. He and the other protesters had gathered there, a few blocks away from Woolcrest's. It was seven-thirty in the morning and the store had already opened. High up to the left, the white fog drifted through the top branches of the eucalyptus grove with a silence that made him shiver. He rubbed his hands together, stood up, then sat down again.

"Shit. Let's go already."

Ken Weaver yawned and sat down next to him. Ken was one of the Black leaders of the march. He wore sunglasses and a white cardigan sweater, V-necked with blue stripes, his hair cut short and neat.

"You nigga motherfucker shit coon pussy," he said to Easton. "Go back home to Africa."

"Morning, Ken."

"Black ape."

"You're not a completely convincing bigot." Easton smiled cordially.

Ken took a sip of his coffee and let out a loud, satisfied sigh. A police car drove by on Oxford Street, the single top-hat siren unlit.

"Just remember," Ken said. "No matter how hard it is, we're trying to make friends out of our enemies."

"I've done this before," Easton said. He'd joined the Congress for Racial Equality six months earlier, after Charles told him about it. Since then he'd participated in a protest every month. "The store is open already. We should go."

"Patience. Not everyone's here yet, and we have to finish the signs. Why don't you go help."

Easton stood up and walked over to the circular brick bench from which he could watch Sandra kneeling down in her gray skirt, drawing large letters on a picket sign. The blond hair on her calves stood up in the cold, but she was concentrating on making the large, round "u" in prejudice.

They'd talked once before, at another rally, when he'd placed himself next to her in the song chain so they could hold hands. She'd raised their clenched fists in the air together, and he stared at their interlocking fingers.

"I hope my father's watching the news," she had said to him. "He'll probably think we're having sex." She was a freshman at the university and a year older than he, originally from Oregon. In Norma, he might have been shot just for standing so close to her.

"This is what I say we do." Charles's voice shook Easton out of his memory. They were both watching Sandra.

"There is no *we* here," Easton said. "There's me and there's her."

"Her? I'm not after no white meat."

"Sure."

"Listen," said Charles. "I'm serious now. I'm talking about the cops. See, the cops expect all of us niggers to be scared and just let the White kids in our group scream and shout, 'cause the White kids don't have anything to lose. But the funny thing is, it's really us that don't have anything to lose, right? But they don't get it. We have to scare them until they realize we're really angry, that they're hurting us and we're going to hurt them back if they don't stop it."

"Why do you think someone like her is doing this?" Easton asked.

"Listen to me, man, I'm serious. None of this 'keep your mouth shut, be they friend' shit."

Sandra started another card and flipped her short ponytail over her shoulder so that her neck showed above the white collar.

Charles continued, "Malcolm said it's fine to be nonviolent, and if everybody'd lay down their guns, then he'd lay down his gun. But if people are still shooting at you, you got to defend yourself."

"That's true. That's true," Ken said as he came over, nodding his head. Easton watched Sandra as the other two got into it again. "But we're doing our damage economically. Nobody ever got anywhere but dead fighting with their fists against the oppressor."

"I guess you never heard of the Civil War."

"I guess you never heard of Martin Luther King, Jr., or Gandhi, or Thoreau."

Easton stood and left the two to their endless debate. He walked over to Sandra, around to the front of the cards, his hands in his pockets.

Easton cleared his throat. "Need some help?"

"Oh. No. You don't have to do anything. I've got it." Her fingernails were perfect half-moons, polished clear and smooth. She pressed on the brown Magic Marker and filled in the circle of an exclamation point.

"I just want to get started," he said. "Please, give me something to do."

"Here, take these signs and nail them to those crosses."

Easton sat and collected the signs. "Did your father see us holding hands?" he asked as he hammered.

She smiled and her ears turned red, almost translucent at the curl. "No. No, he didn't see it."

"Well, maybe today."

"Yeah." She put the marker away and sat up, considering her work. "How's that look?"

He moved around next to her and his heart quickened. "Good. But you spell abolish with an "o," don't you?"

"Do you?" She scribbled out the tail of the second "a."

"I'm not carrying that one," he said.

"No. I'll carry it. I never was so good in spelling. I'm hoping you don't have to spell to be an anthropologist." They were so close that the skin of their arms almost touched. She turned and looked at his face, around his forehead and cheeks, at his lips and hair. He smelled her perfume, a clean alcohol smell, not sweet like his sister's vanilla oil.

"Any other corrections?" she asked. He sifted through the signs intently, as if he were looking for a winning ticket to the lottery. He could feel her eyes on him but was afraid to turn and see.

"Do you have to do anything with your hair?" she asked. "I mean, how do you comb it?"

He touched his head as if he had to remind himself. "I've got good hair. I don't have to do much. I just put in some pomade once in a while and pick it. But someone like my niece, she's going to have to grease it every day or it will get all kinky."

She nodded.

He looked back at the cards. "Nothing else is spelled incorrectly."

"Are you going to go to college? Because I think you should."

"I was thinking about it before. But now I'm more interested in being an artist."

"Painter?"

"Charcoal drawing, mostly."

"Charcoal. That's very . . ." She sat up straight and waved her hands around in the air as if she were trying to conduct her feelings into words. She wore small pearl earrings like he'd seen in the White fashion magazines he sometimes bought, and a silver bracelet around her thin wrist. "It's very sensual," she finally said.

"Well." He laughed. "I just want a job so I can have some cash, you know?"

"So you can take me out, right?"

Easton felt his chest tighten. If he simply said yes, she might be shocked at him for thinking she was serious. He tried to think of something clever but nothing came to him. She stood up and brushed off her hands.

"Okay, signs are ready." Ken walked over with Charles at his side, who was still yelling a point at him.

"No, man, that's because you've internalized the oppressor's propaganda to pacify you. Violence isn't evil in itself, only violence with an evil intent."

"Very nice signs, Sandra," Ken said.

"Yes," Charles said, without even looking at them. "I hope they're not too heavy a burden for y'all to carry."

Ken put his hand on Sandra's shoulder, but she looked straight at Charles and smiled. "I'm willing to do whatever's necessary."

Olaf, the other group leader, ran up the stairs breathing hard. "Sorry. Sorry. Alarm clock." He picked up a sign and held it in the air. "All right. Let's roll."

Charles let out a breath and shook his head. "How come the White folks are always telling us when we can go and when we gotta stay?"

"Sorry." Olaf looked at the ground. "Sorry. I wasn't trying to tell you what to do. I was just saying now that I'm here, we can go. I mean, not now that *I'm* here, now that we're all here, you don't have to wait up for me anymore. I'm just trying to say you don't have to wait up for me anymore."

Ken patted Olaf on the back. "Thank you. We're glad you made it. Don't let Charles intimidate you. It's good to have your leadership skills to help us build ties with the community." Olaf smiled and nodded.

There were twenty protesters and half got to carry signs. Ken took the lead and they marched down Center Street to Shattuck and over to Woolcrest's. Charles was in the back, talking it up with some newer Black members. Easton walked near Sandra, with one young man between them, a blond student in a blue suit who kept smiling and nodding at him as if they were long-lost brothers. Just before they reached Woolcrest's, the man gave him a thumbs-up—for what, Easton wasn't sure.

They made a circle in front of the store. The police were already waiting at the curb, but they stayed in their cars. Usually they let them protest for an hour and then cleared them off. Charles didn't join the circle; he stood at the corner of the building, watching both the picketing and the police.

"Please don't shop here." Sandra handed a flyer to a woman coming out of the store pushing a cart. "They have unfair hiring practices, here and in the South." The woman walked off, holding the flyer away from her body like it might explode.

Shoppers came and went and neither Easton nor Sandra had any luck giving more flyers away. Half an hour later, they still had full stacks of paper in their hands. Most customers looked straight ahead and pretended the protesters were invisible.

Finally Sandra put a flyer in front of one woman and said, "Keep America free." The lady took it. She turned to Easton and shrugged.

To the next man coming out of the store Easton said, "Equal rights for all races." The man put his hands in the air like he was being held up. Then Sandra said to the next man, "Be a good American; support democracy," and he took it. He even smiled at her. Sandra stuck her tongue out at Easton.

"Fight the Commies," Easton said, and a woman stopped and waited for him to give her a flyer. They alternated with new ones:

"Support Kennedy."

"Buy American."

"Feed the children."

"Love the U.S. of A."

"Free America."

Sandra held out a flyer to one man and said, "Free, live American girls," and even then the man had his fingers on the paper before withdrawing his hand and backing away from her.

Charles whistled and pointed to a man and his son skirting around the edge of the circle to get into the store.

"You missed one," he yelled to Easton, who ran after them, but they slipped inside. Easton was about to turn when he noticed a familiar face behind the glass. Mrs. Usher was moving a sign farther from the window, a sign that announced a 50 percent sale every weekend. She looked older, and her arms shook as she gripped the metal base of the stand.

She had long since stopped selling Ruby's line of dresses, not because of his involvement in the protests, but because the store bought exclusively from a national distributor now. Mrs. Usher placed the stand in the aisle and looked up at the doors. She noticed Easton, and as if he'd forgotten why he was there, he smiled and raised his hand in a half-wave. She walked directly toward him, her shoulders forward, her old legs slightly off balance in her high heels. He wanted to run away, as he had that day when he'd begged her for a job. But her intensity kept him frozen there, like she was commanding him to wait. She couldn't have recognized him. It had been three years, and he'd met her only four or five times. And yet he hoped that she might remember, just as much as he hoped she didn't. She pushed the door open a few inches and spoke to him through the opening.

"You're going to have to move, young man. You may be allowed to boycott, but you can't block the entrance. I know that for a fact."

"Mrs. Usher," he said.

She stared at him with narrowed eyes, as if he were a ghost come to haunt her. "Yes?"

"I'm Ruby's little brother, Easton. Love E."

"Oh." Her face changed, first to recognition and relief and then to confusion. "Oh yes. I see now."

"How are you? How's your husband?"

"Why are you doing this? Why are you doing this to me?"

"Oh, no. It's not like that—"

She pulled the door shut before he could explain. He thought he might say that it wasn't personal, that he wasn't trying to get back at her for what she had done, that he hoped she'd forgive him.

"You have to clear the sidewalk," a voice blared from a police megaphone. "You are blocking pedestrian traffic."

"You're blocking the street!" Charles yelled at the cops. "How come you can do anything you want? If we were picketing for an increase of police wages, you would let us march all day!"

Ken walked over to the police car and talked into the open window. The police officers glanced at Charles and nodded. Charles waved to them and yelled at Ken, "Sell me out, brother. That's what they want. You sell me out and then you can smile because the real enemy has been locked up and you can keep your job, holding a sign for the White oppressor that reads, 'Don't worry about me, I'm just going to sing a song if you spit in my face.' "

Ken walked back into the circle and Easton came up to him.

"What did you tell him?"

"I told him we are a nonviolent group, but we won't leave until the store changes its policy."

"What about Charles?"

"I said we couldn't be responsible for what he might do, that he wasn't part of our group anymore."

Easton looked at Charles leaning against the brick building, a pick in his natural and his arms folded across his black turtleneck. Easton walked over to him with his sign down.

"You know they're probably going to single you out," he said to Charles.

"How come you're over here? Did Uncle Ken tell you to come over here? Because you can save your breath."

"I don't think you should let yourself get beat up. I know you, you're just asking for a beating, but this isn't like high school."

"Man, I don't want to be beat up. What I want is to be able to stand here and exercise my First Amendment right to say this place stinks and to close it down because it violates the law and watch them blue boys over there shut the place down. But they aren't going to do it, man. Don't you get it? We've been picketing outside this store almost every weekend for six months, and all they've done is hire one colored elevator man for two dollars an hour, right in the middle of the store where everyone can see him and say, 'Oh deary, what are these radicals complaining about, colored people do work here.' I'm not the one out here starting a fight. I'm defending my right to earn a living. It's self-defense. They're the ones telling you to clear out. I'm just not going to let them clear me out when I have a right to be here."

Two policemen got out of the lead car and slammed their doors. They walked toward Charles and Easton with their clubs out.

"You're going to start a riot if you touch me," Charles said to them. The policemen looked over at Ken, who shrugged. Easton brushed his cheek and then put his hands in his pockets. He smiled at the officers.

"He won't do anything if you leave him alone," Easton said.

"What's your name?" the first officer asked him.

"Who, me?" Easton asked.

"See how it works?" Charles said. "You're going to be in the system now."

"What's your name?" the officer asked again. Easton looked at Ken. Ken shook his head.

"I take my Fifth Amendment right not to say anything." This was part of the training they'd gone through, including the mock beatings and arrests. The rest of the protesters stopped to listen to the confrontation, and the policemen felt them getting closer.

"You don't need a Fifth Amendment right until after I arrest you," the officer said.

"So you don't intend to arrest me?"

"I intend on keeping this sidewalk cleared for the customers." He looked back at his partner, who nodded.

"You mean you're just doing your job," Easton said.

"That's right."

"You're an honest man who believes in what's right."

"Look, I'm asking you nicely"

"I'm just saying that you're a decent human being, that you care about the law, about justice, and morality."

"That's got nothing to do with you blocking the sidewalk."

"That's right. It doesn't. It's got nothing to do with justice. I'm asking you as a person to a person, not as some sort of criminal: Why'd you become a policeman?"

"Listen to this guy talk," the officer said to his partner. "I thought he was taking the Fifth. Seems more like he's been drinking a fifth." His partner laughed, but his smile quickly faded.

"I'm just saying, what are you bothering us for? Isn't it worse what they're doing to us than what we're doing to them? I mean from your point of view."

"I don't have a point of view. I'm just doing my job. Now, turn around."

"You don't have a point of view? What do you mean? How is that possible? Don't you care? Don't you think for yourself?"

"That's enough. Turn around."

"Can't you think for yourself?"

The officer hit Easton in the ribs with a jab of his baton and Easton fell to his knees.

"What did you hit him for?" Sandra yelled. She ran over and stepped between them. The policeman lowered his baton.

"Come on," she yelled again. "Aren't you going to hit me too?" He looked down as if he were being berated by his own daughter. "Aren't you going to hit a defenseless woman? Or is that finally sinking too low for you?"

Charles approached them, and the second policeman lifted his club.

"So now you want to hit me? Now I'm the one needs a whuppin 'cause I want to see what you done to my friend." Charles crouched down and took Easton by the arm.

"Stay back," the first policeman said.

"What's the matter with you?" Sandra continued. "He was just talking, just talking like a civilized human being." She turned around and knelt in front of Easton. Both policemen hovered there for a moment. They looked like they wished to finish the arrest, to maneuver around Sandra and Charles somehow, but instead they squeezed their fists around their batons and waited. Easton looked up at them, frozen there like angry children whose toys had been taken away.

FOR THE NEXT month, Easton recuperated at home. Once in a while he would venture downstairs. In the evenings, the living room was lit by a single curved lamp, and the mellow sun filtered through the burgundy curtains of the Victorian. Corbet sat in his chair with his pipe, smoke floating in front of the single bulb as he rocked beside the phonograph and listened to Charlie Parker. The rug was a dark, blood-red Persian he'd brought home from the shipyard. The polished wooden walls, railings, and windowsills also shone red.

Corbet usually drank a glass of bourbon, slowly raising it to his lips and then placing it down on a circular black cast-iron table imprinted with Chinese serpents. His eyes were often closed, and his back was to the staircase, where Easton would sit and watch him.

Corbet would shake his head and caress his strange pipe and, as if he were invoking some demon, growl softly with the music—sometimes not so softly, like hitting bumps in a road. For a week now, since he'd been laid off, Corbet sat in that chair every day and listened to music. He'd injured his foot, though because of his diabetes, he hadn't known it until it was beyond repair. His foot was now infected and the doctors said they would have to amputate.

"Sit here," Corbet said one night.

Easton did not move from his seat on the bottom steps. He was not sure he had been spoken to, if Corbet wasn't instead commanding some spirit to sit down beside his knee. He'd heard about people from the war having dreams while they were awake. But Corbet raised his left hand and motioned to him with a wave.

Easton stood and straightened his slacks; it took some effort, his ribs were still sore. He passed the kitchen and looked in at Ruby, who'd just come home from the Pearsons' and was fixing supper before going up-stairs to mend pants for a neighbor. She sliced carrots and brushed them into a pot on the burner. Easton was hungry after a long day of taking care of the baby. For two years, while Ruby cleaned houses on the weekends, he had stayed home all day with Lida, keeping her from knocking over picture frames, from falling down the stairs, from drooling on her clothes, wiping her bottom when she went.

Every once in a while he'd go out to look for work. He'd applied to do construction at the postal processing plant, but they wanted some-one at least eighteen. There was no point in trying the trains now that White people were getting Pullman jobs.

Easton approached Corbet in the living room and stopped next to him.

"*Assez-toi, pre de moi.*" Corbet patted the side of his chair.

Easton sat down on the carpet, the curved rocker creaking toward and then away from him. Corbet put his pipe on the table, then reached out and placed his hand around the back of Easton's neck, just below the skull. Easton straightened quickly at this unusual sensation, the first time Corbet or any man had touched him other than to hit him. The fingers of Corbet's large hand stretched all the way from the back of one ear to the other, and Easton soon tilted his head into the full, strong warmth of it.

Corbet's fingers tapped lightly on the side of Easton's neck to the rhythm of the saxophone; they fluttered at frills, stopped at breaks, then dropped one at a time with a long descending scale.

"Hear that?"

Easton nodded his head, but only slightly, afraid the hand might be removed if the lesson was learned.

"Hear that?" Corbet tapped more quickly, higher up toward his ear as the pitch raised. "That: nuh-nuh-nuh-nuh, du-nuh-nuh-nuh-nuh." He rocked the chair and shook his head slowly, his eyes closed. Easton closed his eyes too. He felt the tapping of the sax on his neck, but he listened to the swing of the drums. *Tsst-t-tss, tsst-t-tss, bat ba-boom.* The music entered him: the bass shook his stomach and the snare slapped his chest and he shook his head with the hi-hat. The saxophone fingers tapped on his neck, and he rocked side to side near the chair as the big warm hand pulled and pushed him.

Then—*ting, ting, teeee-ing*—the song ended.

Corbet took his hand away and picked up his glass of bourbon. Easton felt the sudden cold on his neck.

"Now you hear it all in there?" Corbet asked. "That's the Bird flyin free. Saying, I'm not a body. You look at me, but you don't see me. You want to hold me down, you want to put this bird in a cage, but you can't put music in a cage; you can't capture my spirit, 'cause I'm free inside. Inside I'm free."

The record ended and the needle sat in the last groove, going around and around in the silence of the late evening. Ruby called them to the table for dinner, and Easton helped Corbet stand, pulling his arm over his shoulders.

SANTA RITA JAIL

TODAY I READ to you from the *Life of Gustavus Vassa, the African:*

On the passage [from Barbados to Virginia] we were better treated than when we were coming from Africa, and we had plenty of rice and fat pork. We were landed up a river a good way from the sea, about Virginia country, where we saw few or none of our native Africans, and not one soul who could talk to me. I was a few weeks weeding grass and gathering stones in a plantation; and at last all my companions were distributed different ways, and only myself was left. I was now exceedingly miserable, and thought myself worse off than any of the rest of my companions, for they could talk to each other, but I had no person to speak to that I could understand. In this state, I was constantly grieving and pining, and wishing for death rather than anything else. While I was in this plantation, the gentleman, to whom I suppose the estate belonged, being unwell, I was one day sent for to his dwelling-house to fan him; when I came into the room where he was I was very much affrighted at some things I saw, and the more so as I had seen a black woman slave as I came through the house, who was cooking the dinner, and the poor creature was cruelly loaded with various kinds of iron machines; she had one particularly on her head, which locked her mouth so fast that she could scarcely speak; and could not eat nor drink. I was much astonished and shocked at this contrivance, which I afterwards learned was called the iron muzzle. I had a fan put in my hand, to fan the gentleman while he slept; and so I did indeed with great fear. While he was fast asleep I indulged myself a great deal in the looking about the room, which to me appeared very fine and curious. The first object that engaged my attention was a watch which hung on the chimney, and was going. I was quite surprised at the noise it made, and was afraid it would tell the gentleman anything I might do amiss; and when I immediately after observed a picture hanging in the room, which appeared constantly to look at me, I was still more affrighted, having never seen such things as these before.

CHAPTER 5

LIDA SAT AT the bottom of the stairs, where she could see Ruby but not be seen by Easton, who was speaking to a group of people in the living room. She held the torn strap of her dress. She had proof she could show Ruby this time: not just the usual scratches he made, but the broken strap and the teeth marks on her nipple where he'd bitten her when he came on his hand.

The living room was packed with people. A few men sat on the floor between the coffee table and the couch with their knees to their chests. Everyone was in their socks, their shoes all piled up by the door— Ruby's orders. Thirty people stood in the entrance hall and up against the walls by the writing table, blocking the picture of Corbet, their backs pressing into the stacked boxes of record albums.

Lida knew most of the people by name, and the others by sight. The pock-faced man with a short goatee was the guy Marcus bought his weed from. Marcus's father was there too—he'd brought the whole wheat pretzels that Ruby put in bowls throughout the room. Marcus's mother was there, but she sat next to a man in a jade suit who owned the fancy Seagull's Restaurant downtown. Telli, the Jamaican woman who'd sold stationery out of her house across the street before it burned down, sat in Corbet's rocking chair, her poodle on the lap of her red satin dress. Dr. Cott was also there, standing by the vase of pussy willows on the vanity. He'd fashioned Easton's gold cap, the one he licked with the tip of his tongue.

The others Lida had seen only a few times at previous meetings, people Easton knew from Merritt College. They all wore their coats and scarves inside the house because Ruby had opened the window, the fresh air billowing in through the long burgundy curtain. Many of the men wore the same waist-long black jacket that Easton had put on after he was done with Lida.

Now he stood at the front of the living room addressing the gathering, the curtain waving up like a giant robe behind him. She knew that he could not see her white socks on the bottom step. But if she stood up to cross the back of the room, even if she quietly glided on the wooden floor, he would see her between the heads. Her hands tingled at the thought of it. People would turn and greet her. He would say something to her, or about her, before she could reach the entrance of the kitchen, where Ruby leaned against the door frame watching Easton speak, her hands thrust deep into her dress pockets.

"They took Li'l Bobby. They took Bunchy. They took John and Fred, George and Jonathan. But they ain't gonna stop Lionel!"

"Bring 'em back," Dr. Cott shouted at him. "Bring 'em back, brother." There was short applause.

"When we put down the guns, we didn't stop warrin. It's been a long stretch since our party split, since the division: International over there, Central over here. But now it's time for a healing. Y'all know I been down for Eldridge; from the time I was down with him in Algiers, I stood by him tight and took no muzzling of the Panther." There was none of his News English left now, almost the opposite of what happened to Ruby, who'd worked on refining her speech every day.

"From the time he stripped down to his bones and walked out into the street in front of them pigs, I knew he was the bravest man alive. He made me know what I am and what I got to do. But now we got to get together, to take stock in our new power. It's a soft power, but it's real power. Let's give it up for Elaine and our softer side: we have helped our brothers and sisters when the White supremacists would not. We feed the homeless, we have free health care, free legal aid, we be escorting our grandmothers from the Social Security building. We even kill the rats and the roaches, and we got an elementary school too. An now, next April, we're gonna have the first Black mayor of the city of Oakland, California!" Everyone erupted into applause. Ruby clapped with her hands above her head.

Even if she told her, Lida thought, even if her mother believed it had happened, how would she explain why? She could prove there was sex, but not why she'd let it happen, why she had waited to tell after so many times, after so long. She had been afraid that it would look like her fault, like Easton always said it would. She could hear herself say that she'd been afraid, but she only half believed it herself.

"We will have everything though they gave us nothin," Easton continued. "No one gave it to us. Not no White aid from the National Guard. No thanks to the COINTELPRO agents—maybe one of Hoover's boys out in us right now. Not no White kids from the university. Not no Jerry Brown. None of those folks gonna give us this victory. Two hundred years—" Easton bent forward and closed his eyes, his fist clenched against his forehead. "Two hundred years—"

"Take us back, brother," Dr. Cott yelled.

"Two hundred years after this land was sposed to be free and equal for all people—"

"Okay? That's what I'm sayin," yelled Telli.

"We will finally say, here in Oakland, the Wild West—" Easton paused. Ruby laughed, and the smile stuck on her face. Easton went on, "A brother can be elected mayor of a great city, no matter if his great grandady was brought over in chains from our homeland to lick the boots, milk them cows, pick the cotton, and hang from the noose of the White man's rope!" The room erupted in applause again. A number of the men, including Marcus's dealer, shot their fists up in the air.

Lida stood on the step and looked straight at Ruby as if she had to focus on an object at the end of a long tightrope. She did not want to lick the knob of the staircase in front of everyone, so she quickly licked her fingers and touched them to it. Then she started to walk, her shoulders stooped, so she wouldn't be seen above the applauding crowd. The sofa in the middle of the room was the only place not protected by standing bodies. Eight feet of smooth wooden floor and then she would be in the kitchen. There was silence after the applause died away. She reached the middle of the couch and felt the silence stretching on for

an unusually long time. She turned her face to the front of the room
and saw him watching her.

He did not look away. He stared at her with his jaw clenched. Then
a smile grew on his face, first only on one side and then broadly, until
his eyes were shining at her. He lifted his hand toward her and all heads
turned to see. Even Ruby, still wearing the smile on her face, now
looked at her for the first time all night. But the smile was for Easton,
not Lida. She stopped walking toward her mother as if the last door of
a cage had suddenly shut in front of her.

She faced Easton, his arm outstretched. All eyes were now on her.
She pulled the ripped strap of her dress over the scratch on her shoulder.

"There's our hope," he said. "The next kin. The future of the Party.
The first Black governors and senators. The first Black CEOs of oil
companies. The first Black president of the United States of America!"
Everyone in the room applauded and Lida froze, staring at him like a
mouse trapped by his smiling cat eyes. She turned to the kitchen and
saw Ruby applaud too, her loose arms wobbling, tears on her cheeks as
she looked back and forth between her daughter and her brother.

Lida held her hands together at the bottom of her throat, her arms
over her chest as if she were naked. She turned toward the front door
and pushed her way through the applauding crowd. Once more she
glanced at Easton. He laughed, and the whole room laughed with him
at what they must have thought to be her bashfulness.

She held on to the umbrella box and slipped her bare feet into her
Eastmans, kicking his loafers away. The laughter followed her out the
door, down the steps. It echoed in her ears as she ran up the block, as
the pavement blurred beneath her feet, and all she could see in front of
her was his smiling face and his shining gold tooth.

SHE RAN ALL the way to Marcus's East Oakland apartment, not
bothering to hold up the ripped strap of her dress anymore.

"You bleeding?" Marcus asked as he let her in.

She sat on the low yellow sofa next to the guitar and stared at the moss-filled fish tank in the corner. The filter bubbled slowly, each sphere of air building at the top of the spout, pulling up and struggling to free itself.

Marcus moved the guitar and stood back. "What happened to you? You ripped up your dress."

Lida kept her eyes fixed on the tank and spoke softly. "You said you'd kill him."

"Who?"

"Him." She shook her head and blew out through her nose, like a horse shaking off flies.

"Him?"

"Him HIM HIM!" She grabbed a pillow and threw it on the floor. Then she grabbed all the pillows and threw them on the floor, each time yelling louder, "HIM!" When there were no more pillows, she kicked the coffee table, and the brass ashtray banged against the glass.

Marcus moved the guitar. "Listen. Lida, listen. I've been writing a song for you. Listen, girl. It's kind of like 'Wind Cries Mary.'" He strummed and sang: "When you come around, sweet Lida, I see my possibilities."

"NOOOOOOOOOOOOO!" Lida picked up the ashtray and threw it at his clothing shelf across the room. It smashed against the wall and took a chunk of plaster with it.

Marcus put the guitar on the carpet and ran to her, kneeling at her side, but she pushed him back and punched him in the chest. He had to grab her in a bear hug just so she wouldn't hurt him.

"Shhhh. You all right. Shhhh. Stop that." He laughed as she wrestled to get away from him.

"I ain't joking! You said you'd kill him. You're a liar!" She tried to stand, but he pulled her down again. She coughed and vomited a little on his shoulder, and he let go of her and backed away. She spit on the carpet, her face rabid with disgust. She stood up, looked around, and circled the room.

"Where is it?" she demanded. She pulled the clothes off his shelf, then ran to the bed at the far side of the room and thrust her hands under the mattress. "Where's it at?"

Marcus walked slowly into the bathroom and locked himself in. She ran after him and banged on the door, but he ignored her, so she went back into the living room again, which worried Marcus more; at least he knew where she was when she was trying to break the door down. He knelt on the wooden floor in the bathroom closet and moved a white board covering a hole in the wall. From the hole he pulled out a blue shoe box and then a red shoe box, and put the blue box back. The box was filled with baggies of coarse, brown-grain Mexican heroin rolled into tight tubes and taped. He took out the first baggy and put the rest of the box back into the hole, locked the closet door, and dropped the key into the toilet tank. From inside the medicine cabinet, he took a needle and an eyedropper, which he wrapped up with a towel.

In the living room, he found Lida sitting like a stone gargoyle on the bare canvas of the couch, her knees up to her stomach with a pillow in between. He went into the kitchen and took a canteen cup out of a drawer and gently shook the baggy so that a pinch of heroin slid down the edge and onto the metal surface. He added a drop of water into the cup. A strip of paper from an open envelope fit as a collar at the opening of the dropper to keep it tight as he pushed the needle in and made a syringe. He heated the needle over the burner and then brought the cup to the stove. His hand shook as he cooked the mixture over the low flame, watching it bubble and congeal, pulling it away when the handle heated up.

He brought the cup and syringe into the living room and placed them on the wooden table in front of her. She glanced at them and then away, her body still shaking. Marcus sat cross-legged and filled the dropper from the cup, then pulled off his leather belt with one hand.

"You got to tell your mama about him," he said, and knelt down at Lida's side.

"He says I'm gonna be the next president."

Marcus shifted onto his feet in a crouch and took her bare left arm in his hands.

"I shoulda never wore this dress," she said. "It only makes him crazy." Marcus wrapped the belt around her biceps and pulled it tight through the buckle.

"I ain't messin with no needle," she said, but she didn't pull away, she just watched as if he had someone else's arm in his hands.

"It'll calm you down."

"It's gonna hurt like hell."

"I wouldn't ever hurt you." He kissed her shoulder near the scratches. "I'm not like that."

"Fine." She closed her eyes and shook her head. "I don't care if you kill me. I want you to kill me."

"I don't sell no hot shots. This is good for you when you're low. It's medicine, same as like the doctor gives you. Same as I take when I'm low. Horse medicine." He pulled the leather belt tighter around her biceps and handed the end to her. "Hold this and pull. Now make a fist like you gonna hit him."

She clenched her fingers tightly and stared at the needle. He jabbed it into the crook of her arm, and the mixture in the dropper filled with little red clouds of her blood. He waited a second, then squeezed it all back into her.

THE NEXT DAY, Easton sat on the bus-stop bench, his legs crossed, with *The Black Panther* paper open on his lap, reading an article about the election. He laughed and shook his head, turning the page by the corner so no ink would get on his fingers. He was dressed meticulously in black slacks, a powder-blue shirt, black tie, and black leather jacket, his face and neck shaved smooth.

He adjusted his gold-rimmed rectangular glasses, stood up, and looked at the bench, checked for sticky stains, then sat back down.

Marcus walked up to the bench, the gun tucked under his letterman's jacket into the waist of his blue jeans. He stopped at the end of the bench and put one foot up on the seat boards. He leaned over and crossed his hands onto his lifted knee, looking straight at the side of Easton's face.

"Paper good?"

"Mar-*cus*! How you doin, my man? You seen my niece?"

Marcus shook his head. The winter day had been sunny, but now the evening brought with it a windy sting. Marcus looked up and down San Pablo. Directly across the street was an empty storefront that used to be a packaging company, then farther down was a Kentucky Fried Chicken and a fenced-up mechanic's lot with a dog. On their side of the street, behind them, was a closed hardware store; two houses, curtains drawn; and Tobias's liquor store on the corner.

"You want it right now?" Marcus asked. "Or back at your place?"

"Naw, Ruby's back in the shack. You best give me the goods now."

"Sure?"

"Sure. Here." Easton held the paper out to Marcus. "Put it under this and hand it back to me."

A woman came around the corner and they both turned to watch: her copper-colored bangs were greased up into a ducktail, and she wore a thin brown sweater open at the shoulders and large gold hoop earrings.

"Where's the beauty contest at?" Easton said. She smiled at him and kept walking to the liquor store. He turned back to Marcus. "Come on, man. Let's get this done."

Marcus took the newspaper and held it over his ankle. He reached into his sock and pulled out a baggy, rolled it into the paper, and handed it back. Easton opened the paper and looked at the baggy.

"Tremendous. I'll just have to trust that this is what you say. I wouldn't know horse from a horse's ass."

"That'll get you a hundred grains."

"What do you think I'll get for it?"

Marcus shrugged. "About ten a grain. What's Jonny's bail?"

"We'll make it. The Party thanks you. I'll nominate you for Minister of Fund-raising." He put the baggy into his jacket pocket and stood up. A police car passed by them on the other side of the street. They both watched as it slowed, its brake lights coming on. Easton didn't brush his cheek fully anymore, it was more of a flick with one finger. The police car got into the left lane and made a U-turn at the end of the block, then drove slowly back toward them.

"Time to fly," Easton said. They both walked up the block toward Cranston. They bent their heads humbly and looked at the ground, then turned the corner at the liquor store.

The car's tires screeched as the cops sped to the corner and pulled in at an angle just in front of Easton. A bearded officer with a slight paunch opened the passenger-side door and took out his club.

"Officer Monroe," Easton said, and nodded.

A skinny, younger policeman got out of the driver's side and ran around the back.

"Both of you on the ground," Monroe said. "Lay down. Facedown. Hands on your head."

"What's the problem?" Marcus asked.

"Get your ass down on the ground."

Marcus and Easton slowly bent down, first to their knees and then flat on their stomachs.

"Hands on your head. On your head, now."

"We were just walking home," Easton said. "You know I live right across the street."

"Shut up and get your hands back on your head."

As Marcus stretched his hands up, the back of his jacket lifted.

"This one's got a gun!" the skinny officer yelled. He drew his own gun and backed up, stumbling off the curb and behind the car, as if Marcus were aiming at him.

Monroe stepped back to the car and slowly drew his gun. "This one too," he said.

"I ain't got a gun. I ain't got a gun," Easton yelled. He put his hands in the air and shook them.

"I said drop the gun or I'll shoot."

"I ain't got a gun, motherfucker. Shit!"

"I said drop it." Monroe shot Easton in the side of his head, and the skinny cop turned quickly and shot Easton twice in the back. Easton's hands fell to his sides, his face down on the pavement.

Marcus kept his hands locked above his head, his eyes closed. Monroe put his foot between Marcus's shoulder blades and pulled the gun out of his pants. He handed the gun to the skinny cop, then cuffed Marcus and pulled him to his feet, wrenching his shoulders. Marcus looked at Easton, at the dark blood on the sidewalk by his head.

Two women stared out their windows.

If Ruby had come out on the porch, she would have seen the whole thing. But she was sewing, and when she heard the gunshots, she pressed harder on the pedal. revved the small machine's engine until the needle moved faster than her eyes.

SANTA RITA JAIL

TODAY, I READ from *Running a Thousand Miles for Freedom: The Escape of William and Ellen Craft from Slavery:*

There are a large number of free Negroes residing in the Southern States; but in Georgia (and I believe in all the Slave States) every colored person's complexion is *prima-facie* evidence of his being a slave; and the lowest villain in the country, should he be a white man, has the legal power to arrest, and question, in the most inquisitorial and insulting manner, any colored person, male or female, that he may find at large, particularly at night and on Sundays, without a written pass, signed by the master or someone in authority; or stamped free papers, certifying that the person is the rightful owner of himself.

If the colored person refuses to answer questions put to him, he may be beaten, and his defending himself against this attack makes him an outlaw, and if he be killed on the spot, the murderer will be exempted from all blame; but after the colored person has answered the questions put to him, in a most humble and pointed manner, he may then be taken to prison; and should it turn out, after further examination, that he was caught where he had no permission or legal right to be, and that he has not given what they term a satisfactory account of himself, the master will have to pay a fine. On his refusing to do this, the poor slave may be legally and severely flogged by public officers. Should the prisoner prove to be a free man, he is most likely to be both whipped and fined.

The great majority of slaveholders hate this class of persons with a hatred that can only be equalled by the condemned spirits of the infernal regions. They have no mercy upon, nor sympathy for, any Negro whom they cannot enslave. They say that God made the black man to be a slave for the white, and act as though they really believed that all free persons of color are in open rebellion to a direct command from heaven, and that they (the whites) are God's chosen agents to pour out upon them unlimited vengeance. For instance, a bill has been introduced in the Tennessee Legislature to prevent free Negroes from travelling on the railroads in that State. It has passed the first reading. The bill provides that the president who shall permit a free Negro to travel on any road within the jurisdiction of the State under his supervision shall pay a fine of five hundred dollars; any conductor permitting a violation of the act shall pay two hundred and fifty dollars; provided such free Negro is not under the control of a free white citizen of Tennessee who will vouch for the character of said free Negro in a penal bond of one thousand dollars. The State of Arkansas has passed a law to banish all free Negroes from its bounds, and it came into effect on the 1st day of January, 1860. Every free Negro found there after that date will be liable to be sold into slavery, the crime of freedom being unpardonable. The Missouri Senate has before it a bill providing that all free Negroes above the age of eighteen years who shall be found in the State after September 1860 shall be sold into slavery; and that all such Negroes as shall enter the State after September 1861 and remain there twenty-four hours, shall also be sold into slavery forever. Mississippi, Kentucky, and Georgia, and in fact, I believe, all the Slave States, are legislating in the same manner. Thus the slaveholders make it almost impossible for free persons of color to get out of the Slave States, in order that they may sell them into slavery if they don't go. If no white persons travelled upon railroads except those who could get someone to vouch for their character in a penal bond of one thousand dollars, the railroad companies would soon go to the "wall." Such mean legislation is too low for comment; therefore I leave the villainous acts to speak for themselves.

But the Dred Scott decision is the crowning act of infamous Yankee legislation. The Supreme Court, the highest tribunal of the Republic, composed of nine Judge Jeffreys, chosen both from the free and Slave States, has decided that no colored person, or persons of African extraction, can ever become a citizen of the United States, or have any rights which white men are bound to respect. That is to say, in the opinion of this Court, robbery, rape, and murder are not crimes when committed by a white person upon a colored person.

CHAPTER 6

"HERE. THIS IS just for now until I can get you into the house." Love handed Li'l Pit a white plastic plate with mashed potatoes and a barbecued chicken leg. Love had taken his brother, and the bikes they'd stolen from Ace Trey, into the charred structure of the house across from Ruby's. He had to wear a pair of Easton's loafers, which he found in the back of his closet. As night approached, Love lit a candle on a rusted coffee can so they could see. He then sat back on the springs of a half-burnt couch.

Li'l Pit attacked the chicken leg from the top like an ice-cream cone, biting off the bone with the meat. His hands were big already before the rest of him, his nails rotted and covered in the barbecue sauce.

Love smiled, and his high, round cheeks shone in the light of the candle. "You sure are hungry. Didn't anybody teach you manners? You've got the sauce all over your chin."

"Take your stupid chicken, then." Li'l Pit chucked the bone through the rusted security bars still locked to the inside window frame. "I don't need nothin from you, you funny-talking gray boy."

"Don't trip, dog. Don't trip. You hungry, that's all I'm sayin."

"What you laughin at?"

"Nothin." Love shook his head, but then he did start to laugh. "I just recallin you in the lot today, yelling up 'East Side. East Side.' " He looked Li'l Pit in the eye the whole time he spoke. "You like one of those short Li'l Gs, ain't scared of no Mac Daddy. 'East Side.' You crazy, man." He bent over laughing, and his brother laughed too. "That's why you a pit, like me. It doesn't matter how little you are if you're unpredictable. Even big people afraid of a little, uncontrollable dog."

Li'l Pit stood up and danced; his head jutted forward and back like a pigeon's, his hand out in front of him in the East Side flash. He rapped:

Yeah I'm Li'l Pit

Don't fuck with me

I am

The Mac Daddy

My brother is

A punk OG

My daddy up at

Santa Ree.

Love shook his head as Li'l Pit sat again on the ground. "You crazy, dog. You crazy." He looked away to the bars on the window. "You know our daddy ain't up at Santa Rita no more, don't you?"

Li'l Pit cracked his neck and then looked at the food on his plate. "Sure."

"He out in some backyard, toe-up."

"I know." Li'l Pit dipped his index finger into the mound of mashed potatoes and sucked off a scoop.

"You remember him?"

"I met him when I was just a kid." Li'l Pit scooped up more potatoes with his finger. The light of sunset cut through the bars onto the sickle-shaped part in his hair.

"That's a tight fade you got," Love said. "I'm gonna get me a wasp right here over my ear."

"By who?"

"Myself."

"Give me a skull and crossbones right on the back."

"You don't need none of that shit. You too young to be a playah. You should be in school. I'm gonna take you to Prescott next week and set you up."

"No you ain't."

"I'm gonna send you to college."

"No you ain't."

"You're gonna be a computer scientist."

"No I ain't. I'm gonna be a ballah and have me a cherry red Impala."

"You gonna be toe-up, that's what you gonna be if I catch you bangin."

"I ain't got to do what you say. You ain't my daddy. I ain't gonna go to Prescott. I'm gonna kick it wit you and my homies. Yay-eh. I'm West Side now." Li'l Pit stood up and danced again, poking his head back and forth, this time holding up his fingers in the West Side flash.

> I gotta hoo-ride
>
> 'Cause I'm West Side
>
> Gonna have pride
>
> 'Cause my daddy done died
>
> But now I'm West Side.

"I ain't gonna let you be down with no punks," Love said.

"You down."

"No I ain't."

"Yes you is so."

"Well I say I'm not." Love stood up and went to the window to see if anyone was walking around outside. The street was full of tired men and women returning home from work, but the crew was nowhere to be seen. As the sky darkened, a long pink cloud turned gray.

Li'l Pit rubbed his chapped hands over his naked shoulders, which stuck out of his jersey like two thin pencils.

"I'll get you some blankets and a shirt," Love said.

"How come you don't take me in the house?"

"Shoot, dog. I can't just take some strange niggah into her place."

"I ain't no stranger."

"You is to her."

"No I ain't. I came here for Mama once and almost got my shoes

84

took. I ask her for Mama's dress and she give it to me, the yellow one, but it don't fit Mama neither way, and she just sell it for a rock. Anyhow, she know me. She my Nanna too."

"She just got used to being my Nanna last month, dog. You think she want two of us crazy kids wreckin up her place? 'Sides, you got all that lice all in your head. So you got to stay out here a while."

Li'l Pit looked down at the ground lit by the candle. In the dirt lay the remains of someone's crack binge, a half-burnt matchbook, some tinfoil, and an empty box of Arm & Hammer baking soda.

"That's all right. I been use to it anyhow." He reached down and picked up a sheet of newspaper and wadded it up. He held it over the candle's flame until it caught fire. The boys' faces glowed orange as the ball of paper burned toward Li'l Pit's hand. He looked up at Love. The flames reached the tips of his fingers, but he didn't move. He held it for a second more, then threw the ball under the collapsed walls of a baby crib a few feet from them.

Love shook his head. "You ain't got to prove you hard to me."

"I ain't tryin to prove nothin. I just is."

"Course you is, you my blood."

They watched the flame lick the edge of the crib's post and then die away. Li'l Pit picked up the candle and walked over to the post. He held it under the wood until the white paint crackled and caught fire.

"Now!" Li'l Pit said triumphantly.

"That's a shame."

"What's a shame?"

"It gets out a some big ole fire way back, and now you go and light it up."

"Yeah, well, some things was meant to burn up." He held his arms out and warmed them over the small fire. Beige moths raced between the shadows flickering on the walls.

"Some moths look like bees and wasps," Love said. "So they won't be eaten in the day. You know what I'm saying?"

"I think you one of them funny niggahs," Li'l Pit said.

"Just cause I got some learnin don't mean I can't beat your ass."

"Here it is, then." He stood up and bent his butt toward Love. "Come on an beat on it."

"I'm gonna get them blankets before you set your own nappy lice head on fire to keep warm."

"That's what I thought." Li'l Pit lowered his behind.

Love climbed over the fallen railing of the stairway and out through a hole in the wall. He crossed Cranston, unhooked the fence, and climbed the stairs of the red Victorian.

Ruby sat in the rocking chair in the living room, looking out the front window. She wore her suede cowgirl outfit, light brown chaps and matching jacket with long leather fringes. She held a black hat in her lap. The room was quiet and the curtains still open. Love met her eyes when he came in but turned around quickly, closing the door and locking it. He walked by her to the stairs, his hands in the pockets of his white jeans. He climbed the first step, then turned to her.

"Ain't you gonna ask where I been?"

"Will it stop you from going?"

"No."

"Then why should I waste my breath?"

Love turned and jogged up the stairs, then stopped again halfway. "You got another blanket I could have?"

Ruby rocked back and forth a few times then let out a sigh. "You know your mama ain't gonna do nothin but sell it."

"It ain't for my mama."

"I try to get her to a program. Long time ago." Ruby looked at the coffee table. "She lower than low. She ran away from me, you know. But I won't have her in this house till she clean."

"I told you it ain't for her."

"I just don't want to see you get hurt. Everyone else been pulled away from me. You what family I got. But you gonna do what you have to do. I know that. She your mama." Ruby put her hat on the table and stood up. "I'd rather give it to you than have you steal it."

She went into her room and came out with a green blanket, satiny on the edges. Love came back down the stairs and took it.

"Just don't you steal from me. That's the one thing I won't stand for—that's what your papa done. Remember, you asked me and I gave it to you." Ruby sat back down in the rocking chair.

"An where your shoes?"

Love looked down at his feet as though he hadn't noticed. "I lost them."

"You what?"

"I lost them."

Ruby shook her head. "How you gone lose your shoes right off your feet? We can't afford to be given everything away." Love opened the front door.

Ruby yelled after him, "Now don't you give her those loafers, you hear. Those shoes ain't yours."

Love took the blanket back across the street. The crib was still burning in low blue flames.

"Look at this," Li'l Pit said. "I found myself a bed." He lay curled up in an open cardboard box the size of a desk turned on its side, his feet sticking out of the bottom. Love laid the blanket over him.

"I'll tell her tomorrow. Then we can get your head cleaned up and we can stay in the same room."

"That's awright. I don't mind. I got myself a room here."

"I'll come get you in the morning." Love climbed through the wall and over the stairwell again. He stopped in the darkness outside on the street and listened. He could see the crew under a streetlight at the corner liquor store. The guy with the braid and his wheelchair-bound homie with the snake were laughing next to a woman in tight red satin shorts and fishnet stockings. He watched them from a distance until the wind blew and chilled him.

Before he stepped off the curb, he heard Li'l Pit calling to him from inside the burnt house, or maybe singing again. He went back to check on him, and through the hole in the stairs he saw Li'l Pit lying on his stomach inside his box, banging his forehead against his arm and grunting in a monotonous drone, like a car engine struggling to turn over: "Nuh uh uh uh uh uh uh uh uh."

THE NEXT MORNING Love took his usual hour to fix himself up after showering, just as he had at Los Aspirantes. He applied lotion to every inch of his body, rubbing circularly from his wrist to his shoulder, his ankle to his waist, and then carefully greasing the grooves between each finger and each toe. He doused himself in cologne, tipping the bottle against his neck, his chest, and his underarms. He cleaned out his ears with Q-Tips, brushed and flossed his teeth, and then began to dress, laying out each T-shirt on his bed above his white jeans until he narrowed his choice down to two outfits. Then he tried on each shirt twice before coming to a final decision, a red Bull's jersey. He slipped on his loafers and then went back to the bathroom to fix his hair. He picked it out and sprayed on conditioner until it glowed.

He had to wait for Ruby to leave for her cleaning job. Love was supposed to get himself to school. After breakfast and another expedition to the bathroom to wash his hands, brush his teeth again, and reconsider his hair, he put on Easton's leather jacket, which he'd found going through the closets. Then he went outside to check on Li'l Pit in the burnt house across the street.

Li'l Pit sat in his cardboard box, the blanket over his legs, playing steamroller on his lap with two empty cigarette boxes. Love stood by the hole under the stairs and gestured to him with a flick of his head.

"Come on."

"Where?"

"You've got to get ready."

"For what?"

"For school."

"I ain't going to school."

"Well, you want something to eat, don't you?"

Li'l Pit nodded.

"Well, come on then."

Li'l Pit stood up and threw the boxes onto the ground.

The inside of Ruby's house stunned Li'l Pit. The living room was clean and spacious under its high ceiling. The light through the curtains made the room glow softly, as if gold were hidden under the surface of all the wood. He stood silently and put his hands on the blue quilt tucked around the top of the couch. Everywhere were items of comfort and value, soft things to lie on, exotic things to steal.

"I'll fix us something to eat," Love said and went into the kitchen. Li'l Pit felt drawn around the room like a magnet. He studied the sea-shells around the base of the potted plant on the coffee table and the black stone elephants sitting by the record player. When Love came back in the room with two bowls of cereal, Li'l Pit was standing at the far wall, looking at the black-and-white photographs of Corbet and Elise, sliding his hand along the wood frames.

"Sit down here." Love spread red-knit place mats on the table, and his brother sat in one of the tall-backed chairs. He grabbed one bowl and started shoveling the food into his mouth. Love pulled the bowl away.

"I'll let you say grace," Love said. Li'l Pit shook his head and stared at the bowl. "All right. Close your eyes. Thank you for this food we are about to eat and for taking care of us and taking care of our grand-mother and the rest of the people in our family. Amen. Say amen."

"Amen."

"I mixed the Frosted Flakes with the cornflakes so you get some of the good stuff with the healthy stuff." Li'l Pit pulled the bowl back and ate without looking up.

"Now, you've got to chew with your mouth closed. And don't drink the milk out of the bottom. And when you're done, you've got to brush your teeth so they don't fall out."

Li'l Pit finished the cereal, picked up the bowl, and drank the rest of the milk. "I ain't brushing my teeth," he said.

"You've got to."

"It hurts."

"Then you got to use your finger and some toothpaste and rub it all around."

Love took his brother into the bathroom and squeezed toothpaste onto his finger. "See. Don't use too much. Now just stick your finger all around in there."

When they were done in the bathroom, Love made sure Li'l Pit washed his dish and put it on the drying rack, the way the counselors had him do it at Los Aspirantes.

"Now you're ready for school."

"No I ain't." Li'l Pit backed up into the corner against the sink and the refrigerator. It was clear there would be a struggle if Love insisted.

"Then what you want to do?"

"I don't know."

"You want to play hoops?"

Li'l Pit shrugged, which was good enough. Love went upstairs and got the ball from the closet.

"Where the hoops at?" Li'l Pit asked.

"You'll see."

They walked out onto the street and toward the train yard. At the end of the last block they rounded the corner into an alley, the backs of houses and garbage cans on one side and, on the other, a tall concrete wall hiding the train tracks. The hoop was a blue milk crate with the bottom cut out, nailed ten feet up on a telephone pole. Love looked up and down the alley, then, seeing no one else around, nodded and dribbled toward the pole, moving as best he could in his old loafers.

"Yee-eh, boy," he yelled. He jumped into the air, spun almost 360 degrees, and shot it in the crate, leaving the ball bouncing on the pavement.

"Now!" he said, strutting back to Li'l Pit. "Can you say J-o-r-d-a-n?"

Li'l Pit chased the ball down and dribbled it with both hands.

"What's up with that? That's double dribble. Give me that." But Li'l Pit kept dribbling, looking at the ball closely like he wasn't sure if it would bounce straight back up. Love ran to him and swiped it away.

"Do it like this." He bounced the ball with one hand by his side, waist high, nice and basic. But then he couldn't help show off: he bounced it between his legs faster and faster and then went in for a layup. Li'l Pit smiled and chased the ball again. He tried bouncing it with one hand but hit his foot and the ball rolled away.

"I don't want to play. I'm tired," he said.

"You sure is. You the most tired hoopster I ever seen. I'm gonna teach you something. Back in the day, I couldn't do none of this." Love shot the ball into the basket. "But now I'm all that. And I didn't have anyone to show me, like you've got now, see. So you've got to take advantage." He shot a three-pointer from behind a chalk line drawn on the pavement. When he turned around, Li'l Pit was pulling a box of Chinese food from a black garbage bag.

"What you doing?"

"It's for later."

"Put that nasty stuff down. You don't know what kinda AIDS that got." Love snatched the box from him and threw it on the bag. "You've got to have some hygiene. You can't just eat anything. We've got more food inside."

"Hey, hey, nice shoes, punk." The crew from the corner liquor store was upon them without a moment to think, six guys, all bigger and older, including the guy in the wheelchair. A thin stick of a guy punched the ball out of Love's arms and dribbled in for a layup.

"What you doin with our ball and hoop?" said the man standing out in front of the crew. He towered above them with square shoulders and a brow that stuck out over his eyes by an inch, giving him a natural shade without sunglasses. Love recognized him from looking out the window on his first day at Ruby's. He had a long braid of hair down his back, which, Love had heard, was because his father was Japanese.

"Hey Freight Train," the stick boy called to the man. "Watch this." He shot from behind the three-point line but missed. "Man, you-know-what-I'm-sayin, this ball is junk."

The guy in the wheelchair with the boa constrictor around his shoulders rolled up to Love.

"What's up, niggah? You ain't got no tongue?" Love still didn't say anything. He kept his eyes level, staring forward into nothing, as though the crew weren't even there.

"Damn, bro," Li'l Pit said, his body working from side to side as he walked up to the wheelchair. "That's a tight snake."

"Shut up," Love said flatly to his brother.

"Listen here, niggah," the man in the chair said to Love. "You ain't got no bidness talking to a little brother that way."

"What kinda snake this is?" Li'l Pit asked.

"This the kinda snake that eat bitches for lunch."

"Watch this, Curse," the stick boy yelled to the man in the chair. He walked up behind Love and threw the basketball at his head. It hit Love in the ear. Love turned and glared at the boy.

"What you lookin at, niggah?"

It was clear now who they wanted him to take on. This chump in the alley was definitely just a punk who'd be nothing without the crew. He had to stand up for the OGs, but they might not stand up for him because he might still have to prove himself. Love saw no way to leave this alley without a beating. Either he fought and they beat him up but respected him, or he didn't fight and they beat him up every time they saw him. It was going to come down anyway, so Love had to do it while he still had some dignity. He blocked out the pain in his head and ran at the guy.

As he'd expected, the rest of the crew stood and watched while he and this stick boy went at it. They were both good with their hands and got in a few punches before it appeared Love would win, but then the stick boy pulled out a .22. He pointed it right at Love's forehead.

Love closed his eyes. He'd been in this situation before. Closing his eyes helped him keep calm; when he couldn't see the gun and its hole of death, it was like it wasn't there.

"I guess you can't take me with your hands," Love said, loud enough for the crew to hear.

"I could take you with my finger right now, niggah."

Love turned around and looked at Freight Train and the rest of the crew. They waited to see what their homie would do. He hit Love in the temple with the gun and knocked him to the ground. Love put his hand to his head and felt the blood. He spit on the ground as if this would somehow keep his poise, but he couldn't stand up again.

Freight walked over and put his hand out for the gun. The stick boy handed it over immediately. Freight aimed the gun back at him.

"What you doin, Freight?"

Freight didn't answer.

"I had to. You-know-what-I'm-sayin. I had to, 'cause he was dissin us, you-know-what-I'm-sayin." He backed up, and when he'd gotten five feet away, he turned and ran up the alley. Freight shot at him and missed, but the boy fell to the ground and covered his head. He screamed out, practically crying.

"Fuck, Freight, what you shoot at me for?"

"Get up," Freight said in an even tone.

The boy slowly raised himself with his head turned away.

"Come here."

Stick boy walked slowly toward Freight, who held the gun straight at him. Love watched from the ground and Li'l Pit watched from the side of Curse's chair. Nothing moved in the alley but the snake's black tongue, shooting out and quivering, silently smelling the air. The stick boy's chest heaved, but he walked right up to the nose of the gun.

"Would I ever hurt you?" Freight asked him.

The boy shook his head but didn't look convinced.

"When's the only time I'd ever hurt you?"

The boy had a hard time making the sound come to his mouth, but after a few swallows, he said: "If I ever leave you."

"That's right. That's why I shot at you. I love you too much, man, to let your ass go. That would hurt my heart. I was testing you. And now you've come back. So you ain't got nothing to fear." He lowered the gun and grabbed the boy in a long, hard hug that seemed to take the breath out of him. When Freight stepped back, he held out the gun for the boy. "Take it."

He took it and put it back in his pants. Curse wheeled over to the basketball, picked it up and put it in his lap. He rolled very close to Love's fingers and then back to Li'l Pit.

"Here you go, little brother. You can play with our ball for a while." Li'l Pit took the ball and nodded as if he'd been given a special assignment.

Freight turned, and the rest of the crew followed him out of the alley and back up Cranston.

LOVE BROUGHT LI'L Pit inside for breakfast again the next day after Ruby had gone to work. When they'd cleaned up, Love took him outside and walked back around the block to get to San Pablo, instead of going up Cranston and passing the liquor store where the crew always hung out.

"Now I know what we've got to do," Love said.

"Where we going?"

"Prescott."

"Nuh-uh." Li'l Pit stopped. "I ain't, and you can't make me."

"All right. You don't have to." Love turned around and walked past his brother. "Just thought you wanted to come live with us."

"I do."

"Then you've got to go to school. You gonna get Nanna put in jail if you're not in school. And they feed you tacos in school and you get to draw and there are other kids you can hang with. But if you don't want to, then we'll just go on back to your cardboard box and see if there's some more of that Chinese food left in the trash."

"How come you ain't got to go to school?"

"I can't. Got to have somebody working."

"I want to work."

"You will. But now you got to go to school first, and then you can make a lot of money working on computers. You get some of those tight Penny Hardaways and a red Impala. Yee-eh, boy." Love held his fist out, and Li'l Pit tapped it and smiled. They walked toward Prescott and Li'l Pit rapped, his hand waving in the air:

LEAVING

See ya homies later

'Cause I got to go to school

Gonna eat a taco sandwich

Gonna spit it up and drool.

When they arrived at the administration building with all the adults around, they got very quiet and serious. They walked down the hallway and looked for an office where a lot of people went in and out. Li'l Pit stayed by the door as Love went up to the long counter. The woman at the desk did not look up at first. She was typing a letter and had to Wite-Out something on it. Without turning to see who it was, she spoke to him.

"Can I help you?"

"I need to know what class to put my brother in."

"What's his name?" She rolled the paper down and began to type again. Love looked at Li'l Pit and motioned him to come to the counter. "She wants to know your name. Your real name."

"Paul LeRoy."

"Who's your teacher, hun?"

"I don't know."

The woman let out a deep breath and took off her half-frame glasses. "What does she look like?"

"You don't know what you're saying, lady," Love said. "He isn't in school yet."

"You want to register him?"

"Yes please."

She stood up and came to the counter. Now that she was looking at them, she didn't have an altogether unpleasant face. Her hair was braided with gold extentions and tied in the back. When she saw Li'l Pit, she smiled.

"How old are you, hun?"

"Ten."

She looked at Love and shook her head, still smiling a little. "You have to have an adult register him, and it has to be his legal guardian.

You've got to have proof. And you've got to have his birth certificate, or some sort of medical record from the hospital he was born in." She turned back to Li'l Pit. "Were you born near here?"

"Highland."

"And you'll need to get a physical and have your immunization papers. We can't let anyone in until we know you're not going to make the other kids sick."

"I'm not gonna make them sick."

"I know, hun, but we have to make sure. There's a place at the district downtown called Student Services," the woman continued. "Have your mother go there and they'll help her get everything you need. Okay?"

Love had stopped paying attention. He was staring out the window behind the desk into the bright light and the elevated BART tracks above Seventh. This feeling had often come over him at school, and he was surprised to see how quickly it came back. He closed his eyes and then looked back at the woman.

"Can't he just start until we get all that other stuff done?"

"No, I'm sorry. Will it be difficult for you to get the paperwork?"

He shook his head.

"They'll help you pay if you can't afford it," she said.

"That's not it." Love said. Li'l Pit went over to the magazines on a table.

"Does your mother work?"

Love nodded.

"What about your father?" Love looked down at the counter and saw his own reflection in the waxy surface. Li'l Pit turned through the pages of a *Sports Illustrated*.

"Can any adult come in with him?" she asked.

"My grandmother."

"Is she his legal guardian?" Love had enough experience with custody issues to know that it was complicated and that she probably wasn't since Li'l Pit had been living on the street with their mother. But he shrugged his shoulders just to see where it might lead.

96

"Well, have her come in and then we'll know what to do next, okay, hun?"

He nodded. When Love turned away to go, he noticed a sign on the inside door that read MRS. PIKE, PRINCIPAL. He left and Li'l Pit ran out behind him. When they got to the outside of the school, Love kicked the gate.

"What did she say?" his brother asked.

"I'm going to take you to the room and you just sit in there and be good and then the teacher will let you stay. Once I tell Nanna about you and she knows you're in school, then she won't mind you stayin overnight. What grade you suppose to be in?"

Li'l Pit shrugged. Love thought back to the last time he was in a public school. When he was eight, he'd been in third grade.

"You should be in fifth now, but we'll say fourth since you've been out so long. No, we better say third. You're kinda small."

"No I ain't."

Love took his brother's hand and pulled him back into the schoolyard. They walked past the administration building and down each hall until they came to a room with a plaque on the door that said MRS. TERRY, THIRD GRADE.

Love opened the heavy door and stuck his head in. The room was filled with Native American artifacts, kachina dolls on the shelves, painted cardboard drums hanging from the walls with names on them, and a large photograph of an Indian warrior. Mrs. Terry stopped talking and the whole class looked at Love.

"Yes?"

"Mrs. Pike says he's supposed to be in your class." He pulled Li'l Pit into the room.

"Another one? I already have thirty-two." She took a deep breath. "What's your name?"

Li'l Pit didn't answer.

"His name is Paul," Love said.

"Okay, Apaches," said Mrs. Terry. "Let's all give Paul a warriors' welcome." All the kids howled and paddled their mouths.

"Sit over there, Paul, by Jesse."

Love pushed his brother forward and then left. Li'l Pit sauntered to the seat at the far end of the room, his right arm trailing behind his back. He sat next to a kid with freckles on his coffee-brown cheeks who smiled at his new neighbor.

"What you lookin at?" Li'l Pit said. The boy looked down, and a few other kids giggled.

"All right, Paul," said Mrs. Terry. "You have to learn the Apache good-neighbor rules we've written here on the wall. Why don't you read them to us."

Li'l Pit stared at the poster. He began breathing loudly through his nose like a bull. He looked around the room, and every time he met another kid's eyes they hung their heads, but one boy kept looking at him.

"Rah!" he barked.

The class broke out in laughter. Li'l Pit barked again. "Rah, rah."

"We don't allow barking in the class," Mrs. Terry said.

Li'l Pit stood up and barked right at her: "Rah, rah, rah." He moved around his desk toward the front of the room, and as he looked at the other kids, they pulled back, the expressions on their faces caught between a scream and a laugh. Before Mrs. Terry could reach the intercom, he turned and ran out the door.

He ran out of the gate, down Peralta, and caught up to Love on the sidewalk. Love stopped and pushed him back toward Prescott. "What's up? Get back to school."

"They kicked me out."

"Damn, dog, what'd you do already?"

"Nothin. Nothin. They say I can't come back. I ain't allowed 'cause I got to prove I'm a citizen."

"What you talking about?"

"That lady in the office say my mama got to come down and prove I'm a citizen."

"You don't know what you're sayin."

"Well, I didn't do nothin."

"Damn, dog. Whatever." Love turned and walked away from him. Li'l Pit followed, always a few steps behind, picking up pebbles and tossing them at the tall iron bars of the projects.

SANTA RITA JAIL

TODAY I READ to you from the narrative of James W. C. Pennington's *The Fugitive Blacksmith:*

About this time, I began to feel another evil of slavery—I mean the want of parental care and attention. Many parents were not able to give any attention to their children during the day. I often suffered much from *hunger* and other similar causes. To estimate the sad state of a slave child, you must look at it as a helpless human being thrown upon the world without the benefit of its natural guardians. It is thrown into the world without a social circle to flee to for hope, shelter, comfort, or instruction. The social circle, with all its heaven-ordained blessings, is of the utmost importance to the *tender child;* but of this, the slave child, however tender and delicate, is robbed. . . .

Three or four of our farmhands had their wives and families on other plantations. In such cases, it is the custom in Maryland . . . under the mildest of slavery . . . to allow the men to go on Saturday evening to see their families, stay over the Sabbath, and return on Monday morning, not later than "half-an-hour by sun." To overstay their time is a grave fault, for which, especially at busy seasons, they are punished.

One Monday morning, two of these men had not been so fortunate as to get home at the required time; one of them was an uncle of mine. Besides these, two young men who had no families, and for whom no such provision of time was made, having gone somewhere to spend the Sabbath, were absent. My master was greatly irritated, and had resolved to have, as he said, "a general whipping-match among them."

Preparatory to this, he had a rope in his pocket, and a cowhide in his hand, walking about the premises, and speaking to everyone he met in a very insolent manner, and finding fault with some without just cause. My father, among other numerous and responsible duties, discharged that of shepherd to a large and valuable flock of Merino sheep. This morning he was engaged in the tenderest of a shepherd's duties: a little lamb, not able to go alone, lost its mother; he was feeding it by hand. He had been keeping it in the house for several days. As he stooped over it in the yard, with a vessel of new milk he had obtained, with which to feed it, my master came along, and without the least provocation, began by asking, "Bazil, have you fed the flock?"

"Yes, sir."

"Were you away yesterday?"

"No, sir."

"Do you know why these boys have not got home this morning yet?"

"No, sir, I have not seen any of them since Saturday night."

"By the Eternal, I'll make them know their hour. The fact is, I have too many of you; my people are getting to be the most careless, lazy, and worthless in the country."

"Master," said my father, "I am always at my post; Monday morning never finds me off the plantation."

"Hush Bazil! I shall have to sell some of you; and then keep you all tightly employed; I have too many of you."

All this was said in an angry, threatening, and exceedingly insulting tone. My father was a high-spirited man, and feeling deeply the insult, replied to the last expression, "If I am one too many, sir, give me a chance to get a purchaser, and I am willing to be sold when it may suit you."

"Bazil, I told you to hush!" and suiting the action to the word, he drew forth the cowhide from under his arm, fell upon him with most savage cruelty, and inflicted fifteen or twenty severe stripes with all his strength, over his shoulders and the small of his back. As he raised himself upon his toes, and gave the last stripe, he said, "By the ★ ★ ★ I will make you know that I am master of your tongue as well as of your time!"

Being a tradesman, and just at that time getting my breakfast, I was near enough to hear the insolent words that were spoken to my father, and to hear, see, and even count the savage stripes inflicted upon him.

Let me ask any one of the Anglo-Saxon blood and spirit, how would you expect a *son* to feel at such a sight?

CHAPTER 7A

EASTON AND SANDRA walked by the stream on campus, past the eucalyptus grove to a bridge made of redwood planks where they could see the water running beneath them. It was the kind of summer day particular to northern California that felt warm but in a light way, dry and slightly breezy, thin leaves fluttering every few minutes like paper chimes. Because it was a summer weekend, there were very few students on campus, and they were left to themselves to listen to the water and be aware of the space and silence between them.

Easton picked at a pimple by his chin where his thin beard was growing in. He stopped himself before she could notice.

"See," she said to him, pointing through the boards to the stream. "I'm not making it up. Look at the stones. The big one is the eye. See?"

He shook his head. He didn't speak because he didn't have the breath. His chest seemed to push against his lungs. He'd hardly spoken the whole time they were alone that day. He shook his head so that she would keep pointing, so that he could stare at her face as she peered between the wooden boards. She had let him kiss her once, at night by a car around the corner from her dorm. It had been a long kiss, and it had been dark, and he felt so unsure now whether she would ever let him kiss her again, whether she even remembered kissing him at all. He had made a mistake that night, and he worried that perhaps she hated him for it, that she was going to tell him in a few moments that they should only be friends.

They had stopped by a car on the night of the kiss because she didn't want to be seen in front of the dorm, and she couldn't bring him in. There was a wall, a cement wall mixed with pebbles that formed the foundation of the dorm, which was built on raised ground like an unbreachable castle above him. They had stopped to look at the car, a silver Spider with a black leather interior.

"Nice," he had said. She nodded and squeezed his hand.

They had come to hold hands in a very peculiar way. That night was their second date. He had taken her to Blake's to see Dave Brubeck. She was very excited the whole time, watching him explain what he heard and how music was the only way people could be truly free. On the walk back from Telegraph, they had been followed by three young men, all White, one of whom said loudly, "It disgusts me," and spat on the sidewalk beside them. That was when Sandra took Easton's hand. The young men stopped following them at Channing Way; and, though nothing violent had happened, Easton felt he and Sandra had experienced their first intimate moment.

Still holding hands, they turned from the car and faced each other. Everything he knew told him he shouldn't be there and that he should keep still, though he knew what she wanted. He was grateful when she stretched out to him and kissed his lips. They backed away from the car, out of the streetlight, and stood against the wall in the shadows.

Then he touched her breast with his hand. That was not the mistake that worried him as he stood on the bridge. She let him hold her gently as they kissed. It was after they pulled away from each other but were still close enough to hear the mingling of their breath that he said what still echoed in his own mind, as if some stranger had yelled it at him: "How does it feel to kiss a Negro?"

She closed her mouth and frowned. "What do you mean by that?"

He didn't know what he'd meant, only that some part of him urged it on by whispering in him that he must strike first.

"Nothing," Easton said. "I didn't mean anything. I've always wanted to kiss a White girl."

"That's not why I kissed you."

"That's okay with me if it was. I liked it."

"For your information, you are not the first Negro boy I've kissed by a long shot." She wiped her mouth with the back of her arm.

"I didn't mean anything by it," he said.

But that was it for the night, and soon she was in her dorm and he was walking alone back to Shattuck.

On this bright day on the bridge, Easton was glad for the sound of the rushing water, which kept him from talking and saying something stupid again.

Sandra plucked a green leaf from the overhanging tree and traced it against her palm as if she were painting. Then she took Easton's hand and traced the leaf over his palm and wrist, up his arm, along his neck and onto his cheek. He closed his eyes and she brushed it across his face slowly, over his lips and onto his nose, up to and across his forehead.

"You're beautiful," she whispered. "You're beautiful."

He smiled, and she brushed the leaf over the corners of his smile.

"Am I really the first White girl you ever kissed?"

He kept his eyes closed and nodded. He felt her warm lips touch his, and he opened his mouth. The breeze rustled the leaves above them and raised the hair on their arms. Small pebbles turned on the riverbed below, little black and brown stones rolling over each other in the current of the stream. As they kissed, both of them, at different times, opened their eyes and looked at the face kissing them back: looked, and then closed their eyes again, as though leaving and reentering a dream.

THEY DATED ALL summer, and by September, Easton was ready to introduce Sandra to his family. He knew he wouldn't get a word in edgewise, so he took the opportunity to draw her while she sat in the living room. Ruby stayed unusually quiet that afternoon, but Corbet was full of stories.

"See," said Corbet, who sat in his chair drinking, his crutches leaning against the record shelves. "They still didn't trust us to be officers in our own unit. They put us under White folks."

Easton studied Sandra at the other end of the couch. He felt the thick piece of sketch paper between his fingers, the fibrous texture like sacred parchment. He turned to a blank page in the tablet and held the stick of charcoal poised in the air above the center of the paper.

"Jews," said Saul. "They figured that we were the only White people that didn't mind, so all the officers of the Negro companies were Jewish at first."

"That's why Jews pissed me off so much." Corbet laughed. "I thought they ran the army and the school and the government, for that matter. Everywhere I looked, some Jew was telling me what to do." Sandra nodded earnestly, like she was interviewing the president.

Easton began to sketch, brushing the black stick lightly across the top of the paper, his eyes on Sandra, then flicking down every once in a while for a glance at his work. Little Lida walked over and stood across the table from him, staring at his hand and the strokes on the page.

"One day," Saul said, "Corbet, he came up to me and he said, 'We're not going to fight unless we get paid the same as the White infantry.' See, Easton, this is where you get your fire."

"That boy and I aren't blood kin, Saul," Corbet said, and shook his head.

"Doesn't matter. Fire, it leaps around like that. In any case, the whole company sent him up to tell me. And I took him to be telling the truth."

"He just nodded his head and called General Lehey," Corbet said. "That's when I knew he was all right. Then they integrated us, but that was only in the army. Came home and I still couldn't stay in a hotel for my own victory parade. I couldn't take that kind of foolishness anymore. That's why I come out here."

"That's why you disappeared and left Mama," Easton said. He looked up at Ruby, who shook her head at him.

Corbet took a sip of his bourbon. "*C'est la vie.* I know it's tempting to judge me, but life's too messy to simplify like that. You wouldn't even be born if I hadn't."

"Are you going to let us look at your sketch?" Saul asked.

"You're the first person he's done that isn't from a photograph," Corbet said to Sandra. "You ought to be honored."

She smiled.

"She's quiet," Corbet continued. "Watch out for the quiet ones, son. They'll use your own mind to make you crazy."

"She's not so quiet when she knows you," Easton said.

"Is that right? What are you studying in school, young lady?"

"I don't have a major yet. But I'm thinking about anthropology. I also love art history. I brought Easton a book on Picasso."

"Is that right? Let me see that here." She picked the book off the table and handed it to him. "We know Picasso very well. Don't we, Saul?"

"Sure, yes." He looked over Corbet's shoulder while he slowly turned the pages, as if they were precious old pictures of themselves.

"This lady will take you places, son," Corbet said softly. Sandra bowed her head and Corbet spoke up: "Now, do you do that just to look pretty or are you really that shy?"

"Please, Papa," Easton complained.

"Let the boy do his own work," Saul said.

"Sorry. Sorry." Corbet leaned back into his chair and put the bourbon to his lips.

"Just to look pretty," Sandra said.

"Mmm-hmm. See, she's got some spunk in her."

Easton held the drawing tablet away from him. "Okay. I'm done. Here it is."

Sandra took it from him. "Do I really look like this? Oh God, I look so young, I guess. I mean, it's good. Really good. You're really talented. I wish I could do something like that." She passed the tablet over to Corbet.

"See, the real talent isn't the drawing itself," Corbet said. "It's how he caught you smiling and kind of shy. He can see people's vulnerability. That's his real talent." He handed the tablet back to Easton.

Saul went into the kitchen and put on a teakettle. There was a silence, and Corbet watched Lida toddle over to the windup musical bear she got from Ruby. She shook it, and a few notes of "God Rest Ye Merry Gentlemen" chimed out.

Corbet felt Sandra watching him.

"You want to ask me a question?"

"No. It's just that . . . I'm not very familiar with Negro people, and I feel that it's really important that I understand how it feels to be colored so I can be better at fighting for civil rights."

"Mmm-hmm."

Ruby said nothing. She rolled her eyes, stood up, and went into the kitchen.

"You know what I mean?" Sandra asked him.

"I think I know what you think you mean."

"I don't mean to be nosy."

"I know, but first tell me, Sandra: how does it feel to be White?"

Sandra laughed. "It doesn't feel like anything, really. I mean, I guess I don't really think about it."

Corbet sat back and sipped his drink. "Well, that's the difference. I think about it. I think about my skin color because it always mattered, the way you feel when you've got a big old pimple right in the middle of your forehead, like everyone is staring at you because of it, like people won't like you, like you want to cover up, but you know you shouldn't have to."

Sandra nodded and quickly touched her fingers to her forehead.

"But it isn't the same out here," he went on. "It's only because I was spoiled in France. Honestly, you'd have to ask Easton. He's the new generation. My mind is filled with memories and old battles."

"I don't want to talk about it," Easton said. He put the portrait down on the table. "I don't feel colored. I'm just like anybody else. Negro is out there. It's everybody else that's 'Negro this' and 'colored that.' They want to keep reminding you that you come from slaves, that you'll never be the same as them. I don't feel Negro. I just feel like me."

Corbet nodded. He wanted to say something to comfort Easton, but he knew there were no words equal to the task. He settled for: "It's tough when you can't find work."

"Before the war," Saul said, "I couldn't get a job either. I'd go to all the offices, fill out their applications. Nothing. I'd always write my name, Saul Rubenstein, on the top. I was qualified for those jobs. I could even type. But they took one look at me, my name, my yarmulke, and boom—sorry, no job. There had to be a job, or why would they be giving out the applications? Am I right? So one day I come home to dinner and I tell my father, I'm changing my name on these applications. I'm going to call myself Sam Roman, and I'm not going to wear my yarmulke. Of course he goes *verrucht,* out of his head, storms to the icebox, takes out the milk bottle, and pours it onto my plate of meat, then leaves the table. This is a big no-no for us. Next day I fill out my application: Sam Roman, no yarmulke, and boom—first time, I'm hired as a stock manager at Sheraton Office Supply. That's why I wear this yarmulke and clothes now. Shame. It's the very worst. It will eat you from the inside. Don't ever be ashamed of yourself." He smiled at Easton and looked to Corbet for confirmation, but Corbet didn't meet his eyes.

"I'm glad you told me that story," Easton said. "I was about to change my name and go out on more interviews."

Corbet looked at him and they shared a smile. Saul shook his head. "I see. Well, I suppose I'll go and join Ruby now." He stood up and went into the kitchen. While they watched him go, Lida picked up a charcoal stick from the table and drew a line across the portrait of Sandra.

"No!" Easton yelled. "No." He grabbed her wrist with the charcoal in it and squeezed until she dropped it. "Shit."

"It's all right," Sandra said. She went over to Lida and picked her up.

"It's not all right. This is all the paper I've got. I don't have any more charcoal. I can't afford to waste any of it. How come I've got to take care of Ruby's baby? How come she can't take care of her own child?"

No one spoke. Sandra rocked Lida, who stopped crying and played with Sandra's beaded earrings. Corbet stared down at the Picasso book on his lap.

"Ants in the sink again," Saul yelled from the kitchen.

Easton closed the cover on the tablet and lay back on the couch. He let out a long breath and closed his eyes.

CHAPTER 7B

THE FUNERAL FOR Easton was held right around the corner on Tenth, at Baptist AME Church, a square pink building that used to be a movie theater. Inside were rows of seats instead of pews, but there were never any complaints from the congregation who felt it was more comfortable that way. Lida and Ruby sat onstage in folding chairs. The curtain had been pulled aside to expose the screen, upon which the preacher projected slides of the deceased. A large photograph of Easton's face looked down over the room like Big Brother. Lida, in her black dress, shaking her leg, faced away from the screen but could feel Easton's presence through the faces of the congregation who stared above her in the dim light as if she were not even there.

"You can find what you have lost," the preacher said. "Just as sure as you can lose what you have once gained." Lida pulled up the shoulder of her dress, as though the scratches were still visible. Two small children at the back of the church screamed and chased each other, their mother snatching after them. Lida watched the children play in their suits, rolling on the red carpet without a care.

"Before I have Ruby and Lida speak to you, I want to read from the source of wisdom we must cling to in trying times." The preacher bent his head and read from the Bible, which was lit by a small reading lamp:

" 'All go unto one place; all are of the dust, and all turn to dust again. Who knoweth the spirit of man that goeth upward, and the spirit of the beast that goeth downward to the earth? Wherefore I perceive that there is nothing better, than that a man should rejoice in his own works; for that is his portion: for who shall bring him to see what shall be after him?'

"Let us rejoice today in the works of Love Easton Childers. He was truly, as his name portents, love embodied. Many days you could see him here at the church with his friends, handing out free food." The preacher pressed the button in his hand and the slide changed. "He worked tirelessly to elect our new mayor. Many afternoons you could find him at de Fremey Park testing little children for sickle-cell anemia. He was a leader and a giver."

Ruby put her hand on Lida's knee to calm her shaking leg.

"He was a family man without his own children. I want to impart to you my memory." He turned to Lida and smiled. She clenched her fists around the hem of her dress; all eyes were on her. "I remember when you were just a baby, how he took care of you day after day, holding you in his arms with so much tenderness."

Her breathing slowed now, and a familiar sensation came over her that she felt whenever she was trapped, one of submission and numbness, of vanishing and leaving her body. Her mind, almost drunk, blurred and blended the words and the faces together. The preacher continued: "And when he saw that his future, and the future of his whole family, of this community, was headed toward destruction, he put his life on the line to protect us, to challenge us to think, to give us hope. And that is what I want you to take from here today, that spirit of life and hope, which he has passed on to us. Although his life was short, like Jesus', it was plentiful. Many a man has lived twice as long and done half as much in God's glory, and for that, God will reward Easton Childers in heaven."

The preacher stepped toward Ruby and Lida, but Lida pulled back and straightened up. He helped her mother stand and escorted her to the pulpit. Ruby wore a black pillbox hat of her own design from which black lace hung and covered her face, like a widow's. She didn't look up, but stared instead at the pulpit as if a speech were placed there.

"My brother," she whispered. The crowded church fell completely silent. "He had all of you friends." She did not move or add anything, and for a moment it wasn't clear if she intended to continue. Then she cleared her throat. "Thank you all for coming." She turned away, and the preacher ran up to her and helped her to the bench. He gave her an engraved leather Bible and said, "Peace be with you." She nodded and held it to her chest.

The preacher smiled at Lida and held out his hand to lead her to the pulpit. She shook her head a little, but he did not back away. The pressure of all those eyes on her grew until it forced her up. When she stood, it was fast and hard, like a determined witness called to the stand. She straightened her shoulder straps and exhaled loudly. She approached the pulpit. Her eyes were dry, and she stared to the back of the congregation, at the children on the carpet.

"There's a lot of things people don't know about him." One of the children in the back grabbed the other by the lapels and shook him until he fell on his knees. "There's some things you should know." She looked at the faces of the congregation and saw that, although they were silent and waiting, they were not looking at her, but at the screen above and behind her, at Easton. "I don't think you'll believe me when I tell you. Maybe you know already. Maybe it doesn't matter to you. Maybe it shouldn't matter to me anymore 'cause he's dead and I should just let it pass." She shivered and stepped back from the pulpit but felt a hand on her lower back gently urge her on.

She moved to the pulpit again and parted her lips. The people seemed to lean forward in their seats as if to hear her whisper a secret. She felt herself leaving her body again, her ears plugging up, a cold sweat upon her forehead.

"I see he did a lot of nice things for all of you, and that's good," she said. "And I hope he got heaven for that. I really do." A number of people nodded. "But things are just so mixed up," she said. "They look one way, then they change around. And he's dead now. I've been thinking a lot, about how I would say this, now that he can't say anything back, but now it seems like he's always going to get the last word. I should have said it when he was alive. What's the difference now that he isn't coming back?" She waited to see if, in anyone's face, there was some sign of recognition, that she was not alone. But she saw nothing except confusion, even the potential for anger. "You didn't know him like I did, that's all I can say." She went back to her chair and squeezed herself up like a pencil, her legs straight out and her shoulders pressed together. Ruby reached out and touched her arm. Lida had a strong urge to move both away from and toward her mother, but instead, she sat there and waited for it all to be over.

IT WAS A a week after the funeral before Lida stepped foot in the house again. She sat naked on her mother's couch as the silence vibrated inside her chest and arms. After closing the curtains in the living room, she'd taken off all her clothes and wandered around the empty house.

Now she stood up and lifted her arms out like a bird, stretching her fingers to the corners of the room, her breasts pushing forward, her legs apart. She turned around twice like this and then dropped her arms.

She walked into the kitchen and opened the refrigerator. The cold air raised her skin like sandpaper, forcing her to squeeze her body together. She removed an apple from the top shelf and bit into it, then walked back into the living room and contemplated her next direction.

She had not hopped on one foot or licked the knob of the staircase or scratched her arms. She simply wandered the house freely, taking up as much space as possible.

But she hadn't been in Easton's room yet. She turned with determination and walked up the staircase, slowing as she got closer to his door. This was the only room she hadn't wandered through naked, hadn't looked at herself in its mirrors and stretched herself in its spaces. She opened the handle slowly but didn't go in at first. She peered in from the entrance, using the door to block her naked body, as if he might still be inside.

The bed was made, and his charcoal sketches were still on the wall. She took another bite of the apple, then pushed the door wide open as if a trap were set for something to fall on her. Nothing happened. She walked in, swinging the apple at her side like a purse. She strolled up to a sketch of him with Huey Newton and stared at his face. They were looking over a piece of paper with a speech written on it, and Easton was pointing to a word. She tried to read the word, like it might be a clue. But the printing was blurry and crooked.

She looked at the other sketches on the wall, Coltrane and Bobby, and then at the books on the shelf. She traced her finger over the spines of the books, reading the titles and authors: *The Wretched of the Earth,* by Fanon; *The Communist Manifesto* by Marx; *Inside View of Slavery* by Parsons; *Narrative of the Life of Frederick Douglass, an American Slave; A*

114

Documentary History of the Negro People in the United States; The Autobiography of Malcolm X; Rage, all on one shelf, and then below, *Anna Karenina* and Alain Locke's *New Negro Renaissance* and art books of Munch, Picasso, Léger, Dalí, and Schiele. Her breathing quickened as she pulled out the book *Rage,* but the cover just had a picture of Huey on the front, and she put it back on the shelf.

She opened his closet, and his belts clanked against the door. In the darkness, the smell of leather and cologne mixed together like a sharp heat. Jackets hung on one side and shirts on the other. She reached into the pockets of his black leather jacket and pulled out coins and a couple of scraps of paper. She held the papers under the light of the room to read them. One was a receipt from a grocery and the other a chewing-gum wrapper. She threw them both on the floor and noticed boxes at her feet. She bent down, naked in the dark closet, and grabbed one box.

She pushed it out next to the bed and opened it. Inside were photographs, originals for the charcoal sketches, a letter, and other receipts. The letter had a painting on it of two people dancing and inside, written in long, round, cursive:

Greensboro, Alabama, 1967

Sorry I didn't write sooner but I'm real busy. Isn't it funny that so much time passes and seems like a long time and like a short time at the same time. Anyway, I hope you're doing well and say hi to Ruby and Corbet and little Lida for me. We just saw the movie *The Graduate.* I really liked it. It's exactly how I feel: lost. It would have been nicer to see it with you. But anyway, it's actually nicer now, don't you think? I kind of only remember the good stuff. Charles says Hi too. I know you won't believe it, but we really did not plan this. We're not always thinking about it. I don't know if that makes sense. Anyway, I hope you're doing well. Good luck

—*Alexandra*

Lida dumped the box on the ground and sifted through the photographs. She found a picture of Easton and Ruby when they were much younger, standing by a field, a picture from South Carolina. She looked at Easton closely. He was dressed nicely in a Buster Brown striped shirt and a cap; his hands were at his sides—not in his pockets, which might have meant something. He was looking straight ahead. He smiled: a normal smile.

There were not hundreds of pictures of her, like an obsessed man might have. There weren't any of her, really, except one where she was a baby in his arms and Ruby and Corbet stood by their fishing poles at the pier in San Leandro. There were not nude pictures or pictures with women's faces crossed out. There was only one picture with a woman, a White woman, from a long time ago. Easton wore grease-covered blue overalls, and the woman was smiling, like he'd never said a mean word to her in his life.

Lida put down the photo and stood. She looked around the room, at the bulbous red candleholder covered in a fishnet pattern, the poster of John Coltrane in lingering smoke, the wooden stereo speakers—looked for something else, for anything that revealed he might have done to another woman what he'd done to her; that it wasn't because of her that he'd done it.

But she saw nothing. Nothing out of place, nothing unusual.

She stepped up onto the bed and stood in its sinking center. She bent her knees and began to bounce. She bounced up and down. She jumped harder and harder until she started to get a little air.

"Rabbit," she whispered. She had her arms out at her sides, and with every jump, she said the word louder, like she was calling for someone hidden in the room. "Rabbit. Rabbit. Rabbit!" she yelled and filled the whole house with her voice. She bent her legs all the way down like she was going to jump up to the ceiling, but instead, with a second thought, she absorbed all the downward momentum into her body and stopped completely, as if she heard something on the staircase. She waited, spooked, the hairs on her arms raised, like a frightened porcupine. But she heard nothing more. She sat down, got off the bed, and walked quietly out of the room.

Downstairs, she put on her dress and jacket. She picked up the suitcase she had packed and left.

SANTA RITA JAIL

EVERY MAN AND woman needs respect—to feel valuable—and we learn how to get that feeling from our parents and our culture and our peers. When we were babies, if we did something "good," we got a kiss or some food, some kind of safety. And when your friends come up to you and say, Man you are a tight rapper, or man you are smart, then you keep doing what you're doing because you feel respected. We get that food or that kiss or that safety and we feel righteous, we feel like we're getting what we deserve.

Now, each culture's got its own standards for respect, rules that kids learn from their parents and peers that get passed on down. If you do something that the family approves of, you feel good and you do it again. But the knowledge of what your culture thinks of as good can be eliminated.

For fifteen generations your African culture was squeezed out of you; each slave child knew less about getting respect as a free man and learned more about the culture of the slave. During those four hundred years of slavery, there was only one lesson to learn: that we were inferior to the White race. Respect would come in the form of how strong you were, how much work you could do for him, how obedient you were, how much you could get at auction, how many children you could give the master, how attractive you could be to him, or how much you fought against him. It's for him or against him, but it's always about him. There's no respect on our own terms.

Today I read to you from *American Negro Slavery*:

Those on the block often times praised their own strength and talents, for it was a matter of pride to fetch high prices. On the other hand if a slave should bear a grudge against his seller, or should hope to be bought by someone who would expect but light service, he might pretend a disability though he had it not.

You don't believe me. You say you never would have ingested that poison pill of White supremacy. But what if you were a child born into slavery, if you'd grown up as a slave, your father and your grandfather and your great-grandfather were slaves on this same plantation? And you knew the rules, and when you played by the rules, life was as good as it ever got, and when you broke them, it was bad. That was the lesson we were taught every day when we woke up in the morning, when we couldn't speak "properly," when our parents couldn't read or write, when we didn't get rich and didn't wear fancy clothes, when our homes were run-down, and even the smallest White child could tell our parents to pee in their pants. And learning this one lesson helped us survive, helped us keep our fingers from getting chopped off, our backs lashed, and our minds from making us crazy. We couldn't earn respect or sustenance by being educated or running a business or writing books, so we took to the ways of earning respect that were offered us if we wished to survive, the way a man will become a cannibal if there's nothing else to eat.

CHAPTER 8

LOVE CAME FROM upstairs, where Li'l Pit was sleeping for the first time. Ruby drank from a blue ceramic cup of cranberry tea and sat in Corbet's old rocker. She shook her head.

"Near the end of the month, there ain't nothin else coming in to give him." She pulled a black crochet afghan with colored flowers over her knees, one that she'd made for Lida when she was a baby. "All we got is beans and rice as it is."

"I can get money," Love said.

"That's what's bothering me."

"I mean a job."

Ruby nodded her head and rocked slowly with her hands around the steaming cup of tea. "You got a job in mind?"

"Mmm-hm." Love opened up the denim notebook with the insects in it.

"Now, if we was back in South Carolina, I'd just say, go on out and catch us some more fish." She laughed. Love turned the plastic page and straightened the Apollo butterfly.

"There was a red path road that went off to the Edisto River, where Ronal, your granpapa, use to take Love E. And you could catch enough fish for two weeks, that is before the pesticides kill everything. That's what he say. That's what Ronal print in the paper." She stopped and looked into her tea. Love waited for her to continue, but when she began again, she seemed to have lost her train of thought.

"When Love E was 'bout your age, he took a razor and cut off the tail of a dead rattler and he use to take that everywhere, say it's his lucky rabbit's foot. And it came true too. One day he was walkin home from town and there, layin straight across the path, sleepin, was another rattler.

He could a gone 'round in the cornfield, I spose, but that wasn't him. Ronal taught him there ain't no way round a problem but straight head-on. So he take his lucky rattle out a his pocket and start rattlin it. Well, the snake wake up and start slippin toward him, least that's how he tole it. It must a been a girl rattle he had, 'cause it start comin right toward him, but he kept on a–rattlin his rattle and the snake kept a–comin on to him. That stupid bline ole snake come right on up to Love E's foot and blam, he kick it in its head, dead, like that. Least that's how he tole it. Had himself two lucky rattles then."

She took a sip of her tea and smiled.

"How much you think these bugs worth?" Love held up the whole folder.

"You're not to go sellin those bugs."

"They're mine."

"I'll find a way to feed that boy. Don't go sellin those bugs. They yours. You just a chile, and it ain't your burden. What you want me to make you two for Halloween?"

"I'm too old for that shit now." Last year at the home, he'd been a vampire.

"Don't you swear in this house, you hear?"

The two front glass windowpanes exploded, pulling the curtains down with them. At first it wasn't clear what had happened, only that they found themselves on the floor. Then a second gunshot cracked the air and scattered painted macaroni off the heart picture on the back wall above the kitchen entrance.

"Ronal," Ruby screamed. "No! Ronal!"

Love lay flat, the denim notebook over his head, face-to-face with Ruby. She had spilled her tea on the rug. Her eyes were wide, but she didn't seem to be looking at him.

"ESO, Ace Trey!" came a shout from the street. Two more gunshots shattered the upstairs windows. Love closed his eyes, his chest bone pressing hard into the floor with every breath. He knew how this worked. He'd seen it in the movies and on TV. Soon there would be other cars, and they'd enter the house, shoot them in the back of the head with Uzis, spray-paint the room with their tags. He waited for the footsteps on the porch. There was silence. Then the car peeled out and roared up Cranston.

They waited on their stomachs for a moment. A few loose shards of glass fell to the floor. Ruby put her hand on Love's shoulder, her eyes streaming with tears. She pulled herself up to her knees and looked at the shattered bay windows. She shook her head. The night air blew in, and they shivered.

Li'l Pit walked softly down the stairs holding on to the wooden railing, his head shaved clean from the lice cure. He stopped halfway and stood there silently in his new white underwear.

THE NEXT DAY, Love went to the liquor store on the corner. Freight spoke softly to him, putting an arm around his shoulders. "I'm not about hurting people."

They were at the back of the store, behind a row of tomato-sauce jars on perforated white particleboard shelves. The convex mirror on the ceiling showed their reflection to the store clerk up front, a thin, older man with a gray beard. He looked up into the mirror, caught Love's eye, and quickly turned back to watching the World Series on the portable TV hanging by the cigarette rack.

"You don't have to kill no one," Freight added.

Curse in his wheelchair and stick boy hung around just outside the door of the white stucco building, both wearing the same black sweatshirt and blue jeans.

"But you've got to understand, I can't take any chances. You've got to earn our trust. Then we're down for each other. First you got to tell me what's up with these punks jackin up the 'hood."

Love shrugged.

"Do you see my lips moving?" Freight backhanded Love in the chest and sent him stumbling a few steps. Then he ran over and caught him delicately like a dropped fruit. "Don't do me like that, homie. That hurts my heart." He put his arm back around Love's shoulders. "You just have to show me that you trust me. I don't want to see you hurt yourself. You want me to protect you, don't you? Everyone needs to be taken care of." He helped Love stand and brush off his pants. "Tell me who it was. I'll let you pull the trigger."

Love didn't answer, and Freight turned back to face him.

"You're hurting me, blood." Freight pushed him with both hands into shelves of cereal. Love fell down to the floor and crushed a green box of Apple Jacks. "I don't like what you're making me do."

"Hey," the clerk yelled, then looked down and talked more softly. "Come on, FT, that costs us." Freight didn't turn his head or answer the clerk. He was in a locked stare with Love. Curse wheeled himself inside, casually took a look, then wheeled out again.

Love didn't speak but he didn't look away either.

"You got *dokyou,*" Freight said to Love. "You don't let no one push you around. That's something to trust." Freight reached his hand into his sweatshirt pocket and dug around. Love scanned the panel of utensils hanging to his right—can openers, plastic spaghetti strainers—but saw nothing sharp enough to defend himself with.

Freight pulled out a screwdriver. He threw it on Love's stomach.

"I got an old Toyota in Berkeley near the flea market. Bring it back to me here. No one else will ever touch you again."

Love held the screwdriver in his hand, point up. He stood and kicked the cereal to the side.

"What color is it?" he asked.

"How do I know what fucking color it is? Any color you want."

Love waited for Freight to move out of his way. Instead, Freight made himself bigger, put his hands on his hips so the remaining space was filled by his elbows, boxing Love in by the cereal shelves. "What are you waiting for, blood?"

Love didn't say anything. He knew this game. He walked straight into Freight's left arm, then came the slap on the back of his head. Love's eyes teared up, but he continued to walk out the door without looking at Curse or the stick boy.

He crossed Cranston and walked fast, breathing hard through his nose, his jaw clenched. He purposely walked in the path of every oncoming pedestrian. He stared straight forward and narrowed his eyes. Men and women in business suits and some kids coming home from school all walked around him without meeting his eyes. The only one who looked at him was a young man in a purple and blue tie-dye, his ponytail jumping from side to side. He smiled at Love and mumbled something about a nice day.

"What the fuck you looking at, dog!" Love yelled and held the screwdriver up to the man's face.

"I just said hello. God."

"Bitch motherfucker! Fuck you." Love turned and walked on.

Ten minutes later he arrived at the West Oakland BART station. A BART policeman talked to the attendant in her booth. Love waited at a pay phone, picked it up, and listened to the dial tone until the guard left to go upstairs to the platforms. Another passenger got her dollar stuck in the ticket machine, and the attendant went around the corner to help her. Love put his hands on the stainless-steel ticket takers and leapt over the plastic barrier. This was enough to be sent back to Juvi if they caught him, but they'd probably just kick him out of the station.

He pulled his white jeans below his hips, revealing a few more inches of his blue boxers. He took the escalator to the platform and sat on a bench from which he could look over the passengers. If someone was going to start something, it would happen on the platform because you could still get out. The BART train itself was a trap. Each stainless-steel car had doors that could lock. He'd seen a train pull into a station and the doors stay shut while cops hunted down their suspect. One time the cops cornered an older White drunk in a stained jacket playing harmonica and asking for change. The summer before Love left to Juvi, three kids in fur-lined hoods came into the train spitting on the floor. At the Fruitvail station, the cops came on, grabbed the kids, and had them spread-eagled, facedown on the cement platform outside with their hands cuffed behind their backs. Everyone stared at them as the train pulled away, like on the tram at the zoo.

The Richmond-bound train arrived, and Love swaggered to the back, past a woman with two small children. One of the kids looked up at him and the mother pulled his face away and wiped the corner of his mouth. Love sat in the last seat against the wall so he could see anyone coming in before they saw him. This train had originated in San Francisco, picking up Gs from the Mission and downtown.

Love pulled up the collar of Easton's black leather jacket. Most guys didn't fuck with you if you weren't slippin, unless you had done something stupid like take their bikes. You were also fucked if you claimed a rival, but you'd only do that if you had something to prove or if you were being challenged. There were a number of people in the car: one wanna-be G in the last seat facing the other direction, a light-brown-skinned dude with round sunglasses and headphones, but he never looked up. Another brother wore a blue sweater and a blue cap with the gold letters CAL embroidered on the front and was hunched over reading a paperback. There were a few other people, Sunday tourists heading into Berkeley. The only person worth consideration was a Mexican guy in a white and maroon Mighty Ducks jacket, an unlit cigarette in his mouth, his black and white sneaker stuck into the aisle. He looked at Love, and Love turned to the window as if something had distracted him.

He gazed over the houses in West Oakland to the docks and the giant metal structures shaped like white dogs that lifted cargo on and off the ships. The sky was blue all the way across the bay to San Francisco where a tidal wave of white fog rolled over the mountains toward the skyscrapers. But it was blue above the fog and the open space seemed to reach out forever. Then the train dove down into the underground tunnel. Love closed his eyes and let out a breath.

When they pulled into the yellow lights of Ashby Station, he waited to get up until the train came to a complete stop, so it wouldn't make him stumble like a fool or let other people know where to get off if they wanted to follow him.

He got out and took the escalator up with the rest of the commuters but went over by the bathroom alcove. He waited until all the people had exited and then went out the bike gate, wiping his hands on his pants, like he'd just been let in to use the bathroom.

Outside in the fading sun, he faced the flea market, which took up the whole right half of the parking lot: lines of tents and carpets displaying incense holders, record players, irons, hand-me-down clothes, futons, shaving cream, old videos and books; and from somewhere in the center of the market, a pulsating beat of conga drums, clanking hubcaps and bottles. The left side of the lot was all parked cars, plenty of old Toyotas, but there was a police cruiser parked right on the curb out front.

Love walked into the market and eyed the goods. Most people were packing up slowly now that it was getting dark. One old man with a rough, tortoise-skinned forehead sat in front of a blanket loaded with old books and a sporting almanac with a picture of a baseball player on the front.

Love pulled a plastic box out of his jacket pocket and held it in front of his face. Inside was the Hercules Beetle.

"How much you give me for this?"

The man licked his chapped lips and shook his head. "I don't buy bugs."

"It's the longest beetle in the world. Give me fifty bucks."

"I can see what it is, but I don't buy bugs."

"All right, dog."

The old man shook his head and Love put the box back into his pocket. He walked to the end of the aisle and climbed the ivy hillside out of the lot up onto the sidewalk. He crossed Martin Luther King, Jr., Boulevard toward a house covered entirely by pink shingles and turned down Prince Street, away from the traffic and the cops.

This was a mostly Black residential area of Berkeley, with huge houses and rock-bordered gardens of lavender and bougainvillea. There were shiny new cars parked in the wide driveways between each house and children's toys on the lawns. He peered into one backyard at a twisted pipe sculpture in the shape of a pyramid. A calico cat rested on top of the fence and let Love pet him, purring and closing his eyes with a black, mustachioed smile. A small rat-dog tied with a rope ran out onto the back porch and started barking in a high-pitched yelp. Love kicked the wooden fence, and the cat flew off toward the dog. He walked away quickly and turned on to Harper Street, which was lined with high-leafed chestnut and palm trees.

His hands began to sweat and tingle as he looked around for a car. He saw an LTD with its window open, but Freight had said a Toyota. An older man walked toward him with a cane, watching squirrels run across the telephone lines. Love rubbed the tips of his fingers with his thumbs and looked down as the man passed him, yellow leaves crunching under his feet.

"Don't look now," the man said. "I might just smile at you."

Love looked up and the man smiled. Love couldn't help but smile back. But then the man was gone and it was getting darker. The conga drummers were still at it in the distant flea market, their rhythms faster and louder as the night approached.

He spotted a Toyota in front of a triangular-shaped house with a high wooden fence: a bashed-up white Tercel hatchback with a ski rack. As long as it was pre-'85, it would be easy to break into. He'd learned how even before Juvi. He wiped his palms on his pants and walked past it, glanced in, and continued to walk the rest of the block to Ashby. At the corner, he swung around on the pole with the big fish-eyed Neighborhood Watch sign, then headed back, looking around for witnesses.

A silver Honda pulled onto the street and parked a few spaces before the Tercel. Love slipped between cars and sat down on the back fender of a rust-colored pickup truck and bowed his head, his arms and chest shaking, waiting for the people to get out of the car and go away. He smelled chimney smoke and inhaled deeply.

"Pizza?" he heard a man from the car say. "I was thinking more like pasta, or a salad, a great big salad."

"That's fine with me," a woman said. The car doors shut and Love looked over his shoulder. A man, woman, and little girl carrying a red purse entered a yard with a chain-link fence around it. The man lifted up the girl by a tree and she picked a lemon. The woman unlocked the front door and they went in.

Love got up and walked toward the Toyota. He must have gotten up too fast because he felt dizzy. He stopped at the fence in front of the house and wrapped his tingling hands around the top pole. He looked up at the porch. There was a pumpkin on the railing, carved with jagged teeth, and a brown ceramic lamp in the window between the crack in the curtains. In the garden, a tomato plant with small yellow tomatoes grew out of a bathtub up against the fence. He crouched down behind the plant and picked off a firm tomato, the vine pulling and snapping back. He spit in his hands and rolled the fruit around in his palms to clean off the dust, then popped it in his mouth and chewed, the sweet and sour juice squirting into his cheeks.

He savored the taste and rested on his knee as if he didn't have anything else to do. There was only this moment, on this piece of pavement, in this hickory-filled air, the distant drums. He just might not do anything else all night but stay here in this neighborhood and listen to the drumming, and in the morning go from here to the next town. He didn't have to steal the car. There were a million towns and families and gardens in the world.

The yellow streetlights flickered and Love jolted up as if he'd been discovered. At the same moment, a White boy with a Mohawk and chains hanging down from his belt loops came around the corner. His boots pounded on the pavement, and Love turned back to the house and pretended that he was heading inside. The boy was walking right at him with one hand in his jacket pocket. Love opened the gate quietly and went into the yard. The boy looked at him but kept walking. By the time he had passed, Love found himself halfway up the path to the house.

There he was, already inside. That easy. Another world, another life. He took a step toward the porch but then heard the front door opening and quickly turned around.

"Can I help you?" the man from the house asked. He didn't sound angry or frightened, just interested. Love stopped but kept his back to him.

"Are you looking for someone?" the man called out again. "Can I

127

help you?" Already the smell of dinner came from inside the house. Love noticed that there were yellow flowers on this side of the tomato plant along with the fruit.

"Naw, man, I was just mixed up," Love said with an accentuated drawl. He wanted to say something else. But what? Maybe something that would get him invited inside, so then something else could happen—he could show them what a nice kid he was, and they'd want to help him, want to keep him. But what could he possibly hope for from this complete stranger? What about Li'l Pit? What was he thinking?

"Naw, Man. Wrong house. Sorry." He walked out the gate and waited around the corner until he heard the door close.

The front seat of the Toyota was torn up so badly that the foam was missing in the middle. There was no club or alarm. He tried the door handle just in case, but it was locked. The screwdriver fit in the driver's door with a little wiggling. He jammed it into the lock and the button popped up. This only worked with an old Toyota. He opened the door, got in, closed the door, and lay down across the front seats. His eyes moved about in the dark car and his fingers felt for the ignition. He shoved the screwdriver into the keyhole and pushed hard. Something clicked and he tried the steering wheel. The wheel was loose, but the ignition wouldn't turn. He sat up in the driver's seat and worked the handle back and forth, his foot ready over the gas.

After a few tries, the starter turned over and he revved the engine. He'd watched other guys steal cars, but he'd driven a stick only once, on an outing to 7-Eleven with Tom from Los Aspirantes.

He put it in first and pressed the gas, but the car was in gear with the parking brake on, and he stalled. Two bicyclists with helmets turned on to Harper and stopped at a car across the street. They glanced over at him and then looked away. He started the car again and took off the parking brake but let it idle with the clutch in. The bicyclists put their bikes up onto the roof of their car, glancing his way every so often. Love kept the clutch in and put it in first. He turned the wheel and then pressed on the gas. The car revved loudly and then he let out the clutch too quickly, but the car jerked forward into the street.

"Hey," one of the bicyclists yelled and ran toward the car. Love sped up.

"Hey, your lights. Your lights."

Love couldn't bother looking for the light switch. He drove through the stop sign at Prince and kept going on the residential streets, all the way back to Cranston, in first gear.

SANTA RITA JAIL

TODAY, I READ sections in *From Plantation to Ghetto: An Interpretive History of American Negroes:*

The Black Laws regulating the behavior of free Negroes in the Old Northwest were in fact based upon the slave codes of the Southern states. For a period the legislatures of Illinois and Indiana evaded the antislavery prohibition of the Ordinance by enacting laws placing Negro youths under long-term indentures. Thus was perpetuated in modified form the practice of Negro slavery known previously in the Northwest Territory when it had been under French and British rule. The Illinois constitution of 1818 expressly provided for the hiring of slave labor at the saltworks near Shawneetown. Nowhere in the Old Northwest or the newer Western states could Negroes exercise the right to vote or serve on juries. They could not testify in cases involving whites in Ohio, Indiana, Illinois, Iowa, or California. Most of the Western states also banned intermarriage. The Northwestern and Western States attempted to discourage Negro settlers by requiring them to register their certificates of freedom at a county clerk's office and to present bonds of $500 or $1,000 guaranteeing that they would not disturb the peace or become public charges. Toward the end of the ante-bellum period, Illinois, Indiana, and Oregon excluded Negro migrants entirely. Only Ohio, after a long battle, repealed its restrictive immigration legislation in 1849. Though such anti-immigration statutes were only erratically enforced, nevertheless they intimidated Negroes. In 1829 an attempt to enforce an 1807 law requiring a $500 bond precipitated a race riot at Cincinnati and a mass Negro exodus to Canada.

In the Northeast, none of the states provided by law for discrimination in the courtroom and Negro testimony was admissible in cases involving whites. Social custom, however, barred Negroes from sitting on juries, except in Massachusetts where a few Negroes served just prior to the Civil War. Negroes enjoyed the same voting rights as whites in all the original Northern states for a generation after the American Revolution. Then, one by one, between 1807 and 1837, five of them—New Jersey, Connecticut, New York, Rhode Island, and Pennsylvania—enacted disfranchisement provisions. The laws of Connecticut and Rhode Island did not disqualify those already on the rolls, and in Rhode Island the prohibition was repealed in 1842.

. . . Besides legal restrictions in voting rights and the courts, there were other forms of oppression. In Northern cities the most extreme of these was mob violence. During the 1830's and 1840's riots occurred in Philadelphia, New York, Pittsburgh, Cincinnati, and other places. More continuous and pervasive were the patterns of segregation and employment discrimination.

The Jim Crow or segregation laws were largely a product of the late nineteenth century. Segregation by custom, however, and even occasionally by statute, was already common during the ante-bellum period. In the South segregation developed as one of the devices to control the urban free Negroes and the slave population. Separation in jails and hospitals was universal. Negroes were widely excluded from the public parks and burial grounds. They were relegated to the balconies of the theatres and opera houses and barred from hotels and restaurants. The New Orleans street railway maintained separate cars for the two races. Sometimes these practices were codified in law: as early as 1816 New Orleans passed an ordinance segregating Negroes in places of public accommodation. The Legal codes of Savannah and Charleston excluded free Negroes from public parks. Charleston, Baltimore, and New Orleans were among the cities legalizing segregated jails and poorhouses.

In the North, Negroes were not legally segregated in places of public accommodation, nor, except for schools, in publicly owned institutions. Custom, however, barred them from hotels and restaurants, and they were segregated, if not entirely excluded, from theatres, public lyceums, hospitals, and cemeteries. Even in abolitionist Boston, the Negro was considered a pariah in most circles. . . .

Traveling by public conveyance was difficult for Negroes. In Boston there were signs: "colored people not allowed to ride in this omnibus." In New York City Negroes were refused streetcar seats except on a segregated basis. Philadelphia Negroes were restricted to the front platform of these vehicles. Long-distance travel was even more of a problem. On stagecoaches Negroes usually rode on an outside seat, and on the early railroads they often occupied filthy accommodations in a separate car. Steamboats offered the worst conditions, since Negroes were almost invariably excluded from cabins and required to remain on deck even in cold weather. On the all-night trip from New York City to Newport, Rhode Island, they usually had the choice of pacing the deck or sleeping among the cotton bales, horses, sheep, and pigs. . . .

Negroes continued to face discrimination on the streetcars. In 1856 when a minister was removed from a vehicle, the judge upheld the transportation company on the ground that its business would suffer if Negroes could sit anywhere they pleased. This decision was interpreted to apply to omnibuses, hotels, and other public facilities. Five years later a Philadelphia court also ruled in favor of a transportation company's right to bar Negroes by force if necessary.

Recent scholarship has found residential segregation and the origins of the modern ghetto in the ante-bellum city. Actually, before the Civil War urban Negroes generally resided in racially mixed neighborhoods. The homes of the more prosperous free Negro artisans and businessmen were often scattered throughout various parts of the city, singly or in small clusters. There was a tendency, however, for Negroes to be concentrated in certain neighborhoods or wards, but within close proximity to whites. In the Southern towns the slaves who "lived out" tended to move to the edges of the city, where they formed neighborhoods predominantly, though not exclusively, Negro. In Baltimore and Philadelphia there were Negroes living in the alleys between the main streets on which fashionable whites resided. The most impoverished Negroes were the most segregated, often in vice districts controlled by white overlords. New York Negroes were heavily concentrated in a few wards, where poor whites also resided. In Philadelphia the worst slum consisted of a few densely populated unheated rooms, garrets, and tiny wooden shanties lacking even the most modest comforts. In Boston, Providence, New Haven, Cincinnati, and other seacoast and river cities, Negro slum neighborhoods, with names like "New Guinea," developed first along the wharves. Later the Negroes tended to shift to outlying sections known by such names as "Nigger Hill." As discrimination increased all over the North, even the more prosperous colored men were often drawn to predominantly Negro neighborhoods.

CHAPTER 9

LIDA LIVED BY herself while Marcus was locked up. He'd been awaiting trial for forty-two days. But when Lida had visited him the previous Saturday, he said that he could be set free anytime if he'd agree to write a report about the shooting. All he needed to say was that Easton had a gun, or that he might have had a gun, or that Marcus didn't see anything. If he didn't write the statement, they told him that even though he was still a minor, he would get fifteen years for selling heroin and possession of a stolen weapon. Lida told him about the eviction notice, how the landlord came by and said the police informed him about the dealing and wanted them out. She told Marcus to write the statement, and he said he would only do it if they gave him his dope back because he might as well go to jail if he couldn't give Jim the goods.

So she stayed at home and waited. One afternoon she sat on the yellow couch in Marcus's apartment as sweat beaded on her head in the cold room. The low, warm hum of the fish tank drew her attention. She had not cleaned it while Marcus was away, and the algae pushed the lid off the filter. She sat for an hour watching the bubbles form and release from the tube. One bubble stuck to the opening. It grew and wavered in the water, then detached and floated up through the algae. She'd gotten the cap of heroin from Jim, when he'd dropped by to check in on the situation.

At first the ringing was very far away, underwater, in the fish tank; and she smiled as the bubble shook and rang, then floated to the top. Then she remembered the phone, the outside, Marcus, the killing. She stood up and wiped her mouth. The phone was on the bookshelf by the fish tank. She picked up the receiver.

"Yeah."

"Are you sick?" It was Lori, her friend from Lucky's.

"No."

"You're supposed to be on now, you know?"

"Shit. Don't—I'll be there soon. Just don't do anything." She hung up and walked to the closet, sat on the carpet, and slid her red sneakers onto her feet. She grabbed the door handle to pull herself up and then walked directly out of the house into the bright winter day, wearing her blue nylon sweatsuit with gold stripes and matching jacket.

Walking was easy, just one foot in front of the other and no one would know the difference: use the lines in the sidewalk to stay straight. The cracks didn't matter anymore, none of that mattered when she was high. Just one foot in front of the other. Red sneaker toe, red sneaker toe. Curb and stop. Look up. Green light: go. Cross next to the straight white line, and curb, step up, and red sneaker toe, red sneaker toe.

Across East 14th was the big parking lot and Lucky's. She zipped up her jacket to the neck. A woman walked by her with a shopping bag.

"How do I look?" she asked the stranger. The lady didn't answer. Lida crossed the street and walked along the curb of the lot to the front entrance. A man held the door open for her and she thought about smiling at him but just walked straight in.

"Number seven, Lida," Lori yelled.

She went to register seven and put in her key. Already two people raced into her line.

"I had the same flu last week," said the man at the front of the line. "You should stay home and drink chicken soup." Lida nodded and picked up his can of peaches. She pressed in the numbers and it came to thirty-nine dollars.

"I'd go home and sleep it off if I were you," he said.

"Have a nice day," she said. She punched up the soap from the next customer, punched up dog food, soda, candles, punched in the numbers, took the money, nodded to the next customer about whatever she was saying, something about you shouldn't sell grapes because farmworkers' babies were dying.

"Okay. Have a nice day."

It went by mercifully, like the hour staring at the fish tank, not fast or slow, just gone.

THE POLICE LET Marcus out of jail for signing the affidavit. Since he'd been back, the apartment manager hadn't left them alone. He knocked at the door every morning. Lida looked up from the bed at Marcus, who stood at the sink in the kitchen peeling a potato. He froze with the peeler in his hand and waited. The knock came again. Lida slowly lifted the blanket up over her head.

Her breath made a cocoon of warmth under the covers, where she stayed all day when she was home because the heat had gone out. Marcus put down the peeler and brought the potato over to the bed. He jumped in under the covers and rubbed his feet together.

"Oooo. Oooo, you're cold," she whispered.

"Here. Eat this."

"What happened to all the macaroni salad I brought home?"

"I ate it last night before it went bad. Just get some more. Nothing keeps without the refrigerator."

"This whole house is a refrigerator."

He laughed, but only a little, and then took a bite of the hard potato.

"We got to move in with your mama."

Lida didn't say anything and kept her eyes closed. He put his hand out and touched her right breast through her sweater.

"What are you doing?" She jerked away and turned over.

"I was just trying to get things warmed up in here."

"Don't just be grabbing me like that."

"I didn't grab you. I just thought we could have some loving."

"With a potato in your mouth?"

"I was in the coop for over a month, baby."

"I don't feel like being touched." She lay on her stomach but with her face toward him. "I'm sorry. I just don't feel like it."

"You ever gonna feel like it?"

136

She took a deep breath and buried her arms under her body, lying like a beached sea lion.

"Don't you think we could move in with your mama?" he asked her again.

"Far as she know, you got Love E killed. Far as I know too."

Marcus took another bite of the potato. "You're the one who told me to go out and kill him."

Lida curled her knees up to her chest. Now she was in a position that resembled someone kneeling down and listening to the ground. She didn't speak.

"But I didn't," Marcus added. "I didn't do nothing, and neither did you." He put his hand on her back and rubbed.

"I know."

There was another knock on the door. Lida opened her eyes, and Marcus stopped moving his hand.

"Did you tell Jim I'm back?" he whispered.

Lida shook her head. They waited a moment and heard footsteps move off.

"I met some dudes in the coop who might hook me up with a gig."

"From jail?"

"Listen, baby, I was in jail too, you know. But I'm still me. In fact, I'm a better me because I'm not going back there. They wouldn't let me have my fucking guitar. They thought I might use the strings to kill someone. They don't know the difference between a dealer and a murderer. There is no way I'm going back. I don't have to. If you're good at something, eventually it all falls into place." He nuzzled his body closer to hers. "Don't you think?"

"I don't know," she said honestly.

"What about you?" he asked. "Isn't there something you dream of being?"

"I've never given it much thought."

"But deep inside, didn't you think you'd like to do something or be something?"

She took a deep breath and the words came to her lips.

"I guess I thought about being a travel agent."

"A travel agent?" Marcus laughed. "That's not a dream. That's a job."

"Never mind."

"No, no, tell me. I'm sorry. I shouldn't have laughed. Come on. Tell me, Lida. Tell me why you want to be a travel agent."

"I don't know. I guess I like the idea of knowing about all those different places to go in the world, and then maybe getting to go for free every once in a while. You know, flying to all those beautiful beaches with the sunsets and the coconut trees." She closed her eyes and rolled away from him. "I don't like playing these games."

"It's not a game, baby. Trust me. We can do whatever we put our minds to. Anyone who doesn't make it is just lazy or stupid. You've got to make your dreams come true. That's the way it happened for my father. He just worked hard every day and kept at it and bought that shop. That's the way it happens. If you want something, you got to give it one hundred percent. That's the difference between me and them other niggers in the coop. I know what it takes, and I've got the will to do it. You've got to push yourself."

"I don't know."

"Don't you believe me?"

"I believe you."

"I know you do." He put his arm around her and placed his hand on her heart. "I know you do. Don't be scared, baby, it's all going to be good."

Lida shivered and closed her eyes.

THE NEXT WEEKEND Lida went to see Ruby. She sat on the couch in the living room, her black purse on her lap. This was her first visit to her mother's since the funeral, and out of respect, she wore the black dress Ruby had made for her.

They sat in silence and looked around the room like they'd never seen it before. Lida looked for some item to reminisce about to end the awkward distance between them, while Ruby looked for someplace to set her mind and escape altogether. Her mind settled on the picture of Corbet in uniform, and she thought how strange it was that there must have been a last time they had all been together and happy—she, Lida, Love E, and Corbet—but you never know then that it will be the last time, and she couldn't remember it now.

"It's cold still, Mama. Why don't you put the heat on?"

"I'm fine the way I am." Ruby pulled the blanket up higher on her stomach and rocked in the chair.

"How's the quilt coming along?" Lida asked.

"Coming along."

"Almost done?"

"Almost."

They still didn't look at each other. Lida flipped the brass lock on her purse open and shut. Just before she had come over, Marcus was saying all sorts of things to encourage her. They were in MacArthur Park with David, a bass player he'd met in jail, and David's wife, Gina, who'd just had a son. Gina breast-fed the baby as they sat on the bench, her sweater unbuttoned and the baby's head inside against the red knitting. Marcus didn't say anything directly to Lida; he just talked to Gina.

"Look at how that baby loves you. You're mother and child. Couldn't nothing come between you. Isn't that right?"

Gina just smiled. Marcus kept on.

"No matter what your child do in life, you gonna love him and take care of him. Isn't that the truth? Isn't it?" Gina nodded. "Ain't nothing like the love between a mother and her child." Marcus looked up at Lida and she turned away, the way her mother turned away now as they sat in the living room.

"Hear how they burned down the Castlemont Apartments because of the hustlin?" Lida asked Ruby.

"Mmm-hmmm."

"Seems like everybody angry at somebody nowadays."

"Sure do." Ruby closed her eyes and then opened them very slowly to erase whatever feeling might have been coming up on them. "You want something to drink?" she asked. "I'm going to make myself some tea."

She got up to go to the kitchen and took her Bible with her. In the kitchen, she filled the rusted red teakettle and set it on the stove, then came back to the rocking chair and placed the Bible on the cast-iron table beside her again.

"I was thinking about moving back in, Mama."

Ruby made no gesture of response, so Lida moved to the edge of the couch to explain.

"I've still got my job and we could pay for some of the bills."

"Who we?" Ruby looked at her hard.

"Me an Marcus."

"Nn-mmm. That boy ain't livin in this house."

Lida didn't argue. She had never argued with her. When Easton was still alive, she had always been too frightened to think of angering the only person in the house who could have made it safe for her. Now that silence had grown like a deep river between them and it seemed too difficult to cross.

"That boy ain't livin in this house," Ruby repeated again, as if Lida had in fact argued with her. Lida's gaze settled on the leather Bible, so close to her mother's arm it seemed she was touching it on purpose. Lida found herself envying the book. There felt like miles of things she had to explain to her mother, and if she could just explain it all, then she knew Ruby would reach out to her also. She wanted to explain how she used to tiptoe around the house so she wouldn't disturb Easton, how she used to feel so bad about herself, how she always went to Marcus because he would take care of her, and that he didn't sell junk anymore. But then she'd have to explain so many other things: why he had to take care of her, why she had to tiptoe. One thing would lead to more questions, and it didn't all make sense unless she told her what was at the bottom of it all. But even then it didn't make any sense. She couldn't explain why she didn't go to her mother in the first place or how come she had to leave the house even after Easton was dead and it was safe to stay. And when things didn't make sense, they sounded like lies, even to herself.

"I never did know what you saw in that boy," Ruby added. "He stole all that money from his father's store and was into drugs. It's a disgrace, you livin with him, and I have to see his father in church on Sundays." The teakettle whistled, and Ruby raised herself to go back in the kitchen.

Lida looked at the bookcase by the stereo. Two twisted seashells with holes in them sat on the edge of one shelf. She used to put her fingers through the holes when she was a little girl and wear them like gigantic, expensive rings. She stood up and went to the shells. She held one in her hand and slid her finger into it, but it didn't fit past the first knuckle.

"We can't keep our place since he came back from jail," Lida called out to her mother.

"Well, you come live here and let him stay with some friends." Ruby returned and sat back in the rocking chair. "What do you want to stay with him for, anyway?"

"Because." Lida's face burned, and like someone calling for help across a large canyon, she blurted out: "He's the only one who ever loved me." It was the first time she felt like she'd said exactly what she'd wanted to say—and it terrified her.

"What are you saying, Lida? I've always loved you. Plenty of people love you. You're talking crazy."

"You don't understand."

Ruby held her teacup on her lap and stared up at her daughter. She saw a look in her eyes that she didn't recognize and a hard breathing through her nose that was not like Lida, but like a kid after a long fight.

"You're right," Ruby said. "I don't understand. I don't. Maybe I never will. I'm saying you can move back in, but he's not moving in here." Ruby took a sip of her tea as if to settle the matter.

Lida carefully unstuck her finger from the shell and placed it back onto the bookcase. She lifted her purse off the couch and faced her mother, but Ruby added nothing. She walked slowly to the door, fighting the urge to hop on one foot as she used to do, turned the doorknob, and left the house.

LIDA AND MARCUS were evicted. They moved in with Gina and David and their son, Malcolm, across the street from the Kozol Towers. The apartment had a living room, bedroom, kitchen, and a bathroom. Extra tenants weren't allowed, but almost every other apartment had long-term guests. Lida and Marcus hoped not to stay too long, just enough to save up some money for their own place. She had gotten him a bagging job at Lucky's. They both had Monday mornings off, and they lay together on the corduroy couch, which they used as their bed.

Marcus placed his hand on her stomach and looked at her sleeping face. The light crossed below her nose, and he watched as her eyes moved under her lids.

"You love me," he whispered. A curl of her hair shook with his breath, and she made a small noise that sounded like a door creaking open. He smiled and whispered again.

"You love Marcus." She didn't make any noise this time. He blew lightly on her forehead and she rolled over, almost pushing him off the couch.

Now her bare shoulders and upper back were uncovered. Her skin was dark and solid like rich soil. He put his fingertips on one shoulder and brushed them across to the other. He sang to her, softly:

> She's all of the colors
> She's blue on the inside
> She's red in her eyes
> She's green as a child
> She's black in her lies.

Lida rolled back toward him and smiled, her eyes still shut. The sun had moved and now it crossed her mouth and onto his ribs. She opened her eyes and traced her finger along the line of sun on his body. He sang some more.

LEAVING

She's all of the planets

A radiant Venus

And brighter than stars

More helpless than Pluto

More angry than Mars.

"You still have that blue pick?" she asked.

"What blue pick?"

"The one you used to wear in your natural, from elementary school."

"Sure."

"How come you never wear that anymore?" She traced her finger into the small hairs around his nipples.

He smiled at her. "You want me to get it?"

"Naw." She closed her eyes again. "It'd just make me sad."

He reached out to stroke her eyebrows. "What made you think of that old pick, anyway?"

"I don't know. I just pictured you with it."

Kids ran down the building's hallway, pounding on the floorboards. They knocked on the door and kept running, knocking on every door.

Malcolm started crying from the other room.

"Ah no. No," Marcus yelled. They took care of the baby on their days off so David could look for work that wouldn't conflict with band rehearsals. Gina worked two part-time jobs, mornings at Orchard Supply and afternoons at ACE.

Lida threw the covers off. She got her green sweatshirt out of her suitcase and wore it like a dress. She walked through the kitchen and into the bedroom where Malcolm slept on a floor mat beside Gina and David's bed.

Marcus stood in the doorway wearing his blue bikini underwear and watched Lida pick up the baby and cradle him against her shoulder. He was a nappy-haired baby with thin yellow lips and one eye sealed shut with slimy gunk.

"He misses his mommy," Lida said. She held him with her hand across the whole of his back. Malcolm coughed and stopped crying.

"You're good with that baby," Marcus said. "You know how to put up with all that crying."

"He's just hungry." She walked him into the kitchen and got the bottle off of the counter. "See, he was just saying, 'I'm hungry. I'm hungry.' It only sounds like cryin to you. You've got to be able to read a child. They hardly ever say straight out what they really want."

"Crying sounds like what it is: crying. We just about to make love too."

"What do you mean just about to make love? How do you know what *we* just about to do?"

"How come you're always starting something? I just meant we were having a nice time and then . . . never mind." He opened the refrigerator and took out a pitcher of water. He poured himself a glass and went back to the couch, then called back into the kitchen, "How come your mama didn't want us living with her? Did you tell her I didn't have nothing to do with your uncle being killed?"

"She don't like you."

"What'd I ever do to her?"

"Just been yourself."

"Ain't there any way I can make it up?"

"If we were married, then she'd have to let us live there."

"I'll marry you," he said.

"Get serious," Lida yelled back. Marcus got off the couch.

"I am nothing but serious."

Lida came out of the kitchen. "When?"

"I'll marry you right now." He walked over and knelt down in front of her while she stood holding the baby. "Lida Anne Washington, will you marry me?"

Lida laughed.

"Well, will you? I ain't foolin."

"You want to marry me?"

"Yeah."

She turned around and walked back into the bedroom. She laid the baby down on the floor and knelt to change him.

Marcus came to the door and watched her. "So? Will you?"

She took a deep breath and looked away. "Mama still won't let you live at her house."

"Forget your mama. I'm askin you to marry me." She rolled the baby over and took off his dirty diaper. Marcus curled his lips in disgust. She went into the bathroom and came out with a wipe to clean off his bottom. When she finished putting on the new diaper, she placed Malcolm at the top of the bed, then went and washed her hands, slowly drying every finger in the towel, not turning around to face Marcus. Finally she walked to the bathroom door and looked at him.

He stood there in his blue underwear, waiting for an answer. The sun now filled the whole kitchen behind him. The baby was quiet, no cars roared outside, and no one yelled from next door. It seemed the whole world was at a peaceful standstill just waiting for her to answer. She took a deep breath and walked to the bed. She climbed up onto it, and turned around so that she faced the baby lying against the pillows. Her feet sank into the blanket as she stood at the bottom edge of the bed, her back and naked legs toward the window and the rest of the room.

"What are you doing?" Marcus asked. She stood with her arms out and shut her eyes. Before he could ask again, she fell backward toward the floor, her body straight, her face up to the ceiling, the air rushing against her ears and fingers. Neither of them made a sound as she fell. Marcus moved quickly. He caught her just as she became parallel with the floor, and they fell to the ground together.

"You're crazy. What are you doin?"

Lida opened her eyes and looked up at him. She was cradled in his arms, her feet still up on the bed.

"You're crazy, you know that?" Marcus said again.

"Why did you catch me?"

"You'd have killed yourself."

She closed her eyes again as if to hold in her tears. Her breathing was heavy and forced. "I don't deserve you. I don't deserve anyone."

"I want to marry you."

"Even with all the problems I got?"

"They're bound to go away sometime. I'm going to make you so happy all your problems will look like little ants."

Lida listened to the silence of the day. She reached her mind out of the room, out of the building, across the freeway, and out toward West Oakland. She listened and waited for something, some answer from somewhere. But she heard nothing.

"You saved me, so you can do what you want," she said.

"I guess that means yes."

There was another moment of silence as she shook her head. But then she said, "If that's what you want."

IT TOOK RUBY six months to accept that she was really going to be alone, that Lida wasn't coming back, and neither was Easton.

Dinnertime was sacred now. She was her own special guest. The carved rock elephants sat on the center of the table by the tall yellow candle. She laid out two red-fringed place mats, one for the pots and one for her place setting, the silverware imprinted with flowers. She didn't bring up disagreeable conversation topics at this time, that is what she said to herself if her mind wandered. "This is not a time to reflect."

She dressed up each night. She wore her red shawl over a black evening gown. This dress was the last style she'd made, and they didn't all sell. The factories that had moved overseas and the sweatshops in Chinatown now produced a hundred garments at the cost she charged for ten. She hadn't sewn since the burial, when she made a patch-quilt blanket to lay over Easton; she read her Bible instead.

She lit the candle and said grace, then opened the cloth napkin and spread it out neatly on her lap. She picked up the fork and brought the potato to her lips without leaning close or hurrying in any way.

This was a time to taste the yams, to slowly chew their buttery orange sugar. There was the rest of the day to remember Easton, to worry about Lida or bills. This was a time when nothing could be done about those things, and it didn't do any good to think of them and ruin a meal.

This year she would turn forty, and she wondered what she might give herself as a present. And it came to her all at once, maybe because she had been dusting the pictures on the wall earlier, or maybe because she would be forty this year and always thought of her mother as being forty. If she could save, start saving right now, she would take a trip in the fall to South Carolina. She hadn't seen her mother in person for nearly eighteen years, almost half her life. She picked up another forkful of yams and smiled, the first real smile she'd felt on her face in months.

SANTA RITA JAIL

TODAY, I READ to you from C. G. Parson's *Inside View of Slavery:*

"Take off your shoes, Sylva," said Mrs. A., "and let this gentleman see your feet."

"I don't want to," said Sylva.

"But I want you to," said her mistress.

"I don't care if you do," replied Sylva sullenly.

"You must," said the mistress firmly.

The fear of punishment impelled her to remove the shoes. Four toes on one foot, and two on the other were wanting! "There!" said the mistress, "my husband, who learned the blacksmith's trade for the purpose of teaching it to the slaves, to increase their market value, has with his own hands, pounded off and wrung off all those toes, when insane with passion. And it was only last week that he thought Sylva was saucy to me, and he gave her thirty lashes with the horse whip. She was so old that I could not bear to see it, and I left the house.

"Sylva says," Mrs. A. continued, "that she has been the mother of thirteen children, every one of whom she has destroyed with her own hands, in their infancy, rather than have them suffer slavery!"

CHAPTER 10

LOVE PEELED OPEN a six-ounce can of sausages and ate them with his fingers while sitting on the couch watching the *Power Rangers* with Li'l Pit. The room was dark. Though it had been a month since the drive-by, the windows were still covered with wooden boards.

"This is tight. Watch this." Li'l Pit knelt on the floor three feet from the color TV screen. The Power Rangers linked hands and flipped off a cliff together amid fiery explosions, landing flawlessly, ready for more trouble. "Ahhh, that tight." He stood up and went around to the back of the couch, took a running start, and somersaulted over it onto the pillows.

"Shit, dog, watch out!" Love yelled.

Li'l Pit got up and danced, his arms out in front of him, wrists crossed.

> I'm a Power Ranger
> Ain't afraid of no danger
> I'll melt your mind
> Like a TV changer.

"Man, you silly," Love said. Li'l Pit collapsed on the couch laughing, and Love smiled.

"Here comes the grandmother," Ruby said as she climbed down the stairs holding the handrail firmly, shifting her hips with each step. "Time to pretend you studyin."

She walked across the living room and took a seat in the rocking chair. "How you expect him to go to school if you ain't even going? You'll know whose fault it is when he grow up stupid."

Love shrugged and stared at the TV.

"You know the police are going to come take you from me if you don't show up to school, least sometime."

"Poh-Poh don't scare me," Li'l Pit said. "I'll just run away."

"Don't eat those sausages over my couch without a plate."

"I'm going out," Love said. He put the empty can on the table.

"Where to?"

"Just out."

"Don't 'just out' me. I won't let you turn into a rat child and keep on all night. Bad enough we ain't got no more windows."

"That isn't my fault," he said. He put on his leather jacket. "I didn't shoot those windows. I'm the reason why it won't happen again. I'm protecting this family."

Li'l Pit covered his ears and scooted even closer to the TV. Love opened the front door and put on black leather gloves, another of Easton's garments that Ruby had given him. He pushed his feet into his new high-tops, which he'd bought with his first money from Freight.

"I know you doing what you need to," she said. "You almost a man now. But a man can listen to what I got to say and take it or leave it without running away."

Love sighed and rolled his eyes. "What you want?"

"I want you to come back inside and I'll just tell you something."

Li'l Pit let his hands fall from his ears and looked at his brother. Love shook his head and walked back inside.

"Close the door first," Ruby said.

"Come on, dog. What you want from me?"

"I'm not going to have you calling me a dog. You can leave."

"I just say that. It don't mean nothing."

"No." Ruby waved him away. "I won't have you disrespecting me in my own home. Go on. You go on out and you and your other dog friends can go sniffin around the neighborhood or whatever it is you do." Love's hard face broke into a smile, like the embarrassed wizard coming out from behind the curtain.

"What you want to tell me?" He sat back on the couch, and Ruby eased into the rocking chair.

"Turn that TV down so I can talk without shouting." Li'l Pit turned it down and moved even closer to it, his nose a foot from the screen.

"This a story about back in Norma."

"I ain't got all day to listen to a 'back in Norma' story again," Love said.

"I ain't your mother, but you ain't got nobody else, so if you're smart, you'll hear what I got to say."

"What you want already?"

"This has to do with you. This is something for you. I don't have a better way to put it but to tell you a story. Love E used to be scared of these boys who live over at the next farm."

"I ain't scared of my homies. They're my pahtnahs."

"Shush. Listen. All these boys was his senior, and big like one another, and they mean, too. Kalvin Palmer and his two younger brothers, Harold and Louis. They used to throw rocks at him when he was comin home from school over the bridge. And he even once jumped into the water to get away, and then he came home like a wet mop and his daddy, Papa Samuel, that's his blood papa, he ask him what happened, and he said he fell into the water tryin to catch a frog. But Papa Samuel knowd there ain't no frogs round that time a year and he told him to go get a switch. Papa Samuel whipped Love E good and told him he got to fight back against Kalvin and his brothers. Whip him so bad he do his business standing up all week long. Worse than anything them Palmer boys coulda done to him.

"Now, Ronal, your granpapa, he was just a young man, but he took Love E under his wing and he help Love E to read and talked to him 'bout how Papa Samuel couldn't beat up on him forever; he say that in the future, he an Love E gonna be somethin bigger than any these Palmer boys or Papa Samuel could imagine.

"So then one day them boys ambush him on the bridge, Kalvin up front and his two brothers behind. There weren't nowhere to go, 'cause if he jump in the river, then Papa Samuel gonna get him. He couldn't pull out this knife cause then they'd pull out theirs. So he seem trapped, and it seem like he was gonna get it any way he turn. He say it was like being inside a box and every side on fire, and coming closer, too. He didn't see no way out. And then the sky thundered and there was lightning and it was about to rain and he knowd he could jump over that bridge into the water 'cause everyone was gonna be soaking wet that day when they get home, and Papa Samuel wouldn't be wise to him." Ruby looked up to the ceiling, like she could see the rain coming down.

"So he jumped in?" Love asked.

"No, he didn't jump in. No, he just stand there. He just waited right there 'cause he knowd he'd still have to face them boys every day and get beat up sometime. He want it would just get over with. And if he fight, then they'd let him alone, or at least someday they'd get older and move away. He say he just started walking toward Kalvin and thinking of the future, how the only escaping that box was to look on into the future when things'll get better. 'Cause a trap only a trap if you can't see pass it, how it's gonna be different in the future."

"So they beat him up?"

"Sure. There was three of them and one of him."

"Ahhh, that's scandalous."

"And then Papa Samuel beat him good, too, 'cause he looked like he let them boys beat him up."

"No! That's scan-da-lous." Both Love and Li'l Pit laughed again.

"And those boys beat him up again and again, almost every day. But he saw beyond all that. Nothin ever came of those boys. But Love E, he kept going to school, and he turned into something. He was on TV and he was part of something important. Shoulda seen all these people at his funeral. He knew someday he'd be something. So he could look pass his present trouble."

"That's back in the day," Love said. "I wouldn't let myself be beat on like that. I'd take out a AK-47 and stand on that bridge and bloom! Them boys would be divin in that river themselves."

Ruby shook her head. "I guess there's no getting through your thick skull bone."

"Is that all you wanted to tell me?"

"Go on and get." Ruby stood up. "I got so much truth to tell and nowhere to put it."

LATER THAT NIGHT, Love walked up Cranston, nodding his head and practicing his mean mug. He looked at the empty houses and imagined someone staring at him on the neighbor's stoop. He flipped his head back slightly, pushed his top lip up with his bottom, and narrowed his eyes. Even after he passed the stoop, he turned and continued to stare until he imagined his rival backing down. He kept that cut-eye glare as he approached the liquor store.

It was past nine now, and the dark November cold had set in. Freight, Curse, Nat the stick boy, and Solomon were playing dice against the liquor-store wall on the Cranston side. A yellow streetlight off San Pablo just barely lit their game.

"What up?" Love greeted them.

"My dick," said Curse. The crew laughed, though they all knew Curse's dick had been permanently flaccid since he'd been shot. Love went into the liquor store and bought a Snickers, then came back to the game. Freight laid a five on the ground and the others followed, then Freight picked up all the money and held it as he rolled.

Curse turned to Love. "Want a piece of this action? Easier than pussy from a ho."

"Shit, dog," Love said. "You losin that bad?" The other three cracked up.

"Put your cash where your flash is, nigga. Come on, roll them dice. See how hard you laughin when I take your money."

"I don't give my money away."

"Like I always say," said Curse. "If you don't got the dicks, keep out the mix." He laughed and held his fist out for the others to tap, which they all did, except for Freight, who just said quietly:

"If I have to hold on to this money any longer, blood, I might just put it in my pocket." They all shut up.

"What up, niggas?" Li'l Pit yelled. He crossed the street toward them, his hand waving in the air. Love darted out, grabbed him by the arm, and pulled him back to the other side.

"Let go of me. What you doin?"

"You suppose to be in bed," Love said.

"I don't have to," Li'l Pit said.

"Come on." Love pulled on his arm and tried to drag him back home.

"Let go of me. Let me go," Li'l Pit yelled. A light went on in the house behind them.

"Shut that boy up!" Freight yelled from across the street. Love stopped pulling his brother.

"You ain't suppose to be out here," Love whispered.

"Look at that," Li'l Pit said. Love turned to see Tanya, one of Freight's women, dressed in a gold lamé bodysuit, come around the corner by the liquor store. Freight walked with her down the block, had a brief conversation with her, and then took some money. Love watched Tanya's body, the suit tight around her butt.

"That your girlfriend?" Li'l Pit asked his brother.

"That ho? I don't pay for mine, dog."

"Me neither."

Love shook his head. He bent down on one knee in front of Li'l Pit and zipped up his brother's Dallas Cowboys jacket.

"You have to keep quiet and out of the way if you're going to hang with us again."

"I don't have to do nothin I don't want to."

"Whatever." Love stood up, turned away, and walked back to the group. Li'l Pit followed and ran past him, yelling to the crew.

"What up? What up? Hey, hey."

"What up, Li'l Poet," said Curse.

"The moon and the stars." He tapped everyone's fists and then put his hand out in front of the snake's mouth to feel the tongue against his skin.

"Give up a rap," said Freight. Li'l Pit smiled. He looked around the street and began pumping his head and neck to an internal beat.

It was a dark, cold night

By the liquor store

LEAVING

My homies were kickin it
Dicin it, slicin it, smokin it, and mixin it

The crew laughed and nodded their heads as they played.

The sky was purple
And the clouds were gray
My brother said kiss me
I said: hell no I ain't gay.

Your daddy beat your mommy
And your mommy is a ho.
I told you to be better
Or I'll give you to five-oh.

Now you roll a seven
And you get yourself some money
Someone isn't happy
And they say that you are funny.

My name is Li'l Pit
And I rap like Mr. Clinton
I'll check you on the flip
But for now,
I'm fit for quittin.

He stood still and raised two fingers in the air: "Peace-out, niggas."
They all applauded. Li'l Pit wiped his mouth with his fist, squinting
his eyes like a boxer who'd just delivered his knockout punch.

"Who got the smokes?" he asked.

"Right here," said Curse. He reached under his leg and pulled out a
box and gave Li'l Pit a cigarette. Love grabbed his brother's wrist and
ripped the cigarette out of his hand.

"Hey, motherfucker, that was my cigarette," said Curse. He turned on one wheel and faced Love. Love looked down at him in his chair.

"Don't get my little brother smoking."

"Oh, so now you gonna tell me what I can and can't do, punk? Freight, let me kick his skinny little ass down the block."

"Go ahead," said Freight.

"You sure? 'Cause I'm gonna do some damage."

Love tightened his fists.

"Go ahead," Freight said, without watching. Curse considered the focused eyes and the small, unpredictable rigidity of Love's body. He reached under the blanket on his lap and pulled out a small 9-mm pistol.

Love looked over at Freight, who still didn't bother watching. He knew he shouldn't run; he'd seen Nat make that mistake. But this was not the same situation, and Curse was not Freight. Love closed his eyes. He forced his mind to accept it, to embrace it and get it over with. What did it matter? If not now, it'd be later. Cars whizzed by on San Pablo, alternating with the faint singing of En Vogue floating out of the store. He heard the grinding buzz of the fluorescent streetlight above and imagined the swarm of brown moths beating their wings against the encasement of the burning light. If it happened, fast and clean, this wasn't a terrible way to go. He even felt himself drawn to move closer to Curse.

"I didn't want the smoke anyway," Li'l Pit said.

"You sure now, li'l brother? 'Cause you don't got to do nothin nobody tells you."

"I'm sure."

"Well, if it didn't mean nothin to you, then I just as soon let it go. But I don't want no one pushin you around. I'm on the lookout for you."

"It's all good."

"In that case, we all right." He put the gun back under his blanket. "I'll let it go, then." He wheeled around, back into the circle of the game.

Love looked at Li'l Pit, who flashed him a big smile.

A FEW NIGHTS later at the liquor store, Love and Li'l Pit played dice with the crew. Freight put down a ten spot so the rest of them put down a ten.

"I don't got none," Li'l Pit complained.

"I'll cover you," Curse said. He laid down another ten, then rolled a six.

"Six," Freight said, confirming it before they went on.

Nat rolled next, an eight.

"Eight."

Love rolled a seven.

"Seven."

Li'l Pit rolled another six.

"Ha!" yelled Curse. "It's you and me, Li'l Poet." He reached out and tapped Li'l Pit's fist.

Freight rolled a seven, like Love. He didn't say anything or even look at Love. Curse spit to the side of his wheelchair.

It was Curse's turn again. He rolled the die in his hands and blew on them. "Come on, bro, give me a little of your magic breath," he said, sticking his hands out in front of Li'l Pit, who blew on them too.

Curse tossed the die toward the wall and hit a nine. Love didn't smile or look at Curse.

Nat rolled and hit his eight. He jumped in the air. "Yeah, boy! You-know-what-I'm-saying. Money, money, money." He knelt down and picked up the cash.

Freight threw another ten spot down, as did the rest. Curse covered Li'l Pit again.

"First to hit snake eyes," Freight said. No one argued. They went around the circle three times and no one hit. When it got back to Love, Freight held up his hand to stop the roll. "How many sevens there been?" he asked Love.

"Four."

"How many fives?"

"Two."

"Roll."

Love rolled. Eight. They went around the circle twice again. Then Love hit snake eyes. He reached for the cash, but Freight put out his hand.

"Hold on." He looked up at Curse. "How many eights?"

"Four," Curse said.

"How many eights?" Freight asked Love.

"Five."

"Bullshit," Curse yelled. "Four. I been counting."

"It was four," Nat said, and nodded to Curse. They both looked at Li'l Pit. Li'l Pit looked over at his brother and then back at Curse.

"How many eights, Li'l Poet?" Curse asked.

Li'l Pit clenched his fists as if he were about to get into a fight. He looked at Freight, who waited for him to answer.

"I think it was four of them."

Curse smiled and nodded. "That's fuckin right, boy. It was four. Now give me my money."

Freight dropped his hand and leaned back against the wall.

"Five," he said.

"Naw, man," Curse yelled. "It was four, Freight. Don't do me like that." He shook his head as Love bent down and picked up the money.

"Fuck this shit," Curse said, and rolled away down Cranston.

OVER TIME, FREIGHT began to show Love the mechanics of the operation. One day in December he sent him on his first solo run. Curse always spit on the ground when he saw Freight take Love into the liquor store.

Freight put a ten on the counter.

"Four packs," he said to Rick. Rick scratched his beard, took the bill, put it into the register, then took out a single and put it in his pocket.

"Hurry up, blood."

Rick bent down and came back up with a paper bag. He handed it to Freight. Freight wore soft leather gloves, expensive and sleek with rabbit-fur lining. He took off one glove and reached into the bag to feel the vials. He rolled the small jars between his fingers, then shoved the bag into his jacket pocket. He never held the stockpile on him in case the cops showed up.

"What's the count?" Freight watched the TV screen above him, a scene of a soap opera in a hospital room.

"Twenty-two?"

"Right." Freight had an impeccable memory and tested Rick often. They looked each other in the eye for a moment, then Rick looked away. A young man in a blue wool cap, thirsty for rock, came to the entrance of the store, his hands deep in his pockets.

"Get outside," Freight yelled at him.

"This is a store. I can come into a store. It doesn't mean nothing."

"I don't want your kind in here. Get outside. Love, keep this fiend outta here. Shit."

The man turned around and walked out on his own. Freight looked up to the video monitor that showed him in a spectrum of grays standing in front of the counter, but also the whole area up to the entrance.

"Tilt that camera down more, just so it shows this part," he said. He walked out as Rick climbed up on the counter to adjust the camera.

"He said he wanted a soda," Love told Freight outside.

"I don't care what he said. Don't let them in the store." The man in the blue cap stood to the right against the wall on Cranston, cleaning his teeth with his tongue. Freight came toward him and the man began walking away, farther down the street. When he reached a mailbox at a gate a few houses down, the man stopped and turned around.

"It's in there," he said.

"Get back," Freight yelled. The man took a few more steps backward. Freight reached into the mailbox and took out a twenty-dollar bill. He put the bag inside and closed the box. Freight turned and walked back to the store, and the man rushed to the box. He took out the bag, looked in, and disappeared into the burned-out house where Li'l Pit had spent his first week on the West Side.

Love watched this interaction a hundred times a day, and after a while it became a bore. He rubbed his eyes and was knocked off balance by Freight hitting him in the shoulder.

"We'll be clean out in an hour, so hurry up." He thrust his hand inside Love's leather jacket and stuck a roll of money into his pocket.

"Without you?" Love asked.

"Did I say I was coming?"

Love shook his head and got on his dirt bike. He rode up toward Berkeley, his jacket ballooning like a life preserver, and when he reached Alcatraz, he turned and entered a residential area.

A few blocks down, there was a long brown picket fence, high enough that the house inside wasn't visible from the street. Love got off his bike and pulled the string that hung through a hole at one end of the fence, which Freight had shown him the first time they were there together. Nothing happened for a moment; then there was a buzz, and he pushed on the gate. He let the gate click shut behind him and leaned his bike against the inside fence. The yard was overflowing with twigs, overgrown dried weeds, and a low tree, its branches shooting out over the walkway. The front of the one-story house had two windows, both covered with bamboo curtains.

Love walked along the side of the house and around back where there was a small courtyard and a shed. The back door was shut, and a purple curtain hung over the window. He rang the buzzer. After a moment, the metal mail slot lifted and a mouth appeared.

"What do you want?" a woman's voice asked.

"It's Love. I came for Freight." The slot shut.

He heard voices talking inside, and then the woman opened the slot and whispered.

"Give me the money." He took the wad of bills from his pocket, five hundred dollars, if it was the same as before. He pushed the money through the metal flap and it was immediately grabbed from his fingers. Nothing happened for a second more, then the mouth appeared again.

"Okay. Go wait in the shed. And close the door."

Love let out a breath and turned around. The shed was a square concrete building with a thick wooden door. As he walked in, he flipped on the light switch to his left. On the other side of the room was a red wagon with a rusted handle and a cardboard box of firewood in it. There were no chairs, only a wooden table with a clamp screwed into it. The door made a swishing sound as he closed it: there was a plastic cat flap cut into the bottom that brushed along the cement floor. He jumped up to sit on the old table and let his legs swing, rubbing his hands and blowing into them.

A single yellow bulb buzzed in the middle of the ceiling, attached to a bumpy metal tube that went across and then down the wall. There were spiderwebs in every corner of the room. Love bent forward and looked under the edge of the table to see if there were spiders there too, then sat back up and crossed his legs in front of him.

He played with the clamp, twirling the stick around until it tightened onto his left hand, then loosened it and looked at the ridges pressed into his skin. There were no windows or clocks to tell how long he'd waited, but he was used to waiting in the quiet-rooms, and it wasn't so bad except that it was freezing cold, even colder than outside. He was about to put his hand in the vise grip again when the door opened. He jumped off the table, and a thin White man walked in and shut the door. He wore boots and a long blue overcoat. The last time Love was there, the box had just been pushed through the cat door and he never saw a face. This man had straight hair and a little beard. Small crumbs were stuck in the corners of his eyes and he had very thick eyebrows.

"Love's your name?" He kept his hands in his coat pockets. Love nodded.

"Is that your street name?"

Love shook his head.

"How much is Freight paying you?"

Love shrugged.

"Amanda wants to give you the goods, but she told me to come in here first to see if you wanted to make some extra money." He waited. He looked at Love's face and squinted. "How old are you?" Love didn't say anything. He kept his mouth shut and breathed through his nose.

"You don't have to be afraid," the man said.

"I'm not."

"How old are you?"

"Fourteen."

"You know how much money you gave us?" The man leaned on the corner of the table between Love and the door. "You know what would happen if you didn't bring Freight his rock?" Love didn't move, and the man smiled.

"I want to give you forty dollars. Just for you to keep. Okay?" The man took out the bills. "Okay?"

Love nodded.

"It's cold in here, isn't it?" He leaned against the wall behind him and looked at Love for a moment without moving. "If you leave right now, you won't get any rock." He undid the belt around his coat and opened it at the bottom. He wasn't wearing any pants, and his penis sprang out partially erect. His legs were hairy, and he was wearing a white T-shirt.

"Do you know what I want you to do?"

Love looked at the door.

"Don't try to run. I'm not going to do anything to you that's going to hurt you, so you don't have to be afraid."

"I don't want the money." Love put the bills on the table.

The man held himself and moved his hand up and down. "Have you ever seen a White man's penis before? It's not very white, is it? I bet it's not very different than yours. Will you show me yours?"

Love shook his head.

"I'm not going to make you do anything, okay? I could, but I'm not going to. If you don't want another twenty dollars, you don't have to touch me. All right?" He waited. "I said all right?"

Love nodded.

"I'm not going to make you touch me. But remember, if I want, I can tell Amanda not to give you anything. She'll tell Freight you never even came by. You know I could do that?" The man was fully erect and stroking himself faster. "Now all you have to do, and then I'll give you what you want, all you have to do is—you don't have to touch me, which is what I came in here to make you do, I was going to make you do something, but I'm just going to ask in case you might want to anyway for an extra . . . extra hundred dollars—I wanted you to put your mouth on me. Some kids don't mind. But I'm not going to . . . to make you do that. Instead, all you have to do for the money, and then you'll get the stuff, is just show me, just show me yours. You won't have to touch me at all if you do that." Love backed into the corner between the table and the wagon.

"But you have to do that," the man continued, "or else you don't get your rock." He stroked himself faster and pushed his hips forward.

Love turned away and faced the wall with his arms down at his sides. The wall was cracked in the corner. A spider had left a few curled-up ants in an old web, their blood sucked out of them. He could hear the man rubbing himself and walking toward him. The table creaked as the man steadied himself with his other hand.

"Show me your thing," the man said. "You don't have to do anything to me. I'll do it to you. I want to suck it for you so bad," he whispered. "Show me your beautiful little . . . nuh." Everything stopped moving, and the man took a long deep breath.

After a few moments, Love looked back. The man wiped his hand with a twenty-dollar bill and tied his coat.

"I didn't mean to scare you," he said. He put the twenty back on the table and bowed his head. "I just thought you might want some money. Lots of kids want some extra cash." He walked to the door and, without turning back, said: "Don't worry. You'll get your stuff. I wasn't going to keep it from you." He walked out, closing the door behind him.

Love didn't touch the money on the table. He stayed in the corner with his back to the wall. A minute later, a bag slid in through the cat door. He picked it up and stuffed it in his jacket, then slowly opened the shed door. As he came out, the back door to the house slammed shut and the purple curtain gently floated to the glass. Love ran to his bike, twisted the lock on the gate, and kicked it open. The gate swung out and then shut behind him, and now he stood in the empty street, the sun directly above in a hazy overcast light.

He didn't jump on his bike and split, even though he was still just in front of the house. He walked for a moment in the quiet of the open street, down to Alcatraz. He walked slowly, looking at the houses, at trees, at a bird flying overhead. When he reached the corner, he looked at his bike, took a deep breath, and let it out through his nose. He got on and stood up on the pedals, rocking back and forth to balance, like waiting at a starting gate. Then he counted backwards from five, grunted, and took off as fast as he could. He knew he was late and Freight would kick his ass for it.

THE NEXT DAY, Love rode the train from Oakland to the San Leandro BART station, then walked the rest of the way up into the hills to Los Aspirantes. Once they took him back, he'd get them to take Li'l Pit since he couldn't stay at Cranston alone. They had said that they cared about him—Tom had said it out loud—and they would be able to tell he was in trouble, out of school during the day, on his own.

He crossed the bridge over the freeway and walked slowly up the incline of the suburban street. He knew these homes and lawns well, these cars and mailboxes and porches, from driving past them to school every morning from the residential house, from taking walks with Tom to get a Slurpee on special outings. There was a peacefulness about knowing a place well, even if you hated it—no surprises: the steep driveway to the school, the chain-link fence around the playground, the long rectangular buildings of the upper and lower blocks.

When he reached the top of the driveway, he stopped and looked at the administrative bungalow with vines of jasmine creeping up its sides. The front door was open, and he knew Krista would be sitting behind the front desk, her jar of lollipops and candy always open. It occurred to him for the first time that he might not be allowed to leave once they saw him. Krista would recognize him and from there, even if he ran away, they would contact Ruby to find him. Had it really been all that bad at Cranston, bad enough to go back to all the rules and restraints, not being allowed to yell fuck you without having to take a time-out, not being allowed to wear a Raiders hat, not being allowed to listen to Public Enemy? All those times he'd been wrestled to the ground and tossed in the quiet-room for throwing a bowl on the floor. Watched all the time, not able to leave on his own, to have to go to therapy, to have to go to school and sit through those boring classes, to have to go to sleep and wake up when they told you. Was it really worth it?

He could hear the kids playing kickball in the yard: no pushing or cutting, no cursing or hitting. They screamed and clapped for Nita, a girl he knew vaguely from another class. Love walked slowly to the front door and stood by Krista's desk. She was on the phone, but her face lit up when she saw him. He smiled back. She was the most cheerful person in the whole school, if not the whole world, and for on-campus rewards, kids would always ask to go visit her and get candy. She hung up the phone and shook her head.

"Ronald Love LeRoy, what took you so long to come see us?"

Love looked down and smiled.

"How you doing? How's it going at home? You want me to call up to Room 7 and see if they can have a visitor?"

"Naw." Love shook his head.

"Well, have a seat then. You want some candy?"

Love took a piece of butterscotch and sat down on one of the chairs in the waiting area. He unwrapped his candy and pushed it into his cheek with his tongue.

"Who you here to see?" Krista asked.

"I just thought I'd come by."

The phone rang and she pressed a button. "Hold on, honey."

While she spoke on the phone, Love stood up and peered around the cubicle to see if someone in charge was around to talk to. A few of the counselors were waiting around to drive the afternoon buses, but he didn't see anyone he trusted.

When he came back to Krista's desk, she was writing a note that she stuck to the stapler.

"So you just came by to see me, huh?"

"Is Tom around?" he asked. Sometimes Tom worked in Room 7 and sometimes he stayed at the house, so there was a chance he'd be at the campus.

"Tom?" Krista shook her head and took a piece of candy for herself. "Tom Riley? I don't think he's here anymore, Love. You want to talk to him?"

"That's okay. I'll stop by the house."

"No, I mean I don't think he works here anymore is what I mean. I think he quit." Love stood frozen, a stream of cold rushed down the inside of his chest to his stomach. She must have seen it in his eyes, for the smile on her face faded and she picked up the phone.

"Let me just call Lonnie and check." Lonnie was the head of the day-treatment program.

"It's Krista," she said into the receiver. "You know if Tom Riley still works with us? I know. That's what I thought." She shook her head to Love. "Lonnie, you remember Love LeRoy. Actually, he's right here at my desk. By himself." She held the phone to her shoulder. "Is there something we can pass on to Tom for you?"

"Naw." Love shook his head. "I was just going to see if I could come back."

Lonnie must have heard, because all Krista said was "Okay" and then hung up the phone.

"Lonnie is on his way down."

Lonnie was a nice enough man, Jewish with a messy beard. He was short but willing and able to put you in restraint if he had to. He'd had to only once with Love, for kicking a wall repeatedly, but Love didn't hold that against him because no one at Los Aspirantes held it against you for getting restrained. It was as normal as going to the bathroom.

"Love," Lonnie said as he came around the corner. He nodded to him. Lonnie was a no-nonsense guy: he didn't ever cave in, and he wasn't afraid of you; he always gave it to you straight. "You want to take a walk?"

Love nodded and they went back into the parking lot and strolled down the long driveway. Love looked at the ground the whole time, crunching the eucalyptus leaves and pods under his feet.

"So you want to come back?"

Love nodded.

"Why's that?"

Love shrugged. It wasn't that he didn't want to say, but it didn't seem that easy to explain. He hoped Lonnie might ask him the right question to get him to figure out how to say what it was.

"Well, we don't have a place for you right now," Lonnie said. "And even if we did, we'd have to know the reason you want to come back. Things not working out with your grandmother?"

Love shrugged again. It wasn't that his grandmother was doing anything wrong, and he couldn't tell Lonnie he was running for the crew or it might also be used against him to be put in Juvi, which was far worse than Los Aspirantes or the street.

"You know, Tom left after you did. He's doing something new now, too. But if you want, I could give him a message. He may call you. I can't promise he would, but he might."

"Naw."

"Just because he left, Love, doesn't mean he forgot about you, you know."

"I know." Love spat on the curb. Lonnie didn't tell him to take a time-out, and he realized that he almost wished he had.

"Things just aren't going the way I planned," Love said. "That's all."

"You in any danger?"

"Not really."

"Not really danger, or not really bad danger?"

Love shrugged again. If he said he was in danger, then Ruby might get in trouble.

"Can't you just let me stay in the living room at my old house?"

Lonnie laughed. "I wish it were that easy. But it's not. I could have someone come out there, though, and talk to your grandmother, and they might be able to place you somewhere for older kids."

"You mean here."

"Like here, but not here. But I have to tell you that it's a long process and it might take a while, unless there is something immediately dangerous going on." Lonnie looked at Love through his glasses, one eyebrow raised.

"Naw. It ain't nothin I can't handle."

Lonnie nodded for a while, then said: "Let me just tell you, Love, that a lot of kids who leave come back here to ask the same thing, and it's nothing to be ashamed of. But you should know that there's going to be a period of readjustment that everyone goes through."

"Yeah. I know."

They'd walked all the way back down to the freeway overpass, and Lonnie stopped at the corner.

"I can call someone to come out there, but you'll have to tell me more specifically what's wrong."

There were so many cars going by below that Love couldn't hear himself think. He felt an urge to run to the railing and jump over right in front of Lonnie, just to show him how serious it was. But then Li'l Pit would be stuck on his own with the crew, and that was exactly what Love wanted to avoid.

"I'll just give it some more time," Love said.

"All right." Lonnie held out his hand and Love shook it. "It takes guts to come back here," Lonnie said. "I know that. I've always known you were a strong kid, and I mean inside. If it gets rough, you can always come back and talk, okay?"

Love nodded, watching the cars whiz by below. Lonnie patted him on the shoulder, then turned around and walked back up the hill.

SANTA RITA JAIL

TODAY I READ from the *Mississippi Law of 1865,* Chapter 1, Section 3:

All freedmen, free Negroes, or mulattoes who do now and have herebefore lived and cohabitated together as husband and wife shall be taken and held in law as legally married, and the issue shall be taken and held as legitimate for all purposes; that it shall not be lawful for any freedman, free Negro, or mulatto to intermarry with any white person; nor for any white person to intermarry with any freedman, free Negro, or mulatto; and any person who shall so intermarry, shall be deemed guilty of felony, and on conviction thereof shall be confined in the State penitentiary for life. . . .

CHAPTER 11

NOVEMBER 1963 • CORBET 54, RUBY 25,
SANDRA 18, EASTON 17, LIDA 3

BY THE FALL, Sandra had become a regular at Corbet's home. She helped pass out candy on Halloween, and when Kennedy was shot, she immediately drove over and spent the afternoon with the family. They ate dinner, listened to the radio and watched TV at the same time.

Easton reached in and pinched the last grain of rice from his bowl between his thumb and forefinger. He rolled it back and forth, felt the sticky softness of it, then squished it flat and looked at its pure whiteness on his thumb. He scraped it off with his bottom teeth and swallowed it.

"Maybe it's a hoax," he said. Everyone else had retired to the living room. No one responded. Sandra stood by the stereo where she had been from the moment she'd turned it on, her head resting against the side of the bookshelf and tears still in her eyes.

Ruby stood up from the couch and shut off the TV. She shook her head and let out a heavy breath, but she didn't cry. "If they can kill the president, then Lord only knows what they can do," she said.

Corbet sat in his chair next to his crutches, his head bowed. He didn't have anything to drink, and he wasn't smoking. His hands were in his lap, one folded under the other.

"Every president that gets up for the colored folk gets shot down," he said.

"You think it's racial?" Sandra asked, lifting her head for the first time.

"Everything is racial," Easton said. He looked at her sharply, and they locked eyes for a moment. She looked away and rested her head on the shelf again.

"Nothing is strictly racial," Corbet said. "It's all about power and fear. It's like in the war, we're all dug into our little trenches shooting at everybody we can't even see. Takes a kind of blindness to hurt someone."

Lida bent down and picked up a rubber band off the floor. She toddled toward Easton with her gift outstretched. Ruby saw her and quickly came up from behind, lifting her around the waist before she could bother him.

"I have to call my father," Sandra said.

"Use our phone here." Corbet pointed to the phone on the table. Though she'd been coming over to their house for months, she'd never used their phone.

"He lives in Oregon," she said.

"Sure. We know." Corbet smiled at her. She shook her head, but everyone encouraged her and she surrendered.

"I'll pay you back for it."

"You don't have to do that. Call your papa, and then Ruby here is going to call her mama. And let me say hello to her myself."

While Sandra used the phone, Ruby carried Lida outside onto the front stoop. She stood on the porch like she used to do in Norma when Ronald came calling. She could still imagine the dusty steps and the sunlit dirt road, though it had been almost four years since she'd seen them.

"She yours too, Ronal," she had said to him when she found out she was pregnant. Ronald had large stains of sweat under his arms and in the center of his chest. He had walked two miles in his slacks and shirt sleeves from the West River office of the *Tri-County Free Press*, where he was working as a reporter on the pesticide story.

He did not walk up to the porch, but stopped at the bottom and placed one polished shoe on the first step. She sat on the fir chair that her grandmother had made, the wood creaking as it accepted her full body.

"You don't wanna chile wid me, Ronal?"

He wiped the sweat from his gray-black face and closed his long eyelashes so they met like the tips of contemplative fingers.

"You know my plans, Ruby. What am I going to do with a baby at college?"

"She yours and mine together."

"You have always known that I've planned to attend Howard. Why don't you resolve this like last time?"

Ruby looked away from him out across the dirt road to the field, stripped now from too many harvests of cotton. Beyond that, the green fir trees blew gently to the west like giant ancestors bowing and nodding. She was always faintly aware of the steady rush of the river far back in the woods.

"You wanna come in for some ice water?" she asked him.

He looked up the dirt road. "I ought to get back for press. The union is threatening to shut us down. Where is your mother?"

"In town."

He climbed up two more steps. "Where is Easton?"

"In town." The breeze stopped, and the thick heat held them in their places.

"You're going to fix it?" he asked.

"Ice water? It ain't no trouble."

"Come on, Ruby. Not the water."

She rubbed the spot on her rough muslin dress where she'd spilled tuna oil. All the other dresses she'd made went to be sold in town. This was the first one she'd gotten to keep, because of the stain.

"You still want to come in?" she asked.

"I guess now is the safest time there is, anyway," he said. He started up the stairs again to the door. She blocked the entrance and took his hand.

"Here." She placed his hand on her stomach. "Meet your own daughter. She ain't goin nowhere, so you might as well as introduce yourselves."

She held his hand on her stomach. There was no protrusion of her body yet, but they smiled at each other.

Thinking back on that time, Ruby could hardly believe how the unbearable pain she used to feel had melted into the melancholy sweet-ness of memory. As she looked out at Cranston, remembering, she swayed with Lida in her arms, almost too big to hold now. It was a beautiful, quiet day in West Oakland, and not a person was on the street.

In a few minutes, Sandra joined Ruby on the porch, pulling the door closed but not all the way shut. She came up next to Ruby and put her hands on the rail. "I'm all done now, if you want to call."

Ruby nodded her head and rubbed Lida on the back. "You talk to your papa?" she asked.

"Yeah."

"What he say?"

"He thinks it was the Cubans behind it all. He always says it's some foreigner. When the economy gets bad, he says it's the Mexicans, and when crime gets bad, he says it's the Communists or, you know, other people." Sandra spoke quickly, excited by the interest Ruby showed. Ruby didn't usually ask her about herself.

"You tell him where you at?" Ruby asked.

"Nah. I don't talk to him much about my politics. He doesn't go for that."

"I'm sayin, did you tell him where you was callin from?"

Sandra turned and looked at the house as if she needed to remind herself. "You mean here?"

"Yes." Ruby had not looked at her the whole time they were speak-ing, and now Sandra detected more hostility behind the questions than friendly interest.

"Sure." She folded her arms and cleared her throat.

"What'd he think?"

"I told him I was at a friend's house."

"So he don't know."

"Know what?"

"We colored."

"No." They stood in silence for a moment more, and then Sandra headed back to the door.

"You going to tell him?" Ruby asked.

Sandra kept her hand on the doorknob but didn't turn it. "Sometime."

"Not every White man's proud to have his daughter out wit a colored boy. But dey don't hardly never blame de girl. Most always de boy be gettin killed."

"My father isn't going to kill anyone." Sandra came back out and faced her. "You don't like that I'm White, do you?"

Ruby put Lida down but held her hand. The child bent to the floorboards and picked up a tack.

"Give me dat." Ruby took the tack from her, then turned to Sandra. "I'm going to be straight wit you, 'cause you always askin us straight-up about how it is. I don't mind so much dat you White. What I mind is dat you can't tell your papa you seein a colored boy. Either you think maybe you'll hang around and tell him later but you don't know your own mine, or you scared to tell him and you ain't never plannin to tell him; you just figure you wait long enough and den one day you just gonna up and go."

Sandra was about to argue, to get indignant and say she knew her own mind, that she would stand up to her father or any other bigot, and that she resented the accusation. But she looked into Ruby's eyes and saw no anger, just a serious concern, and then resignation.

"I know what you're saying," Sandra replied. She looked at the houses along the street, the brightly painted Victorians with wooden gates. "To be honest with you, I never really thought it through, how I'm going to tell my father and all if it gets more serious. It just makes me so angry that it's such a big deal to be together. I'm not planning to just leave; that's not what I want to do."

Ruby nodded her head. "Well, at least you honest about it. I got to say dat."

Lida toddled to the door, pushed it open, and went inside.

"Well, I got to call my mama now." Ruby followed her child in, and Sandra stayed out on the porch alone, watching the empty street.

CHRISTMAS EVE, RUBY sat at her sewing machine while little Lida slept on the couch. Ruby wet the frayed end of a blue thread with her lips and slipped it through the needle in a fluid rotation of her wrist. Her foot pressed against the pedal, and she turned the light blue chiffon so that the stitches hemmed in the collar.

She was making a dress for Sandra. Perhaps it was a peace offering, or an indirect gift to her brother. In either case, she had always thought that nice clothes made a person more attractive. She would have made a dress for herself if there had been someone who cared how she looked. But that was self-pitying nonsense, and she wouldn't let herself go there. If she could do nothing useful for herself, at least she could help out her brother. Easton was out with Corbet celebrating; he'd finally landed a job at a garage.

Ruby's hands were still young, the skin still tight and smooth. She loved her hands when they turned the fabric. She would finish this dress and then get back to making the yellow banana dresses for the stores. She made only half as much money from the dresses as from cleaning, but she couldn't afford to lose any extra money now. Even if she could, she wouldn't ever stop sewing and let housecleaning be her only job in life; that would be like chewing without tasting.

The water bill, the property tax, the ants, the food, the medication for Corbet's amputation and diabetes, her own rotten tooth, Lida's coughing—it all spun around in her mind. But the needle pumping up and down into the fabric narrowed her focus. She watched her hands and listened to the machine whir, and soon she was back home in Norma, her mother sitting next to her at the dining table in the kitchen, sewing on the pocket by hand. Elise had said on the phone that her hair was getting gray now, but Ruby couldn't imagine that. She saw her mama's chestnut-brown hair wrapped in the black bandanna, her forehead glistening red in the summertime as she told her stories, lived her stories, which never had beginning or end, just endless interruptions.

Ruby remembered how their house filled with light and space in the summer; pollen floated in through the open windows, and the sun made streaks through the slats in the wooden walls. The house was old. Ruby's great-great-grandmother, Pearl, rented the house from her former master, Ruby's great-great-grandfather, after the Union Army burned down Norma and killed most of the White men in the Marlboro family. Elise always looked to the side when telling her stories, as if she were remembering the day when it happened, though it had been forty years before she was born. And Ruby imagined it too, since, as Elise told it, appearances hadn't changed much.

"Nanna Pearl could take one a her shoes and hit a mouse 'cross the room. Wham!" Elise laughed like the wind coming around a corner, a burst of air with no voice. "She could do it in the dark when you asleep: wham! An you sit up. 'JE-SUS, Lord, what was that?' An Pearl'd say, 'Go back to sleep, baby. You safe now.' My Nanna Saluda slep in the same bed wit her mama Pearl till she was 'bout six, and she tell me she never get a night's rest till both shoes been throwed."

Ruby would finish the dress and hand it to her mother, and her mother would always say, "That's another quarter for your pocket." And she was good to her word: a quarter for every dress sold in town. But neither of them ever kept the money; they just put it in the pickle jar for the family—like Ruby did now in Oakland.

Ruby tried to keep her head back in Norma, but the bills started to swirl around. She finished the dress for Sandra and shook it out. Now, one more banana dress and she would finish the stack. This order would bring in another seventy-five dollars, which would pay for the shopping. She felt her sore tooth with her tongue and sucked at it, a warm sweetness in her saliva.

Lida coughed and Ruby turned to her sleeping daughter. Elise had asked on the phone about her, wondered if she had Ronald's beautiful long lashes. She did—those long black lashes. She was going to be a beauty, and she would have any man she wanted, marry a lawyer and never clean a house or sew a dress, unless of course they had their own business together, mother and daughter.

Ruby changed spools and slid the yellow linen under the needle. The foot pedal whirred and clicked in the circular rhythm, speeding up and slowing down, everything under her own effortless control. She turned the fabric between her hands and hummed.

SANTA RITA JAIL

I READ TO you today from *Justice Denied:*

*Thomas James, Jep's second son, had cast his eyes on a handsome young
Negro girl, to whom he made dishonest overtures. She would not submit to
him, and finding he could not overcome her, he swore he would be revenged.
One night he called her out of the gin-house, and then bade me and two or
three more, strip her naked; which we did. He then made us throw her down
on her face, in front of the door, and hold her whilst he flogged her—the
brute—with the bullwhip, cutting great gashes of flesh out of her person, at
every blow, from five to six inches long. The poor unfortunate girl screamed
most awfully all the time, and writhed under our strong arms, rendering it
necessary for us to use our united strength to hold her down. He flogged her
for half an hour, until he nearly killed her, and then left her to crawl away to
her cabin.*

. . . there were often certain concrete advantages to be gained by sur-
rendering themselves to the men of the master race that overcame any
moral scruples these women might have had. In some cases it meant freedom from the drudgery of field labor as well as better food and clothing.
Then there was the prospect that her half-White children would enjoy certain privileges and perhaps in time be emancipated. . . .

The relations between the White men and the slave women naturally
aroused the jealousy and antagonism of the women of the master race.
. . . Sometimes White women used more direct means of ridding themselves of their colored rivals . . . witness the following excerpt from the
family history of a mulatto:

*My father's grandmother, Julia Heriot, of four generations ago lived in George-
town, South Carolina. Recollections of her parentage are, indeed, vague.*

Nevertheless, a distinct mixture of blood was portrayed in her physical appearance. And, because she knew so little of her parents, she was no doubt sold into Georgetown at a very early age as house servant to General Charles Washington Heriot. Julia Heriot married a slave on the plantation by whom she had two children. Very soon after her second child was born an epidemic of fever swept the plantation, and her husband became one of the victims. After her husband's death, she became maid to Mrs. Heriot, wife of General Heriot. From the time that Julia Heriot was sold to General Heriot, she had been a favorite servant in the household, because of the aptitude which she displayed in performing her tasks. General and Mrs. Heriot had been so impressed with her possibilities that in a very short time after she had been in her new home, she had been allowed to use the name of Heriot . . . in the midst of her good fortune, a third child was born to her, which bore no resemblance to her other children. Reports of the "white child" were rumored. General Heriot's wife became enraged and insisted that her husband sell this slave girl, but General Heriot refused.

During the winter of the following year General Heriot contracted pneumonia and died. Before his death, he signed freedom papers for Julia and her three children; but Mrs. Heriot maneuvered her affairs so that Julia Heriot and her three children were again sold into slavery. In the auction of the properties Julia Heriot was separated from her first two children. She pleaded that her babies be allowed to remain with her, but found her former mistress utterly opposed to anything that concerned her well-being. Her baby was the only consolation which she possessed. Even the name Heriot had been taken away by constant warnings.

CHAPTER 12A

EASTON SAT ON a stool and drew Sandra as she lay at the edge of his bed. She wore the light blue chiffon dress that Ruby had made for her. The strapless dress came to just above her chest, leaving her shoulders and neck bare. She posed as elegantly as she could, her head turned away and chin slightly raised. She'd been talking to him, while moving her lips as little as possible, about a gallery her friend had set up in Emeryville for new artists.

"They're into finding what's real. You know, playing drums, reading poetry. They'd like you. I'm sure of it. I bet they'd put up your work."

Easton held the charcoal delicately between his fingers, then lifted it to his nose and sniffed. No matter how hard he washed after work, the smell of gasoline would not come off completely, and he went around smelling everything he touched.

"People would buy it," she added. "I know they would."

He looked at her and nodded, not at what she was saying but at what he was seeing. Sandra was smiling and looking out the window as if in a dream about his success, a smile like a proud mother might have about her child. He began sketching her this way. Now that he saw something other than just the shape of her, now that he saw an attitude, he sketched quickly and easily, drawing sweeping lines and shading them without pausing.

With the sound of Easton working passionately, Sandra stopped talking and waited. She knew it wouldn't be long and believed that she must be still for him to capture whatever it was that excited him.

In five minutes he had finished and put the tablet and charcoal down on his dresser. Sandra leaned toward the picture, but she knew he would want to wait. He crossed his legs, put his elbow on his knee, his mouth against his hand, and contemplated her.

"What is it?" She smiled uneasily.

He nodded. "I think I understand now."

"Well, that's good," she said. She was used to his cryptic statements and was no longer baited by them.

"Yes. You see, all this time I thought you were just playing hard to get. But you were just hard to *get*." He nodded his head. "Uhh-huh. Yes, it was hard to *get* you. But now I got you." She straightened her dress, pulling up on the elastic around her shoulders and then pushing it down again, but not as low.

"Are you going to show me the sketch, or are *you* going to play hard to get?"

"Yes. I want you to see this. Tell me what you think. What do you see?" He picked up the tablet and handed it to her.

She looked at the picture and smiled. "I love it. I think it's beautiful and honorable. I look majestic. It's my favorite."

"Mmm-hmm. You think I captured you, right?"

"Yes. I think you captured my spirit."

He nodded and stroked his small goatee. "I want you to do something. I want to sketch you again. Here, give me the paper. But this time I want you to pull your top all the way down."

She smiled, but when she saw he was serious, she shook her head. "All the way down where?"

"It's for art's sake."

She looked at the door.

"Don't worry. We'll hear anyone coming up the stairs."

In the year they had been dating, he had seen only the shapes of her breasts in the dark while they'd made out. They'd never had sex.

She put her fingers inside the elastic band but didn't pull it down.

"I don't really mind," she said. "It's just that everyone is downstairs."

"I want to sketch you. I want you to let me see you."

She inhaled and pulled the elastic down slowly, edging it to just above her nipples. She stopped and stared directly into his eyes. He waited, hardly breathing. She pulled the elastic down farther, until her breasts were fully exposed. They were small and whiter than the rest of her, milky, with large tan aureoles the size of half-dollars. She stared down at them as if she were unsure herself how they looked, and Easton began to sketch her just like that, her hair falling forward over her face. She heard him sketch and watched his eyes move down her body, along her neck and shoulders, over her breasts, and as if his eyes were brushing against her nipples, they hardened.

When he finished, he stood up and went to the bed and sat beside her. She did not pull up her dress. Instead, she sat straight and looked forward as if she were going to be tested at a spelling bee. He kissed her shoulder without touching her with his hands. He moved his lips up her neck and then gently pushed her back until she lay on the bed. Then, with his right hand, he reached up and caressed her breasts. He touched her softly with his fingertips, the way he held the textured paper in his hands, stroking her over and over again. They had done this petting before, but never in the daylight and never without the sense of where it would stop. He reached his hand up her thigh and placed his palm over her warm underwear. He squeezed, and she responded by squeezing her legs together. Now he was going further, where he had tried to go so often but she had never let him before, slipping his fingers around the edge of her underwear.

Her eyes closed as he pushed into her with his fingers and she moved to the rhythm of his palm. She felt him harden in his slacks and moved her leg between his to press against him. He kissed her, and they moved together for a while, lying intertwined.

Then he sat up and pulled his fingers from her. He unzipped his pants with his other hand while he lifted his wet fingers to his nose and smelled. The potent tang of her hid the stain of gasoline completely. He pulled off his slacks and she stared at him hard in his underwear. He reached up underneath her and pulled her underwear down around her ankles, leaving them there above her feet like a loose rope. She did not move to encourage or discourage him.

When he had taken off his own underwear, he positioned himself above her, his legs on either side. He lifted up her light blue dress and saw her for the first time, swollen and soft, and then, as if he felt he was not supposed to look, he lay against her fully so that they were again face-to-face. He put his hand on her breast and moved himself against her, pushing against her body.

She looked down at their chests together, his brown nipples and black hair against her lighter skin. And it came to her like a movie, Ruby's face on the porch that day, asking her if she'd told her father, explaining why she hadn't, and she still hadn't, not even four months later. She could feel Easton pushing at her, and her body opening to let him in as he slid along her warm flesh; but at the same time, her stomach soured with dread, and like a fist tightening, it rose up into her throat. Then he entered her, and as if she'd been jabbed with something cold and sharp, she clamped her legs together and twisted so that he came out. She pulled her arms over her breasts and turned to her side.

"What's the matter?" he asked. She raised her legs to her chest and rocked.

"What's wrong? What's the matter?"

"I don't know. It just isn't right."

"What isn't right?"

"Your sister is just downstairs."

"She doesn't know. She's busy. Don't worry about her."

"It just doesn't feel right. I'm worried. What if I get pregnant?"

"I'll pull out in time." He moved himself against her, tried to push himself into her from behind.

"No, I can't." She jumped off the bed and stood there above him. "I'm sorry. Not yet." She stared at him. He covered his penis with his hands, like a boy caught playing with himself.

She pulled up her dress and went out into the hall to the bathroom. Easton listened as the water ran. She took a long time, as if she were washing all traces of him out of her, as if he were something dirty or diseased. When she came back, she didn't look at him. She pulled on her underwear and then stood at the foot of the bed.

"I'm sorry," she said. "I just don't feel ready."

"Tremendous." He removed his hands and let himself lie open, naked in front of her, still partially erect, not seductively, but thrusting himself at her as if he were trying to stuff something distasteful into her mouth. He lifted his fingers to his nose and smelled her on them, then reached down and stroked himself.

She turned and saw the portrait of her on the dresser. She held it up like a thin wall between them. "I really love your drawings. You're so good. I don't know. Maybe there's something wrong with me."

"Maybe there's something wrong with me," he said.

"No. That's not it."

"Fine."

She continued to hold the picture up and look at it from different angles. "Can I keep it?"

"Sure. Have both of them. I don't want them. Give them to your hipster friends."

"I think they could really help you."

"If you want." He slid his hands under his head and stared up at the blank ceiling, his legs open and spread. "If it will make you feel better."

She put on her shoes and took both drawings. Before she left, she stopped at his bedroom door and looked back at him again. He knew she was looking, but he didn't face her. He reached down and stroked himself, making himself hard again.

She turned and closed the door. He clenched his body rigid, to listen, hoping to hear her come back. She walked down the steps, said something to Ruby, then opened and closed the front door. He slammed his fists against the bed and stared at the white ceiling without blinking. Even in the silence, he waited, listening to his own breathing. After a minute the ceiling broke into millions of dots and lines and shadows. The white became dark and pulsed with his own temples, and he pushed his mind into those cavernous places between the light and the dark, where patterns shifted and waves pulled him out away from himself, until finally his eyes stung and he had to close them. Slowly the shapes and shadows faded behind his eyelids, and he lifted his fingers to his nose to smell her once more through the returning fumes of gasoline.

TWO MONTHS LATER, Easton sat on the bus-stop bench waiting to go up to Merritt College. He brushed his cheek and then pretended to smooth out his thin mustache. He looked sharp and together on the outside, dressed in his brown suit and his new cowboy boots, the first purchase he'd made after Sandra and he broke up. The one thing he remembered liking about Papa Samuel was his dark black boots.

Waiting at the bus stop, he noticed women glancing at him from their cars. He smiled and nodded back, but his smile faded as they passed by into their own locked-up worlds, somewhere far away from him.

The bus took him up San Pablo to MacArthur, where he had to transfer. In a few months he'd buy a car and fix it up so he could get to campus on his own, but for now he kept his face toward the window and quickly smelled his fingers for signs of gasoline.

Merritt College was located on Grove Street in a block-long, high-walled building like a train station. He found himself in the courtyard, people swarming in and out of all the entrances like bees in a hive. Signs pointed different directions for Summer Registration, Matriculation, Information, Financial Aid, and Photo ID; he wanted all of that, and every line had at least fifty people.

The sign above information read START HERE, but he knew that after he stood in line, they would just tell him to stand in the other line at registration, so he saved himself the time and went there directly. As he waited, he watched all the other students, walking tall with their dreams buzzing in the tops of their heads. There were a lot of other colored kids there—some he recognized from high school—all the serious kids like himself who were headed someplace. There were plenty of White kids on campus too, which meant it wasn't some throwaway place, unless they were all the White kids who couldn't get in to the university. But Sandra was at the university and he was smarter than she; he was smarter than all of these idiots, punch-happy with their independence.

At that moment he heard someone call him from across the courtyard.

"Hey, hey, my Black brother. I see you've finally come to get some education. Those are some slick boots; you be like some Black John Wayne."

"Who are you calling Black?" Easton asked. It was Charles, whom he hadn't seen since the police beating at Woolcrest's. Easton just didn't have the time once he'd started to go out with Sandra. He looked around at the students in line who were staring at this loud man in a green camouflage army suit.

"You Black like me, brother. Black and blue, with the mark of Ham."

"Can't you see I'm trying to get serious?"

"Well, when you get through learnin what they want you to know, you come talk to us and we'll tell you how it really was. You could be a leader, my man. I'm telling you. I saw the way you was. How you stood up for me. You don't have to suck up this assimilation shit."

"Well, I'm just going to keep to myself a while. You know how it is." Easton turned away and shaded his forehead with his hand.

"You come on over to our table and we'll teach you how it is, about your slave name, about your history."

"You see a slave?" Easton turned and addressed the general audience of the courtyard. "I don't see any slaves around here. I'm trying to register for college, if you hadn't noticed. You ever hear of a slave registering for college? Now, find your way back to whatever hole you crawled out of." He felt half off balance trying to move away from Charles but having to stay in line.

"This is a revolution. I'm heading out to Ohio for training next week and then down to Mississippi. Come with me, brother. Don't you want to be a part of history? We're changing the world, and you want to sit at a desk and read about it?"

"You never were much for sitting at your desk," Easton said.

"And what you going to read? You think they're going to tell you how the Blue-Eyed Devil is lynching and beating us into the ground?

No one believes that because it sounds too evil to be true. Soon you'll question: 'What are them niggers doin to deserve all that down there in the South? They must be doing something wrong down there.' Soon you'll be shouting how separate can be equal. Just be careful they don't brainwash you, brother. Like I say. Get it right or get it White."

"Man, I know what it's like in the South. You don't have any idea. You don't know. This isn't about all of that, anyway. This is about me. I'm just going to take some art classes, and maybe a math class. I'm stepping outside of that shit."

"All right. I hear you. I see you." Charles nodded for a moment and stared at Easton. "You're all tied up with Sandra still, so you can't play on our team. That's how you got all turned around."

"Get out of here. Go on."

"Sure, man," Charles said. "You just let me know when that White ball and chain's loose from your neck."

"You don't have the slightest idea, man. Sandra and I are over."

"For real? Since when?"

"A few months."

"How come you ain't given me a call?"

Easton shrugged. Charles smiled and slapped him on the shoulder. "See, I tried to warn you, brother. But don't get so down. I'm saying this is the best thing that ever happened to you. Now you're free. Now you can come on over and hang with us at the table, be with your real brothers and sisters."

"I told you, I'm not part of that anymore." He looked at the White girl behind him, an algebra book in her hand. She turned away, but he spoke to her anyway.

"This man has mistaken me for a Negro. Can you please help him see that I am a college student?"

The girl laughed but didn't look at him.

"You're a Black college student," Charles said. "And you won't never be more or less. Just ask her. Isn't that right, young lady?"

The girl's smile disappeared. She looked to the people behind her and to the side.

Easton pushed Charles in the chest. "Why don't you stop making trouble and try to do something useful with yourself. Get out of my breathing air. You're polluting my space."

"Alright. I hear you. I see you. I feel you." Charles smiled and backed away slowly. "I am you."

He disappeared into the mass of people milling through the yard. Easton bowed his head and felt the eyes of the other students on him. He wasn't like Charles. He had more in common with the woman holding the math book than he had with Charles. She knew that wonderful feeling of taking an unknown quantity and working it through formulas and steps to arrive at an exact answer, to plug it back into the original problem and see it work, prove that it worked. He turned to speak to her, his friendliest smile on his face, an apology already on his lips for Charles's behavior. But she was gone. He spotted her farther back in line behind a tall white man in a football jersey. When he tried to make eye contact with her, she turned her face behind the man's shoulder.

THE LINE TOOK forever in the warm sun. He didn't speak to anyone, and when he finally reached the front table, he found out that he was supposed to have filled out the forms from Information before he could register.

"Then I've got to wait in this whole line all over again?" he pleaded with the woman at the table.

"I'm sorry, but that's just the process."

"But I already waited in this line."

"I'm not the one who makes up the rules."

"Well, then who the hell is?" Easton swore and walked away. The people behind him were probably laughing. But he wouldn't look. When he walked back out into the center of the courtyard, he felt his stomach rumble. He didn't have enough money to register, buy food, and take the bus. He clenched his matriculation form tightly and then shoved it into his pocket as he stormed out of the courtyard and out onto Grove Street. His face itched. His thin beard and mustache irritated it and the sun didn't help. He felt himself starting to explode, but all he needed was a little food. He walked toward the stores, then crossed the street to a Chinese restaurant. Two couples ate inside the narrow seating area, and the chef worked behind a long metal counter; otherwise the place was empty and a little run-down. He took a seat close to the door so that the greasy fumes wouldn't suffocate him.

The chef put down his tongs and came up to his table. He held out a menu, but Easton didn't take it.

"Give me some pork fried rice."

"One seventy-five," the man said.

"That's fine."

The man didn't move. "One seventy-five," he said again.

"You want the money now? Is that what you're saying?"

"Yes, please. One seventy-five."

Love looked at the couples at the other tables, both White. "Did they have to pay first?" he said loudly.

The man looked at them and then back at Easton. "Fine. Pay later." He went back behind the counter and scooped up a single ladle of rice onto a paper plate. He came back and dropped it on the table. He stood over Easton.

"One seventy-five."

"Excuse me?" Easton said.

"Pay, please."

Love turned to face the woman at the closest table. "Have you paid for your meal yet?"

The woman shook her head, and they both looked up at the chef. There were many deep lines in his face, some from age and experience, and others from the way he now clenched his brow down over his nose. He did not move.

Easton stood up, and though he towered over the man, the chef held his ground. Easton moved toward the door. Instead of complaining, the chef nodded as if he expected as much, and he brought the plate of rice back to the counter. Outside, Easton's stomach ached with hunger and his body shook with anger.

He walked directly to the liquor store across the street and stormed up to the counter, where a White man looked at him with some fear.

"I want to get a candy bar. You want me to pay for it now, before I go get it, or can I bring it up here first?"

"You have to get the candy bar first," he said.

Love picked a candy bar out of the box and slammed it on the table, and the man punched it up on the register. A stack of *Vogue* magazines lay by Easton's fist, a picture of a girl on the cover with long, straight red hair and a very short black skirt up to the point that he couldn't help but imagine more.

"I want this too." Easton pulled off the top copy of the magazine and paid for both. He walked out of the store and waited at the bus stop, the image on the magazine burning in his mind. The bus was taking too long, so he began to walk the three miles back home, the cover of the magazine pulling him forward.

Twenty minutes later, the bus passed him. He walked more quickly, sweating under his suit jacket and in his boots. When he finally reached Cranston, he ran to his house. Corbet was home with Lida, and they were both in the living room—Corbet, his crutches leaning against his chair, watching the new black-and-white TV he'd just purchased, and Lida drawing with the crayons Easton had bought her for her fourth birthday.

He walked past them and up the stairs without saying a word.

"You get your classes?" Corbet yelled.

"Mmm-hmmm," he said. Then he went into his room and closed the door. He sat at his desk, put the magazine on top, and looked at the front picture for a long time, not at the face of the girl or what mood she was in, like he did when he was drawing, but at her long, creamy legs and the hair that slid down the side of her face like shiny copper. He put one finger on the top of her thigh and caressed back and forth as he unzipped his suit pants and began to touch himself. She had small breasts poking up in the tight white turtleneck. He touched her chest with his finger and rubbed in a circle. After a while, he put his chin down onto the magazine and licked in the air above the picture, right at the edge of her skirt, right between the tops of her thighs. He looked at her face. She had a cold, distant look, but as he flicked his tongue back and forth, it seemed that the distance was really a look of intense concentration, of clenched teeth and held breath. She was trying not to move, not to give in. But she was going to lose her self-control. She was going to lose it.

Lida threw open the door. Easton straightened and pinched his legs together and yelled, "Close the door!"

"Look." She held up a piece of paper with swirls of colored crayon and walked toward him.

"Get out and close the door," he yelled again. She went back and closed it but stayed inside.

"No," he yelled, but she ran to his desk and put her drawing on top of the magazine. Her face was level with his lap, and she saw him holding himself.

"Get out," he snapped. "Get out and close the door."

She didn't move or say anything but stared at his erect penis. He pulled up his underwear and held the flaps of his pants together.

"Go on. Get out! Leave me alone already."

But she stood frozen, like someone who had suddenly stumbled upon a murder, staring at what his hands now covered.

"What? What?" he asked.

She didn't move.

"What are you waiting for? What are you looking at?" He opened his pants and revealed his erection. "See? Now get out."

She still didn't move and he gripped himself in his hands.

"Go on, now," he said more quietly.

She stood frozen and he moved his hand, his face silent but clenched, breathing hard through his nose. He stared at her, but she watched his hand as if he were playing with a new toy. As his breathing became louder and his hand moved more quickly, she seemed about to step back, to run out of the room—to go tell everything.

But Easton reached out and grabbed her wrist. He pulled her hand to him, put it on him, and moved it up and down, her hand inside of his. Her thin arm flapped from her shoulder as he moved faster, as if it were not attached to her body. He reached to the table with his other hand, pushed her drawing to the side, and stared at the woman on the magazine, at her thighs that seemed to move farther apart with his gaze. The woman smirked ever so slightly and raised her penciled eyebrows, daring him. He pumped himself harder until her smirk became surprised, then fearful, and then he closed his eyes and imagined cumming on that beautiful, defiant White face.

He'd forgotten Lida for a moment, until she moved her fingers in the wetness. He looked down at her dark hand around his penis and let go immediately.

"I told you not to come in here," he said. He grabbed tissues off his desk and wiped both of their hands.

"I told you to leave." He tucked himself in.

She looked down, and tears swelled in her eyes.

"Oh God," he sighed. "What's wrong? I didn't hurt you. What's wrong?" She shrugged and looked at the table, at her drawing that he'd pushed away. There were red and yellow swirls in the corner like a sun, a brown box house at the bottom, and four black stick figures next to it.

"Is this what you're crying about?" He pulled it back to the center of the table.

"Is this supposed to be us?" he asked her.

She nodded.

"Which one's you?"

She put her finger on the last person. It was a little smaller than the others.

"Which one's me?"

She put her finger on the one next to her and stood still for a minute, looking at the picture. He stared at the drawing, the peaceful swirls of colors and the smiling stick figures.

"You know why I yelled at you?" he asked.

She shook her head.

"You can't just come into my room like that. You have to knock first. That's why you were bad. That's why you got in trouble. But I promise not to tell. You understand?"

She nodded.

"Now go down and draw me more pictures, and don't forget to close the door."

She turned and walked away, but before she opened the door, he told her to stop. "Don't tell Ruby what happened or you'll get in more trouble. She'll know you were bad. She'll come tell me."

Lida nodded and opened the door just a bit. She squeezed through the small passage she'd made for herself, then closed the door carefully behind her.

CHAPTER 12B

BY HER FORTIETH birthday, Ruby had saved only twenty-six
dollars in her jar. She would have had more, but now that Easton was
dead and Lida lived with Marcus, she had to pay for all the house expenses, including property taxes, rat traps, and ant poison. Then her
tooth got so bad she couldn't sleep at night, and one morning she was
so tired at work she knocked over one of Mrs. Pearson's ceramic vases
and had to pay thirty dollars for that. So she went to the dentist and
had the tooth pulled, for which she took forty-five dollars out of the
jar. The heating bill went up in November, but she kept it low by
heating up stones and putting them in her slippers and under her blankets
like she used to in Carolina.

Still, the mornings were very cold, and every day it seemed harder
to pull herself out of bed. She remembered then that she had dreamed
about Lida. Ruby hadn't seen her daughter for nine months, since Lida
and Marcus moved in with Gina and David. Ruby had managed to push
Lida out of her thoughts for those nine months, but she couldn't do
anything about her dreams. Lida, as a little girl, walked down the stairs
in her yellow dress and smiled. But her feet were big, very big, like a
man's size fifteen, and as Ruby looked at those feet, they just seemed
to get bigger and bigger.

"Why are your feet so big?" she asked her daughter. But Lida
shrugged and smiled. "But they're so big." And then they were at the
doctor's office and the doctor said, "It's a rare disease." But then they
weren't Lida's feet anymore, they were her own feet, and she sat on the
examining table.

"I'm sorry," the doctor said to her. "We're going to have to remove
them." And she recognized the doctor who had amputated Corbet's foot.

"Remove my feet?" she asked. "But you can't remove my feet." And she yelled at the doctor that he couldn't remove her feet. But he was going to amputate them, she could feel it, and then the dream ended.

Ruby sat up in her bed but didn't get out from under the covers. Her slippers had cold stones in them and the windows were frosted over like a sheet of ice. She put her tongue in the space where her tooth had been and tasted the slightly metallic flavor. The wound had healed up, but it felt like there was still something under it that was sore and infected.

She put her mind on getting herself to work. She'd earn eighteen dollars and forty cents for the day. She divided her daily pay by a formula she'd worked out to make it through the year: fifty cents for transportation to and from work and another dollar for cleaning materials, two dollars for food and two for other groceries; four dollars for income taxes and two dollars and sixty cents for property taxes; one dollar for fixing the roof by June when the rain stopped, and one dollar for gas, electric, water, and telephone; forty cents a day gave her enough for a Sunday-matinee movie, and another dollar a day was enough to eat out once a week for a nice dinner, usually after the movie; she had to get new panty hose and, now that she didn't sew, a dollar-fifty for one new piece of clothing every month, to replace either something that the moths had eaten up or something that she'd outgrown as her body settled in different places; and lastly, another dollar-fifty for the shoes she'd have to get since the ones she had were letting in water and keeping her feet cold. (She was eyeing a pair of red tasseled boots at Sears, but they would cost another extra fifty cents a day.) Every penny was spent before it was earned, except one dollar for the jar, for the trip to see her mother.

She'd thought about renting out a room in the house, taking a boarder to help with the money. But she needed to keep Lida's room free in case she came to her senses and left Marcus. And she wasn't ready to let out Love E's room yet. She could not bring herself to clear off his drawings from the walls or bag up his clothes. She laughed and shook her head: the whole house was already rented out to ghosts.

She reached down and dumped the stones out of her slippers and then walked to the bathroom. The gap in her teeth made her feel old and ugly before her time. She washed her face with the lavender soap that Lida had left, and as she dried behind her ears, she remembered that she would want to be at work today because Tony Pearson was coming back from his college in Boston. She had practically raised Tony since he was three, and she was as proud of him as if he were her own son. She went to the kitchen to make sure she had an extra chocolate bar to bring him, like she often had when he was younger. He would have a girlfriend now and pictures of his school and where he lived. He had written her a letter, to her home on Cranston, and Ruby had her neighbor help her read it, about college and how he had won a scholarship for his writing.

She was excited and awake now as she got ready to go. She put on a flower-patterned dress that he'd always liked. As she brushed her hair, she realized that since it was just after Christmas, she had to bring him a gift. She couldn't give him only a candy bar, but she didn't know what to give him now that he was grown up.

She went into the living room and wandered around, looking for something to bring him. Love E's eight-tracks were no good, and the carved wooden animals were too fancy. She stood in the middle of the room, spinning like a merry-go-round, then stopped, looking at the stairs. She could give him some of Love E's clothes, a jacket, but it might not fit. And Lida's stuff was too girlish. She turned toward the kitchen and thought for a moment. She walked to the counter and pulled the jar from the cupboard above, took out ten dollars, put it in an envelope, and wrote his name across the front.

While she waited for the bus on San Pablo, she found herself smiling at the other women waiting with her. She imagined how Tony would come in the house and see her, how he would give her a big, strong hug and kiss her cheek, like he had when he left. He'd probably be dressed in a suit and tie, his hair cut short, already like a successful lawyer.

She'd never introduced him to Lida, like she'd always said she would. But she'd told him all about her as they were growing up. He'd even seen a picture of her on her sixteenth birthday and said she was pretty. But they went to different schools and didn't know any of the same people. The closest they ever got to meeting was in seventh grade when Lida was supposed to go over and tutor him, but his parents decided to hire someone else.

Ruby leaned against the bus-stop pole. She felt a heaviness trying to fill her, and she pushed all her thoughts of Lida from her mind as quickly as she could. She stared at the pavement to keep the faces from appearing in her mind. But the heaviness grew, and the pole wasn't enough to support her, so she sat down on the bench. The other women asked if she was okay, and she nodded and hung her head.

She heard the engine of the bus coming from down the block, and as always, the women stood up and got in line. The bus pulled to the curb and opened its doors with a long sigh. The women slowly climbed the tall metal steps, pulling themselves up by the metal bar, trudging into the bus like the oldest survivors of the longest war. Ruby waited until the last woman was through the doors, then stood up and got on.

SANTA RITA JAIL

TODAY, I READ to you from *A Bad Seed: My Life as a Slave,* by Branson White:

What is a crime for me? When I stole the kitchen knife and chicken, was I wrong? Was it immoral of me to steal the necklace to have money for my journey? Was it a crime, after a day of building, to run to my children's home in Alabama? Yes, it was, and I was severely punished. Was it a crime to whip me for being late with the water? No, it was not. . . .

What is not justified action against those who enslave me? Was it a crime to kill my master and his family?. . . . Can I choose, now that I am a free man, to abide by my own conscience? Should I choose to abide by the laws of this nation? What will I teach my new child, and what will he know from my eyes? I escaped to the North by the light of the stars, but where is True North on my moral compass?

CHAPTER 13

LOVE DIDN'T GO into the shed to make the pickup anymore. He'd met a kid named Perry who hustled up at People's Park and came by the store to score some smoke. He was a White kid the same age as Love, punked out with a leather jacket, black tips on his spiked blond hair, and thick circles of black eyeliner around his eyes.

Perry rode to Berkeley on the handlebars of Love's bike. Love went inside the gate to drop off the money but then waited outside while Perry went into the shed. He came out with the bag and an extra forty dollars and everyone was happy.

One night on the way back to the store from a pickup, Love saw two police cars parked at the liquor store. Curse was lying facedown in front of his wheelchair, a policeman frisking him and kicking his limp legs open. As Love turned on to Cranston, he saw Freight against the wall with his hands cuffed. Freight yelled at the White cop standing next to him, but loud enough that it was clear he was yelling to the neighborhood:

"Fuck this racist shit! Oppressing the Black man for no reason! We oughta riot in this city."

"Shut the fuck up," the Black cop yelled.

"How can you do this to your own people?" Freight yelled back.

"I could ask you the same question." The cop swung Freight around by the back of his jacket. "It's fuck-ups like you—"

"Naw, it's Uncle Toms like you," Freight spat back.

As Freight was being pushed into the car, he spotted Love standing on the sidewalk. "What the fuck you lookin at, nigga?"

Love rode to his house and carried his bike upstairs.

In his room, he took the bag of coke out of his jacket, went into the closet, and put it into one of Easton's old boots.

Ruby came to the open door in her nightgown. "What's all that fuss at the corner?"

Love shrugged and closed the closet. Ruby came in and sat on the bed.

"You just came from there, but you don't know?" She looked at the closet as Love stood in front of it. "You know I'll go in there if I have the mind to."

Love shrugged again and wandered away to the window. Ruby stayed on the bed.

"I'm telling you, little boy, don't think God ain't watchin. Don't think He don't know."

"I hope He do, 'cause it's scandalous down here."

She shook her head and stood up to leave.

"Ain't you gonna check the closet?" Love asked. "You can go ahead. See if I care."

"I've been down that road before and t'aint gonna do no good. Things'd only get worse. You'd just up and go. Can't be my decision. I'm jus here to help you choose to be a man."

ONCE FREIGHT AND Curse had been arrested, Love became the main presence at the liquor store. At the end of the month, Curse got out of jail, but he couldn't be caught holding or he'd get another strike and be put away forever, like Freight.

Love let Li'l Pit hang out with him on the weekends, but he wasn't allowed to do any of the slinging. One Saturday, while Love stood out front tending to business, a thin, orange-striped cat, not a baby but not fully grown, ran up to the liquor-store building and rubbed against the sunny corner wall. It tilted its head and slowly shut and opened its eyes, flirting with Li'l Pit. He bent down and scratched behind its ears. It smiled and closed its eyes again. But then, as Li'l Pit pressed his hand more firmly into its body, it took off and ran up the block, suddenly frightened by the affection.

Li'l Pit followed the cat. It stopped and turned to let him get closer, then dashed off farther up San Pablo to a vacant lot covered with dry grass. The cat rubbed against an old cement foundation and Li'l Pit bent down again, reached his hand out and stroked the cat. It rippled its body and pointed its tail in the air. He moved closer, inching forward in a squat. The cat let him dig his fingers into the fur around its rump. He put his hands around the cat's body and picked it up, held it close in to his chest, but the cat squirmed and bit him in the fleshy part of the hand.

"Shit," he yelled, dropping the cat, and the cat ran deeper into the lot. Li'l Pit chased after it into the dry grass filled with broken bottles. As he got closer to it, he stumbled and screamed.

"Something bit me!" he yelled. He held up his ankle, hopped out of the lot, and sat on the pavement. "Get it off me. Get it off me." Love walked around the corner and sat down next to his brother.

Li'l Pit lay on his side and held his foot up in the air. Love pulled a thistle from the ankle of his sock.

"What is it? Ow, ow. It's biting me."

"Lay still, dog. You're such a baby. You need some lotion. Look at your skin." Li'l Pit lay silently now, his chapped leg in his brother's hand.

A beeping went off, two quick chirps again and again. Love looked at his beeper, but there was no number flashing.

"You got a beeper?" he asked Li'l Pit. He reeled his little brother up by the leg like a fishing net. He got to his hip and lifted his jersey.

"Stop that."

"What the fuck is this?" He pulled a neon-green beeper off his little brother's hip.

"That's mine. Gimme my beeper."

"What do you need a beeper for?" Love read the number on the top of the digital readout. He didn't need to ask about the number. He knew it by heart from his own beeper, the number to Curse's house, where Freight was relaying all his orders from jail.

Li'l Pit pulled his leg away and stood up. He reached for the beeper, but Love switched hands and held it from him.

"Who gave you this?"

"It's mine. I earned it." He slapped at Love's arms and reached for it.

"How'd you earn it?"

"It's mine. I rapped for it."

"We're going to call this number and find out. And this better be your school calling to say you got an 'A' on your math test." Love stood and walked to the pay phone on the corner by the store. He took a quarter out of his pocket and dropped it into the slot. A bus pulled up and let off a kid about Li'l Pit's age wearing a green backpack with a Bart Simpson patch on it. Li'l Pit stared at him and the kid kept his face down as he walked toward the store.

Love dialed general telephone time and listened to the operator say, "At the tone, the time will be three-forty-seven and thirty-five seconds."

"Who's this?" Love yelled to the recording on the phone. "Curse? What you want? Why'd you give my brother a beeper? I ought to kick your ass. You're scandalous, man. He's only ten years old. All right, what you want?" Li'l Pit pushed into the phone booth and pulled on the metal cord.

"Let me talk. Tell him I'll do it," he yelled. "It's my beeper. He gave it to me."

"He thinks you have something for him to do. I don't want my little brother slinging, Curse."

"I can do what I want." Li'l Pit hit his brother in the stomach.

"Okay. Okay. Hold on." Love turned to Li'l Pit. "I can't hear what he wants you to do." Li'l Pit stopped and waited attentively, staring at Love's face as he spoke into the receiver.

"All right, tell me what you want us to do." Love nodded. "Okay. Uh-huh. I'll tell him. All right. We'll do it. I'll tell him. How much? Okay. Where should we do the pickup? You want me to go too? Okay."

"But it's *my* job," Li'l Pit whined.

"It's his job," Love said into the receiver. "I don't want to go. You want me to go along for backup? You're sure? I'll let him go on his own if you want. All right. If Freight wants me there, then it has to be that way."

"Let me talk to him," Li'l Pit whined. "Give me the phone."

"Okay. We won't call again. The cops got the beeper numbers. Okay. Go then." Love hung up.

"What'd he want me to do?"

"I can't say out here, dog. You want to get yourself locked up? We got to go home and I'll tell you. We can't call him anymore, though. Your beeper might be bugged."

"Let's go. Come on." Li'l Pit skipped ahead down the block and then ran back to him. "Come on. I got a first job. Hurry up."

Li'l Pit ran up the porch stairs and waited at the top for Love to unlock the front door. Love took his time trudging up, thinking of a plan. Even with only two keys, he put the wrong one in each hole and then put each one in upside down.

"Tell me what I got to do," Li'l Pit begged.

"Just hold on. We're not inside yet." When the door was finally open, Li'l Pit went running into the living room almost to the kitchen, as if it were only a matter of getting inside to find out about his job and he could just leave Love behind.

"Where's that black rag Mama gave you?" Li'l Pit asked. "I've got to show my colors."

"First off, that's wrong. See, that's all wrong." Love closed the door and locked it. "You got to not show anything. See. This is why I've got to give it to you slowly, so you know every part of it. You can't make a mistake or else you'll have Freight on us."

Li'l Pit went silent and nodded up at his older brother. Love couldn't help but smile at the earnestness in his eyes.

"How come you want to do this so bad?"

Li'l Pit wrinkled his eyebrows and yelled, " 'Cause!"

"You think this is going to be like some TV show. This shit gets dangerous." Li'l Pit smiled and nodded eagerly. Love shook his head.

"Alright. This is what you've got to do: first, Nanna is home, so you got to shut up. Now, what you've got to do is this." He started to speak more slowly, word by word, to give his brain time to think. "Go upstairs into your room. In your room, look around for something. We need something for the pickup."

"Like what?"

"You need something to carry stuff in, something big, 'cause this is a big job, it's going to be very dangerous."

Li'l Pit nodded his head. "Like that old trunk?"

"Yeah. Okay, take everything out of that green trunk at the bottom of your bed. All them clothes and anything else. Yeah. We have to get that trunk ready. I'll come up when you're done. And put on some of them clothes I got you." Li'l Pit leapt up the stairs by twos and disappeared.

Love looked around the living room in desperation for some inspiring object. Ruby's purse was next to the Bible on top of the table by the rocking chair. The Bible was supposed to be filled with inspiration and advice, but it never kept him from doing something wrong, so it surely wasn't going to keep his brother from it. The canvas notebook of insects was on the coffee table. He hadn't had to take any more out since he started up with Freight. Instead, he'd bought new ones to add to it, a large red ant and a fuzzy caterpillar. He had new black jeans and he even had a savings account at Wells Fargo on Shattuck with four hundred dollars in it, but the account was in Freight's name and he had to get permission every time he wanted to take out money. He got twenty dollars for every run he made, and now he got forty dollars for just standing at the store and giving directions.

His beeper went off and he grabbed it from his pocket. It was Curse calling him. He was bound to come look for them if they didn't respond. He set both beepers to vibrate and took them to the kitchen. He considered putting them in a drawer, but ended up wrapping them in tinfoil and putting them in the freezer.

Ruby came out into the living room and looked around, then spotted Love in the kitchen.

"What you boys up to?" She didn't wait for an answer. She sat in the rocking chair and picked up the leather Bible next to her purse. She opened it and took out the red string that marked her place.

"Come here and help me say this word," she said. Love walked up and looked over her shoulder.

"Which one?"

"This here: 'sour'?"

"Sower." He looked up the stairs, checking for Li'l Pit.

" 'Behold a sower.' Like myself. Why don't you read to your grand-mother?"

"Naw. I don't like to."

"Just this little part."

"I'm busy." He wandered over to the living room windows, which he'd replaced with his own money. He looked out through the curtains, then paced back to the kitchen.

"Too busy to read the truth of the Lord? Now, you must be in real trouble. But there ain't no mess too big for Jesus. No, sir. Read me this here story and I guarantee you'll find your way."

Love looked up the stairs again. "Nanna, how many bad things can you do before you can't get into heaven?"

Ruby shook her head. "The Lord has just got to see that you are trying the best you can and he'll always forgive you if you start doing right."

Love picked up the carved giraffe bookend on the table and slid his fingers up and down its smooth neck.

"I already killed one boy."

Ruby turned and looked at him. "That was a long time ago, and it wasn't your fault. You can still go to heaven. That wasn't none of your fault. Now come and read what Jesus has to tell you."

Nothing else was coming to him, so he went up behind Ruby and read over her shoulder again. He read in a monotone, going right through all punctuation:

" 'Behold, a sower went forth to sow; And when he sowed, some seeds fell by the wayside, and the fowls came and devoured them up: Some fell upon stony places, where they had not much earth: and forthwith they sprung up, because they had no deepness of earth: And when the sun was up, they were scorched; and because they had no root, they withered away.' " Love shook his head. "This doesn't make any sense."

"Just keep on." Ruby had her eyes closed and was smiling like she was listening to peaceful music. He read more carefully this time.

" 'And some fell among thorns; and the thorns sprung up, and choked them: But others fell into good ground, and brought forth fruit, some an hundredfold, some sixtyfold, some thirtyfold.' " Love stopped reading. "There, that's all."

"Mmm-hmm." Ruby nodded.

"This is all about farming stuff," Love said. "It doesn't do any good for us in the city. That's a whole different kind of world than it is here."

"Can't no plant grow in bad ground. That's what it's saying. Just like the cotton ruin all that land back home. In good earth, any seed can grow up and be strong. That goes for city and for country."

Love walked to the front door, checked that he'd locked it, walked back to the bottom of the stairs, then meandered over to his insect notebook. He opened it and tapped a beetle back into place. Ruby rocked and looked at her Bible. There was a sound at the door, and Love stood up straight, but it was only the postman putting mail through the slot and then wheeling the cart away.

"How much does it cost to go to college?" Love asked.

Ruby looked up at Love, a smile bursting in her cheeks, but then she looked back down in her Bible.

"Depends where you go. Could be different now than back then, but Love E used to go to Merritt and didn't hardly cost him nothing. But the university, that may be thousands of dollars."

"Oh." Love nodded and went back to turning the pages of his notebook.

Li'l Pit came running down the stairs, but slowed when he saw Ruby. He was dressed in a new sweater and blue jeans, looking like any other ten-year-old kid on the block who was not part of the crew. It was amazing how much clothes could change his appearance and make it seem like he had never done one thing wrong in his life.

"I'm done. It's all ready," he said.

"What's that?" Ruby asked.

"Nothing." Li'l Pit and Ruby both looked at Love.

"What?" Love said. "Why you always looking at me like I'm doing something? It makes me feel like doing something." He walked up the stairs in feigned resentment, and his brother followed him into his room. Love shut the door behind them and looked at the mess. Lida's old dresses were on the floor and bed. It looked as if Li'l Pit had tried to pile them, but they weren't folded. The green trunk was open and completely empty.

"Give me the key. And take off your sweater." Li'l Pit did so faithfully. "We have to see if this will be big enough. Just get inside and curl up."

"How come?"

"Just get in and I'll tell you."

Li'l Pit stepped into the box and then lay down. It was too small for him, so he pulled his knees up to his chest. "Is this good?"

"Yeah." Love threw the top down and shut the locks. His brother kicked and yelled. Love looked at the chest for a moment as Li'l Pit screamed from inside. He backed away from it slowly, then ran downstairs into the living room.

"What's all that racket?" Ruby asked. Love didn't look at her. He paced to the front door and back, then sat on the couch, then stood up again.

"What's going on?" Ruby went to the stairs.

"Nothing."

"That ain't nothing up there. You tell me right this minute." She began to climb the stairs.

"I locked him in the trunk," Love said.

"What'd you do that for?" She walked more quickly, but Love ran over and pulled on her arm.

"Don't let him out."

"What you mean? Let go of me." She slapped his face, and he laughed nervously.

"Wait. No. Wait, really."

"What you up to? You two boys play too rough with each other. Lida never made this kind of racket."

"I'm not playing."

"What you mean?"

"I didn't know what to do. He's gonna get in trouble."

"Tell me what you mean." She stayed on the bottom step.

"We've got to think of some plan. Something to keep him from slinging."

"What you got him messed up in?"

"Nothing. I didn't. That's why I locked him in. I didn't know what to do."

"But he'll suffocate in there."

"I know. I know. I'm thinking." He went back into the living room and paced.

"You can't go and lock him in a trunk."

"I know. But we've got to do something or he's gonna get in deep." The banging became louder as Li'l Pit made the trunk jump on the floor.

"Now, listen. You tell me what you mean. What might he get into?"

Love smiled again and then brought the smile under control. "See, he thinks he's gonna go on a run," he said.

Ruby shook her head. "What kind of evil you got that boy mixed up in? I'm fixin to lock you up in that trunk yourself once I get him out a there." She turned and started up the stairs again.

"You got to wait," Love yelled, but when he saw she wasn't listening to him, he ran up the stairs past his grandmother to get to the trunk before she did.

"Get me out of here!" Li'l Pit yelled. "Get me out of here."

"Hold still," Love said. "It just fell. Hold still and I'll open it." The trunk stopped moving and Ruby came to the door.

"I had to go get the extra key from Nanna. Just hold still." Love motioned Ruby to leave, but she stayed by the door. He opened the trunk and Li'l Pit burst out and ran to the open window, breathing heavily.

"I was just going to see how it closed, but then it locked," Love said. "I couldn't find the key."

He and Ruby watched Li'l Pit from a distance. He breathed in the fresh air through his nose with his jaw set and tears in his eyes. His hands gripped the windowsill and he stared outside as if he were imagining climbing out and running away. Neither Ruby nor Love went near him, but the long silence seemed only to thicken his distrust, like something setting in concrete.

Ruby looked at the room, the clothes everywhere on the bed and floor.

"Now, what's all this going on up here?" she asked.

Love looked at her and shook his head.

"What's this Love's been telling me . . ." Love opened his eyes and stared at her with a fear equal to anything she had ever seen in Lida or Love E. "This sure is a mess up here," she said instead. "A fine mess." She went to the bed and picked up the clothes, placing them neatly in the trunk. When she was finished, she turned to Li'l Pit, who was still at the window.

"Come on and get your coat and we'll go to Sizzler tonight." She'd taken him to Sizzler once before, and he had said it was the first time he'd eaten in a sit-down restaurant.

"No." Li'l Pit shook his head. "I got some things to do."

"That's not until tomorrow," Love said.

"Then why you want me to get all dressed up now?"

" 'Cause we're going out to dinner," he said. He looked at Ruby. "Nanna told me this morning we were going out and you had to get dressed."

Li'l Pit looked at Ruby. She nodded.

He wiped his cheeks, but his jaw was still clenched. He stared at the planks of the hardwood floor, and a whole minute of silence went by.

Love and Ruby watched his face as he tried to figure out where to put all his anger. At times his nostrils flared and it seemed he wasn't calming down at all. But then he lifted his long, wet eyelashes and looked at Ruby.

"Can we get the dessert bar?"

Ruby nodded. "Of course. You can get anything you want. We're celebrating. This is our New Year's celebration dinner."

"I want the dessert bar."

"Alright, then. Wash your face so we can go." He walked out into the hallway and they heard him turn on the water. Ruby shook her head at Love and he smiled, and then looked away.

CHAPTER 14

EASTON TAPPED HIS package of Kent cigarettes on the cash register at the gas station. He didn't smoke more than one cigarette a day, and he'd already had one in the morning. That was all he would smoke unless he had a test after work, which he did. When he first started smoking, he'd worried that the gasoline on his fingers would catch fire, but all the mechanics smoked on their breaks and so did the attendants, just not around the customers.

On every break over the last year, he had watched Steve, the main mechanic, tear up cars and put them back together. Easton stood over him so it got to the point that Steve asked him to do small things. At first he just handed him oil and filters and parts, until he knew all their names and where they were kept. Then Steve showed him what he did with the parts, putting in the filter, draining the oil, and replacing the fluids. After three months on the job, Easton was doing all the tune-up work so Steve could do more complicated jobs, which he explained later on. After three months, Easton found a broken-down Ford to fix up for himself, and he worked on it in the evenings when he didn't have art class.

This Tuesday morning he was thinking about the test he had that night. He rolled a cigarette between his fingers and then stuck it behind his ear. He'd smoke it right before the test. Five hundred years of Greek sculpture flashed through his mind, slides that the instructor showed one after the other: Poseidon, Hermes, Alexander; and the orders—Doric, Ionic, Corinthian. The hairs on his arms raised like those of an excited cat. It sometimes overcame him, this sense of being a part of academia and the serious study of art, but even more, it was a sense of having a history different from one he'd always been assigned—now he lived in the great tradition of artists. His classmates yawned during the slide shows, but he sat in the front row, captivated: the blank marble eyeballs of the sculptures haunted him, expressionless and chilling, people both dead and somehow alive; the illusion of softness in hardness, the white waves of hair carved into stone, the folds in the gowns, as smooth and flowing as if they were truly made of cloth; the chiseled white perfection of these warriors and gods. He often postured himself at work in one of the common poses of the statues, his jacket flung over his shoulder like a draped toga.

This was how he stood, his head slightly raised, staring through the garage window as if over the Mediterranean, when Sandra drove up. He hadn't seen her since she left him in the bedroom almost a year before. After that, there were a few awkward discussions on the phone. The most he ever got out of her was that she didn't want to hurt him, which, he protested, was exactly what she was doing.

He took the cigarette from behind his ear and lit it as he watched her park by the air hose. She drove a blue '64 Olds, a gift from her father. Her bracelets caught the sun as she turned the steering wheel, the top of her dress open at the neck.

As if he'd suddenly realized that this was not a dream, Easton threw down the cigarette and stepped on it. He turned around, looking for something to do, and, at a loss, got underneath the Chevy he was working on. He stared up at the lug nut he'd already tightened after changing the oil and listened as she walked into the garage, jingling the little bell around the door handle.

"Hi," she said to Steve, who sat reading at the counter.

"Hello, beautiful," he said. There was a moment of silence. "What can I do to make your day more pleasurable?"

"Does Easton still work here?"

"Easton? Right under there."

Easton listened to her shoes swivel on the gritty floor. He could see her calves as she approached the car.

"Hello, Sandra," he said first, just to throw her off.

"Oh. You still recognize my voice?"

"I'm a man of many talents." All he could see was the bottom of the car and her legs.

"I wasn't sure if I should come by," she said. "Or if it would be too painful for you." He didn't reply. There was no proud way to answer that question.

"I hear you're going to Merritt now."

His chest tightened. He hated that she knew anything about him, particularly that he was in college. "Who told you that?"

"Charles."

"Mmm-hmm. I thought he was in Mississippi."

"He didn't make it down there for some reason. I think he was scared."

Easton stared at the metal plating under the car—he didn't want to remember her face. He reached up and touched the cool bottom of the car and then pushed up against it as hard as he could, his chest and neck bursting. Then he let go and breathed out silently.

"I knew you could get into college," she said. "Just two years and you can transfer to Cal."

"What makes you think I want to do that?"

She shifted her weight.

"I don't know. I just thought that's what people did, I guess." She paced at the side of the car. "How's your drawing?"

"Listen, Sandra, what'd you come here for?" She walked away from the car and sat on the bench. Now he could see her legs and dress, all the way up to her stomach. He imagined throwing a wrench at her.

"Did you see that picture of Sheriff Clark beating Annie Cooper in Selma?" she asked.

"Mmm-hmm."

"Did you hear what she did? As she was being wrestled to the ground, she yelled out, 'Don't you hit me, you filthy scum.'" Sandra clapped and laughed out loud.

"So what's your point?"

"I'm going down to Alabama," Sandra said.

He froze for a second, but then crossed his legs at the ankles, casually, where she could see. He was unhappy to find himself wishing she wouldn't go. Even though almost a year had gone by without any contact, somehow her proximity gave him hope that they would get back together.

"They're arresting hundreds of people, schoolkids too. I thought you might want to come be a part of the revolution down there."

"You sound like Charles." But even as he ridiculed her, he imagined sitting beside her in the blue front seat of her Olds, the windows rolled down and the desert around them. He could look at her face as she was driving, wind in her hair, freckles on her ear.

"I've got school," he said.

"Oh, come on. I'm taking the semester off." She got off the bench and knelt at the edge of the car. He could see her now, her hair pulled back in a ponytail, her eyes smiling at him. He was frightened by how beautiful she was to him. She could see him now also, see that he didn't have any tools, that he wasn't working on anything. But she didn't mention it.

"Why do you want me to go?" he asked. He looked straight up at the car.

"I want you to be a part of it. Everyone is down there."

"The Reverend Dr. Chicken Wing?" Easton muttered.

"What?"

"That's what Malcolm X calls him. Didn't Charles tell you?"

"Malcolm X was down there too, for a day."

He pulled himself out from under the car and stood up. She stayed kneeling and he looked down at her, though it felt as if he were the one begging.

"Why do you care if I go? Why do you care?"

She frowned and considered his question. "Because." She shook her head as if she'd never considered it. "I don't know. Because I thought you'd want to. I thought you'd want to do something."

"I see." He turned around and then back to her again, with no place to go. "Is that why you want me around, so I can introduce you to some of my people? So you can be some cool chick showing up with a Black guy in your car? 'Well golly, Shawn, she must really love us niggers; she drove all the way from California with one.' " He brushed himself off. Steve stayed quiet, his eyes still lowered on the paper. Sandra walked outside and Easton followed her. She turned and faced him.

"Why are you getting so upset?"

They were out by the pumps now and the customers stared at them.

"I don't understand why you're doing this," he said.

"I thought you would want to go. Really. I thought I was doing something nice."

"Well, I don't have any reason to go to the South," he said. "I don't need to get hosed down for the cause. I don't have to prove anything to anybody."

He walked over to her car, motioning her to follow.

"Tell me something," he said to her through his teeth when she reached him. He grabbed her wrist and held it tightly. "Do you really have no idea why I'm so upset? Are you that stupid? Because I'll tell you straight out if you need me to."

"I think I know." She adjusted the side mirror of her car with her free hand as if nothing were happening.

"Why? You tell me why," he said.

"Because I wouldn't sleep with you."

"Oh, man!" He threw his hands in the air and turned all the way around, then faced her again. "I'm angry at you because you never told me why. You never explained it. You just up and left, no questions allowed. How would you like someone to do that to you? And now you want me to go on this big trip with you, drop everything I have and be with you again like nothing ever happened. I'll tell you why I'm angry at you. I'm angry at you for coming here and not knowing."

"I left you because I thought it was best for both of us."

"Well, thank you so very much for making my decisions for me." He leaned on the car with a contemptuous smirk on his face. "You know, that's the whole problem with you folks. You think you know what's best for us without ever asking what we want."

"I guess I was right." She brushed her fingertips across her forehead. She let the words hang.

"What were you so right about this time?"

"We could never have gotten past it. I'm not saying it's your fault. It just would have always been 'us folks' and 'you folks.' Never just you and me. That's why I left. That's why I didn't want to go any further with you."

"So you left me 'cause I'm Black."

"No. But that's how you're going to say it was."

"Whatever. I know what I know. Ruby warned me."

"Let's just forget it, Easton." She opened the driver's door and got in.

"Yeah. Let's forget it." He walked away and heard her start up the car. She didn't shift into gear at first, but waited, for what he didn't know, but he hoped that she was waiting for him to come back, because he wasn't going to. He walked into the building and then into the garage. It wasn't until he was behind the garage window that he turned around and watched her leave the gas station. He stared at her car as it pulled into the street, and he stared at the street long after she had gone.

SANTA RITA JAIL

TODAY I READ from *Black Protest: History, Documents, and Analyses:*

Early in the Civil War, when the federal government still adhered to the notion that it was *not* a war over slavery, a debate was carried on among Negroes of the North over whether or not to offer their services. Many did attempt to enlist, but the sentiments of many others equalled that of one man who wrote:

> *I have observed with much indignation and shame, their willingness to take up arms in defence of this unholy, ill-begotten, would-be Republican govern-ment, that summons its skill, energy, and might, of money, men and false philosophy that a corrupt nation can bring to bear, to support, extend, and perpetuate that vilest of all vile systems, American slavery . . . (Wesley W. Tate)*

Yet many Negroes had sought to enlist, and attempts were continued until Congress authorized the use of Negro troops in 1862. Even after rejections Negroes had formed companies or military clubs and drilled, keeping themselves in readiness for the day when the government would decide they were fit, and needed and wanted in the fight. By the end of the war 186,017 Negroes had fought with the Union Army—over 100,000 of them recruited in the South.

Negroes of the South took a stand on the war in other ways also. Some refused to work altogether; others demanded wages for their labor. Many guided Union soldiers and gave information to federal troops. Probably the best known Negro information-gatherer was Harriet Tubman who was a spy behind Confederate lines. In many cases slaves seized the property of their masters when Union troops arrived.

There are recorded cases of slave attack on white civilians in the South, but despite the greatly increased fears of the Southern whites and wide-spread rumors of uprisings, there was no general insurrection. This is not surprising in the view of the militarization of the South during the war which overlay the already established system of repression. In addition many observers agree that a general uprising was precluded by the ac-commodation of slaves to the slave system under the pressures of its elab-orate techniques for preventing communication, and for breaking the will to resist by a combination of punishment and reward. But while there was no general insurrection during the war slaves did reveal their senti-ments, for thousands fled to the Union lines.

Once Negroes were accepted in the Union Army other struggles be-gan. The War Department order providing for Negro enlistment also provided that black regiments were to have only white officers. Despite many appeals and petitions by soldiers, resolutions of Negro organizations, and representations by Negro leaders, not more than 100 Negroes re-ceived officers' commissions during the war. A second struggle of black soldiers was the fight for equal pay. Two Massachusetts regiments, the Fifty-fourth and Fifty-fifth, refused to accept any pay at all until pay was equalized. When the Massachusetts legislature appropriated funds to make up the difference between their pay and that of white soldiers the Negro regiments still refused, holding out for a federal equal-pay order. As Con-gress debated the issue there were threats of strikes and mutinies. One sergeant, William Walker of the Third South Carolina Volunteers, led his company to the captain's tent and ordered them to stack their arms and resign from the army. He was court-martialed and shot for mutiny. The law providing for equal pay was passed six months after its introduction, but even then it had its faults. For those soldiers who had been free at the outbreak of the war, pay was made retroactive to the time of enlist-ment, for those who gained freedom through service in the war, pay was retroactive only to January 1, 1864. Thus, the Congress made a distinction between those who were free before the war and those who became free due to enlistment, providing full pay only for the former. . . .

From the beginning Lincoln had maintained that the aim of the war was to unite the country, and throughout he based his conservative approach on his desire to keep the border states loyal. He cited this when he revoked emancipation orders issued by two of his generals. Then, even when the time came for the admission that slavery was "at the root of the rebellion" the Emancipation Proclamation, so joyously hailed, was itself a reaffirmation of his caution, for it freed only the slaves in the rebel states.

CHAPTER 15

BY TEN-FORTY AT night, Li'l Pit was asleep upstairs after gorging himself on nachos and ice cream from the salad and dessert bar at Sizzler. Downstairs, Love sat on the corner of Ruby's bed while she lay on her back, staring at the ceiling, her shoes off and her feet swollen in her stockings.

Love hadn't been in her room more than twice before, and it seemed like an eerie place, out of time. The bed was thick and so high off the ground that his feet didn't touch. There was a dim yellow light cast by the small lamp at her bedside and a large oak-framed mirror above her dresser. A thick smell of baby powder hung in the air, and the walls were covered in pastel blue wallpaper.

"We could say that he's got to get out if he doesn't quit the crew?" Love turned to his grandmother, but she shook her head.

"He'll jus leave. Then you lost him forever. I been there before with your mama." Ruby rubbed one foot with the other.

"Could lock him in his room."

"And what you think he gonna do when he get out? 'Cause you know one day he gonna get out. Then we that boy's worse enemies, and he goin go an join up with your hoodlums."

Love stood and paced at the foot of her bed. "We got to do something. There's got to be something to do." He stopped and turned to her excitedly. "We could take him to Juvi. We could take him there and have them keep him."

"You know he's got to have done something first."

"That's right. He just has to do something." Love started pacing again, his eyes flashing in excitement. "He got to kill somebody, and then they'll take him to the home and he won't get all messed up here."

"Use your head. You are the dumbest boy I ever heard. You gonna get him to kill someone so he don't get mixed up in crime. What kinda thinking is that?"

"My bad." Love laughed at himself.

"Go in the kitchen and get me a tub of hot water and then I'll tell you what we gonna do. And pour some of them salts in there."

Love went into the kitchen, ran hot water into a metal tub, and brought it back for her. When he returned, she was in her nightgown, sitting at the edge of her bed.

Love watched her touch the water with her toes, pull them out, dip them down a little farther, and pull them out again, all the time breathing through her pursed lips like a woman giving birth. When she finally had her feet resting solidly at the bottom of the tub, she turned to Love and smiled.

"My husband, your mama's papa, your real granpapa, name was Ronal. That's what she named you. Your real name is Ronal LeRoy after your granpapa."

"I know my own name."

"But you didn't know where it came from, now did you? Now hush up and listen. I got something to tell you. Your granpapa was gonna go to college. He wanted to go to college jus like you want for Paul, but he didn't always want to go. He wanted to go 'cause he was scared into it. He tole me this story, that before he was born, his papa was a bootleg. That's when they had no liquor allowed by law, and he made his money running corn whiskey. Now, he work for a Catholic man and they sell their whiskey all the way over to Walterboro. And you could make a lot of money doing that. And so he tried on his own to sell, and got into competition with the Catholic man and they had their problems. But Ronal's papa gave all his moonshine to the police for free, so they leave him alone and he saved up a whole lot a money. Then the law changed and it was legal to sell liquor and there wasn't no more business. Now six years later his wife had Ronal, 'bout the same time I was born. By then, Ronal's papa worked for a coal mine cause he was too old for the war. And he took Ronal out to the mine when he was big enough and showed him how he went down into that hole, way down, and come up all dirty. Now, that hole was dark, and down in there wasn't hardly any space to breathe and sometime it creaked and cracked and it already scared Ronal just looking down into it. On top a that, his papa got up at five every morning and come home every day all tired and aching and had no money, sayin how this was jus like slavery times. This scared Ronal even more, 'cause his older brother was going to work for the mine when he turn fourteen, and he saw what was coming for him. Then one day his papa didn't come home. There was an accident at the mine an his papa was killed. And that's when his mama tole him about all the money saved up from the bootleg days that Ronal was supposed to use to go to college, and if he never been thinking about it before, he never stop thinking about it after that. See, he was scared into it. And that's what we got to do with Paul."

Love shook his head. "Just one problem. Can't no one scare Li'l Pit more than he already been scared. I guess that's the whole difference between now and then."

There was a bang on the front door, like a brick thrown against it.

"Don't get it," Love said. He stared toward the front of the house through the bedroom wall like he had X-ray vision.

"Course I'm gonna get my own door." Ruby slid her feet into her pink fur slippers and trudged up the hall.

"Tell him we're not here. Tell him we're out in San Leandro."

"Who's that?" Ruby yelled through the door.

There was a faint yelling coming from the street. Ruby opened the door and looked down the stairs at the young man in a wheelchair.

"I'm a friend of Love's. I need to talk with him real bad." Love stood at the back of the hallway, almost twenty feet away from the door.

"What you want?" Ruby yelled.

"I need to talk to him."

"It's late. You can talk to him tomarrah."

"I need to talk to him now. It's an emergency."

"He's asleep. It can wait until tomarrah."

"I need to talk to him now, bitch!" Curse took his gun out from under his shirt and laid it in his lap. Ruby slammed the door shut.

"You get on outta here or I'm callin the police," she yelled. "You get on home."

"Listen old bitch," Curse yelled. "You tell that punk to check his batteries. Tell him he needs to call Curse. You tell him that."

"You get. I'm callin the police right now."

"I don't give a shit. They ain't gonna come out here for no tired old lady."

Ruby backed up another step, but then she heard no more yelling. She turned to Love. His jaw was set and his fists clenched as he looked at the door.

"You're the dumbest chile I ever did see."

"He's gonna come back."

"And don't you go and tell me how you gonna fix him when he do."

"I didn't say that. But he is gonna come back, maybe tonight or maybe in the morning, but he's going to come with some other guys who can come up the stairs."

"Well, you're not going to be here when he come."

She walked back down the hall and went into the kitchen. She pulled the stepladder from the pantry, pushed it over to the counter, and lifted up her cotton nightgown so she could bend her knees to climb.

"I'm going to have faith in you," she said. "There ain't nothing you can do now but leave." Love stood in the kitchen doorway and watched his grandmother reach up into the high cupboards where she always retrieved extra cans of tomato sauce. She stretched her arms above her head and felt around blindly, then pulled out a glass pickle jar filled with dollar bills.

"You've got to promise me that you will follow my plan. If you break your promise, don't never come back here, 'cause you'll have lost all my faith left in goodness, and I only got but that much left. You've got to promise me that you will use this for savin your brother. I ain't got nothin but your word, and I'm gonna trust that your word is the honest word of a man. I'm going to tell you what to do, and you got to keep your word like a man keep his word."

Love didn't say anything. He knew a man's word wasn't something you kept by promising you would keep it. It was something you kept by doing what you promised. He knew that from Tom at Los Aspirantes, who just showed up every day and kept at it even though the kids were hitting and kicking him. And he knew it from Freight, who didn't need to say a threat twice. He knew, too, that like the quick sweep of a broom out onto the back stoop, his life was about to start all over, once again.

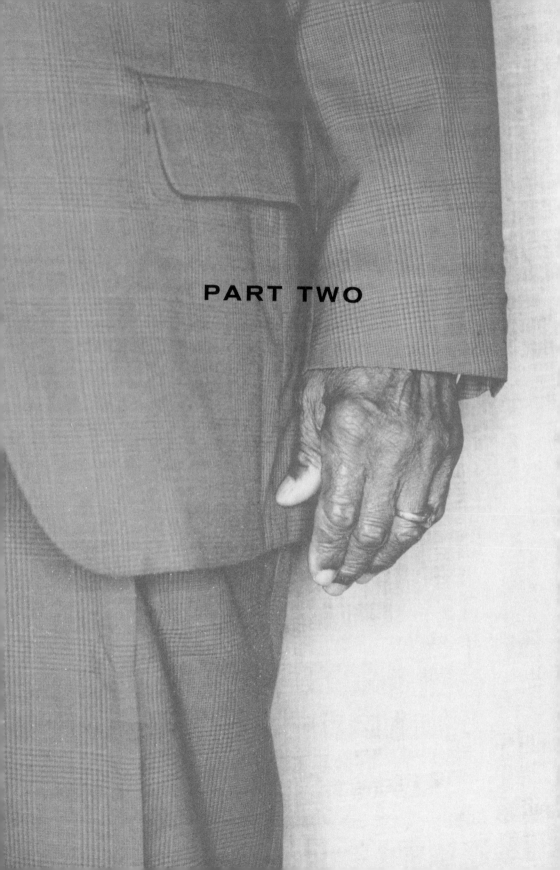

PART TWO

SANTA RITA JAIL

TODAY I START my reading with Booker T. Washington's *Up from Slavery:*

> Early the next morning word was sent to all the slaves, old and young, to gather at the house. In company with my mother, brother, and sister, and a large number of other slaves, I went to the master's house. All of our master's family were either standing or seated on the verandah of the house, where they could see what was to take place and hear what was said. There was a feeling of deep interest, or perhaps sadness, on their faces, but not bitterness. As I now recall the impression they made upon me, they did not at the moment seem to be sad because of the loss of property, but rather because of the parting with those whom they had reared and who were in many ways very close to them. The most distinct thing that I now recall in connection with the scene was that some man who seemed to be a stranger (a United States officer, I presume) made a little speech and then read a rather long paper—the Emancipation Proclamation, I think.
>
> After the reading we were told that we were all free, and could go when and where we pleased. My mother, who was standing by my side, leaned over and kissed her children, while tears of joy ran down her cheeks. She explained to us what it all meant, that this was the day for which she had been so long praying, but fearing that she would never live to see.
>
> For some minutes there was great rejoicing, and thanksgiving, and wild scenes of ecstasy. But there was no feeling of bitterness. In fact, there was pity among the slaves for our former owners. The wild rejoicing on the part of the emancipated colored people lasted but for a brief period, for I noticed that by the time they returned to their cabins there was a change in their feelings. The great responsibility of being free, of having charge

of themselves, of having to think and plan for themselves and their children, seemed to take possession of them. It was very much like suddenly turning a youth of ten or twelve years out into the world to provide for himself. In a few hours the great questions with which the Anglo-Saxon race had been grappling for centuries had been thrown upon these people to be solved. These were the questions of a home, a living, the rearing of children, education, citizenship, and the establishment and support of churches. Was it any wonder that within a few hours the wild rejoicing ceased and the feeling of deep gloom seemed to pervade the slave quarters? To some it seemed that, now that they were in actual possession of it, freedom was a more serious thing than they had expected to find it. Some of the slaves were seventy or eighty years old; their best days were gone. They had no strength with which to earn a living in a strange place and among strange people, even if they had been sure where to find a new place of abode. Besides, deep down in their hearts there was a strange and peculiar attachment to "old Marster" and "old Missus," and to the children, which they found it hard to think of breaking off. With these they had spent in some cases nearly a half century, and it was no light thing to think of parting. Gradually, one by one, stealthily at first, the older slaves began to wander from the slave quarters back to the big house to have a whispered conversation with their former owners as to the future.

CHAPTER 1A

LOVE WOKE LI'L Pit at five o'clock in the morning, before it was light, before anyone from the crew would be on the street. He shook him in his bed, then stripped the covers off him.

"Come on," Love whispered. "We've got to go. Come on. You've got to get dressed and be quiet so Nanna doesn't hear you. We've got to do our business."

Li'l Pit put his arms over his face and rolled away from him. Love shook him again.

"It's time to do your job for Freight, don't you remember?" Li'l Pit turned back toward him quickly, staring at Love until it came to him. Then he sat up straight like a marionette, shaking his head to wake up. Love handed him the red sweater and slacks from the floor where he'd left them the night before.

Love was already dressed. He also wore clothes unaffiliated with the crew, a white button-down shirt and black slacks that he had for church. Over that he wore a blue sweater and then Easton's black leather jacket.

They went downstairs and ate cereal quickly.

"What we gonna do?" Li'l Pit asked.

"Shhhh."

"Don't we need the trunk?"

"We'll get it."

"Where we going?"

"Shhh."

They washed their dishes quietly, and then Love picked up a paper bag from the kitchen counter and stuffed it inside his jacket.

"What's that?"

"Shhhh. You're gonna wake up Nanna and spoil the whole thing."

He climbed the stairs again with Li'l Pit behind him. They went back into the room and Love stood at one end of the trunk.

"We have to carry it. Pick up that end."

Li'l Pit grabbed the leather strap and pulled up; he had to grab it with both hands to support the weight.

"What's in here?"

"I filled it with some things we're going to need. You got that end? You strong enough?"

Li'l Pit didn't answer; he just clenched his teeth and pulled Love forward to the stairs. Love hadn't filled it with much, just some of their clothes and a gun that he'd found in Easton's old closet when he was hiding the dope from Ruby. But the trunk felt heavy to him too, as if its age made it heavier than it looked. They inched their way down the stairs, knocking into the railing, and making such a racket that Ruby surely would have heard them and woken up if she wasn't up already and standing behind her door listening to the whole thing.

"Why we got to take so much?"

"Shhh."

The chest fell from Li'l Pit's hands and slammed onto the floor. They both laughed.

"Shhh, pick it up. Come on."

"What's in here?"

"You'll see. Come on." They squeezed their way through the front door and out of the house, dropping the trunk again on the porch. Love went back in briefly and, pretending to take a look around for something forgotten, nodded down the hallway where he hoped Ruby stood, watching through a crack in her door.

He went back outside, locked up, put the keys deep in his pocket, and checked that the paper bag was in his leather jacket. They carried the trunk single-file down the narrow block, Love walking backward, facing a thin pink-and-orange sherbet sunrise in the east, pulling Li'l Pit along toward the darkness. As soon as they turned the corner, the path widened and they walked side by side, but they still had to work out a common step so the trunk didn't bounce so much. Love counted off: "Step, together, step. Step, together, step."

Ruby had tried to order a cab to pick them up, but none would come to their neighborhood until it was daylight, and they couldn't afford to wait around. So they had to walk the ten blocks to the West Oakland Greyhound station, straight through the projects where Curse lived. Love thought about going around, but the projects were huge and that meant walking an extra five blocks out of the way, which would feel like a hundred miles with the trunk. Besides, it would still be too early for Curse to be out. The business was 24-7, but Curse was strictly 9 to 5 now.

They got to Curse's block and Love pulled them forward. Curse lived on the ground floor where a glittery gold Christmas bell hung, three windows over from the entrance. Love didn't want to stop. He didn't even look toward the apartments. Women and men were trickling out of the entrance every few seconds on their way to work, bundled in their jackets and gloves. A man slept on the sidewalk under a piece of cardboard, and they had to step down into the street and around him.

Love was whispering now, half out of exhaustion, half out of fear that his voice might somehow alert Curse. "Step," he said. He didn't say "together" anymore; instead he just paused before repeating "step."

They lumbered back up onto the sidewalk, and it was clearly time for another rest. They were still just a few windows away from Curse's place, so Love kept pulling them forward, their arms hyperextended, the trunk straps at the ends of their fingertips. Then Li'l Pit let it drop.

"Let's go," Love whispered.

"Naw. I got to rest." He walked away from the trunk, across the cement yard toward Curse's window.

"Where you going?" Love whispered.

Li'l Pit didn't turn around. Love didn't want to shout, so he ran after him and grabbed him by the arm of his sweater.

"What you doing? Curse'll kill you if you wake him up."

"I'm just gonna look in."

"We don't have time."

"I'm just gonna look. We got to rest, anyhow."

"No. We got to go now."

"Not yet. I'm still tired."

"We don't have time."

"Let go a my arm!" Li'l Pit yelled.

Love let go quickly to prevent more yelling. Li'l Pit turned and walked toward the window. Love watched, frozen, staring hard, like he hoped he could draw his brother back magnetically. He could tackle him but he'd just scream. Li'l Pit walked up to the bars on the window and looked in. Love ran up beside him, but against the wall so that he wasn't visible through the window. He whispered: "It's against the rules to be here."

But Li'l Pit was too fascinated to care. He could see only one room. There was a mat on the floor next to a phone, a table with a lamp and a glass of unfinished juice sitting on it next to the mail. There was a poster of Snoop and Dr. Dre on the wall above a metal cage with Curse's snake in it.

Curse wheeled himself into the room, naked from the waist up, lifted the glass of juice, and sipped from it. Love walked away from the building, hoping to draw Li'l Pit back with him. But Li'l Pit stayed to watch. Curse then picked up an envelope but accidentally knocked the glass onto the floor. It didn't break, but spilled the juice and then rolled under the table.

"Fuckin shit. Fuckin goddamn it," Curse yelled. He took a few napkins, backed up, and dropped them onto the puddle. The glass had rolled to the wall and he had to back up more to see it. He unstrapped his legs and then lifted his body with his arms and nudged himself to the edge of his chair. Slowly, he dropped himself down so that he sat on the floor, his legs folded awkwardly underneath him, like a baby just learning to sit upright. He pulled himself forward and onto his belly, then stretched his arms out in front of him and pulled himself flat along the floor, his deadened legs trailing behind him. When he reached the glass, he held it in one hand and stopped to rest under the table, his chest heaving with exhaustion.

Li'l Pit knocked on the window.

Love ran back to grab him but saw that it was too late. Curse stared up at them.

"Hey, what up, niggas!" Curse yelled, muffled through the window. "What you doin lookin in my house, faggots?"

Love smiled and waved. "We're on our way now," he yelled back.

"Stay right there. I'm comin out."

"Come on," Love said and walked toward the trunk.

"Naw," Li'l Pit said. "We supposed to wait."

"But we got to leave!" Love pleaded.

Li'l Pit crossed his arms and faced the building.

"Aw, man. You don't understand. This is s–t–u–p–i–d, stupid."

"You stupid."

Curse came out, his hands in the front tube pocket of his sweatshirt. "What the fuck you doin peepin in my house?"

Neither of them answered.

"Well, where you been, niggas?"

"Here," Love said.

"Here? You ain't been here. Let me see your beepers. I been callin you all day yesterday. We have business. We coulda lost money on account a you and your grandmother. You better tell that old bitch what's up."

"We don't got 'em," Love said.

"What you mean, you don't got 'em?"

"You said they was tapped," Li'l Pit chimed in.

"Can't tap no beeper, fool."

"That's what he said." Li'l Pit pointed at Love. Love turned and spit on the ground.

"We're on our way now," he said.

"What you mean?"

"I thought we had to stay off callin you cause of Poh-Poh," Love said. Curse looked down the block cautiously and then back at him.

"What you mean, you're on your way now? Where you on your way to?"

"We're on our way to take care of that business. I just came by to let you know we're taking care of it so you don't think we're trippin or nothin."

"I'm the one who came by," Li'l Pit said angrily. "I'm the one who stopped."

"Why you didn't call me back, Li'l Poet?" Curse asked.

" 'Cause he told me not to."

"Why you tell him that, nigga?"

"You know, man." Love looked away and spit again. "Cause of Poh-Poh. You told me on the phone you was hiding out. Then our grandmother took us to dinner and we couldn't say no or it would have looked whack."

"You got to tell that old bitch what's up."

"I'll tell her," Li'l Pit said.

"Awright, Li'l Poet, you a true player." Curse backhanded Li'l Pit in the chest affectionately. Li'l Pit smiled and nodded.

"We got the trunk, too," Li'l Pit added. He pointed to the green trunk sitting on the pavement twenty feet away from them. Love shook his head. He thought about running again. It didn't matter where, just keep going, maybe back to the house with the lemons and tomatoes, or even farther back, to Los Aspirantes.

"What you got a goddamn trunk for?" Curse asked.

"To carry it in," Love said.

"What you need a trunk for? You ain't pickin up no dead bodies." Curse headed over to the trunk. Love didn't move. If he stayed far enough away, he could still run if he had to. He had the bag of money on him. If nothing else, he could save his own ass and get away. He watched Li'l Pit follow Curse over to the trunk.

"Wait," Love yelled. Curse fumbled with the lock on the trunk, and Li'l Pit looked just as eager to see what was in it.

"Listen," Love said. "You and Freight got busted, and we ain't takin any chances. You can go ahead an open it if you want, but you ain't gonna find nothin in there but clothes. Fine. Here, look." Love walked over indignantly, almost hyperventilating. He unlocked the trunk with the key and flung the lid open. Li'l Pit's Dallas Cowboys jacket and two sweatshirts covered the contents below, and on top of that, two baggies of meat-loaf sandwiches Ruby had made them. "Look, dog. What'd I tell you. See. Look. We hide the shit in here, cover it up with all the clothes, and then, even if we get stopped and Poh-Poh opens it up, we awright. Right? But no." He slammed the case shut before Curse could dig below the clothes and find the gun. Love walked away from the trunk to get the attention off of it. "You gonna keep us here all day and let everyone know what's up. Damn, dog. Can't you just let us do our job? I mean, let Li'l Pit do his job. You give him a job, now let him do it. Awright? Damn, nigga."

Love had worked himself into a state of irreproachable anger. "We're gonna do what we say, if you just let us do our business. Damn, we don't tell you how to do what you doin, dog."

"Don't call me dog," Curse said.

"Whatever. Cat then. Mouse. Snake. You gonna worry bout the animal kingdom when we got business to do?"

Li'l Pit giggled and Curse glared at him. "You think that's funny? You fucking li'l punk, I'll stuff you inside this trunk and throw you in the ocean." He wheeled over to Li'l Pit, grabbed him by the collar of his red sweater, and threw him down onto the pavement.

"I oughta bust a cap in your ass right here." He wheeled back toward Love but then stopped between him and the trunk. "Now, get your fuckin beepers back, and don't be lookin into my house no more like two perverts." He pulled the hood of his sweatshirt up over his head and wheeled himself back into the building.

Love walked over to the trunk and picked up one of the handles. Li'l Pit brushed himself off and took the other strap, and they started off down the block again. It was brighter now, and cars were on the street. Love looked up past the shoes hanging on the telephone wires to the cloudless light blue sky. He took a deep breath of the yeasty smell coming from the bread factory. He didn't understand why things had worked out—or why things went wrong when they went wrong. His legs began to shake, and at first he thought it was from the weight of the trunk, but then the shaking spread through his shoulders and chest, and by the time he reached the edge of the bus-terminal parking lot, he was doing everything within his power to keep from crying in front of Li'l Pit.

NEITHER BOY HAD ever been outside the Bay Area. The bus hadn't even gotten on I-5 before the city gave way to dry yellow hills and giant power-line towers. They passed Santa Rita Road, in Pleasanton, and the tripod windmills, mounted like alien spaceships on top of the mountains.

When Ruby sent them on their way, she knew from experience that there are at least two ways people leave what they know: one person feels the chains loosen and sees the possibilities of a whole new life and even a whole new personality for themselves in that life; while another person seeks out the familiar everywhere they go, and if the familiar doesn't present itself, this person re-creates it, like a caged lion that still stalks its prey.

Love knew this too. Love had lived a different life at Los Aspirantes, but he'd always been returned to the streets of Oakland and had no reason to doubt that he'd return again after he delivered Li'l Pit to South Carolina. But he could imagine another life for his younger brother, like those of other kids at the home who'd left with foster parents and called back to tell about the house and cars and new life they had, though he knew sometimes it was a bluff. It was the kids who didn't ever call back who must have really made it.

For hours, Love sat in a window seat of the bus with Li'l Pit next to him. As the sun rose across the midmorning sky, it filtered down through the tinted windows and heated Love's forehead while the recycled air cooled his chin from the vent below. There were fields on both sides of the road, the east side plowed and green with dark, rich soil in perfect parallel rows, and on the west side, rough, wild yellow.

"Can you imagine, people actually live out here," Love said.

"You ever been to L.A.?" Li'l Pit had seen that the sign on the bus said Los Angeles.

"Naw."

"They got a lot of drive-bys down there," Li'l Pit said.

"*Locos sureños.*"

"Uzis."

"You don't want to be mixed up in there."

Across the aisle from them sat an older, balding man with a frown. Li'l Pit nudged Love with his elbow and imitated the old man by drooling out of the corner of his mouth. The man glared at them.

"Yo, potato head," Li'l Pit said. "What you lookin at?"

"What are you dissin him for?" Love whispered sternly at his brother. "You want to go and mess this all up right from the start? You better take some chilly powder till we get where we going."

"Shut up. You ain't my mama."

"You ain't my son neither, so just remember that."

"That's right."

"That's right, that's right."

The reek of manure filled the bus as they passed hundreds of cows corralled together by the side of the road.

"Oh, man, what's that smelly fart?" Li'l Pit covered his nose with both hands. A high dust cloud formed above the animals as they battled one another for the troughs.

"What would you do if you was one of them cows?" Love asked.

"I'd kill myself for bein so ugly and smelly."

Love shook his head. "Naw. I'd bust on outta there. I'd get all my homies and we'd knock them small wooden posts down and run on out into that open field with all that grass out there."

"Yeah, and then they'd come out after you and plah-plah-plah." Li'l Pit imitated the sound of a MAC-10. "They turn your ass into beef jerky."

The man across the aisle turned again at Li'l Pit's swearing. He seemed to hold himself back for a moment, then reconsidered.

"Where are you kids headed?" he asked.

Li'l Pit was about to make a biting remark but then turned to Love, just as interested to hear the answer. Love slid his tongue over the front of his teeth and cleaned the back corners of his mouth. He looked the man up and down suspiciously.

"We're going to visit relatives in South Carolina," Love said. At first Li'l Pit squished up his eyebrows and shook his head, but then, as if he'd gotten some wise joke, he smiled and nodded.

"That's right." He turned back to the man. "We going to South Carolina, to see our family and go to church with them, and hold hands."

"You're Christians, then."

"That's right. We Christians for Jesus."

"Well, now, didn't your mother tell you that it's a sin to swear and make a lot of noise?"

"Don't you talk about my mama," Li'l Pit yelled. "My mama don't care what we do. She's a millionaire and she's gonna buy this whole bus company and tell them to throw you on out of this bus and you'll have to sit out there with them stinky cows."

The old man straightened his neck and lowered his chin. "Don't you raise your voice at me. I'll ask the bus driver to let you off at the next stop if you can't behave yourself. Your mother may not care, but I certainly do."

Li'l Pit stood up and burst toward the man, but Love caught him by the sweater and pulled him back down into the seat.

"My brother's just clowning. Tell the man you're sorry. Tell the man you're sorry, dog. He's sorry."

"I ain't sorry. He the sorry fool. He a sorry-ass old potato head." The woman seated in front of the old man turned around. She wore a scarf tied around her head and a pair of octagonal, oversize glasses.

"What you lookin at, telescope creature?" Li'l Pit yelled, and the woman turned back around.

"How old are you?" the bald man asked Li'l Pit.

"That ain't none a your business."

"How'd you get to be so angry? Only a boy, and you're out here making enemies with everyone you see. Wouldn't you rather make friends than enemies?"

"Why you all up in the mix and didn't bring no nuts?" Li'l Pit laughed.

"I'm trying to be your friend. Don't you want friends?"

"Why I want a old dinosaur friend like you?"

"You like ice cream?" the man asked. Li'l Pit didn't answer. "How do you know I'm not the head of an ice-cream manufacturer? Maybe I could get you all the ice cream you want."

"You're not the head of any ice-cream m-a-n-u-f-a-c-t-u-r-e-r," Love said quietly, looking at his hands.

"Very good. I see you're a bright young man. So tell me, why do you think I'm not?"

Love looked right at him. "Because you wouldn't be riding this stupid bus if you was the boss of a store; you'd have your own Ferrari driving past us at a million miles an hour."

"Maybe I'm riding the bus so that I can meet little boys and give away ice cream. Did you ever see *Willy Wonka and the Chocolate Factory?*" Love was silent for a second. They'd shown that movie ten times at Los Aspirantes, and he'd even dreamed about floating in a river of chocolate. He looked at the old man's face to see if he could be telling the truth. The man smiled and Love smiled back.

"You can get us all the ice cream we want?" Li'l Pit's eyes widened, and he looked half the size he'd been when he was yelling. Love hit his little brother with his elbow.

"See, fool, I told you you shouldn't a been playin like that. Now he's not going to give us anything. Say you're sorry," Love yelled at his brother.

"I'm sorry. I'm sorry."

"See," said the old man. "Now, how do you know that woman in front of me isn't my wife?"

"Oh no. My bad. I'm sorry. I'm sorry, lady. I'm sorry. Please." The lady didn't look back. "Can you get those kind with the nuts and chocolate on top?"

"Drumsticks? What if I can? Are you going to be nice to me?"

Li'l Pit nodded his head vigorously, and the man smiled at the boy's jutting ears. Love looked at his brother, so eager and polite. At that moment, he knew they could make it.

"So . . ." The man leaned into the aisle. "You're telling me that if you can get something from me, you're going to treat me very nicely, but if you can't, you're going to threaten me and talk filthy. You think I should really believe you're my friend? Or should I just think you're trying to use me?"

Li'l Pit blinked at the man in confusion. "Are you going to give us some ice cream or not?"

"I'm trying to explain that you don't know who I am, and you should start off by trying to make friends. You catch more flies with honey than you do with glue."

"Yuk! What nasty kinda ice cream you make, anyhow?" Li'l Pit grimaced.

Both Love and the old man laughed, and Li'l Pit laughed with them.

They rode in silence as they passed a small town with gas stations and motels. Within a few seconds, the town was gone and there was nothing but dry grass and fields again.

"You been to L.A. before?" Love asked the man.

"I live there. I was just in San Francisco visiting my brother."

Love nodded and looked out the window. A few seconds later he turned to the man again. "Where does your brother live?"

"Well, I'm not very familiar with the area."

"Did he live by the park?"

"Yes. Not too far from the park."

"Then that's the Richmond. Or the Sunset."

"I see. Thank you."

"No problem." Love looked out the window again. He could feel the man watching him.

"I was actually at my brother's funeral," the man said. "That's why I went up." When Love looked back, the man faced forward but continued to talk to them. "He knew he was dying, so I went up and saw him. He was an antiques collector. Watches especially." He pointed up, and Love saw a little black suitcase with silver locks.

"He got the AIDS?" Li'l Pit asked.

"Yes, he had AIDS."

"Our daddy had it too. But he's all better now."

The woman in front of them turned around again and then quickly looked away.

"Is she really your wife?" Love asked.

The man shook his head and made a sour face.

"You're scandalous," Love said.

"Yes. I guess I am. Excuse me." He stood up. "I must use the restroom."

When the man had gone, Love elbowed his brother.

"Don't bother him no more."

"But what about the ice cream? We got to get the ice cream."

"Just forget it. He don't sell ice cream. He's just playin with us." He turned his head and looked out the window. The plowed farmland outside seemed empty and peaceful. It felt good to finally be away from Oakland, to be away from everything. But they would have to stop traveling sometime. He put on his earphones and turned up Public Enemy. It was like some mixed-up music video: the angry bass beat against the rows of alfalfa and the sunlit Central Valley.

CHAPTER 1B

IT WAS HOT for March, and Easton had forgotten what it felt like in southern humidity. Charles took off his coat and laid it on the top of the car. An airplane passed over, and they looked up and then Easton went back to working under the hood. He'd rebuilt everything in this car, so he could surely fix it, unless it needed a part. Then they were in trouble because Jackson was still at least thirty miles.

"I told you this was foolish," said Charles. He paced behind the car, looking up and down the highway. He had a pen in one hand and he clicked it in and out. "I liked Clinton. Yes, Clinton was a nice place: friendly, the way those boys spit on the car. Maybe it would be better if we took these California plates off altogether. At least then people would think we were just common car thieves."

He had the distinct feeling that Easton wasn't listening to him, so he walked over and watched him work. "You know what's wrong with it?"

Easton had never seen Charles afraid of anything before, at least not openly, and he didn't like the edginess, the kind that got you into unnecessary trouble.

"I knew what it was before I opened the hood," he said. "The thermostat's busted and we got a leak in the radiator. All we've got to do is find some water and a hose and then take it slow. Best if we wait till nightfall. Or we could turn around."

"We are not turning around."

"We've got another day to Selma," Easton said, and closed the hood. Charles folded and unfolded his arms. "Out here's our best chance, anyway. The Black folk will help us before the men at the service station. I'm going to walk up that road and see what I see."

Easton walked fifty feet to a dirt road. He heard Charles walk after him.

"Look," Easton said. "Where you think you're going?"

"I think it's better to stick together."

"You want to go up here and let me stay there with the car? That's fine. I just figured you'd feel more comfortable by the car."

Charles looked up the dirt road. It curved behind some trees and then disappeared. "I don't feel more comfortable anywhere. I'd feel more comfortable in Vacaville State Pen, where they got less trees to lynch you from."

"Whatever happened to 'Fight the Revolution, brother'?" Easton walked back to him. He didn't touch Charles because of the heat, but he got right up beside him and talked softly. "Listen, I grew up in the South. There are more of us in this part than them. This is our land. We built all the fields and homes around here. You're not so far away from home, you just don't know what home looks like. This is nature. Look over there." He pointed to a fish hawk circling above the high top of a pine tree. "That means there's water over there. Why don't you see what you can find that can carry something and go get some water."

He left Charles staring at the bird and headed back up the road. After the curve behind the trees, there was an old wood house with a tractor and a chicken shack. A Chevy was parked out front and he noticed the tires were low, for driving over rough ground.

He climbed the first two steps of the porch and then stopped. A heavy feeling came over him as he looked at the house. Driving the highway was one thing, but here, in the silence of the clearing with this house so much like his own standing before him, he remembered. Below the steps would be the bottles that Papa Samuel hid from his mother. He remembered the feeling coming home after school, wishing he didn't have to climb the steps and go inside.

A dog barked somewhere in the field and shook him back into the present. He tapped his shoes to get the dirt off and walked up to the door. He knocked softly at first, but no one answered. He knocked again and yelled out: "Hello there."

"Yes?" A man came from around the side of the house by the chicken coop, a White man in his late sixties in shirtsleeves and slacks.

"Hello." Easton came down from the porch, slowly. "Hello, sir."

The man stared at him with his hands at his sides.

"Well?" the man asked. "Are you callin for me?"

"Yes, sir. Yes, I was hoping that you could assist me and my friend." Easton wiped his cheek. He could hear the submissiveness in his own words, feel his eyes trailing on the ground—and he hated it. But he couldn't seem to keep it from happening. "We've got ourselves a busted water pump, and I wondered if you might have an extra hose on you."

"Tom," the old man yelled toward the chicken coop. "Dare's a nigger out here say he's lookin for a hose?" He turned back to Easton. "Ya say you're lookin for a hose? What kind a hose?"

A large man in his forties came out, wearing overalls and rubber gloves. He pulled off the gloves and stood by the older man.

"What kinda hose you lookin for?"

"A radiator hose, sir. My car's busted up there on the road. Sure could use a hose."

The younger man wiped his brow and looked at his car. "Where you headed?"

"Us? We're just passing through."

"Where you coming from?" asked the older man. He removed his hat and put his forearm against his head.

"California."

"Oh." The old man looked at the car too, but neither of them moved, like they were waiting for a breeze to tell them what to do. A three-legged dog hopped across the path and sat against one of the tires, panting and smiling.

"What happened to him?" Easton asked.

"Tractor," the old man said. "Don't bother him none, though. Runs fast as before."

"Here, watch this." The larger man picked up a stick and tossed it so high that it hit the upper branches of a tree, and at the same time he whistled two quick chirps. The dog stood, his ears perked. He followed the stick up and then down through the air until it fell to the same height as the car's rooftop. Then he leapt up, his two front legs pushing off with his back one. He caught the stick in the air and brought it over to his master. Tom took the stick and patted the dog between its ears.

"That's a talented dog," Easton said.

"Took him a hardship 'fore he showed his real talent," said the old man. "Was just run-of-the-mill mutt 'fore his accident. Now he's our favorite. Tom's got to show all the strangers come by here his famous dog."

"I can sure see why that is."

"You got some friends out at the car?" Tom asked.

"Yep, yep. One friend. We're hopin to get a hose and fix up the radiator."

"Well, we got hose." Tom walked to the car and popped the hood open. "We can take some of this for now." He pulled off the O-rings and held up a footlong piece of black rubber hose. " 'Bout this long do for ya?"

"Sure. Yes, sir."

"Alright then." The man left the hood open and placed the rings on the fender. With the hose in one hand and the stick in the other, he led the way up the dirt road toward the highway, and Easton followed. Just as they got to the curve by the trees, Tom turned and whistled. The dog scurried up and hopped after them, running just as fast as a jack-rabbit.

CHAPTER 1C

LIDA WAITED FOR her mother to get two glasses out of the cupboard and fill them with milk. It had been exactly two years since she'd been in this house, but immediately the desire to scratch herself returned. Ruby brought the drinks into the living room and placed them on cork coasters.

"When I was pregnant with you, they told me to drink lots of milk. So you finish that whole glass. Go on."

Lida picked up her glass and drank the sweet milk. It was a relief to have an excuse not to speak. She continued to sip and hope her mother would say everything for her, that she wouldn't have to ask to bring Marcus back to the house.

"You don't remember your papa, Ronal, but he was so excited 'bout you coming. He put his hand on me and he ask, 'How you know it's a girl?' and I say, 'I just know, that's all.' "

"Did you really know?"

"Well I guess I did. But you know men, how they don't even think you connected to the baby in no way. Don't you feel you could know?"

"Well Marcus says if it sticks out far then it's a girl, and if it's wide, then it's a boy."

"See, that's just what I'm saying. Menfolk think everything got a shape to it. They've got to look at everything from the outside. You goin over to Kaiser or Highland?"

"I guess Kaiser."

"That's where everyone here go now. Used to be you had a doctor and you knew they name. I don't even got a tooth no more. See here." Ruby pulled her lip up to show Lida the space in her back teeth. "I don't even recollect that doctor who got my tooth." She took a sip of her milk, and they sat in silence for a moment.

"Well I think it's a boy," Lida said.

"Well then it got to be a boy. Ronal sure would have loved a little grandson. What about his daddy? He want you to have the child?" Ruby never said Marcus's name.

"He is thinking up names already. He hopes it's a boy."

"He wanna call him after his self, I suppose."

"No. He doesn't want that. He's thinking Jimmy or Keith, or some other names."

"What about a name from the Bible, like Matthew?"

Lida laughed.

"Why's that so funny? Just 'cause he don't go to no church? He gonna marry you in a church, ain't he?"

"Yes." Lida sipped her milk.

"He say he was going to marry you, didn't he?"

"Yes."

"Did you have to tell him or he asked you?"

"He asked."

"Well that's good. Least the boy has some pride in him."

Lida nodded, and her stomach growled.

"Why didn't you say you was hungry? I'm hungry myself now that your stomach remind me. Isn't he feeding you nothing?" Ruby stood up and went into the kitchen. "What kind of job he got? He got a job, I hope. A real job."

"Yeah. He's working at Lucky's."

Ruby pulled down two bowls and took out a pot of stew from the refrigerator. She put the pot on the stove, and they stood in the kitchen and talked while Ruby stirred the food.

"You got the child to think of now, you know. You have to keep him away from all that junk you-all be doing."

"We don't do that anymore, Mama."

Ruby didn't argue. She shook some salt into the stew and then tasted it with a big wooden spoon. She got brown sugar from the cabinet and dumped in a stream of it, then tasted it again.

"You can't give it too much salt or too much sweet or it gets rotten. Hard to know exactly what it needs."

"We're all through with that junk, Mama. I swear we are. He didn't have none since he's been outta jail."

Ruby turned to her. "You sure he's the papa?"

"Mama! Yes, I'm sure."

"I'm just asking. Love E told me you were sleeping 'round with all kind of men."

Lida felt a burning in her face. It took a moment before she could bring any words to her mouth.

"An you believed him?" she finally asked.

Ruby turned off the burner and got a ladle out of the drawer. She scooped the stew into the bowls. "He was my brother."

"I'm your daughter."

"But look what kind of boy you took up with."

"You don't even know." Lida shook her head. "You don't even know what you're talking about." The smell from the stew nauseated her and she walked out into the living room holding her stomach, as if poison had just filled it. She paced by the front window until Ruby came in holding the steaming bowls.

"Get me those red place mats out of the drawer," Ruby said.

Lida turned.

"Marcus is the father of my child. Don't you talk about him like he's nobody. You didn't even know all the things going on right under your own nose, but you think you know all about him and me." The words came from her without her permission, as if she'd filled up with them and now they were overflowing. "You got no right to call him out of his name. He was a hundred times better than Easton. A thousand times. I don't care if you never let us back in this house again, but you should have to know the truth, 'cause Easton was a liar. He was worse than a liar." She shook her head. "I can't eat none of that now. I just can't eat."

Ruby brought the bowls back into the kitchen and placed them next to the sink. She stood over the counter and kept her back to Lida.

"What did Love E ever do to you that was so awful?" she asked, just loud enough for Lida to hear in the living room.

Lida didn't answer. She didn't know where to begin. Everywhere she looked in that house, she could picture him, could see a moment when she felt terror. She saw him smiling at her from the couch as he drew pictures, eating at the table, sitting in the chair listening to records. She closed her eyes.

"It doesn't matter, Mama, 'cause he's dead now. I just want to go on. I just want to get this baby out of me and go on."

"You have space for a baby where you living?"

"No. Why?"

Ruby dumped the stew back in the pot. " 'Cause there's so much room I got here."

"You saying we could all move in back here?"

"I don't know why you won't tell me what Love E did. I know he didn't mean it. He never did anything to hurt someone on purpose."

"I definitely can't live here, Mama, if you're gonna keep bringing that up on me."

"But if you just tell me, then we won't have to bring it up anymore and it will be done with."

"You aren't going to believe me anyways, and you'll just hate me more than you already do."

"I don't hate you, Lida. I love you."

"Then you've got to pick, Mama. 'Cause it's got to be him or me. You've got to promise to never talk about him."

"But Lida, why do you want to hurt me this way? Can't you at least let me have my memories?"

"That's what I'm doing. I'm letting you have your memories, the way you want to have them."

"You're talking crazy. I don't know what you're saying." Ruby sat down on the stepladder by the counter and held her head. "It's not fair of you to make me choose like this."

"There's nothing to choose. I won't make you choose, Mama. I can't live here again, anyway. This place makes me shiver. It's like coming back to some kind of nightmare."

Lida left the kitchen, and Ruby stayed on the ladder holding her head, looking at the floor. Lida picked up her purse from the couch and was almost out the door when she stopped and saw her old pair of Eastman shoes by the mat. She touched them lightly with the tip of her foot, like nudging a small animal to see if it was still alive.

"This was a good idea of mine to leave these shoes down here, wasn't it, Mama?"

Ruby didn't answer, and Lida let herself out.

SANTA RITA JAIL

I READ TO you today from Mississippi law known as the Black Codes:

3. Mississippi Vagrant Law; Section 2

All freedmen, free Negroes and mulattoes in this State, over the age of eighteen years, found on the second Monday in January, 1866, or thereafter, with no lawful employment or business, or found unlawful assembling themselves together, either in the day or night time, and all white persons so assembling themselves with freedmen, free Negroes or mulattoes, or usually associating with freedmen, free Negroes, or mulattoes, on terms of equality, or living in adultery or fornication with a freed woman, free Negro or mulatto, shall be deemed vagrants, and on conviction thereof shall be fined in a sum not exceeding, in the case of a freedman, free Negro or mulatto, fifty dollars, and a white man two hundred dollars, and imprisoned at the discretion of the court, the free Negro not exceeding ten days, and the white man not exceeding six months. . . .

4. Penal Laws of Mississippi; Section 5

If any freedman, free Negro, or mulatto, convicted of any of the misdemeanors provided against in this act [including "insulting gestures" or "exercising the function of a minister of the Gospel without a license"], shall fail or refuse for the space of five days, after conviction, to pay the fine and costs imposed [up to one hundred dollars], such person shall be hired out by the sheriff or other officer, at public outcry, to any white person who will pay said fine and all costs, and take said convict for the shortest time.

CHAPTER 2A

AT TEN P.M., after winding through Bakersfield, the bus arrived at the L.A. terminal. Love and Li'l Pit were tired and groggy as they got off and wandered into the main waiting area, a cavernous hall flooded in fluorescent light. The room was crowded and the floor tiles were covered in ashy dirt. In the center were rows of long wooden benches, divided with a wooden bar every three feet so people couldn't sleep on them. They sat down and looked around. There was a video arcade off to the side with loud laser explosions and flashing lights. At the entrance to the building, three teenagers stood against the wall, looking around at the passengers and every once in a while whistling across the street. Li'l Pit sat at the end of the bench and put his feet up.

"What we got to do now?"

"We got to wait."

"Here, in this old toilet?"

Love nodded.

"What about our trunk?"

"I told them bus people to hold it for us until we're ready." The loudspeaker announced a departing bus, and a few passengers began to run. Li'l Pit laughed and then started to drone and nod his head.

"Yuh yuh yuh yuh yuh."

"Cut that shit out," Love said.

"YA YA YA," Li'l Pit yelled louder, but then stopped. "I'm going in there." He got up and walked into the darkened video arcade. After wandering around looking for quarters on the floor, he stood next to a taller kid playing Street Fighter. As he watched, he shook his head.

"Here," Li'l Pit said. "I'll get you a free man." He grabbed the controls and pushed the kid to the side so he wouldn't have time to argue. He played the game for a minute and got an extra man.

"Here," the boy said, trying to get his play back.

"Just a minute." Li'l Pit was fighting intensely and pushing the controls. A minute later the boy spoke up again.

"Here, let me play." He pushed Li'l Pit, but Li'l Pit didn't budge, so the boy wandered off. Love came over and watched his brother. Li'l Pit punched the enemy one more time and the game awarded him another new man.

"Bet you wish you was that good for real."

"This is for real," he said. "There ain't no one in the world can beat me at this, and that's for real."

A policeman came up to them with his hand on his club. He tapped Love on the shoulder.

"Outside, both of you."

"What for?" Li'l Pit said.

"Out."

"I was just getting him extra men. He said I could play."

"Now."

"Shit, man. Can't never do anything nice for no one."

Love and Li'l Pit walked out of the arcade, shaking their heads, the policeman following them. Li'l Pit started to babble: "Libily libily libily."

"What's wrong with him?" the policeman asked.

Love shrugged. "He's not doing it on purpose."

The policeman thrust out his arm and pointed to the wall. "Stand over there."

"Damn. Poh-Poh ain't gettin none at home," Love mumbled, and his brother laughed.

"Is this them?" the cop asked. Love turned and saw the bald man who'd sat across from them in the bus.

"What'd we do?" Love yelled.

The whole bus station seemed to be watching them. The man nodded and the cop came up behind Love and handcuffed him. He then patted Love down all over his body.

"Get your hands off me, faggot."

The cop reached into Love's jacket and pulled out the paper bag. He looked in and then rolled it up.

"Give me that back," Love yelled. "You don't have any right to take my stuff."

"Lay on the ground."

"Give me my bag!"

The cop pushed on Love's shoulder and forced him to his knees and then flattened him onto his stomach.

"You too," he said to Li'l Pit. Li'l Pit began to bark: "Rah rah rah rah! Rah rah rah rah rah!" But when the policeman raised his club, he got down and lay on his stomach.

"What'd your bag look like?" the cop asked the old man.

"It was a black case, a soft briefcase, with silver locks. There were watches in it."

"We don't have his stupid bag," Love yelled. The cop went into the arcade. Passersby stared at the boys, handcuffed and on the ground, some with convinced looks, nodding their heads, others with convinced looks, shaking their heads.

"I don't see your briefcase in there," the cop said. "They may have put it somewhere or sold it already. They have a bag here with money."

"That money is my money," Love yelled. "My grandmother gave me that money."

The cop continued to speak as if Love were just one more video game screaming in the background.

"I'll tell you what you can do. If you want to press charges, I can take them in and confiscate the money. We can call up the kids' parents. If we can prove they took the watches, then the money is yours. But I don't think you'll probably see your watches again. In fact, there's not much chance we'll prove they took them, and then they keep the money. You can fill out a report, though, if you want; but my feeling is to just take the money and send them on their way. That's just my suggestion. But you can do what you want."

Love stood up and shouted, "That's my money, motherfucker. You can't keep my money. We're supposed to use that for food money. You can call my grandmother. You can't steal my money."

"Get down on the ground, now." The cop took out his nightstick and approached him. Love lay down again.

"I don't know if he took my bag for sure," the man said.

"He took it," the cop said, standing over Love. "I've seen his kind a thousand times. They dress up nice and hang around here all day and snatch people's stuff. Believe me, he took it and sold it right outside. Then they use the money to buy drugs and turn that around for more money."

"We're going to South Carolina. You can look at my tickets," Love groaned.

"Maybe we should look at their tickets," said the old man.

"Listen," the cop said. "If you don't want me to do my job, then why did you ask me over here? I don't care if they got tickets to Kal-amazoo. Where do you think they get money like this, huh? And in a paper bag." He held the bag open in front of the man's face. "They take a bus, they steal some luggage, and then they get money to buy crack outside the station to sell for even more. I see it every day. It's a gang thing. It's an initiation. They've got to steal somebody's stuff and then they can be a part of the gang."

The old man shook his head.

"I know it's a sad thing to see," the policeman continued. "But when you're out here like me, seeing these kids stealing and killing day after day, getting away with everything, you don't feel sorry for them any-more. You got to stop looking at them like kids. They're rotten seeds. By this age, it's already too late. You got to just lock them up and throw away the key."

The old man was looking at the boys lying on the dirty ground, Li'l Pit in his V-neck red sweater, babbling in a quick monotone.

"I can't prove they took it," he said. "But I can't see anyone else on that bus taking that case."

"What do you want me to do?" the cop asked.

"What will happen to them if you arrest them?"

"If they have records already, which they always do, then they might go to Juvi, or to a camp. Either way, they'll be out again in a few months and you'll be minus your money. If I book them, I've got to keep the money as evidence."

"We're going to South Carolina," Love said in a whisper.

"We should just at least look at their tickets," said the old man. The policeman went to Love and rolled him over like a carpet. Love lay perfectly still as the cop unzipped his jacket and got the tickets from his inside pocket.

"Yep. Norma, South Carolina. Probably some national gang ring. If you want, I'll put them on the bus. They'll just hop off at the next stop. But then you can have your money and at least they'll be out of my hair."

"Yes. I guess that's what I want you to do, if you don't mind."

The cop shrugged. "Here's the money; it's obviously yours." He held the bag out to the man.

"I don't know. I guess so. It's so hard," the man said. He looked at the boys on the floor and shook his head.

"Damn right it's hard," said the cop. "Every day of my life I wonder how I keep going."

TWO HOURS LATER they sat in silence on the midnight bus out of L.A., thinking of how the old man and cop screwed them over. Every once in a while Love would look down and shake his head. Upon seeing him shake his head, Li'l Pit would shake his head too. But then they'd go off into their own thoughts again, staring at the back of the seat, or out the window into the darkness.

Li'l Pit's mind was racing so fast that he couldn't speak. Every time he was going to ask Love a question, a more important question popped into his head: Why did the man think they took his bag? Why did the cop make them lie on the ground when they were already in handcuffs? He would have liked to have hit that old man, stand on top of him and take the cop's club and smack him right between the eyes. But the man did let them go because Love had the tickets to South Carolina. But why did Love have tickets to South Carolina? It must have been just in case something like this happened. But if they were really going to stop in Dallas on the way, as the bus driver had announced, maybe he could go to Texas Stadium and see Emmitt Smith. But then Freight and Curse would kill them. Except Love had said at first that they were going to L.A., so they must be waiting to get off at the next stop. But how were they going to buy the stuff now that the cop had their money? That cop was just lucky he had that club, or he would have tore him up. There was no excuse for putting them on the floor like that in front of all those people. Li'l Pit shook his head. Love looked at him and shook his head too, and they both smiled.

THE BUS PULLED off the freeway and stopped outside a small terminal in Indio, California.

"Five minutes," the driver said. He opened the door, left the engine running, and got off. Li'l Pit looked at Love, but Love put his head against the window and closed his eyes.

"Ain't we gettin off?" Li'l Pit asked.

Love rolled his forehead back and forth against the window. It was just past two A.M., and the three-day trip to Norma included three more transfers, one in Dallas, another in Atlanta, and the last one in Augusta, Georgia.

"Ain't we goin back to L.A.?" Li'l Pit asked again. "You afraid that cop still there waitin for us? We don't have to go back in through the station."

"We can't get another ticket back to L.A. What money are we going to use? We only have this ticket to Carolina."

"We could sell it back."

"You can't sell nothing back once you got it. You got to just keep on going."

"Shouldn't we call Curse and tell him what's up?" Li'l Pit asked.

"No. Definitely no."

257

"We have to. This is my job, and I'm saying we should go back. I'm getting off."

"You can't."

"Watch."

Love grabbed him and Li'l Pit screamed: "Let go of me!" The passengers turned and stared.

"Listen. Wait," Love said.

"Naw. It's my job."

"But you don't know something."

"I know we sposed to be in L.A."

"No. Something else that you've got to know before callin Curse."

"What already?"

"You've got to sit down before I tell you. I'm not going to yell this all over the bus."

"Fine." Li'l Pit sat in the seat.

"Okay." Love's face stretched into a smile.

"Stop playin."

"Okay, okay. This is real important. I'm just smiling because it's so important it's making me nervous."

"Hurry up. The man's gonna come back."

"Okay. You can't call Curse because Curse doesn't know we're down here." Love's smile returned.

"Yeah he do." Li'l Pit moved to the edge of his seat, as if he were about to get up and go.

"This is real, what I'm saying to you. You got to know sometime. There was no job. I made all of that up."

"Curse told us to go on the job."

"Curse thought I was talkin about some other job, some job for Freight."

"What other job?"

"I don't know. Some other job he had in mind when he paged you."

"What you mean?"

"I mean, we really are going to South Carolina."

"For Freight?"

"No. We're going to South Carolina to get you all out of that mess."

"When we going back?"

"Listen, dog, you're not going back. From now on we only going forward. You've seen the last of Oaktown and all that G thing."

"What you mean we goin to South Carolina?"

"We got family there."

"What about Nanna?"

"She's the one who wanted us to go. Haven't you been listening to nothing I said in the station? She's the one who gave us all the money."

"I don't get it."

"Oh man." Love put his hand over his forehead.

"We sposed to be pickin up somethin for Curse, that's what you said. We got to call and tell him. They gonna kill us."

"They don't care."

"They will when they find out you lyin."

"They already probably found out, dog. But now we gonna be long gone."

"But what about when we go back?"

"I told you, dog, we ain't goin back."

Li'l Pit shook his head like he was hoping all this confusion would shake itself into place.

"But what about Mama?"

"Forget her."

"You can't just take me, that's stealin," Li'l Pit yelled. "That's kidnappin." People in the bus shushed him but he didn't care. "Naw. Naw. We got to get off." He ran down the aisle and off the bus.

"Fine. Go on." Love closed his eyes and gave all his weight over to the cool glass of the window. He put his headphones on to show how completely disinterested he was, but after a few seconds he opened his eyes and watched his brother out the window.

Li'l Pit walked toward the station with the determination of someone who knew he was being watched and had a point to prove. He walked up to the door just as the driver was coming out. He said something to the driver, and the man pointed inside the adobe building.

The driver let the door to the terminal shut behind Li'l Pit and labored back toward the bus under the yellow light of the parking lot. Halfway across the dirt expanse, he threw his cigarette on the ground. He hoisted his pants and cracked his neck. After taking a look up to the stars, he climbed the steps of the bus and sat down, adjusted himself in his seat, opened his side window, and pushed a button that shut the door with a loud hydraulic swish. Love stood up and climbed into the aisle.

"Wait," he yelled. The bus moved forward and swung around in a U-turn toward the parking-lot entrance.

"Wait," Love yelled again when he got to the driver.

"Calm down, son."

"My brother's still in there."

"I know he's in there. Have a seat." The bus slowed down. "I'm just pulling up to the door." Love stood there, half crouched, looking through the front windshield at the terminal. The door swung open, and Li'l Pit ran out of the building waving his arms.

"Wait," he yelled. "Wait."

Love quickly walked back to his seat and pretended to be asleep. The bus driver pulled up to the curb and opened the door again. Li'l Pit ran up the stairs. Out of breath, he bent over and put his hands on his knees.

"I thought you were leaving me," Li'l Pit spat out.

"I ain't leaving you out in the middle of nowhere, little man. Don't worry."

"I thought you were," he said again.

"No one's going to leave you."

"How am I sposed to know that?" He shook his head. "I was just in the bathroom."

"I know where you were. Wasn't I the one who told you where to go?" He started the bus moving again. "Think I forgot about you?"

Li'l Pit shook his head.

"You better take a seat now."

Li'l Pit walked back to the middle of the bus where Love was sitting, his head against the window, eyes closed, and headphones over his ears.

Li'l Pit kept walking and sat in the empty row of seats behind his brother, watching him through the crack.

As the bus drove onto the freeway ramp, Love opened his eyes, and when he saw no one next to him, he jumped up and looked around the bus. Li'l Pit laughed from behind him.

"You're hilarious," Love said, and sank back down into his seat.

They remained in their separate rows. For half an hour, as the bus traveled across the desert at night, neither of them spoke or looked to see if the other was asleep. There were no lights on in the bus, nor were there any lights outside. The darkness was complete and impenetrable, except for the few dots of light in the sky. Time went by slowly, and they never seemed to gain any ground against the desert.

"I'm hungry," Li'l Pit finally said.

"I know."

"When we gonna stop again?"

"Probably not for a long time."

"But I'm hungry," Li'l Pit whined.

"What you want me to do? Ain't you never been hungry before?"

Li'l Pit didn't say any more. He knew the hunger would pass. First it would get worse, turn into pain, like a piece of glass cutting him from inside, and then just as he would think it unbearable, it would vanish, as if his stomach had been lying to him all that time. But until then, until it stopped poking at him, he knew he couldn't get to sleep. He took a deep breath and let out a quiet chant as he did when he was banging his head to sleep: "Uh uh uh uh uh uh uh." He stopped to inhale, and after every deep breath, he let out the chant again, each time a little louder.

"Shut up, dog," Love whispered between the seats.

"Fuck you." Li'l Pit punched at Love's face, and when Love pulled back, Li'l Pit rose up and reached over the top of the seat, attacking Love, hitting and grabbing at his head.

"We sposed to be on a run," he yelled. "We sposed to be going back." Love batted his hands away. When Li'l Pit couldn't reach anymore, he kicked and punched the seat from behind.

"Settle down," the bus driver called to them. "I'm not going to have any of that on my bus."

"Stop it, dog. Stop it." Love stood up, went around to Li'l Pit's row, and grabbed at his arms.

"Naw! Fuck you!" Li'l Pit punched at him through his tears, but Love caught him by the wrists. "What you doin? Let go of me, faggot! Let go of me!"

"Quiet down back there," the bus driver said over the speaker.

Love pulled his little brother toward him and hugged him from behind, restraining him like they'd done at Los Aspirantes. He sat in the aisle seat with his brother wrapped in his arms like a straitjacket. Li'l Pit slammed his head backward against Love's chest, aiming for his chin, but Love knew this trick and avoided the blow. He held on tightly, and finally his brother stopped struggling. His body still shook, and his tears dropped onto Love's arms as he hyperventilated.

After a few minutes, Li'l Pit's chest heaved in a long, deep breath, and the convulsing also stopped. He began to hum in a monotonous tone, accompanying the hum of the bus engine. Finally, after many miles, his throat tired, and there was only the steady hum of the bus as it traveled through the darkness. They sat like that in the calm, numbing silence, uninterrupted for minutes on end, and then broken only by the occasional flash of headlights and rush of a car speeding in the other direction on the two-lane highway.

"I want to go back," Li'l Pit said quietly.

"We can't go back. Nanna don't want us there. It's just us now." Love relaxed his grip on Li'l Pit's wrists but knew better than to let him go altogether.

"Why you doin this? Why didn't you just let me be with Mama?"

" 'Cause you my heart, bro. I want to see someone I love do good." He let Li'l Pit pull his hand away to wipe his nose. " 'Sides," Love continued, "I don't have anyone else I can trust to do your job. I need someone to watch my back. That's your new job. You watch my back. You got a new job now, okay?"

A Jeep passed them and they looked over. When the tailights faded away, they saw their own dim reflections in the window, like two ghosts looking back at them.

"Okay?" Love asked. He squeezed his brother once to get a response. Li'l Pit nodded and put his wrists back into Love's hands.

CHAPTER 2B

EASTON FIXED THE water pump properly in Jackson, and they drove to Meridian by nightfall. They stayed at a boardinghouse run by a Mrs. Walker. She had lost her domestic job for registering to vote, so she had made her home into a motel by nailing a VACANCY sign onto her front porch. During Freedom Summer, the year before, the COFO workers from the movement felt obliged to keep her house full until the fall. But she rarely had any paying guests anymore, so she was very pleased to see Charles and Easton. She was an old woman with a limp, an injury she'd gotten from fighting with her past husband when he was drunk. But even with her limp, she was quick to set up a cot in the living room with a bucket on the floor for spitting, though she was the only one who chewed tobacco.

In the evening after supper, Easton drew a picture of her and gave it to her before they went to bed. For the gift, she said she'd cook them breakfast for free in the morning, although Easton told Charles she would have done that anyway. Easton lay on the cot while Charles shared the couch with a longhaired cat. They all had their eyes open and stared at the ceiling in the dark.

"I can't believe you grew up around here," Charles said.

"I didn't grow up anywhere near here. South Carolina's five hundred miles away."

"Yeah, but it's the South, man. All these places is like going into a time machine."

"No it's not."

"I mean it, man. I feel like standing up and screaming at these folks, 'What you crazy people doing down here?' Don't you know what I mean?"

"South Carolina wasn't like this."

"It had to be something like this."

"I don't know. It always seemed different. At least in the South you know who likes you and who doesn't." Easton turned on his side and closed his eyes. He lay in silence for a moment, then a dog barked twice and a bottle broke somewhere outside, which reminded him of his father, Papa Samuel, but he pushed that thought out of his head with a picture of Sandra, sitting the way he had sketched her that day on his bed, the top of her dress pulled down over her shoulders.

"I got to go," Charles said. "Where'd you say the bathroom was at?"

"Bathroom?"

"Yeah."

"Out back."

"You mean outside?"

"Just watch out for them spiders. And them cottonmouth snakes that live in the bottom of the pit."

"That's not funny." Charles pulled on his socks.

"You don't have to worry about none of that. The smell will kill you 'fore you sit down."

"I don't know how I let you talk me into coming down here."

"You're the one who wanted to come before me."

"That was for the movement, but you let Sandra drag you down."

"You don't understand."

"Damn right I don't. And I don't think you do, neither."

"Maybe not. But when the feeling's this strong, it's like you know it's got to work out right. It feels like everything is riding on it."

"I don't know how you get so excited about a White girl." Charles slipped on his shoes.

"So," Easton said, "you like girls with a big booty and nasty hair?"

"What's nasty about their hair?"

"I'm talking about objective beauty," Easton said. "I'm talking about hair that isn't all in knots, and smooth skin that isn't chapped all the time, and little firm asses and blue eyes. You're gonna tell me that sparklin blue eyes that look like a swimmin pool aren't prettier than brown holes you can't even see nothin in but your own reflection?"

"Like yours, you mean."

"Yeah, like mine. Sure. I'm not beyond self-awareness."

"You got about as much self-awareness as a floor mat. Haven't you ever been with a Black girl?"

"No, man, I couldn't."

"What you mean you couldn't?"

"I don't know. There's something about just the thought of it, makes me feel kind of wrong, you know, kind of unnatural."

"Man, you are one sorry-ass nigger."

Easton threw his shoe at him and apparently hit something vulnerable.

"Aw man, that's cruel. I've got to go." Charles stood up. "If I don't come back in ten minutes, send out the National Guard."

"Don't hold your breath before you go in," Easton called out. "You'll only end up having to take a deeper one right in the middle of it all." Charles shuffled off through the kitchen and out the back door.

Easton lay in the living room alone, but for the cat. He closed his eyes and listened, and at first there seemed nothing to listen to, but then he heard the crickets in the distance, and it made him nervous. He wiped his cheek. There was a particular smell as it cooled off at night that brought him back to sitting by the Edisto River. He took a deep breath, but he could not shake the unsafe feeling that there was something out in the night. He opened his eyes again and strained to hear better, beyond the crickets, but their creaking became louder, as if they were moving closer, filling the streets, surrounding the house. Soon their call occupied his whole mind and all the darkness around him, and he could hear and think of nothing else but their screaming at him from every direction.

The screen door slammed and the sound of the crickets receded. Charles ran in. "Oh God. Oh man." He jumped onto the couch and slid his feet under the covers. "Get this mangy old cat away from me."

"Let me ask you something, Charles." Easton cracked his fingers one by one and let out a long breath. "What do you think it means to be crazy? I don't mean all wild and crazy—I mean, just how mixed up inside your head do you have to get before you're not sane anymore?"

"Anyone who lives down here is definitely crazy."

"No, man. For real."

Charles sat propped up on the couch and gazed out the front window. The half-moon, like a torn sheet of paper, rose up over the house across the dirt road.

"You thinkin you might be crazy?" Charles asked.

"I'm just asking."

"You hearing voices? You seeing ghosts of dead people?"

"Naw, man. But I wonder. I mean, how much control over your own feelings are you supposed to have? You know what I'm saying?"

"Because you like White women?"

"No, man, I'm not talking about that!"

"Then what are you talkin about?"

"I mean about feeling confused and angry and all mixed–up like."

"Okay. I hear you."

"Yeah?" Easton sat up and looked at the shape of his friend. "I mean, like this thing with Sandra. I didn't come down here when she offered, 'cause she did me wrong, you know? I was pissed off at her, and now here I am, going down on my own to see her. It's like I can't get hold of myself. And all I can think of is, well, I'm gonna walk up to her and spit in her face, you know, 'cause I'm so angry at her for making me come all this way. But I know it can't be just her, man. I couldn't have done some stupid drive all the way across the country just 'cause of her." He shook his head repeatedly like he was trying to fight through a fog. "It's like this statue we studied about in class: this girl, she got stolen by Hades, the god of the underworld, and when she was down there, she ate some pomegranate, and then, when she was finally rescued and brought back up into the light, she still had to go back down to Hades for part of every year because she had that pomegranate inside her. You know what I mean? I've been thinking about that story ever since I decided to come back here. You don't just think about things for no reason. It must be that I couldn't help it. I just had to come here, like if I could just get down here, I could dig that little red seed out of my stomach and just . . ." Easton had his fists out in front of him like he was shaking someone by the shirt. "Man! I'm going out of my mind. I feel like I've got no sense of myself."

"Everybody feels like that."

"Not everybody."

"I know I do. I feel like I'm bustin in my own skin sometime, like my whole body wants to yell 'cause I'm not being myself. The only time I feel right is when I'm fightin the fight, like those days out at Woolcrest's, and now goin to Selma. I feel like I have a purpose. You just have to figure out what gives you purpose. Everybody feels like this. It's not crazy. Unless everybody's crazy."

"I don't know." Easton lay back down and put his hands under his head. "I can't believe everybody's walkin around feelin like this. This world would just fall apart."

"It is, brother." Charles stood up again.

"Where you going?"

"I've got to go back outside," Charles mumbled.

"Already?"

"Yes."

"Didn't you go?"

"I couldn't see nothin in there."

"Didn't you take the flashlight?"

"What are you talking about?"

"The flashlight by the door," Easton said. "You didn't take it?"

Charles didn't answer.

"Ah, man. You one sorry-ass city boy. You've got no country sense at all. Maybe you're right, maybe this ain't where we belong after all. Maybe this whole thing was a big mistake."

THEY ENTERED SELMA on Sunday afternoon. It was cold again, as if the sun had hidden its face. Easton could see his breath as he drove through the neighborhood looking for Brown's Chapel on Sylvan. They eventually found the redbrick building with its three distinctive white stone arches. A large crowd had gathered around the building, and there were four long black ambulances, like hearses with sirens on top, parked across the street.

"Maybe we're too late," Charles said as he got out.

"Do you see her?" Easton climbed on top of his car and looked over the crowd. There were only a handful of Whites, but none of them women. "Maybe she's inside."

Men, women, and children lined up in silent apprehension. Most of the men wore long overcoats, some fedora caps, sweaters, and ties. The women were also dressed formally, some with large gold earrings. A little boy went to his mother and hid in her coat. His father came and picked him up and brought him to the sidewalk crying.

"Do you see her?" Easton asked again.

"Who?"

"Sandra. I don't see her. I'm going inside."

"I'm lining up," said Charles. "This is what I came here for."

A man in a tan overcoat walked to the top of the chapel steps and addressed the crowd. A deep, concerned line ran down the middle of his forehead to the top of his nose.

"If you'd listen up here, please." He raised his hands, and an invisible wave of silence swept over the crowd. "We're going to get into two lines. One behind me—I'm John—and another behind Hosea. Remember: we are a peaceful people marching to Montgomery. Ignore the taunts and protect yourself as you've been shown. If they become violent, do not let yourself be cheapened by becoming like them. We have the moral high ground, and there will be newsmen and cameras, but Wallace has said he will not let us march to Montgomery." He stroked his thin, downturned mustache. "If anyone wishes to stay back, we won't hold it against you. I cannot promise you anything."

Easton jogged up the steps of the church, and Charles walked over to the front of the line. Before going inside, Easton turned and watched the marchers leave, the two lines of people, silent, walking into the distance like a slow funeral procession.

When they'd turned the corner and were out of sight, Easton entered the church. There were a few people praying, some by the podium, while others sat silently looking at the floor. One woman put out bandages, scissors, and tape on a table. Easton walked up to her.

"Excuse me," he said. "I was wondering if you'd seen a woman I'm looking for, a White woman."

"What's her name?"

"She's blond, with some freckles on her cheeks, skinny, and about your height."

"What's her name?"

"Sandra."

"Sandra? Yes. I may have met someone like that, but I don't know where she is. I just arrived last night with supplies and it has been pretty busy around here. She may be on the march. The march started, you know?" She looked at Easton with her eyebrows raised, like a mother telling her child it's time to go to school.

"Yes. Thank you." Easton walked around the side of the pulpit and looked out onto the main floor.

"She's probably on the march," the nurse said again.

"I already looked."

"Well maybe she was going to join up with them at the bridge."

Easton took one more look around the church and then nodded. He jogged back outside, down the steps, and up Sylvan. At Water Street, he saw the ambulances trailing the march. He ran and caught up to them just as they turned onto Broad Street.

"Make sure you got your runnin shoes on," someone yelled to him from the sidewalk. Easton turned and saw a team of White men leaning against a building.

He smiled at them and then ran between the ambulances and up to the tail of the marchers. He could see ahead of him that John and Hosea had just started up the incline of the Edmund Pettus Bridge. The two lines of marchers moved to the sidewalk even though the highway was completely empty in both directions. There was no traffic on the bridge that day, and the police kept the ambulances from following them.

Easton moved through the line slowly. After passing a few people, he stood on his toes to see if he could spot Sandra farther up front. He didn't see her, but if she was wearing a scarf over her head like many of the other women, there would be no way to distinguish her until he got up close. He pushed past more people and then jumped up to see again. As he came down, he landed on the heel of a little girl in front of him and nearly knocked her over. Everyone looked at him, too tense to speak.

"I'm sorry. I'm sorry." He picked up her white purse and handed it back to her. She took it and just stared at him, her eyes already wide with fear. He moved forward through the center of the two lines. The protests he was used to were always full of singing and shouting, but everyone here seemed peculiarly quiet and moved aside for him without a word. He'd made it more than halfway to the front of the line when he reached the top of the bridge. The marchers suddenly slowed. He looked down the decline, and there, less than a hundred yards away, blocking the street, were helmeted state troopers with gas masks, their nightsticks out in front of them. Behind them were men on horseback, guns in their holsters.

Easton stopped in his tracks. For a second, he forgot all about Sandra. The marchers continued forward, though more slowly and closer together, down the bridge toward the troopers. Easton fell into one of the lines and for the first time felt trapped within the river of people around him. He could no longer see in front of him or to the side. A middle-aged woman with a long, lean nose blinked at him as she took his hand. His arms began to shake, and he felt squeezed between this woman and the back of a man's jacket. He considered turning around, but the people were like a strong current forcing him ahead. He tried to walk on his toes to see what was happening. Photographers ran down the open street of the empty bridge, swarming around them like mosquitoes. Down below, the troopers slapped their nightsticks in their palms. Easton lowered himself back on his heels and stared again into the man's jacket. And there, on that black wool canvas, not more than six inches from his face, he pictured Ronald, bloody and beaten. The cold memory flashed into Easton's mind and made him shiver. He brushed at his cheek. But too much remembering was impossible, for the immediate danger kept him in the present.

He let go of the woman's hand, and though she did not let go of his, he shook himself loose and fell farther back in line. People bumped and jostled his shoulders as they passed. Though he'd slowed, he still reached the other side of the bridge, and Hosea and John led the lines across the street to a grassy strip in the center of the highway.

The marchers stopped ten yards away from the troopers, who looked like flies with round cans of oxygen attached to their plastic gas masks. One of the officers addressed them through a bullhorn: "It would be detrimental to your safety to continue this march, and I'm saying that this is an unlawful assembly and you have to disperse. You are ordered to disperse. Go home or go to your church. This march will not continya."

Easton started to turn around, but no one else moved, and shame held him in his place.

"Is that clear to you?" the officer yelled.

Hosea asked if he could have a few words with the man.

"I've got nothin further to say to you," the officer replied.

They all stayed put. It wasn't too late to go back, Easton thought. To one side of the highway was a Volkswagen van with the ABC emblem on it. The press men were separated and placed in front of a car dealership. In addition to the reporters, there were almost a hundred White spectators, and farther back was a place for Negro spectators.

Easton saw a familiar face in the group of White spectators. It looked like Sandra with sunglasses on and a scarf, but he could not be sure. She turned away quickly, as if she had not wanted to be seen, but then he saw another woman who looked like Sandra too, but larger.

He was still looking into the crowd when the troopers moved forward toward the marchers, slapping their nightsticks in their hands like starving men licking their lips. Their ranks began to gather together in the middle to meet Hosea and John head-on like a battering ram. Easton felt the people around him tighten together even more, squeezing the breath out of him. The troopers kept coming as the marchers stood their ground. It did not seem possible: even looking into each other's eyes, it seemed as though neither side believed it could happen, and yet it seemed unavoidable, like the drivers of two trucks heading toward each other without brakes, bracing themselves for impact. The troopers walked right into Hosea and John, pushing them back. The people in front were smashed into Easton, and the people behind him pushed him forward. The line collapsed into itself, and those in the front were knocked to the ground. There was screaming all around as the troopers continued to advance, stepping on the fallen marchers, beating them down with their nightsticks. At first Easton was in shock, but then others around him turned and ran back toward the bridge.

The White spectators cheered.

He turned and ran as fast as he could, faster than many of the others around him, and yet he heard the officers on horseback now, catching up to him from behind. One swung down with his club and hit him in the back of the head. The blow seemed to smash his brain into the upper palate of his mouth. He fell to the ground and heard shots, and then a cloud of tear gas filled the air. His hands burned and ripped against the pavement. The officers on foot were still advancing. Easton stood up, pressing his torn palms against his ears to stop the pain in his head. Just before the smoke reached him, he turned and saw Charles and two other men carrying an injured woman to the side of the road. He went back toward her but choked on the gas and pulled his shirt over his face. The men on horseback circled below them again and chased the crowd. Easton turned and ran up the bridge, but the sounds of the horses clopping on the pavement grew louder, so he tensed himself, ready for another blow to the back of his head, his temples already pounding with pain.

As he got closer to the Selma side of the bridge, the men whom Easton had seen lounging against the building earlier now blocked the way. They attacked the fleeing crowd with whips and electric cattle prods, but the horsemen and tear gas behind the marchers forced them into the ambush.

The little girl he'd stepped on earlier was in front of him, her braided pigtails whipping from side to side. Easton crouched with his hand on his head and followed her through the posse. They seemed to leave her untouched. But then his eye caught the eye of one man with a bullwhip, and as if that momentary connection had irrevocably fated them together, the man hollered and ran toward Easton, his hairy arm raised. With a reaction deeper than thought, Easton ducked behind the little girl and shielded himself. She screamed, as much at Easton as at the attacker. The whip sliced the air and cut her neck. The man froze in a moment of shock, and Easton dashed past the girl.

He ran forward again blindly, not knowing any longer which direction it was to the church. He ran through the streets of Selma with screams behind and around him. He ran as fast as his tired legs would take him, and as if a tunnel surrounded him, he saw nothing but the light of a clearing far off in front of him that he had to reach. He ran for that clearing, but never seemed to close in on it as the noise continued to suffocate him. He turned the corner on to a side street and there was a loud crash behind him. He put his hands over his ears as the throbbing became a ringing and the ringing became a high squeal, like the long, pained whistle of a train. The tunnel around him narrowed, and the clearing in the distance became more and more remote until finally it closed and there was nothing ahead of him but darkness.

WHEN HE CAME to, he was inside of Brown's Chapel again, in a makeshift infirmary where doctors and nurses bandaged people's ribs and wrists and carried others out on ambulance stretchers. His face was pressed into the white uniform of a nurse's stomach as she wrapped his head with cool, wet gauze. The relief was so great that he wanted to reach out and put his arms around her and fall asleep against her belly as he used to in Ruby's lap. She stepped away to dip more gauze in a bucket of water, the back of her neck visible below a straight line of blond hair. It was Sandra.

She hadn't been on the march at all. She'd been safe in this church with all the angels looking over her. He could feel his head start to throb again and he closed his eyes. This was the woman he'd traveled two thousand miles to see. She looked different, though. He couldn't be sure he wasn't hallucinating. She wore glasses and had cut her hair. She directed another nurse to bring her a pair of scissors.

She finished wrapping his head and looked at him, her face filled with concern. He turned away. She dipped a towel in the bucket of water and wiped down his chest, which he realized was naked.

"You need to go to the hospital," she said. "You probably have a concussion."

"I thought I saw you at the front of the march."

"No. I've been here. We listened on the walkie-talkie. Your tooth's broken. Doesn't it hurt?"

He reached up to touch it. "I thought you would be in the march."

She shook her head. "SNCC decided not to be a part of it because we knew something like this would happen. I didn't even know you were coming."

He lay back in the chair. He was sure there was somebody laughing nearby—or were they crying? He didn't want to open his eyes to figure it out.

"What happened out there?" she asked him.

"We were surrounded. Ambushed."

"Oh God," she said. "God. I knew this would happen."

He opened his eyes just enough to see her face close to his, washing the cuts off his cheek. She was focused on the job, concerned, but like a careful archaeologist. She went to the sink and wrung out the towel, then returned to stand in front of him.

"Why weren't you marching?" he asked.

"What do you mean?"

"You're the one who said I should come."

"I thought you decided not to."

"I did."

"But you came."

He stared at her face, her puzzled look, as though she could not even fathom his motivation. He couldn't tell her, not if it wasn't obvious to her already. But to come all this way and not be sure, not force the point.

"I came for you."

"For me?" She stepped back from him with the towel to her chest. "You didn't come for me."

"Yes I did."

"Not for me."

He didn't reply.

"But I didn't ask you to come for me." She shook her head as if she were being accused of causing an awful accident. His head pounded again. He could see in her eyes the same frightened look she had when she'd left his bedroom, as if she were being forced into some obligation. She would only resent him more now. He must have seemed pathetic, like a beggar—exactly what he had sworn he'd never be, especially to her.

Charles trudged into the infirmary cradling the little girl whom Easton had used as a shield. He laid her on a table and then went back outside. Easton grabbed the towel from Sandra's hand and covered his face.

"I don't know why I came," he said. He stood up, his head still dizzy. He staggered to his shirt, which hung from the handle of a cabinet. He put it on, and when Charles came in again, he took his arm.

"Come on, man," Easton said. "We're leaving."

"What?"

"I'm taking off." He was bent forward as if he couldn't hold up the weight of his head.

"Where are you going?" Sandra said, but Easton didn't answer her, saying instead to Charles, "Are you coming, man?"

"But we're right in the middle of it," Charles said. "There are a hundred and fifty officers with rifles and shotguns out on the street."

"Well, I'm taking off. I've had enough. You were right. You've been right all along."

"About what? Where you gonna go?"

"Wherever."

Charles hesitated and looked at Sandra.

"You can get a ride with me or someone else around here," she said to him.

Easton turned sharply and stood up straight with a rage greater than his pain. He put his hands on her shoulders and pushed her to the wall. He gripped her so hard that she shrank down.

"Why are you doing this?" he yelled. "Tell me why you are doing this!" A sharp pain shot through his head with every word.

"What?"

"I mean all this! Why did you come all the way to Alabama? I don't get it. I don't get why you are here with all of us. Why don't you get out of the way and let us take care of our own problems? You're one of them. You're the enemy, don't you see that? When all these niggers look at you, you know what they see? They see some spoiled rich White girl who's coming in for a little guilt time, and then you'll go back into your daddy's safe White world."

"Hey, brother," Charles said. "Let the sister be."

"I am not your brother, *brothah*." He pushed Sandra away in disgust. "And she is not our sister."

He looked around the room, and everyone was staring at him as if he'd changed into some sort of werewolf.

"Why don't you stay?" Sandra said. "You're hurt."

"No. I'm not hurt. You didn't hurt me. I'm fine. Don't ever think about me again." He stormed toward the door, hiding his face as he passed the little girl, a nurse dabbing at her bleeding neck with iodine.

THE PAIN THROBBED inside Easton, compounding the confusion. He drove the residential streets of Selma until he realized that the main road was the blocked bridge. He pulled into a gas station, parked by the air pump, and stared at the wooden fence in front of him, his mind still trying to come to some resting place, some sure decision about what he needed to do.

Nothing seemed to pull him, as though he were an empty shell without a clear sense of himself. What did he know for sure about who he was? He wasn't certain how he felt about Sandra or the movement or school or art. It all seemed to be about something else that wasn't him. Every direction he wanted to turn felt full of half-truths and ulterior motives that he couldn't bear. There wasn't one thing that felt pure and true to himself. What did he have at that moment that he knew was good and pure and himself? He had the car, which he'd built with his own sweat and the knowledge of how to do it. And he had the trip, this trip that had destroyed everything, but was inside him. It was still inside him. Seeing Sandra had only made it worse. In some way, he had to get it out. He leaned his pounding head onto the steering wheel and closed his eyes.

It was getting into evening, and the crickets were creaking softly beyond the station and the houses. Somewhere between resting and dreaming, Easton pictured Ronald's face again, and then he remembered the night five years ago. He was almost fourteen, lying in bed, falling asleep. His room was right next to Ruby's, so he was awakened when Ronald climbed in through her window from the porch, breathing hard and laughing. It was a few days after Ronald's article about the pesticides came out in the paper.

Easton got out of bed, crept to the door, and peeked into Ruby's room. It was lit by the moon, and he could see their shapes. His half sister slept naked in the summer, and he often watched her make love to Ronald. She held open the muslin spread at the top as Ronald tunneled his way down, kissing and tickling her pregnant belly.

"Shh. Love E right in there," Ruby said.

Easton stepped back behind the wall for a second, holding his breath as Ruby got up and closed the door. But as soon as he heard her walk away, he crouched down onto his knees and looked through the keyhole.

Laughing, Ruby flung herself onto the bed as Ronald undressed, carefully folding his slacks into quarters and placing them on his shirt and socks. He got in bed and they began to kiss.

"Your breath smell like tomatoes," she whispered. He nodded but did not stop kissing her. They moved together for a while and then threw the covers off their sweaty bodies. They were joined only at the hips and where their fingers traced along each other's warm skin.

Easton went back to his bed and touched himself, thinking of his half sister's dark black body heaving in pleasure. With the song of crickets returning to lull his mind, he fell asleep. Not long after, from within a dream, he heard tires rolling slowly over the pebbles outside the house. Car doors opened but did not shut. The porch stairs creaked. He sat up and stared at a small circle of light across the ceiling, not sure if he was yet awake. The crickets still screamed in his ears. Then something crashed through the window in the other room. Easton jumped up and ran into the room to see.

"What was that?" he asked. A chair lay on the floor in the middle of broken glass.

"Get under the bed, Easton," Ronald said. He stood and pulled on his slacks, his eyes wide. A man with a light strapped onto his forehead entered though the bedroom door and another man climbed in the broken window. Easton rolled under the bed frame as he'd been told. He could see everything as his face rested against the dusty floorboards.

Ronald charged at the man in the door, and a dark bar hit him in the head. Wetness sprayed Easton's cheek and Ruby screamed from the bed above him. More men ran into the room from all sides. Easton heard the swish of the bar through the air again, and Ronald fell to the floor beside him, holding his head.

"Stan, weh dat gun?" a voice asked.

"Here."

"You tell me how our chilren spose to eat. I got four chilren, you ugly piece of black shit." The shot from the gun shook the floor and Ruby screamed again.

The men surrounded the bed, their dirty boots lined up close to Easton's face. He moved under the middle of the mattress and shut his eyes.

"Free piece of poontang," one of them said.

"We aren't like that," a second man said to him. "We done what was right. We done justice. Now let's go."

"But she saw everything. She seen who we are."

Easton watched one pair of boots lift from the floor, and the bed creaked as the man crawled upon it.

"You don't live here no more. You hear? Go far away. Leave for your own good."

There was no answer.

The man crawled off the bed and they all left the room.

Easton listened to the boots shuffle out of the house and down the porch. Doors slammed shut, the car started, and the engine whined in reverse. Easton slowly reached up to his cheek and wiped at the wet spray of Ronald's blood.

A MAN KNOCKED on the passenger window and Easton jumped. It was a White gas-station attendant. Easton rolled down the window a crack.

"You should get on home," the man said. He was young, Easton's age, his hands dark with oil. "There's a curfew for Negroes and they'll arrest you, even if you're drivin."

"How can I get toward Montgomery? They got the bridge closed down."

"Just take this road and turn left. It follows Route 80. You can get back on after a few miles down."

"Thank you."

"My pleasure." The man wiped his hands in a rag and walked back to the station.

Easton started his car and backed out of the parking lot. He didn't decide to go anywhere for sure, just to get going, but he knew he couldn't return to California yet; something was still unsettled. So he drove east through the backwoods as he was told, until he reached the next town and got onto the highway.

His sense of being in a dream remained. The dusk of evening lit the side of the highway, dense with stripped trees just beginning their budding. The white, gray, and brown branches pointed in a thousand directions, but they were beautiful and calming in their stillness. Row after row of trees waited confidently for the spring to renew them, their bare arms toward the sky. After his dream, the recent past of the march was not as sharply in focus for him as the more distant past of his childhood. But now it was not the childhood of Ronald's death or of Papa Samuel's beatings; it was the clouded, removed feeling of drifting through a less complicated world.

The sky was large and open above the road as he traveled farther into the countryside. Hidden in that thicket by the highway were wooden shacks and brick tract homes. Somewhere a boy searched for something to do, trying to start fires by striking rocks together and then, with frustration, throwing the rocks at lizards that dashed for cover under the mulch of pine needles and dried leaves. Somewhere in the woods, as in Norma, there was a distant river running over brown rocks, and lakes with catfish twitching their whiskers in the stagnant pools. Easton remembered standing as a child with Ronald by the side of those pools, holding a stick for a fishing rod, to which he'd tied a piece of string and a hook. Even with no bait, at least once a week, a catfish would bite that hook as it snapped the surface of the water like a mosquito. At least once a week, he'd hold that fish in his hands, remove the hook, and take it home to show his mother and father.

CHAPTER 2C

FOR THREE MORE months, Lida and Marcus stayed in Gina and David's living room. Lida lay next to Marcus one night on the couch in the dark and held her pregnant stomach. Inside was this person growing, pushing her body out of shape. The closer she got to being a mother, the more she wished she could push it back down into itself. She would be glad if it wasn't a girl, but she wished it didn't have to be a boy either. A girl would get nothing but taken advantage of in this world. But a boy—how was she supposed to love this boy, this man-to-be? She couldn't even bring herself to love Marcus. She used to think she loved him, when she lay with him and had that feeling of forgetting in his arms, but was that love? It was not toward him that she felt something at those moments, but away from everything else. It was maybe the closest she could get.

The baby kicked. It was a boy, she could tell: obstinate, aggressive. She couldn't teach a boy not to be a man, just as she could not keep a girl from being used by men. The world had already made up its mind, and it was much bigger than her own desires. The only thing she could do was to drink and smoke to make it small. That's what Gina had done with Malcolm, so he wouldn't hurt as much coming out.

It was after three o'clock in the morning when Marcus came home from practicing with David and the band at Eli's. They were preparing for a short tour of the blues clubs from Santa Cruz to L.A., a three-week circuit in preparation for a bigger one to the Midwest later. David said that before any record company would sign them, they had to get their name out and build a following.

Marcus woke Lida up, as he did every night when he came home, sliding under the covers on the couch and then starting to toss and turn. It wasn't much use getting back to sleep when she felt so warm anyway. She got off the couch and lay on the floor. Her back had hurt for months, but she wasn't about to go beg her mother for her old room again.

There was a gunshot outside, but Marcus just turned and put the pillow over his head. Lida rolled on her side and got up to get some food. She had to be quiet because the door to Gina and David's room was at the other end of the kitchen. She opened the refrigerator and stared at the food. They each brought home something from Lucky's, so the refrigerator was always full, mostly with snacks.

She took out a carton of cherry ice cream and a can of beer. The TV was at the foot of the couch, but it didn't seem to bother Marcus when she watched it with the volume low this late at night. She sat on the floor a foot away from the TV and wrapped a knitted blanket around her shoulders as she sipped the cool beer and ate ice cream. The movie was a black and white from the fifties. A rich White woman who talked funny was supposed to get married to a guy who talked funny.

Gina came out of the kitchen in her slippers and bathrobe. When she saw Lida, she went and got a beer and then came and joined her on the floor.

"What you watchin?"

"Some bullshit." The flickering TV lit up Lida's face.

"I couldn't sleep neither before Malcolm come out. Let me touch." She put her hand on Lida's belly. "I don't feel him. He must be sleepin."

"Yeah, he's sleeping, now that I'm up. David wake you up?"

"Shots. Or maybe sympathy feelin for you, I guess."

Lida smiled and laid her head on Gina's shoulder. She continued to stare at the TV. The woman in the movie went into a little house to change into a bathing suit and swim in her pool.

"I don't want to have this baby," Lida said.

"Girl, it's a little late for that now. You just about due next month."

"I know."

"It ain't so bad." Gina rubbed Lida's head.

"Shush!" Marcus yelled and pulled the pillow tighter over his ears. The two women looked at him and then went back to talking.

"Don't you want a baby, someone who's gonna love you with all its might?" Gina asked.

"No. I don't want nothin to love me like that." Lida sipped her beer. "I can't do nothin but let it down. I can't hardly take care of my own self. And look at this place. What kind of world is Malcolm growing up in, with people shootin outside and all us livin here? Now we gonna have two babies in this house? Uh-uh, I ain't lookin forward to it."

"Honey," Gina said. "You just feelin low-down, that's all. You gonna get past it."

"I'm thinking of just jumping off the Bay Bridge."

"You got to jump off the Golden Gate," Marcus said from under the pillow. "That's the proper way to do it."

"You shush up," Gina said.

"All right, honey," Lida said to Marcus. "I'll make it the Golden Gate just for you."

"Why don't you go do it now, so I can get some sleep."

"Fine." She stood up and went to the front door, dressed in just her shorts and a large pink shirt.

"Shut up, Marcus. Lida, you ain't goin nowhere." Gina grabbed her sleeve.

"Let go a me."

"See now, Marcus?" Gina yelled. "See what you doin? You a pig, Marcus, tellin your wife with a child to go and jump off a bridge."

"Shut up, bitch."

"Don't you call me a bitch in my own house."

Marcus took the pillow off his face. "This our house too. We pay our rent and we sleep out here on the couch and get no sleep. So I'll call you a bitch if I want to."

David came out from the kitchen, his shirt off and his blue jeans unbuckled. He kept his eyes closed and yawned. "Why you callin my wife a bitch, Marcus?"

" 'Cause she is one. She tellin me how I'm supposed to talk to my own wife."

Lida opened the front door and walked out of the apartment.

"See what you doin?" Gina yelled. "He told her to jump off the bridge. Now is that the way you supposed to talk to your wife?"

"Goddamn." Marcus put the pillow back over his head. "I hope she just do it. I'm so sick of her talkin about it. I wish she'd just do it, if she's going to, and get it all over with."

David scratched his stomach. "Damn, Marcus, you ought to let up on her."

"So now you're telling me?"

David waved his hand and went out after Lida. He followed her down the stairs and found her on the bottom landing, sitting on the cement floor and crying. He sat down next to her without touching her.

"I remember how Gina was," he said.

Lida didn't say anything until she could keep herself from crying. They sat beside each other, the moths flying into the light above.

"I feel awful," she finally said.

"I know."

"I mean it. I can't take this shit."

"It's just another few weeks and then you'll be light again."

"I can't take another few weeks. You all out every night till forever and I got to have this child. I need to sleep. I need something. I need something more than just this beer and shit. What you got on you?"

"What you mean?"

"Don't play with me, David. I need something."

"You don't really want to get back into that again, do you?"

"What kinda pusher are you? Just tell me what you got for me or leave me alone."

"I got a cap on me." David dug down into his pocket and pulled up a small baggy with a twisted-off corner of heroin.

"I'll pay you later. Just turn me on now to get through tonight. Just a little taste, not to get hooked again."

David handed her the cap and she opened the baggy. She stuck her nose into the corner and sniffed, alternating with each nostril until it was gone. Then she leaned back and put her head against the wall.

"I feel so awful," she said.

"You don't look so awful."

"Ha."

"Really. You always look good."

"Very funny."

"I always tell Marcus you're the finest woman I've ever seen."

Lida wiped her nose and looked over at him out of the corners of her eyes.

"I ain't lyin. You look twice as good pregnant as most women look regular."

"Hmmm," she said, and closed her eyes.

David put out his hand and touched her shoulder. He let it stay there for a second and then, as if he were afraid to keep it there too long, he took it off.

"You don't feel bad to me. You feel pretty good."

She laughed.

"Come on," he said. "Come on upstairs." He stood and reached his hands down to her. She shook her head.

"I don't want to see him," she said.

"You don't have to. He'll be asleep. Come on. You can stay in our bed." She opened her eyes and looked at him suspiciously.

"Really," he said. "Come on."

She took his hands and let him pull her up.

"I'm so tired," she said.

"You tired now, just wait till you have the kid. 'Baby' ain't a four-letter word for nothing. Shit. You two got to get yourself a place. It just isn't right for you to be in our living room raising a child. It's no wonder you two always on each other."

She held on to the handrail and took the first step, and he went up behind her, supporting her, his hand on her lower back.

TWO WEEKS LATER, Marcus went to see Ruby. It was a Sunday, and Cranston was alive with people in their nicest clothes coming back from church. First he stopped at the corner market. He wanted to buy gum to freshen his mouth, anything to lessen the offense Ruby already felt toward him. He also bought a rose to give her.

Ruby's was the seventh house down on the left side. He couldn't believe his own nervousness, as if he were going to ask Ruby for Lida's hand in marriage. He walked up the steps and rang the doorbell, then brushed at a spot on his slacks where some water had dripped off the rose. As he expected, nobody came to the door. Ruby sometimes worked on the weekends, but this was right after church so she was bound to be coming home soon. He'd planned it this way so she couldn't ignore him by not answering the door.

He sat on the top step and picked the thorns off the rose stem as families walked past. The sun shone brightly, and he nodded at the women in their hats, and they smiled back at him with his flower. He'd known most of these women as kids, and now they had kids of their own.

"How you doin, Marcus?" one of the women yelled.

"Fine. Fine. How you doin?" He shaded his eyes with his hand to get a better look at her, but he still didn't recognize her.

"Fine," she said. "We moved into Acorn Projects just a few months ago."

"Seem like everybody moving there, these days."

"Sure do. All the rich movin out and all the rest goin to Acorn." Her husband pulled at her arm. "Well, good to see you. Take care now."

"You too." She walked away and he stared after her, trying to remember something about who she was. So when Ruby came down the street, he didn't see her at first. She wore a white dress that she'd embroidered with shell patterns. It fit snug around her large shoulders and hips.

"Lawd, if it isn't the prodigal son hisself come home. Help me up these stairs here, Marcus." She seemed as relaxed and happy to see him as if she had set up the meeting herself. Marcus took one of her arms as she pulled on the railing with the other.

"Whoo-wee, them stairs keep gettin taller." She wiped her brow and then dug in her purse for her keys. "Preacher said today was the day we need to start forgivin our enemies, but then again he always sayin that."

"See now, that's what I don't understand. Why am I your enemy, Mrs. Washington?" She opened the door, pulled her swollen feet out of her shoes, and placed each shoe neatly next to the doormat. Marcus did the same. Ruby glanced at the rose as he struggled to get his shoe off with one hand.

"I guess that flower's for me. Why don't you get a jar from the kitchen and fill it up with water." She sat down in the rocking chair and closed her eyes. "Why don't you get me a glass of water too, while you're at it."

Marcus got two jam jars out of the cupboard and filled them with water. He brought them into the living room and put the rose on the table between them. He had to break off the lower part of the stem to make it stay.

"Just give me mines over here on this stand. Now hand me that Bible right next to it." Marcus delivered the water and handed her the leather-bound Bible, then sat down on the couch. Ruby raised her reading glasses onto her nose and took a moment to page through St. Luke.

"What you make of this, Marcus?" She pointed at the place on the page and waited for him to stand up again. He came around behind her and read:

" 'If any man come to me, and hate not his father, and mother, and wife, and children, and brethren, and sisters, yea, and his own life also, he cannot be my disciple.' Now what you think that mean? Christ hisself say that."

Marcus shook his head.

"The preacher told us that you must first plan before you go on and build a tower or fight some war, but I still don't see how that's got anything to do with it. Lessen it means you got to be down before you can follow the Savior."

"Could be that, Mrs. Washington."

"Marcus, you my son-in-law now, so call me Ruby. I see you wearin your Lucky's pin and got yourself all fussed up for me so that I'll say you done changed your ways."

"Yes ma'am." Marcus wished he had his guitar in front of him. He always felt better with his guitar between himself and others.

"You lost but now you found. That what you sayin?"

"Yes ma'am." Ruby took a sip of water and put it back on the cast-iron stand.

"Lida at work?"

"No. No, she's not feeling so well right now."

"She sick?"

"No. Nothin like that. She just gettin down to those last weeks, you know. Ready to have the child. That's why I think she needs to be here. It ain't good for her where we're staying. It's too crowded and she needs some better space."

Ruby rocked back in the chair and nodded her head. "You got a name for him yet?"

"I was thinking about a name from the Bible." He smiled at her. "I was thinking about Paul."

Ruby stopped rocking and looked at him angrily. "What you know 'bout the Bible, Marcus? You haven't been to church since the day you was last in your father's house. You leave your own and take mines from me and come around here expectin that I'm gonna fall right into your little game? Paul! You tell me one thing you know 'bout Paul."

Marcus took a deep breath and patted down his hair. "He was a friend of Jesus."

"Sure 'nough. That all you got to say about him? You gonna name your very own son after him and you don't know nothin about the name. How you know he ain't some sort a thief or devil?" Marcus shook his head. "I'll tell you who he was: he try and convert all the Jews, but they won't listen. He travel all 'round the world teachin in the name of the Lawd. An he seen Jesus rise up again from the dead. He was bitten by a poison snake, and nothin happen to him 'cause he had God's promise."

"I remember that part."

"You remember the poison." Ruby sat back in her chair. "Well, I hope so. I hope you remember all that poison you put into yourself. Something 'bout where you been. You can't just let go of the past and think it all gonna be fine."

"I'm all through messin around with that junk, Mrs. Washington. I know you don't care for me much, but I'm askin for Lida, for the grandchild's sake."

"I already said she could move back in here."

"You did?"

"Yes, I did. She the one who ran out the house and said it wasn't gone be no good. She went on screamin 'bout me never sayin Love E's name again. She didn't tell you? Lawd, you don't even know your own wife."

"But she said you wouldn't let her move in if I came along."

"That was a long time ago."

"So you'll let us move in?"

Ruby put the Bible down on the table. She rubbed her eyes with the palms of her hands, then let her fingers drag down over her face.

"You got to answer one question first, Marcus."

"All right." Marcus moved to the edge of the couch.

"You got to tell me why Lida hate Love E so."

Marcus looked away from her, up to the pictures of her family, her parents, and Easton. He remembered all those times Easton let him come over and use his records. He wiped his hands on his pants and stood up.

"Let me just get us some more water and I'll tell you why," he said.

"You better stay right there and answer my question or you can just keep going right on out of my house for good."

He sat back on the couch and nodded, looking again at the records stacked up under the pictures. He knew exactly where to find *Electric Ladyland*.

"She didn't hate Easton," Marcus said. "She didn't hate him."

"Then why can't I even say his name around her? Why she leave and go live with you? What you tellin me these lies for? God's lookin down on you now, Marcus, and you got a chance to come clean. And I'm tellin you that if you want to live here, you got to answer my question."

Marcus reached out and tore the remaining thorn off the rose. Without a place to throw it, he dabbed its point onto the tip of his finger, testing its sharpness.

"She was just jealous of all the attention you give him. That's what she told me."

Ruby took a deep breath and stared at him. He couldn't tell if she was waiting for more or just contemplating whether to believe him.

"She came to me because I treated her special," he added. "She always felt like you loved him more than her. That's what she told me, at least," which was part of the truth, so he was able to look her in the eye.

She stood up in front of the photographs with her back to Marcus. There was a long silence as she studied the pictures. She reached up and straightened the one of Easton, then Corbet's and her own, as if she had thrown the whole lot of them off center by moving just one. Marcus wasn't sure if she planned on answering him or had even heard his response.

"I guess I see how that might be," she finally said. "It was always hard for me to look at Lida without thinking of Ronald and bein pained, and maybe that's why I didn't show her 'nough how I love her."

"Well, I can understand that. I'm sure she could understand that." He threw the thorn in the jam jar, then stood up and brushed off his hands. Ruby turned back to him.

"That can't be all of it, though. I mean, she didn't just hate me, she hated him, too."

"Sure."

"So what he do?"

"Well, he wasn't all that nice to her always."

"How wasn't he nice? How so?"

"You know how it is between family."

"What he do? He yell at her? He yell at everyone now and then. She can't hold none a that against him. It must a been something."

"She just wanted to feel special, that's all."

Ruby shook her head and took another sip of water. She looked out the front window, through the new white lace curtains, at the faceless shapes passing on the sidewalk, the bright sun behind them. The light wasn't too bright to look at when it came in filtered by those curtains. It was softer and colored the room with a tolerable glow.

"I guess I could see how I loved my brother too much," she said. "That's a sin I can live with. I guess I sinned 'cause I thought he was perfect. Nobody is perfect, the Lawd knows that. It won't hurt me none to think of him as more human. I can live that way. I don't see why Lida can't even hear his name no more, though. But comin from her position, I guess she think he could do no wrong in my mind."

"That's how it is," Marcus said. He watched the thorn float in the water.

"I'm sure my grandson gonna do some wrong someday too, but he have a much better chance comin up in this home than out in that small place of yours." She sat back down in her chair.

"That's all I care about."

"Yes. I can see how I was always leavin her with Love E and she think I don't love her 'nough. Well he gone now. I guess I got to go on with the living. You got to let her know I won't say his name 'round her if I can help it."

"I will do that. I will. You think we might move in here tomorrow?"

"Tomorrow?" Ruby sat up in her chair and put her hand to her collar. "You believe she might want to come back so soon?"

"Well, with all you said."

Ruby stood up and went to the bottom of the stairs as if she were on her way to do a chore, then paced over to the front door and back to the couch.

"I guess that's fine if she want to come."

"Now don't be surprised when she comes in. She's not feeling so well. Promise you won't say anything about how she looks sick or any-thing. She's just getting ready to have our child."

"All right. All right. I just have to go into her room and dust off. I kept everything the same for her, but she may not want all her old things in there from before." She turned to Marcus with her hands clasped in front of her, almost reaching out to him. "It seem as if some-one finally hear me up there. Let me ask you, Marcus, what do you think of callin your chile Ronal, after his grandaddy?"

"That was the other name we were thinking about."

"Never mind, it's no matter." She had turned before he'd even an-swered and started up the stairs again.

"Don't go to no trouble, Mrs. Washington. She'll just be so happy to come home."

She stopped at the top of the stairs and looked down at him. "You think so?"

"Sure."

"All right." Ruby nodded and walked slowly toward Lida's room. "You go ahead and let yourself out," she yelled behind her. "Your house too, now, I suppose."

SANTA RITA JAIL

I'LL READ A 1905 oral narrative collected in *The Life Stories of Undistinguished Americans as Told by Themselves:*

I am a Negro and was born sometime during the war in Elbert County, Ga., and I reckon by this time I must be a little over forty years old. My mother was not married when I was born, and I never knew who my father was or anything about him. Shortly after the war my mother died, and I was left to the care of my uncle. All this happened before I was eight years old, and so I can't remember very much about it. . . .

I was a man nearly grown before I knew how to count from one to one hundred. I was a man nearly grown before I ever saw a colored teacher. I never went to school a day in my life. Today I can't write my own name, though I can read a little. I was a man nearly grown before I ever rode on a railroad train, and then I went on an excursion from Elberton to Athens. What was true of me was true of hundreds of other Negroes around me—'way off there in the country, fifteen or twenty miles from the nearest town.

When I reached twenty-one the Captain told me I was a free man, but he urged me to stay with him. He said he would treat me right, and pay me as much as anybody else would. The Captain's son and I were about the same age, and the Captain said that, as he had owned my mother and uncle during slavery, and as his son didn't want me to leave them (since I had been with them so long), he wanted me to stay with the old family. And I stayed. I signed a contract—that is, I made my mark—for one year. The Captain was to give me $3.50 a week, and furnish me a little house on the plantation—a one-room log cabin similar to those used by his other laborers.

During that year I married Mandy. For several years Mandy had been the house-servant for the Captain, his wife, his son and his three daughters, and they all seemed to think a good deal of her. As an evidence of their regard they gave us a suite of furniture, which cost about $25, and we set up housekeeping in one of the Captain's two-room shanties. I thought I was the biggest man in Georgia. Mandy still kept her place in the "Big House" after our marriage. We did so well for the first year that I renewed my contract for the second year, and for the third, fourth and fifth year I did the same thing. Before the end of the fifth year the Captain had died, and his son, who had married some two or three years before, took charge of the plantation. Also, for two or three years, this son had been serving at Atlanta in some big office to which he had been elected. I think it was in the Legislature or something of that sort—anyhow, all the people called him Senator. At the end of the fifth year the Senator suggested that I sign up a contract for ten years; then, he said, we wouldn't have to fix up papers every year. I asked my wife about it; she consented; and so I made a ten-year contract.

Not long afterward the Senator had a long, low shanty built on his place. A great big chimney, with a wide, open fireplace, was built at one end of it and on each side of the house, running lengthwise, there was a row of frames or stalls just large enough to hold a single mattress. The places for these mattresses were fixed one above the other; so that there was a double row of these stalls or pens on each side. They looked for all the world like stalls for horses. Since then I have seen cabooses similarly arranged as sleeping quarters for railroad laborers.

Nobody seemed to know what the Senator was fixing for. All doubts were put aside one bright day in April when about forty able-bodied Negroes, bound in iron chains, and some of them handcuffed, were brought out to the Senator's farm in three big wagons. They were quartered in the long, low shanty, and it was afterward called the stockade. This was the beginning of the Senator's convict camp. These men were prisoners who had been leased by the Senator from the State of Georgia at about $200 each per year, the State agreeing to pay for guards and physicians, for necessary inspection, for inquests, all rewards for escaped convicts, the cost of litigation and all other incidental expenses.

When I saw these men in shackles, and the guards with their guns, I was scared nearly to death. I felt like running away, but I didn't know where to go. And if there had been any place to go to, I would have had to leave my wife and child behind. We free laborers held a meeting. We all wanted to quit. We sent a man to tell the Senator about it. Word came back that we were all under contract for ten years and that the Senator would hold us to the letter of that contract, or put us in chains and lock us up—the same as the other prisoners. It was made plain to us by some white people we talked to that in the contracts we had signed we had all agreed to be locked up in a stockade at night or at any other time that our employer saw fit; further, we learned that we could not lawfully break our contract for any reason and go and hire ourselves to somebody else without the consent of our employer; and, more than that, if we got mad and ran away, we could be run down by bloodhounds, arrested without process of the law, and be returned to our employer, who, according to the contract, might beat us brutally or administer any kind of punishment that he thought proper. In other words, we had sold ourselves into slavery—and what could we do about it? The white folks had all the courts, all the guns, all the hounds, all the railroads, all the telegraph wires, all the newspapers, all the money, and nearly all the land—and we had only our ignorance, our poverty and our empty hands. We decided that the best thing to do was to shut our mouths, say nothing, and go back to work. And most of us worked side by side with those convicts during the remainder of the ten years. . . .

The troubles of the free laborers began at the close of the ten-year period. To a man they all refused to sign new contracts—even for one year, not to say anything of ten years. And just when we thought that our bondage was at an end we found that it had really just begun. Two or three years before, or about a year and a half after the Senator had started his camp, he had established a large store, which was called the commissary. All of us free laborers were compelled to buy our supplies—food, clothing, etc.—from that store. We never used any money in our dealings with the commissary, only tickets or orders, and we had a general settlement once each year, in October. In this store we were charged all sorts of high prices for goods, because every year we would come out in debt to our employer. If not that, we seldom had more than $5 or $10 coming to us—and that for a whole year's work. Well, at the close of the tenth year, when we kicked and meant to leave the Senator, he said to some of us with a smile (and I never will forget that smile—I can see it now):

"Boys, I'm sorry you're going to leave me. I hope you will do well in your new places—so well that you will be able to pay me the little balances which most of you owe me."

Word was sent out for all of us to meet him at the commissary at 2 o'clock. There he told us that, after we had signed what he called a written acknowledgment of our debts, we might go and look for new places. The storekeeper took us one by one and read to us statements of our accounts. According to the books there was no man of us who owed the Senator less than $100; some of us were put down for as much as $200. I owed $165, according to the bookkeeper. These debts were not accumulated during one year, but ran back for three and four years, so we were told—in spite of the fact that we understood that we had had a full settlement at the end of each year. But no one of us would have dared to dispute a white man's word—oh, no; not in those days. Besides, we fellows didn't care anything about the amounts—we were after getting away; and we had been told that we might too, if we signed the acknowledgment. We would have signed anything, just to get away. So we stepped up, we did, and made our marks. That same night we were rounded up by a constable and ten or twelve white men, who aided him, and we were locked up, every one of us, in one of the Senator's stockades. The next morning it was explained to us by the two guards appointed to watch us that, in the papers we had signed the day before, we had not only made acknowledgment of our indebtedness, but that we had also agreed to work for the Senator until the debts were paid by hard labor. And from that day forward we were treated just like convicts. Really we had made ourselves lifetime slaves, or peons, as the laws called us. But call it slavery, peonage, or what not, the truth is we lived in a hell on earth what time we spent in the Senator's peon camp. . . .

When I was first put in the stockade my wife was still kept for a while in the "Big House," but my little boy, who was only nine years old, was given away to a Negro family across the river in South Carolina, and I never saw or heard of him after that. When I left the camp my wife had had two children by some one of the white bosses, and she was living in a fairly good shape in a little house off to herself. . . .

Today, I am told, there are six or seven of these private camps in Georgia—that is to say, camps where most of the convicts are leased from the State of Georgia. But there are hundreds and hundreds of farms all over the State where Negroes, and in some cases poor white folks, are held in bondage on the ground that they are working out debts, or where the contracts which they have made hold them in a kind of perpetual bondage, because, under those contracts they may not quit one employer and hire out to another except by and with the knowledge and consent of the former employer.

One of the usual ways to secure laborers for a large peonage camp is for the proprietor to send out an agent to the little courts in the towns and villages, and where a man charged with some petty offense has no friends or money the agent will urge him to plead guilty, with the understanding that the agent will pay his fine, and in that way save him from the disgrace of being sent to jail or the chain-gang! For this high favor the man must sign beforehand a paper signifying his willingness to go to the farm and work out the amount of the fine imposed. When he reaches the farm he has to be fed and clothed, to be sure, and these things are charged up to his account. By the time he has worked out his first debt another is hanging over his head, and so on and so on, by a sort of endless chain, for an indefinite period, as in every case the indebtedness is arbitrarily arranged by the employer. In many cases it is very evident that the court officials are in collusion with the proprietors or agents, and that they divide the "graft" among themselves. . . .

But I didn't tell you how I got out. I didn't get out—they put me out. When I had served as a peon for nearly three years—and you remember that they claimed I owed them only $165—when I had served for nearly three years one of the bosses came to me and said that my time was up. He happened to be the one who was said to be living with my wife. He gave me a new suit of overalls, which cost about seventy-five cents, took me in a buggy and carried me across the Broad River into South Carolina, set me down and told me to "git." I didn't have a cent of money, and I wasn't feeling well, but somehow I managed to get a move on me. I begged my way to Columbia. In two or three days I ran across a man looking for laborers to carry to Birmingham, and I joined his gang. I have been here in the Birmingham district since they released me, and I reckon I'll die either in a coal mine or an iron furnace. It don't make much difference which. Either is better than a Georgia peon camp. And a peon camp is hell itself!

CHAPTER 3

EASTON SLEPT IN his car by the side of the road and in the morning drove from Selma to South Carolina, seventeen miles past Aiken toward Orangeburg, across the Edisto River, and onto the small white sand roads of Norma. On both sides, pine trees hid the tract houses in the backwoods. Just after a low grass field on the right, he turned in to a driveway by the black cast-iron mailbox. Here there was no number on the mailbox or the house, for all the families and homes were well known to the postman. He drove slowly, the sand and pebbles crackling under his tires. Nothing seemed to have changed in his five-year absence: the NO TRESPASSING sign still lay on its side from the time he and Ronald shot the post out from under it with Papa Samuel's shotgun; the rusted iron horseshoe spike stood by the dogwood tree; even the patterns of shadows seemed familiar as they shifted in the slight breeze over the windshield of his car.

A deer stood in the middle of the road, looked up at him, and slowly walked into the thicket, rubbing its antlers on the low myrtle branches. Then the tunnel of pines gave way to the house and the adjacent cotton field. The field had died long ago, and hollow thistles stood up in the dried grass.

There was no car parked out front, but there never had been. Elise had never owned a car, and Papa Samuel took his tractor when he left. Easton pulled right up to the steps below the porch. It looked older than he'd remembered it; the thin grayed wood had splintered, and the roof had blanched. The front doorknob was still missing.

He turned off the engine. Though he'd come all this way to see it, he had no desire to enter the old house. He got out of the car and stood beside it.

"Mama?" he yelled. There was a slam, which Easton knew to be the breeze opening and shutting the back door. He put his foot up on the first step leading to the porch as Ronald used to do talking to Ruby, and it felt strange to know he was now nearly the same age as Ronald had been then.

"Mama?" he yelled again.

She wouldn't be home in the middle of a weekday; she'd be in town selling her dresses or tending to the feed shop. He gladly turned away from the house and looked across the field to the trees that hid the river. It was still bright, though the cold evening was coming and in the thicket the darkness could overtake you swiftly. He walked across the field. His head no longer hurt, but he still felt a cloudiness as he walked, like a thought had just escaped him. The field went on for fifty yards and then turned into tall weeds and small saplings. The path to the river was still clearly beaten down, though branches had grown across at shoulder height, or perhaps those branches had always been there and he'd been too short to notice before. As the woods grew thicker, the air became damp, and he could hear the river rushing in the distance like a breeze blowing through leaves. He walked more quickly, swiping branches out of the way with impatience. It had been warm earlier in the week, so the water would be high. The pine needles crunched beneath his feet and hidden animals ran in the side brush. He knew he was close to the river when he passed a piece of barbed-wire fence: two posts stuck in the ground to the side of the path with one rusty wire between them.

The river roared as he reached its side, the swift water splashing against the larger rocks that still peeked above the surface. This was by no means a rapid, but the swollen tide ate away at the dirt banks and revealed the roots of trees dangling at its edges. The other side of the river was a stone's throw, perhaps thirty feet across, yet the sheer force and volume of water made the distance seem untraversable.

The bridge to town was a quarter mile downstream on an inland path cut by the schoolchildren and laborers from the surrounding farms, but the spot he used to go to with Ronald was upstream, not nearly as far but less well traveled, on the edge of the river, lined by blackberry vines entangled with poison ivy.

Easton walked carefully along the muddy shore until he found the spot, a fallen log covered by moss, just large enough for two, and a large rock, waist-high, perfect for resting fishing rods against to let the lines dangle into the carved inlet. He leaned himself over the rock and looked down into the water, searching for catfish or trout. But nothing below the surface was clear. The water was too wild in the main part of the river, and even the depth of this private alcove churned with soil and sand.

He sat on the damp log and put his feet up on a shelf of the rock—his legs used to stretch straight out across, but now he bent them at the knees as Ronald used to do, sitting forward with his elbows on his thighs. Finally at rest, he let the sound of the river fully engulf him. Ronald said the river was a healing force: the loud, steady sound cleaned out the noise in your own mind. But now the rushing river brought with it memories.

"Why is he so mad at me?" Easton once asked Ronald after the required moments of cleansing had passed.

"He's just mad. He's not mad at you. Some people get mad at so many things that happen in their lives that they forget what they're mad at and just take it out on anyone they can. And Samuel is a person like that."

"When I'm mad, I know who I'm mad at."

"And who are you mad at?"

"I'm mad at him."

"Anyone else?"

"And I'm mad at them Palmer boys. They the ones who done something to me."

"They're the ones who did . . ."

"They're the ones who did something to me. And my papa. He can't just beat on me like I was his mule. I ain't his mule. I ain't nobody's mule."

"You sure you aren't mad at anyone else?"

"I told you I'm not."

"Tremendous. I just thought you might be—but as long as you don't forget who you're mad at, then you're all right."

"He's stupid if he doesn't know who he's mad at."

Ronald nodded. They fished in silence for a while, and just after letting enough time go by so that Easton knew he'd been heard and respected, Ronald gave him a little more to consider.

"Sometimes it takes longer before things get more complicated. Sometimes you get less sure of yourself with age."

Easton nodded his head, sitting alone, older now, listening to the river. He was mad at everyone it seemed, and no one in particular. He felt the anger in his belly and his chest. He was mad at himself the most, for all the things he'd done and hadn't done. How had Ronald been so wise? Or did he just know what everyone knows when they get older but doesn't do them any good to know: that it all gets more complicated as time passes.

The sun was setting and it was beginning to get cold. There was a snap of twigs and Easton looked up to see his mother staring at him with a smile. Elise hadn't changed all that much; she looked like Ruby wearing a pair of black plastic-rimmed glasses. Her head was wrapped in a red bandanna, and her body sagged under the weight of her thick wool coat.

"Look at you," she said. "Look at you. You a man now." Easton stood but did not go to her, and she did not go to him.

"I'm not a man, Mama. I'm just your little boy grown bigger."

"You got a nice car. Is dat your own car?"

"I built it."

Elise shook her head. "I went to de house and saw it and wondered who was out here. But here you is. Your sister say you might be comin, but I didn think so soon. Not before Sunday. I'm so glad to see you. Why didn you call and I could a fixed somethin for you?"

"I didn't want you going to all that trouble."

"Well, come on and we'll have cake. You hungry?"

"Let's just sit here a minute."

"In dis cole?"

"Just a minute."

Easton sat back down on the log. He patted the space next to him. "You come sit here next to me and listen, Mama. I want you to hear this."

"I'll jus meet you back at de house when you get done." She turned away and began to edge back along the path.

"All I'm asking for is one little minute. Can't you give me one minute after all this time? And I come all this way. Shit."

She stopped and looked at him. He turned away.

"I guess I could stay if it mean dat much to you," she said.

She moved cautiously, turning her large body sideways between the vines and the river. She brushed off the log next to him and sat. He didn't move to touch her or even look at her.

"Just listen," he said. The water rippled over rocks and around snags into small falls. But the rush of the river did not feel calming to him anymore. He felt her impatience, and the roar of the water only seemed to push them further apart.

"What you want me to hear?" she asked after a few moments.

"Just listen. Listen to the water."

"What about it?"

"Mama, you're not giving it a chance. The water's supposed to take all your thoughts away, all your worries."

"I don't have no worries, chile. You have worries, June Bug?"

"No, Mama." He shook his head. "No. I just meant it's peaceful here."

"Well, it's peaceful *and* warm back at de house. We can get de stove burnin. I worked hard all day and I need to res my feet. You come along when you feel de need." She got up and brushed off the bottom of her coat.

She walked up the path, but Love didn't watch her. He sat for a minute more, staring at the river until he could no longer hear her push aside the branches, until he saw that she really wasn't going to wait for him.

THERE WERE NO piles of clothing on the dining table, no pieces of broken thread by the sewing machine, and no needles stuck in a bar of soap like there used to be. Elise had a job as a textile worker. "Now I just makes de fabric and imagines de clothes," she told Easton.

That night he told her about his life in Oakland, and she fell asleep right after supper. He went with her to the mill the next day and got hired on for temporary work so he could make enough money to get back to California. The work was tiring, and again they talked little at night before falling asleep.

At five A.M. the next morning, before work, Easton stood in the kitchen by the wood-burning stove, rubbing his hands together while his mother patted down rice cakes to take for lunch. Then they ate breakfast in silence, as they had for the last two mornings. They were heading into a ten-hour day of clattering machinery, so deafening that it stayed in their heads long into the night and entered their dreams as waterfalls and trains rushing down tracks, so in that way it was nice to have the silence. Yet it was uncomfortable, as if they were pulling on each other with invisible threads. Every once in a while Easton looked at Elise as if he expected her to say something, ask him something about his life, though he'd already told her everything he could think of that first night.

After breakfast, they left the house and crossed the field toward the shortcut to town by the river. Easton didn't want to drive and use up any of the gas. He thought about his finances as he swiped away branches. At a dollar-fifteen an hour, he'd earn enough money for the trip in a few more days.

He turned around and noticed that he'd lost sight of his mother. She walked more slowly than he but at a steady pace, with a more forceful consistency, her eyes lowered and her feet moving in equally spaced steps, landing on whatever flower or vine happened beneath them. He waited for her to catch up, and without looking at him, she continued past, as if her feet couldn't stop once in motion.

They reached the river path while the sun was still below the horizon, and the sky turned a light gray, almost blue, in the east. The opposite bank overflowed with a tangle of pink and white flowers from which sprouted a live oak, one of its green arms arching over the water toward them. All the colorful growth was mirrored at the water's edge so clearly that there was no distinguishable boundary between the plants and their reflections.

Easton hurried his step, in part because he was cold, and in part because his mind kept wandering into the past. This was the way he'd walked to school most mornings when the river hadn't flooded. Even without a heavy rain, the path turned to marsh in unexpected places, and many days his feet were wet and muddy, the water leaking into his shoes where Elise had sewn the soles back on. Remembering his mother, Easton stopped himself on the trail and waited for her again. When she came astride him, he put his arm in hers, so that he would not move away from her so quickly this time. As he did so, he looked at her face for some reciprocation of his affection, but her face remained unchanged and she plodded forward. Before long, he unhooked his arm and walked ahead of her once again.

After walking a quarter of a mile, they reached the bridge to town. Easton looked around, half expecting to see the Palmer boys. But they worked on their farm now, his mother had told him, except for Kalvin, who was in jail for beating up a police officer. Others joined them, though, adults and children, bundled in their coats and scarves, coming from the main road.

The water ran swiftly under the bridge, and Easton shook his head watching it, to think that he'd ever jumped in from there. That river never seemed as dangerous as he knew it to be now, and never as beautiful either, surrounded by lush cypress and azalea, the smell of narcissus floating up to him on the morning breeze—all those times fishing and fighting on that bridge.

He'd lost track of his mother again, ahead of him this time, and he jogged to catch up. Once over the bridge, they were nearly to the Negro school. The Negro school, farther outside town than the White school, had been held in a converted brick storehouse that had been used for keeping cotton before the boll-weevil pestilence destroyed the harvest in 1921, when many of the farms switched to growing soybeans and peaches. He remembered how the Palmer boys laughed at him and told him to go off to his nigger school and learn to talk nigger, even though he couldn't hear any difference between the way he spoke and the way they spoke. He remembered how he longed to keep walking into town, how he longed to have a school with a chalkboard and a White teacher who dressed in a pink dress, and separate grades for older kids, and books he could write his name in.

"Why are you so black?" he had asked Ronald once as they were fishing at their private spot. Easton was eight then and liked to think of Ronald's skin as Negro compared to his own, which he considered ginger.

"Because I'm not part White, like you."

"I'm part White?" He remembered the feeling at this revelation, as if he'd found out about some secret fortune he was due to inherit; he stood up against the rock but turned away from Ronald, knowing already that there was something shameful in that ecstatic hope he felt. "I'm not White," he said delicately.

"Sure. Your great-great-grandfather was White. He owned this land. You and Mr. Marlboro are related."

Easton walked to a bush and picked off some wild blackberries to toss in the water, to keep his smile hidden from Ronald. "You mean," he asked, "if my mama had married a White man instead of Papa Samuel, I'd be even Whiter?"

"It sometimes works out that way and sometimes doesn't."

That next week at school, he stood up in class to inform Miss Moore that from now on she had to call him "sir" because he was White, and all the other kids laughed; but many in turn came up to him privately and asked how it might be true. At home he asked Elise if it was true that they were related to Mr. Marlboro, and she told him, "We all brothers and sisters under de eyes of de Lawd."

On the way to the mill, Easton and his mother passed the Negro church. It was a small brick building with a steeple, and on the doors, Minister Aimes had painted the words *Let the heavens be glad, and let men rejoice: and let men say among the nations, the Lord reigneth*. These were the first words Miss Moore had taught them to read—standing out in the cold morning, a morning very much like the one Easton was walking through now, the whole class, ages five through thirteen, came to read those words on the first day of every year.

The edge of town was now clearly in sight; the big white mansions stood back on the side of the road, some three stories high, with columns and porches that wrapped all the way around and palmetto trees in the yards. The main crossing downtown was Longstreet—named for James Longstreet, the Confederate general—and Doby, renamed so in 1948 for a local Negro boy who helped the Cleveland Indians win the World Series, the same year Negroes got to vote for the first time in the Democratic primary. Shops stretched out for half a block each way at this crossing. In the last ten years, Norma had almost doubled in population to a town of three thousand, due to the new mill built next door to the old one. The clothing store at which Ruby and Elise used to sell their dresses was on Longstreet, attached to Laurel's five-and-dime, and across the street from Carol's, a combined grocery and restaurant, from which they had bought most of their goods all their lives. Elise had been allowed to eat there for the first time in just the last year. The *Tri-County Times* West River office, where Ronald used to work, was an office on top of the tire company. Its press was in a brick building four blocks away on the Negro side of town, connected to the African Methodist Episcopal Church, which sometimes paid for the paper's printing with community donations.

They reached the mill at seven. It was across town, away from the shops and residential area. Elise and Easton worked in a large room spinning yarn out of cotton. The room was as large as the plantation it had been built on, a hundred yards in each direction, with the spinning machines, each fifteen feet long, lined up end to end, row after row. Each steel pillar holding up the ceiling had a yellow circle taped to it with a smiley face that Jane Sloan, the spinner behind Elise, had made to brighten up the place. This was a newer facility, and now that every-one was allowed to work there, White and Black worked side by side in their departments.

Easton worked a number of rows away from his mother, but close enough that he could see her face between the pillars. It struck him as funny and absurd that here they were once again in Norma, and now they worked together in the same building. Every few minutes he would think about her and look to see if she was looking at him, but she never looked, not that he could see.

EASTON STAYED FOR a week. After working at the mill, Elise walked straight home. Easton took his walk home through Norma, stop-ping on the way to stretch his back a few times and say hello to some of his old friends who worked at the shops in town. He'd saved enough money to get back to California, but he didn't feel ready to leave, like he hadn't gotten what he came for.

When he arrived back at the house, it was already dark. Easton took his sketchbook from the car and joined his mother inside. He sat at the dining table where Elise and Ruby used to sew, and he watched his mother under the naked yellow bulb as she prepared a loaf of corn bread. He kept his stick of charcoal poised over the page, hoping for that moment when she would reveal herself to him. She patted the dough with her hands, almost unconsciously, her eyes staring forward into noth-ing. She had a persistent gloss in her eyes, like a shell over her soul. There had been something impassable between them since he'd arrived, and though they'd been physically closer to each other than they had been in five years, he felt like they were standing on opposite sides of a glass wall. Much in Norma felt that way to him, his old friends, the river, the house and farm, but most of all his mother.

Part of it was the silence. Most of the day they were away from each other in the mill, and at home Elise seemed to be closed up in her own world. She was happy to see him, she'd said that enough times. They'd done some catching up since he'd been there, but they'd never talked about the past, as if nothing of substance had happened between them before this visit.

Elise bent down slowly to put the bread pan into the oven, extending her other hand against her knee to keep her legs from giving out: that was how he would sketch her, although it still was not exactly right.

"How old are you, Mama? You seem like a hundred-year-old woman."

"Truth be tole, chile, I feel like a hundred-year-old woman." But even in that very breath, she firmed herself up, straightened her hair, and pulled back her shoulders.

As he watched, Easton let his fingers trace the charcoal over the page, the slight friction of the textured paper vibrating in his fingers.

"You didn't say how old you really are."

"Don't draw me like this, June Bug, with my hair all mussed up." She pulled her bandanna out from her hip pocket and tied it around her head. She had a slight, shy smile, like a young schoolgirl worrying about the boys getting a look at her, though she was a grown woman who'd been married twice, had two children, worked in a mill all day and came home to work some more; a woman who'd seen a dead man in her daughter's room. But still she concerned herself with a trifling vanity. Easton turned the page and started a new sketch, just a bust this time, with his mother turned slightly away with that smile.

She placed the dirty pans out on the porch to wash them in the morning and then came back in to finish a prairie-rabbit stew she was fixing, which was just her fancy name for muskrat.

"Corbet let you draw him like that?" she asked, as she washed off cabbage greens and carrots.

"Sure. I've done a lot of him."

"Is that right?"

"Sure."

"You got some of him with you?"

"Yeah. In this book." He flipped through the pages to find one he was proud of, one of Corbet with his eyes closed listening to music— one that wouldn't show him without his foot.

Elise dried her hands on her apron and came over to look. "Mmmmm-mm. There he is, all right. Sleek as a cat."

"What you mean sleek?" Easton held the picture up toward her as if she had missed what he was getting at—a calm, peaceful man—but she had turned away and gone back to the sink.

"I mean sly as a fox an handsome as a movie star."

Easton went back to his sketch of her as she broke off the carrot heads. He worked quickly to catch the wrinkles and curve of her mouth, the slight tilt of her head, and her stare, which, instead of looking no-where as usual, seemed to look at something pleasant inside herself. They worked in silence for a few minutes, and the chirping crickets filled in the space around them.

"I'm so glad you come to visit me," she said once again. He looked up and saw something new in her face, not the smile of memory or the gloss of hardness, but a sad smile, one of loneliness. She dried her hands on her apron, came over to him in his seat, and pulled the back of his head to her stomach. "You know I wished you never had to leave."

He closed his eyes and let himself fall back into her, and everything felt right for a moment. His shoulders dropped and he let his hands hang at his sides as she ran her fingers over his forehead.

"I need you to stay around and take care a me," she added. With that, something changed inside him, like a small crack in a dam. He didn't want to notice it, but anger began to seep into him again. He felt like pulling away from her. The smell of onions from her hands became stronger and mixed together with lavender from her apron. He wanted to pull away, as if she didn't deserve to hold him like this for her comfort. It was she who should be there to comfort him, not the other way around. She seemed to sense him pulling away and let go. She went back to the kitchen and picked up the chopping knife. As soon as she walked away from him, he wished she would come hold him again, and it angered him even more that she didn't know this without his having to ask.

He went back to sketching the image of her smiling shyly, but he no longer felt a pleasure in doing it.

"When did you meet Papa Samuel?" he asked.

"Jus before de war. Well, no, I guess I knowd him since we was children, but I got to really know him once Corbet was gone to de war."

"Weren't you still married?"

"Course we was." She went to the refrigerator and took out the carcass of the muskrat. She let out a deep breath as she held the animal under the water. "Dere's a lot you don't know about, a lot a parent don't tell a chile, 'cause it's not good to burden him. I don't want to burden you wit all dis even now. Why don't you jus draw an let me fix us supper."

"I'm not a child anymore, Mama. It's more a burden not to know."

She turned off the water and looked at him. "No. I guess you ain't."

"So weren't you still married to Ruby's papa?"

"Sure. We was married still." She took the muskrat by the leg, sliced the stomach open, and pulled out the insides. "Corbet never put foot back here long enough to get a divorce. So Sam come around and we got to keepin each other company. Folks sometimes gets lonely. That's how dey make mistakes."

Easton shifted in his chair. He couldn't be sure if she was referring to him as a mistake, but it made one more crack in the dam.

"How come you liked him?" Easton had to say it quickly to get the question out at all. He was no longer drawing, his fist clenched around the charcoal.

"You sure is full of questions tonight," she said. She opened the oven and checked the bread, then took some radishes out of a paper bag. She washed them and sliced them on the counter.

"Why did you like Papa Samuel, Mama?"

Elise stood straight and thought for a moment.

"Why do anyone like some people sometime? God's doin, I guess."

"But why him?"

"I felt he was handsome," she said. "And I needed someone at de time."

Easton sat stunned into silence. It seemed so random. He pictured another time, or a hundred times rolled into one, when his mother was in the kitchen, just as she was this day. He pictured her through the rungs in the back of the chair he sat in now—at those times he was on the floor, on his knees, holding on to the chair seat, his pants pulled down as Papa Samuel used a switch on him, on his back and on his head. And through the rungs in the chair, he could see his mother at the counter. She never looked at him.

"Why was Papa so angry all the time?" Easton began to move his charcoal again in his book without realizing it, quick lines back and forth on the page across the picture he'd begun of Elise.

"He wasn't like dat all de time. Sometime he was a good, kine man."

"Then how come he beat on me?"

She turned to him. "I don't know, chile, but I'm awful sorry dat he did."

He waited for more, but it didn't come.

"How come you didn't do nothin about it, then?" His voice was low and tight. He didn't look at her.

"What you mean, chile?"

"How come you just stood there and let him beat me?" He stared down at his paper, unseeing.

"Well, I didn't let him, June Bug. He jus did it, and I couldn't stop him, dat's all."

"How come you didn't make him leave?"

"I was scared, too. I did, jus as soon as I could. I made him go."

"Ronald made him get out." Easton looked straight at her. "That was Ronald."

"Well, I couldn't do it all myself. You know what kine a man he was."

Easton closed his sketchbook. His body was shaking too much for him to keep asking questions. He got up, walked across the room slowly with deliberately soft steps, then pushed the front door open, making sure it did not slam behind him. He would not be the one to alert her to his anger.

He stood on the porch looking out over the field and took a deep breath of the cool air, then looked up and blew toward the stars. The insects and animals were everywhere out in the darkness, blindly calling to one another. The stars were bright and clear in the night, millions and millions of them going back into that space until he couldn't see them anymore, only sense that they were there in the darkness behind the darkness that went on forever. He put himself up into that space, an image of himself floating off into the distance, away from the porch, from Norma, away from the earth, from all people and life. His mother called to him from inside, but he didn't answer. He purposely made her call to him again.

THE NEXT MORNING they got a call from Ruby. Corbet's diabetes had worsened. He fell into a seizure while smoking his pipe, drinking bourbon, and listening to the phonograph. Easton took the phone and made Ruby tell him herself. He listened in silence. Ruby had called for an ambulance, but it took a long time to arrive, and by the time they reached the hospital he was dead.

"Okay," he said, and held the receiver down by his chin.

"Shouldn't never pick up de telephone early in de mornin," Elise said. She went back to the kitchen where she was fixing lunch for both of them. He watched her hands slice carrot sticks, the knife pressing into their skins and then snapping down to the board.

"I've got to go back," he said. He could see his own breath in the air.

Elise rolled the carrots in napkins and put them in both lunch bags.

"Didn't you hear me?"

She put one lunch bag on the table and went to the door. "I've got to get to work."

"I mean," he said, "I'm going to leave today."

"All right." She nodded.

"Just as soon as I pack up."

"Well, I guess I was lucky to see you as long as I did."

Easton stood up at the table and faced her, but neither of them moved toward each other. He massaged his forearm where he felt a slight aching.

"You could fly out and see us sometime," he said.

"You know how I feel 'bout flying."

He nodded and turned away from her. He picked up his drawing pad and placed it in his box of materials.

"You know how to let yourself out," she said, "so I'm jus gonna go on."

Easton nodded again.

"I'm not gonna say good-bye," she said. "I'll jus say we gonna see each other real soon."

He placed a charcoal stick back into its case and heard her feet scuff on the porch floor.

"Mama?" he said. She stopped and turned around, looking at him through the open door.

"What is it?" She waited quietly for him to speak, but he could see the look of impatience in her eyes.

"I came down here to see you," he said.

"I know you did." She smiled quickly, then turned and walked down the steps.

He gathered his belongings and left the house as he'd found it, quiet and empty, and walked down the front stairs to his car. He started the engine and let it warm. It hadn't run in a week. Every day—for every useless day of his entire journey—inside him something cracked a little more. He put the car into gear, turned around on the dirt driveway, and drove back down the road through the tunnel of trees, past the horseshoe and the mailbox and out onto the highway. As he drove, he thought about her eyes, the look on all of their faces—his mother, Papa Samuel, Sandra in the church and the day he tried to make love to her, Charles, the little girl, the cops at Woolcrest's, Lida when he'd grabbed her hand, and Mrs. Usher. He could see how they all misunderstood; they all looked at him as if he were asking too much from them, as if he were some sort of hungry monster and they couldn't wait for him to disappear. And he could never explain, he could never convince them that he was anything else, and he could feel the anger move through every sinew of his body.

PART THREE

CHAPTER 1

LIDA AND MARCUS moved into Ruby's house in the beginning of June, but for nearly a month, Lida hadn't left her bed except to go to the bathroom. Mostly, she had been staring at the telephone across the room. Marcus told Ruby that the doctor said she had to stay on her back or else she might lose the baby, so Ruby brought her food and took care of her like she was a little child again.

But the truth of it was that Lida just couldn't get herself out of bed. When she woke up in the morning, remembering that she was pregnant made her tired again. The idea of getting up, of walking down the stairs and through this house, and having to talk to her mother all made her tired. She felt warm and safe in her bed, so she fell back to sleep. But this morning, she woke up and her hands started to shake in the old, familiar way, as if her body had never forgotten the craving, as if it had always been waiting just under the surface.

She didn't move at first. She hesitated, in part because she didn't want to disappoint Ruby any more, or be forced to move out if she was caught. She was also afraid of getting hooked, although she'd always believed she could do it just every once in a while and still be all right. She wasn't hesitant because of the baby inside her; in fact, the thought of the baby only made her want to take it more. What made her body so heavy, what kept her from going to the telephone, was that she didn't want to give in to him again, not after she'd finally moved back with the promise of never hearing his name—she couldn't still be so unhappy; he didn't still make her hurt that much. It seemed impossible that something from so long ago could control her.

Yet she did want to do it, and she felt ashamed of her own desire, which itself swelled the desire that much more. Her chest now trembled with the need. The more she felt ashamed, the more she shook and didn't care for anything but to end the shame, to end all the feelings.

"Rabbit, rabbit, rabbit," she said softly, partially for old times' sake, but also because it felt right and necessary. She threw off the covers and put her feet over the side of the bed. It took all her energy to get up—the deep bending of her knees, pushing off the bed behind her. Her legs were not accustomed to working with the extra weight they carried. She hated herself even more for putting so much energy into getting a fix when she couldn't convince herself to get out of bed for anything else. But she continued, as if her thoughts were scratching at an itch far below the surface of her skin.

When she was fully erect, she straightened her long pink shirt over her stomach and thighs and let everything inside her adjust. She looked again at the telephone on the desk. She could walk the other way—the desk wasn't any farther than the bedroom door—out into the house, down to see her mother, maybe have a productive day helping her sew or clean up. But she had decided already. Just one more time. One more time before the baby came.

She walked to the desk and put her hand on the receiver, as much to steady her body as to make the call. Her arm shook even though she gripped the phone tightly. As she looked at it, she saw that it was not her arm, it was some body part acting independently of her own will. The rest of her body was the same way, growing, breeding, moving, breathing, all against her wishes. And then there was the heroin that it wanted against her will. She didn't want it: it wanted it. She looked at herself in the mirror above the desk and was overwhelmed with disgust, her face dented from the pillow and chapped, her lips white in the corners. She picked up the receiver and dialed, her swollen fingers barely fitting into the holes. She looked at herself in the mirror as the phone rang, her heart pounding, as if it were Easton himself waiting to pick up on the other end.

DOWNSTAIRS, RUBY WAS finishing up the original for her first new line of clothing. Since Lida had moved in, she had been thinking of making a baby and children's line. She'd already made a bodysuit, and when she finished putting the tassel on the cap, she would take the outfit up to show Lida.

She hadn't realized how much she missed sewing, or the feeling of having someone else home while she sewed, and sewing for them. At first she was sad when the Pearsons had let her go, but now she saw it more as a blessing, as His way of telling her to go back to what made her happy and be home to take care of her child and grandchild. It seemed that for the first time in the three and a half years since Love E was killed, she could imagine the future again: the baby playing in her house, money coming in from her clothes, maybe even her mother coming to visit from Norma.

A few hours later she was finished. She cut the thread and tied a knot on the inside of the cap, then turned it right side out. What made her baby line special was the kinte cloth, with orange, black, and green African designs.

She stood and gathered the suit and laid it over her arm for presentation, hiding the cap underneath. She climbed the stairs quietly, knowing Lida would probably be asleep, unless she was still up from when her friend David had stopped by earlier that day. The wood planks creaked, but not as badly as before, since she'd lost some weight. She could lay the clothes out on the green trunk at the foot of Lida's bed, like she used to when Lida was in school, so that when she woke up, they would be there to surprise her.

She reached the top of the stairs and stopped to catch her breath. Love E used to say that if she would bring him breakfast in bed every morning, then she would be in great shape to get a man. But Love E's door was closed for good now.

She turned and walked down the hall past the bathroom to Lida's room. She turned the doorknob and opened the door gently, but still the hinges creaked. At first when she saw that Lida was not in her bed, she turned around and looked down the hall toward the bathroom again, but she had already seen that no one was in there. Then she heard a soft scraping and saw Lida on the floor, sitting against the closet door, rolling her head slowly from side to side, her naked legs sticking straight out in front of her below her pink shirt.

"What you doin down there, chile? That cold floor ain't no good for you. You just get back into bed so you don't hurt nothin inside." She put the clothes down on the trunk and took Lida by the arm to help her up.

As Lida stood, water ran all down the inside of her leg. She looked at it and shook her head. "I'm sorry, Mama," she said. "I'm sorry." Ruby looked at the puddle on the floor where Lida had been sitting.

"Oh baby, it's coming now. You got to get to the hospital. We got to call Marcus. Come on with me. We'll get a cab to drive us. Come on, baby. Don't be so slow. We got to get you some towels."

RUBY STOOD ALONE in the hospital elevator with the warped silver reflections of herself on the walls around her, each a little different depending on the angle. She fixed her hat and pulled on the shoulders of her dress. Soon she would be a grandmother. Or perhaps she already was a grandmother. There was a dignity in that, a sort of achievement to having gotten this far: on her own in California for twenty-one years and she had kept the family line going. And Ronald a grandfather. She looked up toward the elevator numbers and spoke out loud. "Yes, I know you're with me, but I wish you could be down here to hold your grandchild."

The elevator stopped and the doors opened onto the fifth floor. As she stepped out, two men wheeled a gurney around the front counter and up a hallway.

"Excuse me," she asked the woman at the reception desk. "I'm looking for my daughter, Lida Washington. I brought her into emergency about two hours ago."

"She's in Room 556, down that hall and on your right." Ruby almost asked about the baby but realized she wanted to find out for herself. She unsnapped her purse and got out her package of tissues. Already she had to blot down her tearing eyes. She took a deep breath before entering and then opened the door.

Lida was asleep. A woman with dark licorice-colored skin stood next to her adjusting an IV. There was no baby in the room.

"She's sleeping now," the woman said. "I'm Dr. Matthews." She extended her hand to Ruby.

"I'm her mother. Has she had the baby?"

"The baby is in the premature-care ward. But he's going to be fine. Your Lida is just sleeping. She's going to be fine too. She just needs to rest." The doctor closed the curtains to the room. "I would like to ask you something, if you don't mind."

"What's that?"

Dr. Matthews walked to the door as if she wanted to bring Ruby as far away from Lida as possible.

"Well, the baby came out prematurely, which isn't so unusual in itself, but your daughter was already sedated when she arrived. Is she on some sort of medication?"

"Medication? I don't think so. She's just been feelin real low-down the last few weeks."

"But you don't know if she's been on any other drugs?"

"No. Lida's been in my home now for the last month, and she hasn't been taking anything. I've fed her practically every meal myself."

"I see. Well, you may wish to ask her when she wakes up. The baby just has to stay here a few days so we can watch to make sure he's strong enough to thrive on his own. But congratulations, Mrs. Washington."

"It's a boy? Can I see him?"

"The baby? Sure. You can't hold him, but you can look through the glass, if you wish. Come on with me."

Ruby followed the doctor down the hallway.

"This is your first grandchild?" she asked Ruby.

"Yes. Yes he is. The first."

"Do you know who the father is?"

"Of course."

"Are they married?"

Ruby turned on her angrily. "Sure they're married. What kind of question is that? The father's her husband. He's a fine young man. He's comin from work right now."

"Well, if he gets here, he can fill out the name on the birth certificate."

"Well, I can do that if it's got to be done right now," Ruby said. "I know what they been meaning to call him."

"I'm sorry, it's got to be a parent that names him, if they can."

"All right then."

The doctor led Ruby into the care unit and pointed at the fourth baby in the second row.

"There's your grandson, Mrs. Washington."

He was attached to a breathing tube and heart monitor. Ruby put her forehead against the glass. He was tiny and didn't seem to be moving.

"Is he gonna be all right?"

"Well, there are no guarantees. But I think he's got a good chance. We're just keeping him for observation."

Ruby took a deep breath and moved away from the glass.

"So what name are they going to give him?" the doctor asked. Ruby shook her head.

"I don't want to say yet," she said. "We oughta wait to see what happens. He look so small in there. Just like a tiny bird that fell out of a tree."

"Yes. Well, if his father shows up, he can name him then."

"Why do you keep on sayin that: 'if he show up'?"

"I'm sorry, Mrs. Washington. Often when the baby is born early and the mother comes in on narcotics, there's not a father in the picture."

"What you sayin? I told you she been in my house all month. She been in bed."

"I'm simply saying . . . I'm sorry, Mrs. Washington, I'm sure her husband will be here soon. Or you can wait for Lida to wake up, and she can name him."

Ruby turned back around to look at the baby. She felt so helpless behind the glass wall. If she could just hold him, or if she knew more about medicine, then maybe she could do something. She imagined how he felt: he was so tiny and everything around him seemed so big. She closed her eyes and prayed. "Dear Lord, let this child live."

She felt a hand on her shoulder and turned to face Marcus.

"Which one?" he asked.

"Right there, with the blue cover."

He looked through the glass. He didn't say anything as he stared at the steady, jagged heart rate on the monitor.

Ruby finally cleared her throat and said: "That's your son."

"He sure is small."

"The doctor say she was on drugs." She looked at Marcus's eyes.

"No she wasn't." He patted down his hair.

"The doctor thought she was on some sort of drugs already when she came in, and that's maybe why the baby's so early."

"You know she's not doing any of that."

"That's what I said."

"You know these doctors," he said. "Just see some Black girl and they think they're on drugs."

"This doctor was Black herself."

"Well." Marcus wiped his nose. "Then I don't know."

"Don't give me none a that stupid look. You better not be keepin somethin from me, Marcus. I sure ain't beyond kickin you out, even if you is that boy's father."

"I told you, I don't know what you're talking about."

Ruby shook her head. "That's my grandson in there. Just remember that."

"I know. It's my son."

They stood in silence, looking at him through the glass. Ruby continued to shake her head and then spoke up again.

"She say you've got to go name him on the certificate."

"Right now?"

"Go on over there to that woman."

Marcus went to the counter and filled out the forms. He came back with a big smile on his face.

"You sure proud all of a sudden," she said to him. "I never seen such a big grin on your face."

"I named him Ronald Love LeRoy, after Love Easton too. How do you like that?"

"What are you doing?" Ruby yelled. "You can't go an name him Love. What are you tryin to make up for? If I didn't think she was on drugs before, I know she is now."

"I swear, Mrs. Washington, if she's on something, I don't know about it. When I left her this morning, she was asleep upstairs in your house."

"You better not put no 'Love' down on the certificate. Lida'll chop off your testimonials."

"Too late. Besides, she ain't never gonna see the certificate anyway."

"Now why not?"

"They gave the copy to me."

"Well, I'm gonna know 'bout it, and she's my daughter. How'm I suppose to trust you when you willin to lie to my daughter?"

"I was doin it for you."

"You ain't done one thing in your life for anyone but yourself."

"Never mind. I don't need this shit."

"Where you goin?"

"I got to go."

"What you mean you got to go? You just had a son. Your wife's here waiting for you."

"She's sleeping, and there isn't anything we can do right now. I've got rehearsal, which can't wait. I'll come on back in a few hours. We're leaving to L.A. on Saturday."

"Marcus, you are not going anywhere."

"What can I do here right now? I've got to think of the future for that boy. I've got rehearsal." He put his leather cap on his head and walked away. The doctor came back into the ward just as he was leaving.

"That's the father," Ruby said to her. "He's got to get back to work."

The doctor nodded, and Ruby turned back to looking at the baby.

LOVE SOON THRIVED, overcompensating for his rough start. Rather than sucking his thumb, he put his whole fist in his mouth. When they brought him home, his cries from the bedroom could be heard in the kitchen downstairs. After Ruby taught Lida the proper way to breast-feed, Love insisted on staying attached all day long, as if he needed to make up for the time he'd lost while in the incubator.

To Ruby, having a new baby around filled the house with a sense of purpose. It was no longer a place to keep up, to clean and repair, to pay for with no reason in mind; instead, it was a place to prepare for the new life, for the hope of what it might become. Every pot washed and every carpet laid was done with the baby in mind. Germs had to be killed, the floor had to be soft, rats had to be chased out with a stray cat they found and fed and named Lion. The new life burst beyond the child and into both women. Ruby sewed ten children's outfits a day, and Lida learned to embroider names while holding the baby in the crook of her arm. The children's clothing line was now going to have personalized names on each pocket. They talked with energy about their new business together as Ruby had always imagined it, as she had once had with her own mother.

At night, the baby slept in Lida's room, in a white crib that a neighbor gave to them. Lida no longer wished she didn't have him. From the moment she saw him, she knew there was nothing else in her life; she existed only to love and care for this baby, named Ronald, Marcus told her, after her own father whom she had never met.

After three weeks and two days, Marcus held his son for the first time. Marcus had gone on his scheduled tour to L.A., missing his son's homecoming. He walked in the door without his guitar, just as Ruby was clearing off plates from dinner. Lion ran past him into the house as Marcus stood with the door open.

"Well, look what the cat dragged in," Lida cooed to her sleeping baby. "Who's that scary man just walked in the door?"

"It's his famous daddy who's gonna make him proud." Marcus slipped off his shoes and put them next to the doormat.

"Who's that lyin good-for-nothin man just walked through the door? Huh, little Ronny?"

"Now don't be givin our boy a bad idea of his own father."

"Oh, it's your daddy, he say." She looked up at Marcus. "What you come back for? You forget something?"

"I come home to see my wife and son. And my lovely mother-in-law, grandmother of my child."

"You want some leftovers, Marcus? We got some artichokes in the pot," Ruby offered.

"Uh. Yeah. I'd dig some artichokes." He came around the back of Lida's chair and looked at his son cradled in her arms, sleeping with his fist in his mouth.

"He got your big mouth," she said to him.

"And your kinky hair."

"You want to hold him, or you afraid he might wake up and not recognize you?"

"Sure I'll hold him." He came around to her side and started to scoop him up.

"Don't try to swing him around. He ain't no guitar."

Marcus lifted Love into his hands, weighed him in the air. "He sure is a beautiful baby. You done a fine job. Amazing. He's a whole person in there."

"Hold him closer. Put your hand under his head."

"I know. I got him." He walked around the living room rocking his son.

"Don't wake him up, now."

"I know." He walked to the front door and, cradling the baby with one arm, turned the handle. Lida stood up.

"What you doing?"

"I'll be right back. I got to show the boys."

"What are you talking about?" She looked out the door and saw a white Pontiac parked out front with the rest of the band in it. Marcus walked down the stairs in his sock feet. David waved to Lida from the passenger side, but she didn't wave back. The sweet smell of marijuana seeped through the air.

"This is my son, Ronald LeRoy," Marcus said to them, holding him up to the windows.

David got out and took the baby from Marcus's arms.

"Hey, Lida, how you doin?" David said.

"Don't wake him now," Lida whispered loudly. She put on her shoes and walked down the steps. She couldn't stand to see her child passed around like a trophy, especially to stoned folks. Love woke up and started to cry.

"Give him on back," she said. She took Love from him and walked up to the top of the stairs.

"Come on, man," David said to Marcus. "Let's get set up."

Marcus slowly walked up the steps and got his shoes from inside.

"Where you going?" Lida asked. Marcus looked at the baby's face, squished like a dried-up apple.

"We got a gig tonight at Blake's." He tried to kiss her on the forehead, but she pulled back.

"I thought you was stayin. What about the artichokes?"

"I'm sorry, baby. Keep them warm for me. I ain't got time right now. Save them up for when I get back." He ran down the stairs and opened the driver's-side door.

"When's that gonna be?"

His bandmates shook their heads and started talking in low voices.

"Baby, don't make me tell you when I'm comin home. I'm a grown man. I'm tryin to make somethin of myself. I'll be home when I'm done. " He got in the car, then yelled out the window, " 'Round three, probably."

MARCUS WAS HOME at three, and again at three every Friday and Saturday night for weeks. When he came upstairs, he woke Love, who started crying. Lida fed him; then she laid him in his crib, and

Marcus played an arpeggio to lull him back to sleep. Lida lay against his shoulder and closed her eyes.

"At first it doesn't make sense," Marcus said in a soft, deep voice, continuing an ongoing conversation he'd had with Lida during these late nights. "And then it doesn't seem it could be any other way. It seems like it's all just randomly put together, that they could have put the strings in any order." He played as he spoke. "Jimmy James played his upside down, with all the strings reversed, 'cause he was a lefty. Lefty Diz from Chicago played it like that without changing the strings. But how come six, how come not five strings, like the number of fingers? Or how come it skips back a fret after the G?" He paused to finish the arpeggio and then began speaking again as he started a new progression. "But it's all planned out; over all the years and centuries that it's been passed down and changed, it kept getting better. It came over the ocean, and then this Spanish brother, Torres, he made it sound better. People just naturally used what worked until it was made right, so that I can just move down and play the next notes in the scale. Over time, things got better. They naturally have to get better, 'cause you try until you get it right. You don't even have to think about it, really, because time takes care of that."

Lida breathed deeply in her sleep. Marcus stopped playing and leaned the guitar against the bed. He slowly moved out from under her and put a pillow in his place. The floor was cold on his feet, but he got up and walked to the crib with his toes stretched up. He stood above his child. Ronald Love LeRoy was asleep, his face turned to the side and his small tongue just visible in his mouth. He panted quickly like he was having a bad dream, and his body shook in the kinte-cloth baby suit. Marcus reached down over the side of the crib and placed his open hand lightly on the baby's warm body, covering the boy's whole chest and stomach. He kept his hand there and his son's breathing calmed.

After two minutes, Marcus's feet were freezing. As he slowly pulled his hand away, the baby opened his tiny eyes and looked at him, not at everything in front of him like a big blur, but at Marcus, into his eyes, at the person standing over him. They simply looked at each other for a few seconds; then Love closed his eyes again and slept.

In September, when Love was two months old, Marcus went on a tour with his band to the Midwest. When he didn't return at the end of the month, as he was supposed to, Lida took a job at Sears on Telegraph because AFDC wouldn't give her any money when they found out that her address was the same as her mother's and that her husband supposedly worked at Lucky's, though the store had him on a leave of absence. They told Lida that Marcus would have to come back to Oakland to prove to them that he was in Chicago.

She explained this to Marcus in a letter, and he wrote back that David and he had a regular gig and he was going to stick it out and make so much money that it wouldn't matter, anyway. And Lida half believed it, or didn't want to lose all hope. So she got the job and wrote him from work when it got boring. He wrote her back every week during October. Then he stopped writing, and at the end of November, the third month he'd been gone, Lida got this letter of explanation:

Dear Lida,

Good news! We're making a record. I'm not sure how many more weeks we're going to have to stay out here. I'm as antsy to get back as you are to see me. This regular gig is good and this one cat has us pegged to do real well once we have an album, and he hooked us up with a studio. So we're going to make an album and I've been trying to work something new out so I haven't had time to write. I hope you're holding up good and the baby too. Tell him to get ready for his big star daddy to come home. I'd like to see my father's face when he sees my name on an album. Anyway, I maybe have to be here longer. I just don't know right now. There's some real nice people out here, though, so don't worry none about me.

Lida took a couple of hours off work to bring the letter to the Welfare Office. She told them she couldn't pay all the expenses for herself, the baby, and Ruby on her salary of three-ten an hour. They said that now that she had a job, she was earning too much to get any aid. When she got angry, they had the security guard show her out.

IN JANUARY, LIDA was walking up Broadway to Telegraph and she noticed a familiar figure in a red-and-white-striped sweater. As she got closer, he ducked into an office building. She went in after him and found him by the pay telephones.

"David!" she yelled and gave him a hug. He hung up the phone and patted her shoulder. "I can't believe you're back. Where's Marcus?" She stood away from him and noticed that he would not look her in the eye.

"How you doin, sugar?" he said.

"Fine. Fine. What's the matter? You look like I caught you with your pants down." She laughed and hit his arm.

"Girl, you did. You caught me just now when I was about to make a call to somebody important, and you surprised me. I'm just a little disorientated, you know. Half of me is still in Chicago. How you doin, sugar?" He picked up the phone, put in a dime, then hung up again. He reached his finger into the return slot and fished out his money. "Man, I am out of it. How you doin?"

"Fine. Fine." She looked at his eyes to see if he was on junk, but his pupils seemed normal.

"So, where's my man at?" she asked.

"Your man? I don't know where he at."

"Maybe he's waiting for me at home."

"Could be. I haven't seen him in a while. For all I know, he still in Chicago."

"What you mean?"

"Yeah. I haven't seen him since we broke up the band."

"I just got a letter from him last month about the band."

"Then he's probably out there still."

She dug in her purse and looked at the letter; the red postmark did say Chicago. "He never said nothin about you breaking up. He said something about working on a new gig and a record."

"Well, that must be it. Listen, sugar, I got to get, if you know what

I mean." They walked out together into the winter afternoon, the sun directly above them so that neither they nor the buildings cast any shadow. He started to walk away in the direction she had come from. "I'll catch you later."

In an instant, she was alone on the sidewalk, holding the letter, completely baffled. She ran after him and grabbed his shoulder from behind.

"You got to tell me what's happening. All I've got is this letter. What happened? Why did you break up?"

David looked down the street as if he were anxiously waiting for a bus to come.

"Lida, I'm going to tell you all I know. There's probably some I don't know, so don't think this is everything." He looked at his big hand and picked at a callus on his thumb. "It didn't work out like we planned. They told us they'd pay us seven hundred for the gig at the Regal, but the booker gave us three hundred, which wasn't enough to get us all back. Marcus had the idea that we try to find a regular gig, and we got one at the Orchard for the door, which got us enough to eat. But we couldn't stay at my auntie's place forever, and we ended up in this motel on the South Side." David stopped and shook his head.

"But then our drummer quit on us. That was the beginning of the end. He came back here, so we lost the gig at the Orchard. We got this one cat to sit in, but that didn't work, and I said we should come back home and get ourselves together as soon as we worked up enough money. But Marcus wanted us to make a record. Said he'd found a place that we could pay for studio time. There are so many bands out that way tryin to make it. It's worse there than here, so he couldn't find a gig to get up the cash for the album. I suggested we should use the last of the money to turn around some smack, just so we could get the money to come home, or to, you know, hold us over until another gig showed up. And we did make some money on that deal, but he kept on insisting that we spend the money on an album, that once we had an album, we'd be all right. He said he didn't want to come back empty-handed. You know, he wanted to make his son proud. But I wanted to come back, so we split up the money. We'd been stayin at my auntie's again in the Horner Projects, and one day last month, Marcus stole her purse right off the table and all the rest of the money. I'm not saying I'm still mad at him, but I didn't see him after that. I worked at a hamburger joint for two weeks and then came back here. That was a month ago. I don't know what happened to your man, but I don't think he's got his guitar anymore, so I don't think he's out there playing music. You know what I'm sayin?"

Lida shook her head.

"I'm sorry you had to hear it," David added, "but I know you want the skinny. Listen, if you want to come on by my place, it'd be good to see you. You know, I'll take care of you. But I've got to leave off and find someone myself right now. Things is hard again. You take care, and if you see Marcus, tell him to come on around and hook up with me."

This time David jogged across the street, dodging the traffic, putting a solid but shifting wall between them. Lida watched him disappear and then sat down on the sidewalk against the building, the cold wall burning through her shirt.

SANTA RITA JAIL

HE CAME TO the front of the room holding *The U.S. Riot Commission Report* and *Black Protest*.

We are floating on our raft down the River of History. Yet many of you say, I'm not a part of the South and all that Jim Crow mess. I'm a city man from the West or the North. You say, I'm not a part of that Mark Twain, Huckleberry Finn, river-raft shit; I'm a modern man in modern times. My problems all start and end with the ghetto, and the ghetto is something that started after Jim Crow, when we were free to be a part of the American Dream.

But that's the blindness caused by the rushing river, brother. At times it seems to move so swiftly that we don't even see how we got here and where we've been. We don't even see that we've been floating in the muddy waters of the ghetto for a whole century and it brought us to this future, the present we are living, here in 2020.

It started with the Great Migration.

After 1910 there were months when ten thousand of us would leave the rural South. Over one hundred thousand a year during the wars. In the beginning of the century, ninety-one percent of our ten million brothers and sisters lived in the South, but by the mid-sixties, when we were twenty million strong, half of us lived in the North or West, mostly in the cities, where there was work to be found.

We'd see advertisements for better wages and freedom. The employers would pay for our train rides to the "Promised Land." In 1944 the cotton gin, the mechanical cotton picker, all but exiled us southern sharecroppers. Between the forties and the seventies, almost six million of us moved out. Once we arrived in Chicago, New York, Detroit, East St. Louis, Phoenix, Oakland, or wherever they needed cheap labor, we moved into the old sections of town, like the immigrants before us. But unlike other immigrants, we were not free to live in the White parts of town. This is the very definition of a ghetto, a place in which a particular group is concentrated and to which they are restricted.

The Whites fled the cities to the suburbs. With them went their money, businesses, and the tax base for schools and municipal services. When the Depression hit, or when the boys came home from the wars and there were fewer jobs to be had, we lost jobs first. This is how it started. The poorer we got, the less desirable the neighborhood, the fewer jobs available, the worse the opportunities, the worse the dropout rates, the worse the crime, the worse the drugs, the worse the health conditions and sanitation. The ghetto became our next prison: overcrowded, deteriorating, and for many, inescapable.

Why are we so angry? Many people look at the most recent riots and see them as an isolated eruption of some crazy and lazy niggers taking advantage of a hyped-up case in the media. But you're not seeing the River. Maybe you remember reading about the riots in Los Angeles after Rodney King, or you may have studied the first nine months of 1967 when there were riots in 39 cities, 217 "civil disorders" nationwide, 83 deaths, and 1,897 injuries. Or maybe you recall San Francisco and Oakland in '66; Watts in '65; Harlem, Rochester, Cleveland, and Philadelphia in '64. But do you know about Detroit and Harlem in '43 and '35; Tulsa in '21; or D.C., Omaha, Charleston, Longview, Knoxville, and Chicago in 1919; Chester, Houston, East St. Louis, and Philadelphia in 1917.

And many of these riots were not started by angry Blacks, but by angry Whites. When there wasn't enough housing, the Black areas started to expand into the White neighborhoods, and we weren't welcome. There were bombings and crosses burned, garbage thrown and fires started. There were drive-by shootings. Police machine-gunned a whole apartment building in Detroit. It all started a long time ago.

Here, I'll read to you from *Black Metropolis: A Study of Negro Life in a Northern City*:

The sporadic bombing of Negro homes in 1918 was but the prelude to a five-day riot in 1919 which took at least thirty-eight lives, resulted in over five hundred injuries, destroyed $250,000 worth of property, and left over a thousand persons homeless. . . .

The Chicago riot began on a hot July day in 1919 as the result of an altercation at a bathing beach. A colored boy swam across the imaginary line which was supposed to separate Negroes from whites at the Twenty-ninth Street beach. He was stoned by a group of white boys. During the ensuing argument between groups of Negro and white bathers, the boy was drowned. Colored bathers were enraged. Rumor swept the beach, "White people have killed a Negro." . . .

Pitched battles were fought in the Black Belt streets. Negroes were snatched from streetcars and beaten; gangs of hoodlums roamed the Negro neighborhood, shooting at random. Instead of the occasional bombings of two years before, this was a pogrom. But the Negroes fought back. . . .

One result of the Riot was an increased tendency on the part of white Chicagoans to view Negroes as a "problem." The rapid influx from the South had stimulated awareness of their presence. The elections of 1915 and 1917 had indicated their growing political power in the Republican machine—a circumstance viewed with apprehension by both the Democratic politicians and the "good government" forces. Now the Riot, the screaming headlines in the papers, the militia patrolling the streets with fixed bayonets, and the accompanying hysteria imbedded the "Negro problem" deeply in the city's consciousness.

Civic leaders, particularly, were concerned. They decided that the disaster demanded study, so Governor Lowden appointed the non-partisan, interracial Chicago Commission on Race Relations to investigate the causes of the Riot and to make recommendations. . . .

The Commission was very specific in its charges and did not hesitate to allocate responsibility for the conditions which produced the Riot. Even governmental agencies were asked to assume their share of the blame. To the police, militia, state's attorney, and courts, the Commission recommended the correction of "gross inequalities of protection" at beaches and playgrounds and during riots; rebuked the courts for facetiousness in dealing with Negro cases, and the police for unfair discrimination in arrests. . . . The City Council and administrative boards were asked to be more vigilant in the condemnation and razing of "all houses unfit for human habitation, many of which the Commission has found to exist in the Negro residence areas." In such matters as rubbish and garbage disposal, as well as street repair, Negro communities were said to be shamefully neglected. Suggestions were made that more adequate recreational facilities be extended to Negro neighborhoods, but also that Negroes should be protected in their right to use public facilities anywhere in the city.

The Board of Education was asked to exercise special care in selecting principals and teachers in Negro communities; to alleviate overcrowding and double-shift schools; to enforce more carefully the regulations regarding truancy and work-permits for minors, and to establish adequate night schools. Restaurants, theaters, stores, and other places of public accommodation were informed that "Negroes are entitled by law to the same treatment as other persons" and were urged to govern their policies and actions accordingly.

Employers and labor organizations were admonished in some detail against the use of Negroes as strike-breakers and against excluding them from unions and industries. . . .

As to the struggle for living space, a section of the report directed toward the white members of the public reiterated the statement that Negroes were entitled to live anywhere in the city. It pointed out several neighborhoods where they had lived harmoniously with white neighbors for years, insisted that property depreciation in Negro areas was often due to factors other than Negro occupancy, condemned arbitrary advance of rents, and designated the amount and quality of housing as "an all important factor in Chicago's race problem." The final verdict was that "this situation will be made worse by methods tending toward forcible segregation or exclusion of Negroes."

Not all of the Commission's advice and criticism was directed at public agencies and white persons, however. The Negro workers who had so recently become industrialized were admonished to "abandon the practices of seeking petty advance payments on wages and the practice of laying off work without good cause." There was an implied criticism of the colored community, too, in a statement urging Negroes "to contribute more freely of their money and personal effort to the social agencies developed by the public-spirited members of their group; also to contribute to the general social agencies of the community." Negroes were also asked to protest "vigorously and continuously . . . against the presence in their residence areas of any vicious resort" and to assist in the prevention of vice and crime. . . .

In addition to the specific recommendations of the type referred to above, the report proposed a long-range educational program grounded in the belief that "no one, white or Negro, is wholly free from an inheritance of prejudice in feeling and thinking. . . . Mutual understanding and sympathy . . . can come completely only after the disappearance of prejudice. Thus the remedy is necessarily slow."

The long, slow river of leaving.

CHAPTER 2

FOR ALMOST THREE years, Lida didn't hear from Marcus. Love could walk up the stairs on his own now, holding the rungs under the handrail. Ruby had given up on her new line of clothing after the majority of it was returned to her as remainder from the department stores. She'd applied for the civil-service exam but could not read and write well enough to pass it. She took the first jobs offered to her: at the age of forty-five, Ruby worked as a crossing guard for Prescott Elementary from two to four every day and then went to the Calison Calculator Company on San Pablo to clean the offices from six to eleven. This allowed her to spend mornings with Love.

In the afternoons, Love stayed home by himself until Lida got back from Sears. He watched TV most of that time. The TV was set right in front of the living room window, and he sat on an oval rug two feet away. Lida left pretzels for him to eat, and he sat for most of the afternoon with a pretzel in his mouth, his tongue jutting in and around it, licking off the salt.

Some days he watched the raindrops on the windows, the tapping all around him. He'd kneel on a chair and put his finger against the pane, touching the drops from the inside, following them as they slid to the bottom. The first time there was thunder, it rattled the glass and he ran to the couch and put the pillows over his head until he fell asleep.

A million little events transpired every day that he never found the words to talk about with anyone else. In the middle of the afternoon, during *Electric Company,* the mailman walked up the stairs to the porch, and then the mail dropped through onto the floor. One time, a truck pulled up outside. A man carried a package to the door and knocked. Love stood in front of the door and waited for the package to come through the door. When the man stopped knocking, Love looked through the metal slot and saw the truck drive away.

Every day after *Spiderman,* kids walked down the block coming home from school. Some waved at him through the window, most ignored him, and a few others stuck their tongues out at him. He liked these kids the best because they paid him the most attention: if he stuck his tongue out at them, they'd point their middle fingers up in the air. He looked up to where they were pointing but never saw anything except the clouds and some seagulls.

One time a man came and peed by the steps and left a gold can. Love begged Lida to give him the can when she got home, but she just crumpled it up and threw it away. Another time two cars crashed, and the men got out and yelled at each other. Then one of the men went to his car, came back, shot the other man, and sped off. The ambulance came, and two men lifted the shot man off the street. Then the police came and started talking to the people who gathered around the accident. They came and knocked on his door, but went away when nobody answered.

One day Love ran out of pretzels and went to get more from the kitchen. He knew where his mother kept them, in a bag in the cupboard over the counter. He climbed up on a chair that got him to the top of the stove and walked across the cold burners onto the counter. His head reached to just below the bottom of the wooden cupboard doors. He reached up and pulled on the brass handle. Inside were shelves of cans and then, above that, a shelf of jars with metal clasps. Each jar contained a different-color food—red beans, white beans, yellow twisty pasta swirls. And behind the jars was the blue bag of pretzels.

He reached up above him blindly, stretching on his tiptoes, pushing aside the jars. His fingers grasped the foil pretzel bag, and when he'd pinched it a little, he pulled it out quickly. As his toes and ankles gave out on him, the bag pulled down the big jar of white beans. He watched it, his mouth open and the bag of pretzels clutched to his chest. The jar fell from the cupboard, down in front of his face, onto the counter, rolled a few inches to the metal stripping, and fell off the counter. It smashed on the floor, beans and glass everywhere. Love stayed still a moment, holding his breath, hoping that it might pull itself together and fly back up to the cupboard. But nothing moved.

He knew he would have to clean it up before his mother came home; some days when he'd messed up, she'd come home and scream at him, which was okay because later she would apologize and hug him and give him a dollar; but other times she would see whatever he'd done—broken plate, spilled juice, pee on the couch, knocked-over lamp—and she'd go straight upstairs and lie on her bed and wouldn't talk the rest of the night. This was how it was most times now, so he had to clean it up.

He crouched down on the counter and, facing the cupboards, lowered one leg down over the edge and then the other. When he got to his stomach, his arms could no longer support his weight, and he simply slid onto the floor, his foot landing on a shard of glass.

He screamed and hopped out into the living room. The blood dripped from his heel and he collapsed on the floor, holding his foot in the air. He began to cry but then looked around the empty house and stopped. The glass was a single triangle that he could grip at the end. He pulled it out and looked at the long tip that had been inside him. He then looked at all the bloodstains on the carpet and knew he was in big trouble. So he stood and slowly hopped upstairs and hid in his mother's closet. He sat down behind her dresses and her pants in the dark and squeezed his foot, the smell of his own blood mixing with the perfume of his mother's clothes.

Lida came home that night and found blood all around the living room and the glass on the kitchen floor. She yelled for Love, but he didn't answer. She followed the trail of blood upstairs into her room but didn't see him in the dark closet.

"Ronald!" she screamed as loud as she could. He could hear her crying. She sounded as if she had been injured herself.

"Mama," he said, "I didn't mean to."

LIDA CALLED DAVID to drive them to the hospital. He showed up and carried Love to the car. David waited with them for the three hours it took for the doctors to give Love a shot and stitch him up. Afterward Lida asked David if they could stay with him for the night.

Gina had left David and taken their child when she found out he was dealing again, so he let Lida and Love sleep in the bed with him. That night he rubbed his hand along her back until she fell asleep.

She wouldn't get up for work the next morning and stayed home all day, so it seemed to Love that things had worked out for the best after all. But she didn't talk much or want to play. She stayed in bed that day and the rest of the week without making a sound, except once every few hours she would call for Love in a desperate voice and wouldn't stop until he came and held her hand. She stayed at David's a week, then returned home and went back to work, but she put a padlock on the kitchen door so that Love would not hurt himself in there again.

ONE RAINY AFTERNOON while Love was home alone watching TV, he heard Lion meowing and scratching to come in. Love spent ten minutes trying to pull the front door open; the knob was just above his head, but the door was locked. As he pulled, the knob turned on its own. Love stepped back and the door opened. Marcus stood in front of him, soaking wet, holding a small paper bag in one hand. He smiled, and Love hopped away from him on his healthy foot.

He tried to make it up the stairs but slipped on the edge of a step, and his bandage came loose. He looked up at the strange man to see what he would do.

Marcus put down the paper bag on the vanity, then went to his son and picked him up under the arms. "What's wrong with you? Why don't you watch your step?"

Love turned away from the sour-beer breath and the wet hair that dripped on his face. Marcus looked up the stairs to the second floor. "Hello?" he yelled, and then he turned back to Love when no one answered. "Your mother gonna blame me for this for sure."

He put Love down and went to the kitchen, his feet leaving large wet prints on the floor. "Hello?" he called again into the house. "Ain't nobody home?"

He tugged at the kitchen door and then saw the lock. "Shit. What they want me to do, starve to death? How am I gonna get me something to eat?" He turned back to Love, who sat on the stairs, pressing himself in between the rungs of the railing.

"Hey," Marcus said. "Let's you and me walk down to the store and get some food." Love didn't say anything.

"Naw," Marcus said. "I guess it's too wet out. What'd you do to your foot? Come on in the bathroom and let me take a look at that." Love shook his head. "Come on, it looks like it's bleeding. We got to get you fixed up." He took Love by the arm and pulled him to the downstairs bathroom. He wet a hand towel with cold water and squeezed it out.

"This will keep it cold. Just squeeze it around there." Marcus put the towel on Love's foot. He then pulled open the mirrored cabinet and looked inside. He took out a bottle of prescription painkiller, read the label, and then stuffed it in his pocket. He found a Band-Aid and peeled it open across Love's stitches.

"What'd you do to yourself?"

Love scratched his nose.

"Don't you talk yet or nothin?" Marcus asked. "How old are you?" Love didn't reply.

"Don't you know who I am?"

Love nodded.

"Who am I?" Marcus smiled. "Tell me who I am."

"Lion."

"Lion? That mangy old cat?" Marcus laughed. "Naw, I ain't Lion. I'm your daddy, Marcus. M-a-r-c-u-s. Spell my name. M-a-r-c-u-s. Marcus. Can't you spell yet?"

Love shook his head.

"Don't you remember me?"

Love hesitated and then nodded, but he didn't recognize this man whose wet hair stuck flat onto his face.

"I know I been away for a long time, but that wasn't my fault. They locked me up, and I couldn't come back to see you. But believe me, I wanted to. You're a mighty big boy now. I bet you could play a guitar already. Soon as I pick me up a new one, I'm gonna teach you some chords. All right?"

Love was staring at the Band-Aid, which had fallen to the floor. Marcus shook him. "All right?"

Love nodded.

"Let's you and me get dried off and then get some rest."

Marcus dried himself off with a towel and then walked back into the living room. He lay on the couch, put his feet up on the armrest and a pillow under his head. He watched the cartoons until his eyes closed.

After a few minutes, Love quietly walked out of the bathroom. He stood by the couch and watched Marcus until he was sure that he was asleep. Then he sat down on the floor and watched TV.

THIS WAS HOW Lida found them when she came home with wet bags of groceries in her arms. Love hardly looked up at her, just enough to make sure it wasn't some new stranger.

Her first impulse was to yell at Marcus to get the fuck out of the house. But she stopped herself, seeing him there asleep. She would still yell, but first she wanted a minute to look at him again. As she watched him sleep, she wished she could lie down there next to him and have them wake up together like nothing had ever happened.

She shook her head and went to the kitchen door. She quietly opened the padlock and placed the bags on the counter without looking back out toward the living room. One item at a time, she unpacked the groceries; opened the refrigerator door, put the butter in the drawer, closed the drawer, walked back to the bag, took out the cheese, went back to the refrigerator, and opened the drawer again. She repeated this mechanically and, without deciding to, went and got the butcher's knife from the counter.

She walked into the living room with the knife held behind her.

"Ronald," she said sternly, loudly enough to wake Marcus, "go on up to your room." Love looked at Marcus, then did as he was told.

Marcus sat up on the couch and watched Love disappear up the stairs, then smiled at Lida. She brought the knife out for him to see.

"What are you doin with that?"

"Don't ask me any questions. Don't *you* ask *me* any fucking questions. I'm gonna gut your belly right here on the couch is what I'm gonna do." She walked toward him, and he scrambled over the top of the couch, laughing at her.

"I know you're angry. You got a right to be angry. Just listen to what I have to say."

"I don't have to listen to a goddamn word out of your lyin mouth. Who the hell you think you are? Give me back them keys to this house. Where the hell you been?" She held the knife out at him, more like a pointing stick, an accusation rod, than a weapon.

"I've been in Joliet. They locked me up for dealing. I'm telling you, I didn't want to stay away."

"No." She covered her ears. She didn't want to hear it. She didn't want to hear any excuses, especially any legitimate reason. She wanted him to have been cheating and running around so she could kill him and kick his body onto the street. It wasn't fair to take that away from her after three years.

"Why didn't you call me or write to me or send word or nothing? Don't tell me they don't got no pencils and paper in prison."

Marcus shook his head. "I was going to, baby. Every day I told myself I was going to call you. But I figured you knew from David and . . . I know I should have called you, baby, but I was ashamed. I'm sorry. I just thought I'd do my time and come back a new man."

"Don't give me that shit. You get the fuck out. You think you can just leave us and come back in here so easy, just walk back in here and lay down and rest." She jumped up on the couch and climbed over the top, holding the knife over him.

"Watch out, baby. You're gonna hurt yourself with that."

"Get out a my house."

"This is my house too."

"Don't tell me whose house this is or ain't. Get the hell out!"

He picked his paper bag up off the counter.

"I'll kill your sorry ass." She came at him, and he backed out onto the porch, then down the steps into the rain.

She watched him from the doorway. He pulled his jacket collar up, covered his head with the paper bag, and walked up the block, looking back at her and smiling. She wanted to slam the door, make it thunder in its frame, loud enough to shake the sidewalk under his feet, but she could not move from the doorway, from watching him walk away huddled under his jacket until he turned the corner into the liquor store.

EVERY DAY FOR the next two months, Marcus came to the house, sometimes with flowers, dressed in a nice secondhand blue suit, and other days drunk or stoned with a bag of beer in his hand, his shirtsleeves stained.

One Monday evening she returned from work to find him playing on the porch like a cat tapping at the window, waiting to be let inside. He was talking to Love through the glass, pointing to different things in the house and telling him to bring them over for him to look at.

"That's an ashtray. Spell 'ashtray' for me, Ronald. Ash—."

"What does he need to know how to spell ashtray for?" Lida dragged herself up the steps and took out her key.

"Don't open it," Marcus said. "Watch, I taught him how." He tapped on the window. "Ronald, go open the door for Mommy."

"Oh great, Marcus, now my child can get out the house by himself. Thank you. Would you please stay away from here when I'm not home?"

"So when you are home?"

Lida shook her head. She let him in, not because she forgave him but because she was lonely.

"I need some cash, baby."

"Well, get a job." Lida put her purse down on the vanity. Marcus looked at it and then put his hands in his pockets.

"I'm working on that, but I need some funding right now, just to hold me over, and you're the only one I can ask." Marcus jumped over the top of the couch and landed on the cushions like a cowboy.

Love stood up in the middle of the living room, half listening to them, but turned toward the TV, watching the news.

"I should be asking for money from you, Marcus," Lida said. "We're tight as it is. How about three years of child support and then we'll talk."

"I told you before, I'm gonna take care of that when I get back in business. You'll get all that and more. I'm just in need of a quick fix."

"Haven't you seen the inside of prison long enough, or do you plan on another three-year vacation?"

Love turned around and looked at his father.

"Baby, don't you know how hard this is for me to ask in front of our child?"

Lida opened the padlock to the kitchen and went to the refrigerator. "Ronald, come in here and give your mama a hug." Love ran into the kitchen and grabbed his mother around the hips.

"I don't want you going to that window anymore when he's around," she whispered to him. "Okay? You hear me?" Love nodded. "Now what do you want for supper? You want some lasagna?"

"That sounds good to me," Marcus yelled in from the living room.

"You need to be out a here before Ruby comes home. She's already told me she'd chop off your privates if she sees you again, and she's not foolin."

"Listen, baby, I need that money. I can reciprocate it to you by tomorrow."

"Aren't you ashamed, asking your own wife for money?"

"That's what I'm saying. Sure, I'm ashamed. This is hard for me, baby. You think this is what I wanted to be? But a man comes out of prison with nothing—I'm flat broke, and besides, who's gonna hire me? When times was hard for you, wasn't I down for you? If it wasn't for me, you wouldn't even be living back here no more. I'm not trying to say you owe me, Lida. I'm just saying how come you can't help me out when I'm down too?"

"Because you left for three years, Marcus."

"Never mind." He turned and walked out of the kitchen through the living room. He got to the front door and opened it.

"Where you going?" Lida asked.

"Out."

"To do what?"

"What do you care? I'm going to do what I have to." He opened the door and put on his hat.

Lida marched out to the couch and yelled at him, "How come after you leave me, I'm the one that feel bad?"

" 'Cause you know it ain't my fault. You know I always helped you out when times was rough. But don't worry, I ain't asking for nothing from you. This time I know what I got to do." He turned to the door.

"Don't do anything crazy. Don't go off and make me be alone again. I can't." She shook her head, and it was clear she was trying not to cry.

"You know I didn't want that. You know I wanted the best for us."

"Just come back in here and shut your mouth." She walked into the kitchen, and Marcus followed.

"We don't have any extra money, Marcus." She pulled a chair over to the counter and stood up on it, almost exactly where Love had been reaching for the pretzels. She took the money jar off the top shelf.

"This is not mine," she said. She opened the lid to the jar and took out a handful of bills. "You better have this back by tomorrow."

"Spot me twenty and I'll never ask for money from you again. I promise."

"Oh, I know you won't, 'cause I ain't givin you any more."

She clasped the lid back on and stepped down with the money in her fist.

"Don't come back here without this money." She put it into his hand, and he counted it. "Don't ask for anything more."

He stuffed the money in his pocket and smiled up at her. "How about a kiss?"

She didn't answer him. Love watched his parents. Marcus leaned forward and kissed her cheek. Lida closed her eyes.

TWO MONTHS LATER, Ruby stood in the entryway of her house and surveyed the living room. The black-and-white TV was twenty years old, so it wasn't that valuable. But it had a soul value, like anything that has been with you for long enough that it becomes a traveling companion. The stereo-turntable was as much a piece of Corbet as the picture of him on the wall or the records on the shelf. Other things had been stolen too: the crystal ashtray, the giraffe bookends from Love E's trip to visit Eldridge Cleaver in Algeria, and what hurt her most of all, her sewing machine. The only thing left was the Bible on the cast-iron table.

She was tired from cleaning at the calculator company and didn't have enough energy to do more than shake her head and sit on the couch.

Lida watched her from the table. She had spoken with the police and given them a report.

"They took your jewelry too, Mama." Ruby didn't move.

"Go get your Nanna some water," Lida told Love.

"I don't want any water," Ruby said.

Love didn't move from the tall chair at the table where he sat staring down at his reflection, his hands in his lap.

"The police said they must have come through an open window 'cause there was no sign of breaking in."

"Why should he break in," Ruby said, "when his boy's gonna let him in?"

"This has nothing to do with Marcus," Lida said.

"Then how did he get in? Ask your son. He was here." Lida looked at Love. He reminded her of how she used to sit when she was around Easton, making herself small and invisible.

"Don't you think I asked him? The police asked him too." She turned to Love. "Was your daddy here today?"

Love shook his head.

"Well, what's the boy going to say?" Ruby whispered. "Don't you think Marcus told him not to tell."

"Did your daddy tell you not to tell?"

He didn't answer.

Ruby sighed loudly from across the room, closed her eyes, and folded her hands across her stomach in resignation.

"Now, you look at me when I'm talking to you! You tell me." Lida stood up and grabbed Love's chin. "Was Marcus here today? I want to hear your voice, Ronny."

"No."

"I swear, God's gonna keep you outta heaven if you've been bad." She squeezed his face even harder, her thumbs sinking into his cheeks.

"I didn't see nothing."

"The child was here all day," Ruby said. "He had to see something."

"He was in his room." Lida let go of Love's face, and he turned away from her.

"Now, how you gonna tell me he was in his room while all this ruckus was goin on down here?" Ruby asked.

"He was sleeping in his room."

"That drug-addict fool of a father of his better not show his face 'round here ever again. I'll have the police lock him up permanently." Ruby got up and went into the kitchen. She saw the chair by the counter and looked at the open cabinet above. Some last reserve of energy seemed to leave her body, and she hung her head. She couldn't bring herself to see if she still had money in her jar. She went into the refrigerator—at least they hadn't taken the food—and took out the carton of orange juice. The words came to her as she was pouring, and she said them loud enough for Lida to hear.

"I don't want you speaking his name in this house. I got my forbidden people, and now you got yours. You should have been celebrating the day he left and never came back. I told you to keep clear of him, and now look where it's got all of us. We've been stripped naked by that beast." She came out of the kitchen with a glass of orange juice. They stood face-to-face.

"You never gave him a chance," Lida said. "You'd have blamed him for this even if he was still in jail."

"Listen to yourself. In jail. In jail for robbin and lyin and stealin someone else's away from them. Yes, he's a fine, upstanding young man."

"I trust Marcus. I trust him more than I trust anybody. He could have stolen anything from here any time he wanted, but he asked me for money, and I gave it to him. And he gave it back the next day. He knew he could ask if he wanted more."

"What money'd you give him?"

"What does it matter? He paid it back. What? I can't give him money if I want to? He's done more for me than anybody else ever done. He's done more for me than you ever did. He's the one who brought me back here in the first place. You should be thanking him. You should be on your knees thanking him if he ever comes back!"

"Lida," Ruby begged. "Baby, why are you acting like this? Why are you saying such mean things?"

"I want him to move back in here. I'm gonna ask him tomorrow to move back in here."

"He's not coming near this house. You can't have a thief in this house."

"He's no thief. You don't know what he's done for me."

"I jus don't know why you want to live with that man after what he's done to you. I don't understand you, Lida. I don't understand you." Ruby shook her head and sat back on the couch, facing away from Lida toward the empty shelves against the wall. She pulled a knitted blanket over her legs. "I don't think I've ever understood you."

"That's right, you haven't."

"From the day you was born, I loved you the best I knowd how. But I always felt that wasn't good enough for you. I know how you always been jealous of Love E. Marcus done told me all about that. That's one thing that man has cleared up."

Lida gaped at her mother, as if the lie she thought could never get any bigger had just swallowed everything around her.

"No." She shook her head. "That's not how it was."

"It's all right. I don't mind. I've gone and accepted it in my heart. Now I put you first. The truth always sets you free."

Lida walked up to Ruby slowly and stood above her. Ruby reached up and took her hand and their eyes met.

"He raped me," Lida said. She'd imagined saying these words out loud so often that she wasn't sure if she'd really said them.

"Oh baby, no." Ruby squeezed her hand. "And now you want me to let him move back in?"

"Not Marcus." She looked straight into Ruby's eyes; they were soft and filled with more compassion for her than she'd ever remembered, and she nearly stopped herself. But the words flowed to her lips, and she felt herself fall into them as she had fallen into Marcus's arms off the edge of the bed so long ago.

"Love E raped me."

She let the silence hang because there was nothing more to add; after so long, those words had become the only fixed point in her life, the most distilled truth. Every time she had imagined saying this to Ruby, her mother responded in a different way, sometimes yelling, sometimes reaching out and holding her. And a part of her regretted having said it, if only because in a moment, it wouldn't be possible to imagine or to hope anymore.

"What are you sayin?" Ruby asked. "What are you sayin?"

But Lida didn't answer. Now that this piece of her was out, she felt herself cave inward, bow her head and curve her shoulders. She felt herself run away into the center of her chest as if she'd done something terribly wrong. Ruby pulled her hand away.

"You need to explain yourself. You need to talk to me right now and tell me what you are saying to me." Ruby blinked her eyes as if sand had been thrown in them. Lida felt the tightness of her jaw, so strong that she couldn't have opened her mouth if she'd wanted. Ruby stood up and the blanket fell to the floor.

"Don't feed me no lies," Ruby yelled. "Just because you're jealous of the love I had for him. I won't let you drag in any ole piece of drug-selling trash. You don't tell me something like that unless you mean to explain yourself. My brother loved you like you was his own. You was like his only chile. He took care a you all your life, and now you up and slap him when he gone so you can bring that man back in my home? You shameful and disgraceful and I can't stan to look at you." She walked away and faced the front windows, the couch now between them.

Love sat quietly at the table, his feet crossed at the ankles.

"Then I'll leave," Lida said softly.

"That's right you'll leave." Ruby turned to her and held on to the spine of the couch to keep herself steady. "And this time you don't have to bother comin back. I've had enough of your lyin and shuckin for this man. Look at my home. Look at what he robbed me of. I don't even got money to go back and see my own mother now. I been saving. For three years I haven't even let myself speak his name, but I'm not gonna let you take the little memory I got left a him, the little decent part of my life I got after the two of you been through me. You love him so much, if he's such a—a fine man, you can let him take care of you. You shameful. I don't know what kind a hook he got in you, but it's clear I can't never get it out."

"That's right, Mama, you can't never do nothin for me. Come on, Ronny." Lida grabbed Love's arm and pulled him off the chair.

"Where we going?" he asked.

"Upstairs to pack." She dragged him to the stairs.

"I don't wanna go."

"We have to go."

"No. I ain't gonna. I didn't mean to." He pulled back and forced her to turn around. "I'm sorry. I didn't mean to."

"Shut up!" She slapped him across the face. "Now. Come on. Don't make me hit you again."

AFTER LEAVING HER mother's, Lida and Love moved in with David at the Terrace Apartments. Marcus was already staying with David. With Marcus and Lida out of work and sleeping on the sofa together, it wasn't long before Lida was pregnant again. It took them six months to finally get their own place in the same building. When Section 8 came through, they moved into a one-bedroom on the third floor. They decided to have a special housewarming celebration on the Fourth of July, Love's birthday. They had a barbecue on a picnic table that was bolted to the cement in the back behind the first building, between the laundry room and the low wooden garages that the tenants used for storage.

David had a hibachi, and he bought the food. Marcus poured an ample amount of lighter fluid on the charcoal, and the smoke rose up into the buildings; one by one, the neighbors slammed their windows shut. Marcus placed a portable radio on the table and listened to KMEL pump out the tunes. It was a warm day, the chicken smelled sweet, and they drank Bitter Motherfucker out of the bottle, a mixture of port wine and lemon juice.

A man came downstairs with his German shepherd to put in his laundry, and Love ran over to play with the ragged dog. He grabbed his tail, and the dog snapped at him.

"Get back here, Ronald, before I slap your face!" Lida yelled.

"You better go on over there." The man nudged him.

Lida looked at the man suspiciously. Though the neighbors were friendly enough, she knew people in the complex thought she didn't belong there if she was a friend of David's because he was slinging junk.

The man gestured to Lida's stomach with his chin and smiled. "Got yourself twins on the way?"

"Don't even." Lida laughed. "Second one's bigger, that's all. Ronald come out like a rabbit, but this one's drivin his own truck."

The man walked away with his laundry, then David slid over to her on the bench.

"I'm glad you got your own place now, but I'm sure gonna miss you."

Lida smiled and nodded.

All afternoon they ate and drank. Marcus passed out chicken and hot dogs on paper plates. Love didn't sit still with his food. He ran over to the Dumpsters and, chicken leg in his hand, climbed up onto the roofs of the garages. From there he could see his mother and father and David talking. They didn't seem to even notice that he was gone. There was a large oak tree next to the garage with one of its branches reaching out across the rooftop. Love put the drumstick in his mouth and climbed onto the branch. He skirted down toward the trunk and then hugged the tree, slipping and scratching himself all the way to the ground. He looked over at the picnic table, but still no one was watching. He stood up and started to cry, looking at his punctured and bloodied arms, but his mouth was full of drumstick, and he was able to get out only a soft moaning.

Later that afternoon, the man with the dog came by again to pick up his laundry. He carried his basket on his head, like a village woman returning from a river with water. Love ran over and grabbed the old dog's tail again, and the dog barked.

"I told you to keep away from that dog!" Lida yelled. She stood up and came at Love, who laughed and ran behind the man. The man stopped with the basket in the air and let Love use his legs as a shield. Lida came up to the man and grabbed at Love's shoulders.

"That boy's going to make me lose my temper."

"Here," the man said, bending down to Love and handing him the basket. "Why don't you carry this?"

"You best not drop that man's clean clothes," Lida yelled.

"Look, look." Love lumbered forward hugging the basket in his arms, his face buried sideways in the clothes so that he could still see the picnic area. Marcus turned to see but never stopped talking to David, then quickly turned back to their conversation, as if they were involved in a very important business deal. Love stumbled and fell, but the basket landed flat on its bottom and no damage was done.

"That's enough of that." Lida swiped at Love's face as he lay on the ground, but he rolled away. The dog barked at her, and she stepped back.

"That's all right," the man said and picked up his basket. "It was my fault. I asked him to do it."

Lida turned away and walked back to the bench. Both men stopped talking as she slid over to Marcus. David got up to take care of the leftovers on the grill.

"I could use just a little snort," she said to Marcus. "What you got on you?"

"I don't have a lot, and I don't have enough cash to get any more."

"Well, can't you ask David to front us?"

"Listen, come on upstairs. I might have something."

"Well, I got to get upstairs anyway. My Lord, this baby is pushin on my bladder somethin fierce. Hold on, baby, I'm comin."

They left David with the chicken and the grill while Love entertained himself amid a pile of discarded newspapers.

Upstairs, they entered their new home. It wasn't a large apartment, just a living room with an attached kitchen and a bedroom at the other end, but it was spacious because they didn't have any furniture yet except the stools that came with the kitchen counter. They hadn't gotten any curtains either, so they used white towels they'd borrowed from David.

"David's cool, don't you think?" Marcus asked through the bathroom door.

"Course." Lida came out of the bathroom and wiped her hands on the window towels. Then she eased herself up onto a stool. Marcus took a baggy of smack out of his pocket.

"You found something for me?" she asked.

"I can't afford to just give you mine all the time. You've got to buy your own."

"Well, I don't have anything, and I can't do nothing until this baby of ours is born. You know how it all got taken."

"I feel real bad about what happened to you and Ruby, how you lost all your stuff," he said. He waited for her to say something, just to see what kind of mood she was in and if this was a good time to go further. She had her arms crossed above her belly and leaned on the kitchen counter.

"I was thinking real hard about how you're just getting by," he continued, "and what we could do to get some cash flow. And I came up with something that's real easy and fast and there ain't no risk."

"I already been buying the lottery every Friday, Marcus."

"That's not it. There ain't no guessing with this."

"You going to put us in jail."

"It's not like that. I was talking with David about old times, and he was saying how it's a shame you so low right now. But he was looking for some way he could help out."

"Well, he could spot me some for now."

"He can't do that. See, he's got to earn a living too. But he said he wanted to do something for you. He always liked you. You know how he always thought you was real fine."

She felt an urge to scrape her arm, but instead, she laughed and cupped her hand over her forehead, feeling the bumps of acne that had returned, like in her adolescent years.

"Naw, really. He always told me I was the luckiest man. I didn't hold it against him none, 'cause it's true. But we got to talking, trying to work out a solution to your problem, and it got me to thinking about what we came up with. There ain't one thing in this world a woman has more valuable than her looks. It may not be fair, but it's the truth. In fact, I wish it was like that for a man. No matter what, if a woman got her looks, then she's got somethin. She don't never have to be down too low."

"I ain't no supermodel, Marcus."

"You don't have to be no supermodel for this. There plenty of people who think you're pretty. But that ain't the point. The point is, David still thinks you fine."

Lida didn't say anything but her lips parted.

"Let me tell you where I'm comin from," he continued. "When I was in Chicago, I would have given anything to be a woman and not have to do the things I did to get by. You been through some bad times with me, but you don't know how bad it can get."

"I'm not in the mood to be brought up on your time in Chicago, Marcus."

"That's not where I'm goin. Just hear me out. I want to help you stay on your feet. But I'm flat broke myself. Even if I get a steady job, it's going to be a while before we see any money. And you hardly got anything right now, and with this new baby comin, things bound to get thin. I'm just talking from experience. If I was a good-looking woman like you, I tell you what I would have been doing in Chicago. I would have made myself a quick friend. You know what I'm talking about?"

"You talkin about whorin?" She shook her head. "I'm not whorin myself out to no one!"

"I'm not talking about whorin, baby. This ain't like whorin if you friends with someone. You think David's a nice guy, don't you? I mean, he don't smell bad and he looks nice. You might a been with him for free if I wasn't in your way. You lucky someone like him wants you, and he's even willing to pay for it. It's just a nice thing you can do for him and he can do for you. It's like friends helping each other out."

"I'm your wife, Marcus!"

"I know you're my wife, that's why I'm telling you all this. I care about you. I love you. I want you to be happy and I want my kids to be happy. It can be just a onetime thing, even. I'm saying you can have enough money for the rent and for the clothes and for anything you want. You don't have to listen to no boss or wake up early or go no-where, and it pays good."

"Why are you so interested in me doing this? How much you gettin out of this, selling your own wife?"

"Baby, no one's forcin you to do this. I just found a way to help you if you want. Sure I get a little somethin from it, 'cause I'm the one who brought him to the door. And I'm the one who'll keep him away too, if you don't want to see him, just like I done before with your uncle. You know I stand by you."

Lida shook her head and licked her dry lips.

"You know I love you, baby," Marcus continued. "I wouldn't want you to do anything you don't think is best for you. People make this out to be such a bad thing. It's just like them rich folks shakin someone's hand and kissin ass for all their money. Just think how quick it'll be over and then you got a hundred dollars. It's not like you lose anything. You may even like it. Fifty dollars for fifteen minutes of somethin you never run out of."

"When I'm pregnant like this?"

"He don't mind. He even thinks it's sexy, and you can't get pregnant twice, so then it's even better."

Lida looked at the baggy in his hand, then squeezed her shoulders up to her ears like cold water had just been thrown on her back.

"He's down there waiting for an answer," Marcus said. "You got your chance right now. Let me tell him to come up. I'll tell him to be real gentle with you, 'cause you're my lady. You want, I can give you some of my stuff for now if I know it's the last time—to make it easier." She shifted herself back onto the stool and put her face on the counter.

"It's fifteen minutes and it's all over, like nothing ever happened," Marcus said softly.

She sat up and rubbed her palms along the thighs of her blue jeans. "You'll give me a taste first?" she asked.

He kissed her forehead, opened the baggy, and removed a popper. He pulled her shirtsleeve up to see her veins.

"Where you gonna be?" she asked him.

"Where you want me?"

"I want you right here."

"No. Not in here. I'll be just outside."

"No. I want you in the house." She pulled her forearm away from him.

"Baby, it's not going to be that bad."

"I know how it's going to be. You don't know!" She let him take her arm again and stick her with the popper.

"Relax, baby," he said. "I won't let nothing bad happen to you."

She sat back on the stool and closed her eyes and waited.

"We'll be right back," he said, and left.

She turned to the kitchen and rested her chin on her arm. The sink of her new apartment was empty, and there were grease stains running down the front of the cabinets like brown tears. In the corners of the ceiling, cracks ate their way through the paint on the walls. Outside, from the street below, she could hear the music from a thousand parties and barbecues, like the old days on Cranston, listening to the sounds of the neighborhood.

SANTA RITA JAIL

TODAY I READ from Claude Brown's narrative, *Manchild in the Promised Land:*

Most of the time, I would go up to Harlem on the weekends, because this was the only place I knew to go when I wanted some fun. It seemed that if I stayed away two weeks, Harlem had changed a lot. I wasn't certain about how it was changing or what was happening, but I knew it had a lot to do with duji, heroin.

Heroin had just about taken over Harlem. It seemed to be a kind of plague. Every time I went uptown, somebody else was hooked, somebody else was strung out. People talked about them as if they were dead. You'd ask about an old friend, and they'd say, "Oh, well, he's strung out." It wasn't just a comment or an answer to a question. It was a eulogy for someone. He was just dead, through.

At that time, I didn't know anybody who had kicked it. Heroin had been the thing in Harlem for about five years, and I don't think anybody knew anyone who had kicked it. They knew a lot of guys who were going away, getting cures, and coming back, but never kicking it. Cats were even going into the Army or jail, coming back, and getting strung out again. I guess this was why everybody felt that when somebody was strung out on drugs, he was through. It was almost the same as saying he was dying. And a lot of cats were dying.

I was afraid to ask about someone I hadn't seen in a while, especially if it was someone who was once a good friend of mine. There was always a chance somebody would say, "Well, he died. The cat took an O.D.," an overdose of heroin; or he was pushed out of a window trying to rob somebody's apartment, or shot five times trying to stick up a place to get some money for drugs. Drugs were killing just about everybody off in one way or another. It had taken over the neighborhood, the entire community. I didn't know of one family in Harlem with three or more kids between the ages of fourteen and nineteen in which at least one of them wasn't on drugs. This was just how it was.

It was like a plague, and the plague usually afflicted the eldest child of every family, like the one of the firstborn with Pharaoh's people in the Bible. Sometimes it was even worse than the biblical plague. In Danny Rogers' family, it had everybody. There were four boys, and it had all of them. It was a disheartening thing for a mother and father to see all their sons strung out on drugs at the same time. It was as though drugs were a ghost, a big ghost, haunting the community.

People were more afraid than they'd ever been before. Everybody was afraid of this drug thing, even the older people who would never use it. They were afraid to go out of their houses with just one lock on the door. They had two, three and four locks. People had guns in their houses because of the junkies. The junkies were committing almost all the crimes in Harlem. They were snatching pocketbooks. A truck couldn't come into the community to unload anything any more. Even if it was toilet paper or soap powder, the junkies would clean it out if the driver left it for a second.

The cats who weren't strung out couldn't see where they were heading. If they were just snorting some horse, they seemed to feel that it wouldn't get to them. It's as though cats would say, "Well, damn, I'm slicker than everybody else," even though some slick cats and some strong guys had fallen into the clutches of heroin. Everybody could see that nobody was getting away from it once they had started dabbling in it, but still some people seemed to feel, "Shit, I'm not gon get caught. I can use it, and I can use it and not be caught."

Guys who were already strung out were trying to keep younger brothers away from stuff. They were trying feebly, and necessarily so, because guys who were strung out on drugs didn't have too much time to worry about anybody but themselves. It was practically a twenty-four-hour-a-day job trying to get some money to get some stuff to keep the habit from fucking with you.

There was a time when I'd come uptown on the weekend and cats would say things like, "Man, let's have a drink," or "Let's get some pot," or "Let's get some liquor." But after a while, about 1955, duji became the thing. I'd go uptown and cats would say, "Hey, man, how you doin'? It's nice to see you. Look here, I got some shit," meaning heroin. "Let's get high." They would say it so casually, the way somebody in another community might say, "C'mon, let's have a drink."

I'd tell them, "No, man, I don't dabble in stuff like that." They'd look at me and smile, feeling somewhat superior, more hip than I was because they were into drugs. I just had to accept this, because I couldn't understand why people were still using drugs when they saw that cats were getting strung out day after day after day. It just didn't make too much sense to me, but that was how things were, and it wasn't likely that anybody was going to change it for some time to come.

Then money became more of a temptation. The young people out in the streets were desperate for it. If a cat took out a twenty-dollar bill on Eighth Avenue in broad daylight, he could be killed. Cats were starving for drugs; their habit was down on them, and they were getting sick. They were out of their minds, so money for drugs became the big thing.

I remember that around 1952 and 1953, when cats first started getting strung out good, people were saying, "Dam, man, that cat went and robbed his own family. He stole his father's suits, stole his mother's money," and all this kinda shit. It was still something unusual back then. In some cases, the lack of money had already killed most family life. Miss Jamie and her family, the Willards, were always up tight for money because she spent the food money for playing the numbers and stuff like that. This was the sort of family that had never had any family life to speak of. But now, since drugs demanded so much money and since drugs had afflicted just about every family with young people in it, this desire for money was wrecking almost all family life.

Fathers were picking up guns and saying, "Now, look, if you fuck wit that rent money, I'm gon kill you," and they meant it. Cats were taking butcher knives and going at their fathers because they had to have money to get drugs. Anybody who was standing in the way of a drug addict when his habit was down on him—from mother or father on down—was risking his life. . . .

CHAPTER 3

OVER THE NEXT few years, Lida's habit grew worse. She was in a deep nod most of the day, scratching her arms and staring at parts of her body for hours. When she wasn't nodding, she was turning tricks to make a quick buck. Her habit cost her seventy dollars a day, and usually she found the money. David had introduced her to a few of his friends, and she didn't need to go on the street to sell herself. At first, she always knew a man willing to give her ten dollars for a blow job, even in the last months of her pregnancy. She had felt pride in that aspect of her life, that she was not some street whore, but more of an in-house friend of friends. When she called on her customers, it was an implicit rule that they talk to her nicely, offer her a beer, ask her about Ronald and Paul. But word had gotten around and the wives and girlfriends of the male tenants gave her nasty looks. Even Gina, who'd come back to live with David, wouldn't talk to her in the hallways. Her in-house clientele slowly dwindled while her habit increased.

When he came home from practice, Marcus could see Lida was ill, sweating and grabbing at her stomach, but he didn't talk about dope in front of the kids. Paul was asleep in the bedroom, and Love was in the living room sitting on a pillow in front of the wall where the TV used to be, the one Lida had pawned the night before. He had his legs stretched out in a triangle, his feet against the wall as a trap for a cockroach. He used a butter knife to flip the bug over every time it got close to the perimeter of the world he'd made for it. But the cockroach was fast, and he ended up smashing its back legs and tail by mistake.

"What you doin over there, Ronald?" Marcus asked. "Where's our TV at?"

"I'm real bad, baby," Lida whispered.

"Sweetheart, why don't you go on up to seventeen?" he asked her. "See Sammy." Marcus always had something on him, but he couldn't afford his own habit if he gave it to her.

"I've been there, baby. I've been to everyone, and they're not home or they wives is in. Just give me a small taste."

Marcus knew better than to let her get beyond begging. Soon there wouldn't be anything left to lose and she'd do what she had to.

"Ronald," Marcus called out. Love didn't turn his head. "Stop that banging and get me some p-e-a-n-u-t b-u-t-t-e-r." Love spelled it back to himself and then dashed for the refrigerator. Inside was a stick of butter, jam, and old bread. He knew there wouldn't be any peanut butter but he had to find the empty jar. The jar was on the counter from lunch and he brought it to his father.

"You are the smartest little nigger I know," Marcus said. Love bowed his head and Marcus scrubbed him on the back of the neck. "Here. I'm gonna give you this and you get us more peanut butter and get a g-r-a-p-e-f-r-u-i-t too. You understand?" Marcus took out his wallet and pulled a ten from the rows of cash inside.

Lida wiped her lips with her arm and swallowed. "Baby . . ." she said to Love, but she didn't continue.

"Get on outta here, Ronald," Marcus yelled. Love pushed the money down into his pocket and opened the front door. He turned down the hallway and headed for the stairs, then realized that he didn't have his shoes on. He went back to the apartment, but the door was closed and he thought better of knocking. He had a key of his own, but he heard his father yelling.

"What'd you do with our TV?"

"That was our TV, Marcus! You took that TV from my mama, so I can sell it any time I want."

"Now you gonna take your mother's side after what I've done for you."

"That ain't what I'm saying. I'm just ill, that's all."

"You'd sell my own children if I didn't come by to check on them. Look at this place."

"Marcus, please, I can't hear any of that right now."

"I know, baby. I'm sorry. Listen. Here. I got some rock for you. Hold you over."

There was silence for a little while. Love turned around and looked down the hallway. It wasn't a large building, but to a seven-year-old, it seemed monstrous, especially the dark staircase that loomed ahead. He walked toward it silently, barefoot, listening for anyone who might be waiting to mug him.

He could afford to take his time. He knew better than to get the food right away and come back too soon. A year ago he'd done that and found his mother and Marcus sitting naked on their mattress, his mother nodding in the corner and Marcus playing guitar. Love had been sent out for cereal that day. He placed the box of Cocoa Puffs on the counter and then Lida called to him.

"Ronald, baby, come here to your mama." Her voice was deep and lazy. Half of him wanted to go to her and half of him wanted to run out the door, but it wasn't often that she asked him to be with her and his father, so he walked over slowly and stood in front of them. He looked down between his father's legs but the guitar was covering him. Marcus sang, " 'Papa don't take no mess, ha!' " and played three high chords over and over.

"Come sit here between us, Ronald," she said. It wasn't her naked-ness that scared him, it was being so close to her and the way she held herself, her dark body curved forward, her legs spread open like for-gotten toys. Lida patted the carpet once more, and Love squeezed be-tween their bodies, his arms pressed into his sides. Marcus sang to himself and didn't seem to notice or care that Love was there.

A few minutes went by this way. White towels hung over the win-dows and a faded gray light filtered into the room. There was one coffee table and a chair near the food counter and the bed mat on which they sat, and that was all the furniture they had.

Love felt his mother shake, and at first he thought she had hiccuped, but then she sniffled and he saw tears run down her face. Her body spasmed against his. He'd heard of a boy's mother on his floor who'd died of an O.D., but he didn't know what an O.D. looked like. Marcus didn't seem concerned.

"What's the matter, Mama?" She continued to cry, and her curved body shook even more as she stared forward, her breasts dripping milk over the folds of her stomach. Love took her hand and rubbed on the inside of her forearm, just below the track marks.

"Mama?" He began to cry also, and then Paul began crying in the other room.

They cried for ten minutes. It was like Lida's whole body was filled with water and it leaked and leaked out over her. He got scared she might cry herself out of breath or that she was hurt somewhere inside and he couldn't stop it. Love buried his face into her ribs and he heard her heart beat like a washing machine with shoes in it, but soon it sounded like it was slowing down.

Then she stopped crying all of a sudden, and that scared him even more. He stopped crying also, so he could hear if she was choking. There was a long silence, and then she spoke:

"Don't hate me," she said into the air.

"I don't, Mama," Love said. There was silence for a long while again. The wind blew the towel on the window a little and Love felt Lida's skin rise in goose bumps all over.

"I hate you," she said softly. Love looked up at her, but she wasn't looking at him.

"Why?"

"I hate you," she said even louder. "I hate you!"

"Why, Mama, why?"

But she didn't answer him. She rolled onto her side and curled up in the corner with her back to him and closed her eyes.

This time he would stay out all evening and come back when he was sure they'd be asleep. When he saw the light from outside, he ran down the last dark steps and out onto the street. Ten dollars in your pocket wasn't a bad thing to have, even if it was supposed to be spent on groceries. Marcus always let him keep the change anyway, and Love put his mind on figuring out how much might be left for himself. He couldn't figure out complicated math yet, but it seemed everything cost one dollar and so one jar of peanut butter and one grapefruit would be two dollars, and he knew ten dollars was a lot more than two dollars. Then he could buy pizza for dinner with a Coke and have ice cream too, and maybe buy a water gun, but maybe that was too much.

The street felt exciting and alive, if not exactly safe. There were many older kids out as the evening came on. One group of boys threw a football across the street, another played dice and yelled at girls as they walked past, and others sat on the stoops of buildings listening to music. They wore gold earrings and bracelets, laughed and pushed each other around. They tapped each other's fists and took part in secret business through the windows of doubled-parked cars. He loved the way adults coming back from work walked with their arms close to their sides, weaving through the teenagers as through a minefield, afraid of accidentally setting one off with the wrong look.

It was not that frightening to him. Most of the kids seemed to ignore him, or if they tripped over him, they'd just push him away or say something like "Watch yourself," and then be off.

He knew the two blocks to the liquor store well, and only one spot posed any danger. At the first corner was a doorway to an inside staircase that was hidden from the street. It was impossible to see who might be in there, but almost always there were bottles thrown out of it at random and the sound of men laughing. Once he saw a woman stop in front of the doorway and look inside after someone had shouted to her. A man's hand reached out and grabbed her arm, and as she struggled, another pair of arms reached out and pulled her in, ripping the purse off her shoulder, seemingly sucking her into the darkness and laughter.

To avoid this corner, Love crossed to the other side where two boys his age sat on steps and laced up shiny black Rollerblades. Love stood on the curb and watched them, his mouth open, unaware of himself. The two boys finished lacing their skates and stood up, grabbing onto the posts for balance, then wobbling forward. One was overweight, and it seemed the boots might crack and burst under him, the wheels bending at an angle. The other boy had no hair, his head smooth as a brown egg.

"What up?" this boy said to Love with a slight yell, the way all the older kids on the block greeted each other.

"What up," Love said back. The two boys skated and stumbled to the next staircase and grabbed on, the larger one following the eggheaded one and running into him. Love watched but did not laugh, for even the attempt at skating seemed a triumph to him.

"I'm Durrell," said the bald one to Love. "He's my twin brother, Turrell. He don't look like my twin 'cause he's fat." Turrell looked at him and smiled. "He don't like to talk neither," Durrell continued. "He could talk. He talks to me, but he don't talk to no one else. He don't even talk to our mama." Durrell started off across to the other staircase again.

"How'd you get your head so smooth?" Love asked.

"That's its natural way. I can't grow no hair. My mama says it's 'cause I got the same blood as my great-grandad. His head was bald too. Somehow the blood got carried on through my granddad and my mama and then on to me. But my mama ain't bald. Anyway, what you doin?"

"Goin to the store."

"Where your shoes?"

"At home."

"You got money?"

Love knew he shouldn't say but felt that it was so obvious he couldn't lie, so he nodded.

"How much money you got?"

"Ten dollars," Love heard himself brag.

"Your mama give you ten dollars?"

"My papa, for peanut butter."

"What you gonna buy, a whole cow?"

"Grapefruit too."

"That ain't gonna cost no ten dollars."

"I know."

"You want to buy Turrell's blades?"

Turrell heard this and shook his head.

"You gonna sell 'em for ten dollars?" Love asked.

"Naw. You got to pay twenty dollars for blades like these. But I got a way you could get ten more dollars that's real easy. You just got to come with me."

"I got to go to the store."

"Well, when you come back from the store, we might not be here, and the man giving away all the money might be gone too. And it only takes a little bit of time now."

Love shrugged his shoulders. "That's all right."

"All right." Durrell pulled Turrell to standing, and they both went across to the other staircase and back again.

"Where's the man at?" Love asked.

"You got to have ten dollars to start with. Show me you got ten dollars."

Love shook his head.

"All I want to do is see you got it. You can stand over there and just hold it up."

Love walked to the opposite staircase and held out the ten-dollar bill.

"Okay, I see it," Durrell said. "Now come on with me. You don't have to do it if you don't want. Just come on and see how I mean for you to get it."

Love walked behind the twins as they skated across the street and turned the corner on to a block that Love had never been on before. This was even more crowded than his own, with people filling the streets and yelling at each other like at a party, and no cars driving through.

In the middle of the block, a group of older kids stood in front of a staircase that went down to a cellar, their backs to the street like a wall. He heard someone yelling behind the older kids.

"The middle one, man, it's the middle one. Aw man, you got to watch more closely." And the whole group groaned in disappointment.

"I always wanted to do this, but I never had any money," Durrell said. "But I always know the one to pick. Watch this."

He pushed his way between two boys and made room for Love to peek in. A young man crouched on the ground facing the crowd. He moved three walnut shells around very swiftly in front of him.

"Play your money, friends. Keep your eyes on the prize." He quickly lifted the middle shell and revealed a green pea, then went back to shuffling. He showed the pea in the middle every time he called out. "If you've seen it by chance, keep your money in your pants. If you've seen it twice, got to roll the dice. If you've seen again, you're sho to win." He stopped shuffling, and Love was sure he knew the pea was in the middle. In fact, the man had gone real slowly the last time, and it seemed like you'd have to be stupid not to know.

"Who wants to play? Pick the shell with the pea and double your green." There were no takers at first, and Love couldn't understand why no one bet, but they'd been watching longer, so maybe they knew better.

"It's in the middle one," Durrell yelled.

"Show me your money, half-pint," the man said.

"I ain't got none. My friend's got the money."

"Well, have him lay it down."

Before Durrell could beg Love, a very tall man with dark sunglasses spoke up. "I think the boy's right," he said. "Here's my money." He took out three bills and carefully counted them, tossing them separately onto the ground. "Twenty . . . forty . . . sixty dollars. Now show me that pea."

The man lifted his hand and there, in the shadow of the shell, was the dried-up pea. Everyone, including Love, jumped in the air and screamed with pleasure

"I told you! I told you," Durrell yelled. "How come you didn't bet? You've got to give him the money."

The man with the shells shook his head and took out a thick roll of bills. He counted the money just as the tall man had, slowly, throwing the bills on the ground so everyone could see. The tall man bent down and grabbed all the bills, then held them up to the rest of the people, and they clapped. The man on the ground began to shuffle the shells again. "It's that easy, friends. Maybe I'm not as fast as I used to be. Or maybe that boy there's got an eye for gold. If he were a pirate he'd be Long John Silver, if he were a bomber he'd have hit Qaddafi smack on

the head. Now take a good look, 'cause I'm gonna show you the pea."
He lifted up the shell in the middle and the pea was there. Then he
shuffled again. "Do you know where it is? Are you following it?"

"It's in the middle," Love yelled out.

The man lifted the shell and there it was. "The boy's right."

"Ten dollars. Give me ten dollars."

"You've got to put the money down first, half-pint."

Love pulled the money out of his pocket and held it in his fist as the
man shuffled again. The man's hands moved slowly, and Love followed
the shells the whole time. This was the easiest way to make money ever.
He would bring back the money to show Marcus. He could buy the
food and buy the skates and his mama wouldn't have to beg Marcus for
money anymore. He could buy his brother something too, maybe a toy
or a bottle. The man's hands stopped.

Love threw his money in the circle.

"It's in the middle. I call it. It's in the middle."

"The boy says it's in the middle. Does anyone else want a piece of
the action?" The rest of the kids grumbled and moved around, but no
one put any money down. They looked at the tall man, but he shook
his head.

"I didn't see it this time," he said. "I think I saw it under the middle,
but I lost my concentration."

Seeing that there were no other takers, the man on the ground turned
the shell over with a slap. The pea was there.

"I won! I won! I won!" Love danced and hugged Durrell. "Give me
my money. I put in ten dollars. Give me ten dollars."

The man shook his head and took out his roll of bills. "This is not
my day. I guess I'm gonna have to go home and practice some more."
He put the money on the ground, and Love picked up the two ten-
dollar bills.

"See, I told you. I told you," Durrell said. "Give me some money
so I can play."

"Naw. I won this money for me."

"But I showed you. You got to give me some too."

Love shrugged. He could always win again, and anyway, this was the first real friend he'd ever had.

"What you gonna do? You gonna bet?" Love asked as he handed Durrell one of the bills.

"Yeh, I'm gonna make me a million dollars."

The man on the ground shuffled his shells again and called to the crowd. "All the little boys out here making money today, but the grown-ups is too scared to trust they own eyes. See, here's the pea. Now watch if you can as I shuffle around real fast." But he didn't shuffle real fast, and then he asked again:

"Who's gonna take some candy from a baby today? Who knows where that little green pea is at? Who's gonna double what they made all week, all month, all year, in just one tiny second?"

"I got to put it down this time," said the tall man. "I've seen it for sure under the middle." The man put down all his money, one hundred and twenty dollars. "I just wish I had me some more." Then it was like a dam burst, and everyone else in the crowd threw their money on the ground. "I got ten on the middle." "I put down one hundred." It was hard to tell whose money was where. Both Love and Durrell joined in and threw their money down with smiles stretched across their faces and grabbed each other's hands.

The man on the ground slapped the shell over. It was hard to see at first, or maybe just hard to believe, but they had to blink twice before they saw clearly. There was nothing but pavement underneath.

"No way, I saw it!" yelled out a large boy with a gold watch.

There was a second of silent shock, but before anyone else could think to speak, the tall man yelled out: "Five-oh! Here come the cops." Love and Durrell turned to look around, as did everyone else. They looked both ways but didn't see a car or even any bicycle cops. When they looked back, the money, the man on the ground, and the tall man were gone.

"Aw shit!" one guy yelled. "That son of a bitch got all my money."

"You mean he won it all," said his friend, laughing.

"I got to buy peanut butter and a grapefruit," Love said. His eyes began to fill with tears. He was afraid to think what Marcus and his mother might do to him if he showed up with no money and no food.

"Ten dollars ain't so much to go cryin over," Durrell said. "I know how we can get ten dollars easy."

Love shook his head.

"It's easier than this. You just have to follow my plan and we can get money from a cash register. My older brother, Murrell, does it all the time. And you don't need no money to do this."

Love walked away from the stairs through the crowd of people, with Durrell and Turrell skating behind him. The pea had to be under the middle shell. He'd seen it. It had to be there. The man had tricked him. The tall man and the man with the shells and Durrell too. They'd all tricked him out of his money.

"Give me your skates," Love demanded. Durrell stopped, and Turrell ran into him.

"Why you want my skates?"

"Give me my money back."

"I don't have any money."

"Give me your skates then," Love said again.

"Naw. I ain't gonna give you my skates."

Love rushed him and grabbed him by the shirt and shook him from side to side.

"Give 'um!"

Durrell fell backward, pulling Love on top of him. Love punched Durrell as hard as he could in the face and in the stomach, just like he'd seen older kids do on the street. He put his head down and punched as Durrell swung back wildly. A crowd gathered around and the teenagers started yelling.

"Get him. That's Snapple's little brother."

"Look at that boy punch," another one yelled. "That boy's tearin him up. He's a pit bull."

"That little boy's from my building. His mama's a ho."

"He's got a whole lot of dog in him. Look at this boy. This boy's gonna mess him up."

Love felt encouraged by the shouts and hit Durrell even harder. Turrell took off his skates as fast as he could. He held one in the air and went over to where Love straddled his brother and hit him over the head with the rubber heel-stop.

"Oh, that got to hurt!" one boy yelled, and the crowd laughed as Love fell off Durrell. The laughter of the crowd angered Love more than the hit on the head, and he got up after Turrell now.

"He gone take on both a them. I got my money on that pit bull."

As if a bolt of lightning rushed through him, Love began pounding Turrell.

"Give me my money. Give me my money," he screamed. He struck out as if he were in a sticky spiderweb that he had to swing and swing through until he was free. Durrell pulled him off his brother, and without interrupting his swings, Love switched targets. He didn't think about the skates anymore or about his money or about Durrell. He had no thoughts but to hit as hard and as fast as he could until there was no more to hit or until he was no longer able to hit.

Durrell's nose was bleeding and he'd stopped fighting. He just turned to the side and protected his face. But Love hadn't gotten all the fight out of him yet. He jumped up and went after Turrell, but Turrell ran away with his skates in his hands.

"I hate you!" Love yelled. The crowd laughed, and some applauded. "I hate you!"

Love stood in the center of the circle by himself now. He felt the throbbing of his swollen hands and the pounding in his head and his burning knees, but he felt good, better than he'd ever felt before, like everyone there had given him ten dollars, a hundred times over.

A WEEK AFTER the fight with Durrell and Turrell, the older kids of the neighborhood took Love into their set. Even Durrell's older brother, Murrell, had to tolerate him because the OGs liked him. It was an OG known as Soda Pop who had given Love the name Pit Bull at the fight, and Soda Pop brought him to their crib the next time he saw Love on the street.

The crib was an abandoned room on the sixth floor of the corner building. The laughing demons in the darkened doorway were sentries for the crew, tweakers who got free rock for watching the entrance. Now they nodded to Love and cleared the center of the hallway as if he were a rap star coming out to the stage. He had free passage into the tunnel and up the stairs. Next he'd run up the stairwell, two steps at a time, until he reached the fifth-floor landing, where another guard stopped him and used a walkie-talkie to let them know he was coming. They always radioed back saying exactly these words about him: "He cool."

When he got to the door, he knocked once, paused, and then three times quickly, for 13th Street, Ace Trey. Ace Trey controlled the blocks from 11th to 14th, High Street to Fruitvale. All the pushers went through them, including David, although he saw them simply as the only suppliers in the area, like Lucky's was the only supermarket.

In general, it was safe to claim Ace Trey anywhere on the East Side of Oakland. The rivalry with West Side had started before anyone could remember, but Carlyle, another member of the set, explained that it had to have started around the time the Cypress Freeway went up, when many of the people left West Oakland and built up East Oakland. Love knocked the secret code and Onion came to the door, named so because his smell alone was enough to keep people out. He was over seven feet tall and had a cut-eye look, as if he thought you'd called his mama out of her name. Only people in the set knew how nice he was. He opened the door, looked straight over Love's head, and put his hand to his brow.

"I thought I heard someone knocking." He turned back into the room. "You guys hear something?"

"I'm here," Love yelled from below him.

"That! You hear that? Like some sort of mosquito. Oh well." He began to close the door, and Love pushed against it.

"Oh, it's Pit Bull." Onion grabbed Love and swung him up on his shoulder like a plank of wood and then dropped him in the kitchen.

The next best thing after getting in the crib was going around and tapping everyone on the fist. Carlyle was in the kitchen making pancakes on the flat iron burner. Carlyle was always cooking, and Love was always hungry, so they naturally became good friends. Carlyle gave him a tap and then Love went into the living room. The windows were boarded up and the room was lit from each corner by a naked bulb, casting long shadows across the walls. Web and Sam, two Lebanese brothers, played dominoes at the table with their girlfriends, Sandy and Letreece, whom everyone called Puke for her bulimic tendencies. Love went over and tapped each one of them.

Murrell sat on the couch with his shoes up on the windowsill, smoking a jay and listening to his headphones. He was eleven and used to be the youngest member until Love was let in. Love walked over to tap him, but he closed his eyes.

"What the hell's that, Snapple!" Soda Pop yelled at Murrell as he came out of the bedroom, five of the older members behind him.

Snapple shrugged. "What?"

"Pit Bull, get back in here. You can't let this punk dis you like that."

Love turned slowly, knowing that even coming back was like calling Murrell a punk.

"I didn't do nothing, Pop," Snapple said.

"You best watch yourself. Pit Bull gonna catch on to your shit and take you like he did your brothers. Now give him some love."

Snapple tapped Love's fist with a covert hardness as Soda Pop walked past them. Snapple didn't wait for Love to tap him back.

"You two are going on a mission," Pop said. "You're going to get me a chili burger from Adam's."

"I can do it on my own," Snapple protested.

"So can I," Love said.

"So could I," Soda Pop said, "but you two are going together, to keep an eye on each other. Here." He handed Snapple some cash and both boys headed downstairs, Snapple moving too quickly for Love to keep up.

"Come on. Pop wants his food fast." Love did his best to catch up as Snapple yelled questions to him.

"Where you live at before?"

"Cranston."

"West Side? You a traitor."

"No," Love said, losing his breath.

"You better not be."

"I'm not." They reached the hallway on the first floor and ran through the addicts blocking the passage.

"What your daddy do?" Snapple asked.

"He's a m-u-s-i-c-i-a-n." Love spelled it exactly as Marcus had taught him.

"What's that?"

"A musician."

"He ain't no musician."

"He is so."

They got onto the block and Love ran faster, but so did Snapple.

"What about your mama? What she do?"

"Slow down."

"I thought you was fast. You want me to slow down for you? All you got to do is ask."

He slowed to a walk, panting hard himself. Love caught up to him.

"Everyone know what your mama do," Snapple said.

"So?"

"Never mine. You too young to understand."

"No I ain't."

They turned left on East 14th, past the Army Supply and Bait Shop.

"What your mama do?" Love asked.

"She a nurse."

"What about your daddy?"

"He in the air force. He fly jets."

"Hornets?"

"No, fool. Airplanes."

"I ain't no fool."

"Yes you is." Snapple spit near Love's foot.

"You a F-O-O-L," Love spelled.

Snapple stopped and bent over in exaggerated laughter.

"What?" Love asked.

"You can't even spell fool."

"Yes I can."

"Fool is F-U-L."

"No it ain't."

"It is so. What you know? You cut school too long. You don't even know your ABCs." Snapple began to walk quickly again.

They reached the parking lot for Adam's, a small burger joint with a single row of stools behind a glass wall.

Snapple stopped at the corner and put his finger close to Love's face. "You got to stay outside and guard my back in case some dudes come looking for me."

"Who?"

Snapple waved his hand in front of his nose. "Damn, dog. Now I know why they call you Pit Bull. That breath smell like Purina Puppy Chow."

Love pulled his lower lip out and tried to smell his own breath.

"Just be on the lookout for any angry-looking dudes."

Snapple went inside and got in line at the counter while Love stood to the side of the glass door and surveyed the parking lot. The street was busy, and cars came in and out of the lot every few seconds.

When Snapple came out of the restaurant with the food, he walked straight past Love, who had to jog again to catch up. Then he slowed down, and when Love got out in front a little and led the way, Snapple stepped on the back of his shoe and gave him a flat tire. Love turned with his fists clenched.

"Oh, sorry, dog," Snapple said. "I didn't mean to. I thought you was speeding up. Here, let me get you some candy for that. I'll go get you some candy from a store I know." Love looked at him for a moment, the anger swelling and then receding inside him.

"Come on, you . . ." Snapple mumbled something that sounded like "pussy."

"What?"

Snapple smiled, "What? Come on, I'll get you candy."

Love followed him to a liquor store five blocks away. He was angry at Snapple but didn't know what to do, like when his mama slapped him on the head.

Snapple took him inside the store, and they stopped in front of the candy shelves directly across from the counter.

"Get what you want. You can get ten candy bars."

"Ten?" Love couldn't help but smile.

"Yeah. I got to get something to drink from the back for Pop." Snapple slipped away toward the refrigerated section. Love picked up and replaced different candy bars from the shelves while the owner, a large West Indian man, watched him closely.

"You going to get some of that candy or just touch all of it?"

Love looked at him and then went back to picking out his candy. He knew that he couldn't eat ten candy bars at once, so it would be important to get some that he could eat right away and some that wouldn't melt. He couldn't get too many chocolate bars, but he didn't like hard candy except for the kind that tasted like sour apple. He also wanted to get something for his little brother, something he could suck on like a Blow Pop, but he didn't know if Snapple would consider a Blow Pop a whole candy bar or just half, since they cost less. Just as he put back the sucker and picked up a pack of gum, there was a large crash in the back.

"God damn you," the owner yelled. "What you doing in the back there?" He ran around the counter and up the aisle. At the same moment, Snapple materialized from another aisle and went up to the counter where all the scratch-off lottery tickets were locked up in large rolls of silver and gold.

"Shit!" the West Indian man yelled from the back of the store. "Why don't you watch what you're doing?" Snapple lifted himself up on the counter, reached over to the cash register, and pushed all the buttons. The register rang and the tray opened.

"Hey!" the owner yelled and came running back up the aisle. Snapple grabbed as many bills as he could, jumped off the counter, and darted out the door.

"Run," he screamed to Love, and laughed. In an instant, Snapple was gone, but the owner reached the door and blocked Love's way. He grabbed Love by the biceps and yelled after Snapple, "I'm going to kill you, you motherfucking rat!"

He lifted Love up by his arm and dragged him behind the counter. With his other hand he dialed the police on the phone.

"I've just been robbed and I have one of the rats, and I'm going to kill him if you don't get over here fast." He hung up the phone and took a gun out from under his counter. He pointed it at Love.

Love had never stared up the barrel of a gun before, and he was frightened, not by the knowledge that it could kill him as much as by the knowledge that it would make a very loud sound right in his face.

"Get down on the ground." Love sat down. "Now lay down on your stomach, over here." Love lay on his stomach, and the man stepped on his back with one heavy foot as he counted the money left in his register.

"What's your friend's name?" he demanded. Love could hardly breathe under the weight of the man's foot. He didn't answer, and the man pressed down even more.

"What's his name, you little shit?"

"Murrell."

"Murrell what?"

"I don't know."

"You worthless piece of shit. You know you're going to go to jail and be beat up every day by murderers and rapists. The police are going to come get you and take you away and you'll never get out alive. You'll rot in jail and then you'll rot in hellfire forever. Kids like you go to hell."

Two policemen eventually showed up. They walked in slowly with their hands on the butts of their guns.

"You called us?"

"He's back here," the owner said. The policemen came around the counter and cuffed Love with a plastic twist-tie device as the owner explained what happened.

"You should lock him up for good," he added. "These kids are just going to get into more trouble if you let them out. They're a plague on society and us hardworking people."

"All right," the policeman said, lifting Love up and walking him out of the store. "We'll make sure he doesn't bother you again."

They threw him in the back of their police car and got in.

"I didn't do nothing," Love mumbled from under his tears.

"What's your name?"

"Ronald LeRoy. L-e-r-o-y."

"What was your friend's name?"

"Murrell."

"Where does he live?"

Love shrugged, though he knew Snapple lived at the crib.

"Where do you live?"

"Terrace Apartments."

The cops drove him home, and one of them walked up the stairs with him.

"This it? This where you live?" Love nodded. The policeman knocked. There was no answer and he knocked again.

"You live with your parents?"

Love nodded.

"Know where they're at?"

Love shook his head. The officer took a deep breath and let it out loudly. The radio on his shoulder spewed information and he talked back into it, then faced Love.

"I guess I'm going to have to take you to CPS. You're too young to be on your own. And without any shoes on either."

"I have a key."

"Well, your parents shouldn't let you out by yourself and then not be home. I'm supposed to take you with me."

"No," Love cried. "I'm not going." He shook his head. He'd heard of kids in his building being taken away from their parents by the cops and never coming back.

"Hey, hey." The policeman laughed. "It's okay. Stop crying. I can't take you now, anyway. I've got to go." He looked up and down the hallway and then took out a piece of paper from his belt. "Tell me what your parents' names are."

"Lida and Marcus." Love wiped his eyes and spelled their names for the officer.

"Okay. I'm going to leave you here, and then I'm going to send somebody out from CPS. Now, you understand that if you do anything like this again, if you even go into his store, I'm going to take you to jail. You understand?"

Love nodded. The cop cut off his plastic handcuffs.

"Okay. Now go on inside." Love waited for the cop to leave, but he didn't move. "Go on," he said. "I just want to make sure you get in okay."

Love took out his key and opened the door, then slipped inside and slammed it shut. The policeman laughed and talked through the door: "Okay. Now you stay there until your parents get home."

Love heard the cop walk away.

The room was empty except for the mat on the living room floor. He walked into the bedroom, but no one was home and Paul wasn't on his blanket.

He rubbed his wrists and went to the window. He pulled aside the white towel and watched for the cop to leave. There were people staring at the police car and kids playing kickball in the street. He recognized a guy from Ace Trey on a bike, riding up and down the block ringing his bell, warning the dealers.

There was a thump from the bathroom, and Love turned. There was another thump, and he went to check it out. He found Paul sitting in the empty bathtub in a pool of his own urine, kicking the tub with his heel.

"How long you been here?" Love knelt by the side of the tub and turned on the water. It was cold for almost a minute, and he let it run over his wrists until it warmed up. He plugged up the drain with his palm and the water filled in around his brother's legs and waist, mixing with the urine.

"I got busted by the cops," Love said. Paul looked at him silently. Love watched the water rise, slowly swallowing his brother's body. When it reached his own elbow, he pulled his hand away from the drain and the water emptied at nearly the same rate as it poured in. He took an old towel from the shower rack, soaked it under the faucet, and rubbed the warm cloth around the back of Paul's neck, across his thin ribs, and over his small potbelly.

NO ONE FROM CPS ever came to check on them as far as Love ever knew. He continued to hang with Ace Trey, and when Paul got old enough, he brought him to the crib too. The crew called Paul Li'l Pit since he was Pit Bull's little brother.

Carlyle made Danish pastry braids for Li'l Pit's fifth birthday. He'd seen how to do it on *Julia Child* which he reserved the right to watch every afternoon at three. Soda Pop was up for it, bought him all the ingredients he ever wanted. Love was up for it too, and so was Li'l Pit. Pop had them stay in the kitchen while the rest of the set worked in the living room, planning. Ace Trey was going to war. They were going to war for the Tigers against Four Deuce after Four Deuce sent Fletcher Washington to the hospital with a bullet in his spine. Everyone knew it was Claude Sonny who took out Fletcher because Claude just came out of Fulton for trying to get Fletcher two years earlier. There wasn't anything else to know except that Ace Trey protected the Tigers and the Tigers protected Ace Trey.

Li'l Pit sat on a stool at the kitchen table and Love stood at the counter. Love got to mix the flour and eggs, mash the berries, and add the sugar.

"Give me the measurer," he told his brother. Li'l Pit brought him the waxed-Pepsi cup on which Carlyle had drawn measuring marks. "Now!" Love poured in twice the amount of sugar called for. "Taste this." He dipped his finger in and held it out for Li'l Pit.

Snapple sauntered in from the living room with a smile. "How the womenfolk all doin? We got some hungry men waitin out here."

"Seem like some niggahs don't want no food," Carlyle said to Love.

"Damn, dog, I'm just playin wit you." Snapple tapped Carlyle's shoulder. "Smell good. Like some serious jam. Well, you little girls keep yourself safe in here." He walked out again, sure to return, as he had all morning. There wasn't much for him to do in the living room. They let him watch, but he was still too young to speak up.

"These fools ain't gonna let me do nothin," Snapple said when he kicked the kitchen door open a few minutes later. "They too scared I might go crazy and kill a whole lotta niggahs just 'cause I feel like it." He bumped Li'l Pit off the stool with his hip and sat down.

Li'l Pit stood up and began to bark at him loudly.

Snapple laughed. "Damn, you a sick puppy, Li'l Pit."

"What you doin, niggah?" Love walked up to Snapple, his fists clenched at his sides. "Give my brother back his stool."

"This ain't got nobody's name on it."

Li'l Pit continued to bark at Snapple, baring his teeth.

"He was sittin there," Love said.

"I was sittin here yesterday. I was sittin here 'fore your tiny butt was born."

Carlyle stepped between them. He was tall and thin, and it was known that he hadn't hit anyone even once in his life, but he stepped between them, a cookie sheet in his hand.

"Snapple, why you hanging out with the young kids? You growing up or down?"

Snapple spit on the kitchen floor near Li'l Pit's feet.

"Why don't you go on out with the big boys?" Carlyle said to him.

"Naw. I got to be in here." Snapple turned his head to the side and cracked his neck.

"That punk gonna get a lip full," Love said to Carlyle.

"Yeah," Snapple replied. "A lip full a your ass."

"I'm gonna count to three," Carlyle said, "and then I'm gonna step out the way and let happen whatever happens. But then I'm gonna have Pop beat both your asses, and no telling what he's gonna do on a day like this." Carlyle counted out loud slowly. Snapple waved his hand in front of his nose.

"Man, what's that burning? Somethin in the oven burning." He went over to the oven, opened it, and looked in. There wasn't anything in it yet. Li'l Pit got back on the stool.

Love laughed. "It's not even on."

"Well, something smell like it's burning."

Carlyle went back to the table and rolled the dough out into long rectangles. He gave Li'l Pit a butter knife.

"Cut these like this, in little triangles."

Li'l Pit took the knife and cut. Snapple stood by the door. Every once in a while, they could hear someone raise his voice in the next room. Carlyle turned on the radio to a jazz station, and Li'l Pit cocked his head to the beat, then started to sing.

> I do the cutting
> You do the baking
> I do the dough and
> You do the jam.

"That's right," Carlyle said.

"Fuck this noise. I got to go," Snapple said. "I got to go home and see my brothers." He put his hands in his pockets and waited.

"What's keepin you?" Love asked.

"Don't want to see my pops."

"I thought your daddy was in the army?"

"He is."

"The army of God," Carlyle added.

"No he ain't. He over there fightin in Panama. I just got a letter."

"Show it, then," Love said.

"I lost it."

"You lost your mind," Carlyle said, and put the pastry in the oven. He laid out a new sheet of dough, and Li'l Pit cut it into triangles, singing his song again. Love helped press down the edges as Snapple watched silently from the corner.

"Y'all is whack," he said. "I got places to be."

"Be there, then," Carlyle said.

Love pushed his brother off the stool in front of Snapple and sat down. Li'l Pit looked stunned but didn't bark this time.

Snapple spat on the ground, halfway between them.

"You gonna clean that up, you know," said Carlyle.

"I can spit if I want."

"Not in my kitchen. Now grab a rag and wipe that up."

"The hell I will."

"Didn't your mama teach you nothin?"

"My mama taught me not to hang around with no little faggots."

Love walked toward Snapple again with his fists ready, but then Li'l Pit started to bark and they all stopped to watch. This time his barks were not like an angry dog, but like a sick, rabid dog, foaming and sloshing with spittle. He wiped his hand across his mouth and nose, leaving a long strand of shiny mucus. Immediately he threw his arm against the tray of dough triangles and sent them flying onto the floor, covered with his saliva.

He stood over his mess, and the rest watched him as he seethed.

Snapple burst out laughing. "Damn. Those look like some good snot tarts you made there, Li'l Pit." Carlyle reached out to slap him but missed. Snapple backed to the door, smiling.

" 'Didn't your mama teach y'all nothin?' " he said. "You gonna have to clean that up, you know?" He laughed and went back into the living room.

"What up, bro?" Love asked Li'l Pit. Li'l Pit just turned around and sat on the floor.

Soda Pop opened the door with Snapple behind him.

"See," Snapple said.

"Who the fuck did this?" Pop asked.

"It was Li'l Pit," Snapple said. "I told you."

"Why the hell do you let him in here?" Pop yelled at Carlyle. "You know how he gets."

"It wasn't his fault," Love said.

"Didn't he throw them on the floor?" Snapple yelled in.

"Shut up, Snapple," Pop yelled, then turned back to Carlyle. "If you can't keep control of the kids, then get them the fuck out of here!" He closed the door, but not before Snapple got in one last smile.

THE NEXT MORNING the war table was used for breakfast. The first battle had not gone well the night before. Puke, Sam's girlfriend, was supposed to entice Claude Sonny. She'd given him her number the week before, and they were supposed to go to the barbershop on 27th to get him a haircut, and while he was in the chair, Soda Pop was supposed to come in and shoot him in the head. But someone had tipped him off, and Sonny took Puke to an abandoned house where she was raped by five guys. So Ace Trey and the Tigers went and shot up the house, but by then Four Deuce was long gone.

Carlyle served scrambled eggs with mushrooms and diced tomatoes, English muffins with leftover strawberry jam, and a concoction of lemonade and grape juice he called Get-the-Fuck-Up! It was Snapple's favorite thing to say, and he often finished four glasses of it in one sitting just to ask for more.

"Get-the-Fuck-Up," Snapple said to Love, his hand reaching for the pitcher. This was not a morning Pop would tolerate any bickering. Love paused, then handed him the juice and shook his head.

"What's your problem?" Snapple said.

"Nothing." He went back to eating his eggs.

Li'l Pit sat on the other side of him. He didn't eat, just squeezed the eggs in his hands. No one told him to stop, because they knew from experience that he would start throwing food. Soda Pop sat directly across the large round table. Fourteen members of the crew were there that Sunday morning, and the TV was on behind them, playing the U.S. Open. Soda Pop was a big golf fan and a member of the Lake Chabot Municipal Golf Course, where he was going to take the younger set to watch him tee off later in the day. He usually let them drive the golf cart and putt on the greens.

When breakfast was over, they were all told to wash up the dishes so the older members could plan another attack to go down later that evening. Love called drying first, so Carlyle washed, which he would have done anyway since he didn't trust the others to get the plates clean. Snapple rinsed, but in order to reach the sink, he had to stand on a milk crate they kept for such occasions. Li'l Pit sat on the stool by the table.

Love and Snapple stood right next to each other. They both knew that if they caused any trouble, one of them was bound to be left at home when the rest went golfing.

Carlyle got the lather up in the first sink and then let the water run over Snapple's hands. When Snapple was through rinsing a plate, he handed it to Love up high, like he was teasing a kitten with a piece of food.

"Don't drop this. It's very slippery."

"Just give it."

"I'm just making sure you know."

"Well then just give it and stop playin."

"Why you a playah-hater?"

Love dried the plate with the clean T-shirt they used for a towel and placed it on top of the table in front of Li'l Pit.

"You know I'm going to hit a hole in one today," Snapple said.

"Uh-huh," Carlyle said. "You gonna hit a hole in one of them trees."

"You see. You want to put money on it?"

"You got a hundred dollars?"

"Sure."

"All right," Carlyle said. "I'm gonna put a hundred dollars on it. But you got to hit a hole in one, not just from the place it land on the green."

"I'll put a hundred on it too," Love said.

"You ain't got no money yet," Snapple said. "You got to do some slinging first."

"I got money from Pop."

"You got money from yo mama's snatch," Snapple said. He hung a plate out for Love to take.

"Shut up," Love said.

"Don't tell me to shut up, bitch. It ain't my fault your mama's a ho. I'm just tellin it like it is."

"Shut up, Snapple," Carlyle said.

"You just angry 'cause you like to be with these little boys and touch they things."

"That's it." Carlyle threw the plate into the sink and grabbed Snapple in a bear hug so that his arms were trapped.

"Get off a me, faggot! Help, the faggot's trying to rape me."

"Get his legs," Carlyle yelled to Love. Snapple kicked, but Love was able to hold on to one foot after he pulled off a shoe. They carried Snapple out of the kitchen into the living room, where the rest of the crew sat around the war table, watching TV. Snapple yelled again:

"Pop, get these faggots off a me," but no one moved. Li'l Pit ran and grabbed Snapple's loose foot, but Snapple kicked him away, and he stepped back and followed them into the bathroom, the only room with a window that opened, which was in fact perpetually open to air out the smells.

Carlyle pulled Snapple to the window and put his head out of it faceup so that all he could see was sky. Snapple got his hands loose and grabbed on to the walls around the window to keep from being pushed out farther, but Love let go of his feet and punched him in the stomach.

When Snapple let up for a second, Carlyle was able to force him out the window along his back, all the way to his knees, which he hooked around the windowsill like a gym bar.

"Fuck you faggots," Snapple yelled as he clawed behind him. "Let me up, you fucking faggots." Love looked back and smiled at his brother, who stood in the doorway.

Carlyle peeled Snapple's legs from the windowsill and held them, locking them over his forearms. Snapple didn't kick at all anymore.

"Here," Carlyle said to Love, and gave him Snapple's right ankle to hold.

"Please let me up," Snapple cried out. He lifted his body with his stomach muscles so that both boys could see his face before he fell back against the building again with a thud.

"On the count of three, we're going to let go of you," Carlyle yelled.

"No you ain't, motherfucker. Let me up! Pop, tell them to let me up!"

Carlyle nodded at Love with a smile and a wink, and Love smiled back.

"One."

"One," Love repeated.

"I'm going to kick your ass, Pit Bull, unless you pull me back right now," Snapple yelled.

"Two."

"Two." Love nodded at Carlyle, his arms stretched out of his shoulder sockets with the weight of Snapple's body. Then they both said together:

"Three."

Love let go of Snapple's ankle and thrust his hands into the air triumphantly. Snapple screamed and his body flew to one side as Carlyle tried to hold on to just one leg. He had him by the foot and grabbed at his pants, but Snapple was swinging back and forth from the momentum and his other shoe came off in Carlyle's hand. Like the tail of a snake, Snapple's foot slid the rest of the way out of the window. They watched him fall six stories down to the cement.

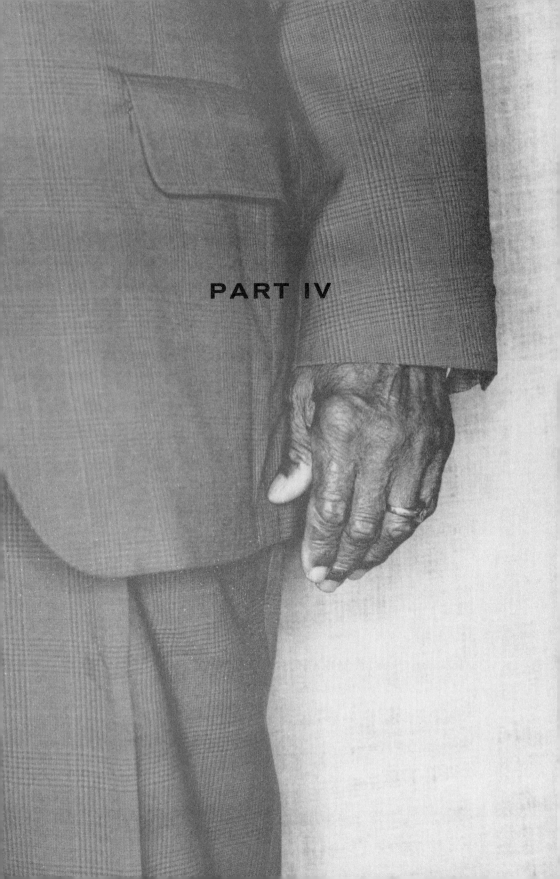

PART IV

SANTA RITA JAIL

TODAY I READ to you from Proposition 209, entered in to the State Constitution by Californians in 1998:

AMENDMENT TO ARTICLE I

Section 31 is added to Article I of the California Constitution as follows:

SEC. 31. (a) The state shall not discriminate against, or grant preferential treatment to, any individual or group on the basis of race, sex, color, ethnicity, or national origin in the operation of public employment, public education, or public contracting.

CHAPTER 1

LOVE AND LI'L Pit finally fell asleep on the bus as it left California, and they woke up the next morning at the stop in Phoenix. They had forty minutes to scrounge up some food. There was a restaurant in the terminal, but without the bag of money from Ruby, the kids were completely broke.

Li'l Pit went to a table that hadn't been cleared, and he scooped up the remains of scrambled eggs with a piece of half-eaten toast. But the waitress noticed him and removed the leftovers from all the other tables. She dumped the extra food into the trash and then took the busing tray into the kitchen.

"I'm going around back," Li'l Pit said to his brother. "You comin?"

"You ain't gonna catch me eatin out of no Dumpster," Love said. He hadn't had to do that since before his time at Los Aspirantes, and if there was one thing he'd been told over and again there, it was that you needed to be clean and sanitary. Li'l Pit shrugged and left Love staring at the menu above the round cases of doughnuts and bear claws dripping with white glaze.

The restaurant filled with passengers from early-morning bus routes. The sizzle of bacon and scraping of metal spatulas gnawed on Love's stomach as the chefs ran around the kitchen yelling out orders and placing food on the service counter. He stared at a plate of sausage and pancakes as the waitress passed by him.

There was a wait for seating now, and Love went up to the first man in line. He had a long beard and long hair, wore blue jeans and a T-shirt.

"Excuse me," Love said. "Can you spare a dollar for some food?"

Everyone else in line, within earshot, immediately straightened up and looked away.

The man rolled his eyes and shook his head but reached in his pocket with a look of obligation. "Here's all the extra I've got." He handed Love a quarter.

"Thank you." Love took the quarter and went to the next few people, who, before he asked, shook their heads. He looked at the hanging menu again, but the least expensive item was a doughnut for sixty-five cents. His stomach was so hungry it pulsated like a pounding fist. He went out into the general seating area and looked for the pay phones. He spotted them by a gift shop, but a thin old man in dirty clothes was already checking the return slots.

Love went into the gift shop. The shelves were loaded with desert memorabilia: ceramic sculptures of cacti and snakes, leather Indian tepees and moccasins, the jawbones of a coyote and the horns of a steer. There was also a rack of books and, under the register, a shelf of candy and gum. But all the candy bars cost over fifty cents.

"Can I see one of them radios back there?" Love pointed to the Walkman behind the cashier. When the cashier turned around, Love grabbed a handful of candy bars and lifted them to his pocket. But then he saw a security guard at the edge of the store with his eyes on him.

"This one?" The cashier held out the Walkman.

"How much is it?"

"Thirty-nine ninety-nine."

"Naw. That's okay." He put the candy back and nodded to the security guard as he left the store, like they were old friends.

Around back, beyond the bus stalls, was a large rust-colored Dumpster surrounded by a high gate and barbed wire, so that even people desperate enough to look in the trash couldn't. But the huge quantity of waste was too large for the terminal to keep up with, so there was a line of additional trashbins outside the gated area waiting to be unloaded.

Li'l Pit went to the last of the Dumpsters in line and stepped onto the wheel carriage. He pulled himself up over the rim and balanced himself on his chest so he could take a look at the offerings. It was only half full. The restaurant's garbage was mixed in with the mechanic's and janitor's garbage, so that under small piles of paper and lint were empty cartons of milk and cans of beans, all surrounded by greasy bottles of oil and darkened rags. In order to reach the food below, Li'l Pit leaned over the edge of the Dumpster, his stomach pressing into the rim, his legs straight out in the air behind him. He sifted through the pencil shavings and paper clips, below the paper towels and gum wrappers. By the time he dug deep enough, his stomach hurt from the edge of the Dumpster. So he let himself slide all the way in like a diver, hands out in front of him. Then he stood up inside, on top of the trash.

His feet sank beneath him and he found himself knee-deep in seating foam and applesauce. He laughed out loud, as if he were being watched by his old crew. But then he began to dig through the top layer of trash, un-covering an area of mostly food items. There were pieces of toast, half-used jam containers, orange slices, bacon strips, and lettuce leaves. He found many partially eaten or uneaten pieces of food, which would have been perfectly edible if they hadn't been mixed in with the other garbage; but as they were, each was stained with some bit of oil or Liquid Paper. He then spotted a Styrofoam take-out container with a lid and dug it out care-fully like a buried skull. He popped it open and found the food still orga-nized into separate compartments, some scrambled eggs with catsup and two and a half sausage links. The links were covered in some white-ish liq-uid that was probably milk, though he lifted one and smelled it to be sure. He also found an unused plastic orange-juice container with its aluminum-foil top still sealed. Although it was damaged, bent at the side and leaking, there was still enough in it to accompany a meal.

Li'l Pit was too hungry to wait. He stood in the Dumpster and scarfed down the sausage links and eggs, then peeled off the orange-juice top and drank it down quickly. He finished and tossed the containers to the side. Nothing else looked salvageable in this Dumpster, and he decided to check out the other ones. He tried to move to the edge of the bin but found he had sunk up to his waist in trash.

As he pulled his left shoe out and over onto the top of the heap, he noticed it was soaking wet with something very similar to the color of grape juice. He had to lie forward onto the trash in order to get both legs fully out, which put his face an inch away from a powerful smell of fish and ammonia. As he pushed with his hands to stand up, they quickly sank into the pile and he smashed the side of his face into a wet mush. His arms were now deep in the garbage, and as he pulled each one out, they too were streaked with dark oil and an unidentifiable white liquid. The front of his shirt and pants were also covered with jam and coffee grounds. He was literally covered in garbage to the point that he seemed to be a part of it.

"Hey!" he yelled, sinking down with every attempt to turn and get on top. He kicked the side of the Dumpster and made a thunderous banging. "Hey, I'm stuck! Hey."

A bus started and the engine drowned him out completely. He stopped yelling and struggled some more. Then, without warning, a bucketful of garbage came over the top of the Dumpster and rained on his back.

"Hey, there's somebody in here, you know!"

A Native American man's face appeared at the edge.

"Don't you look where you're throwing things?" Li'l Pit yelled at him.

"No. Not usually."

"Well, are you going to help me out?"

The man reached his hand down and Li'l Pit grabbed it. He catwalked up the slick metal wall, and the man lifted him the rest of the way and put him on the ground.

"Did you find what you were looking for?" the man asked.

"That ain't none of your business." Li'l Pit brushed himself off as best he could.

"You sleep in there last night?"

"Naw! I didn't sleep in no garbage can. What you think I am, a rat?" He walked away from the man, across the parking lot to the terminal, and just as he reached the door, Love came out to meet him. He panicked when he saw Li'l Pit.

"What happened to you? They ain't gonna let you on the bus like that!"

"Where you think I'm going? I'm about to find the bathroom." Love walked with his brother back inside, trying his best to shield him from the view of the other passengers. They went into the bathroom and Love pulled out a pile of paper towels as Li'l Pit took off his shirt and dunked it in a sinkful of water.

"Did you get food?" Love asked.

"A little."

"I was just about to come see what you got. These people ain't nothin but s-t-i-n-g-y," he spelled.

"I'm still hungry."

"I feel ya. We got to get some money."

"I'm gonna ask for change. They always pity a little kid like me."

"You do look awful pitiful right now. I just hope they let us back on the bus with you all smelly like that."

Love washed off his brother's face and legs and squeeze-dried his shirt. By the time Li'l Pit came out of the bathroom, he looked like he'd been swimming with his clothes on.

"We got to hurry up," Love said.

They stood by the entrance to the terminal, and Love let Li'l Pit do the begging, holding out a plastic beer cup.

He tried a few different approaches. First he was sad and scared: "Please, don't you have any extra money for food for two little kids?" The few people who looked at them shook their heads and smiled apologetically. Then he tried to push them: "Come on, man, I know you got some money." No one took well to the accusation. He eventually started insulting them when they didn't give anything. One woman shook her head and put on her sunglasses. "Ugly ole bitch," Li'l Pit said. "Probably couldn't earn nothin for yourself last night."

A few people who were standing in front of the terminal waiting for rides kept glancing back at the boys. In a quiet moment, when no one was passing through the doorway, Li'l Pit began to rap toward them:

> I know you hear us
>
> 'Cause you standin near us
>
> You keep turnin 'round
>
> Then lookin at the ground.

> All we askin for is dimes
>
> But you ain't got no time
>
> To help us get some food
>
> And you know that you just rude.

One of the women in a yellow dress turned, smiled at them, and dropped a few coins in their cup.

"Thank you, thank you, thank you!" Li'l Pit said genuinely. He grabbed the change and counted it.

"Fifty-five cent."

"Keep rappin," Love said. This time he laid down a back beat for his little brother that went "Boom, ba-*boom*-boom, ba-boom-*bap!* Boom, ba-*boom*-boom, ba-boom-*bap!*"

> We the LeRoy boys
>
> Comin in from Oaktown
>
> You can listen from your rear
>
> To our beefy phat sound.

> Put your money in our cup
>
> so our stomachs can fill up
>
> We could come out there an take it
>
> Or our mama could go make it
>
> But we comin to you for change
>
> So to keep us outta gangs.

Every other person seemed to drop something in their cup now. One man put in a whole dollar bill, and a kid put in a Canadian penny, which Li'l Pit said he would save for a collection. After ten minutes of rapping, they'd earned enough money to each get the $1.99 egg, hash brown, and toast breakfast. But there was no time to eat at the station.

They bought their food and started to chow down as soon as they got on the bus. When they finished eating, Li'l Pit made up new lyrics for the next stop, and Love wrote them down for him. Then they talked about their dreams, not of getting spare change, but of being discovered and getting a record contract when they got to South Carolina.

AFTER PHOENIX, THEY rapped for money in Tucson and made enough to split a dinner. It was the last long stop until Dallas, eleven hours away. They left at six-thirty, and Love slept through the short stop in El Paso, but at one in the morning, he was wide awake again and hungry. A pocket of emptiness pulsated in his stomach as he pushed against it with his forearm.

The hunger was awakened in him by the smell of food coming from somewhere in the bus cabin. He stood up and noticed a single light over a pair of seats six rows up. He didn't know how he would do it, but he had to get some of that food. He walked up the aisle and heard the chewing. He smelled garlic and tomatoes, not that he knew the exact smells, but he knew it was spaghetti sauce or maybe a meatball sandwich or lasagna.

He heard whispers and saw hair wound up like a cobra's on the head of a girl in an aisle seat; through the space between the seats, he saw the face of the girl sitting by the window, an oak-colored face, with short red hair as short as velvet. This girl by the window had a large red apple in her hand and opened her mouth as tall as a lion's, as if her jaw unhitched. The juice dripped from the apple onto her chin. She laughed and quickly wiped it with the sleeve of her sweater, then chewed as she shoved part of it into one cheek.

Love slid into the empty seat across the aisle from them. They were older than he, maybe sixteen, and bigger. The two girls turned to him, the one closest, with the cobra hair, covering her full mouth with a smile. She was eating spaghetti with a plastic fork out of a Tupperware container. Love ignored her and talked to the one by the window.

"Let me have a bite of that apple," he said.

"This apple?"

"Yeah. Come on."

"Why should I give some nappy-headed playah like you some of my fine red apple?"

" 'Cause you're a nice person."

She switched her speech from streetwise to gentle Texan: "I'm sure you must have me mistaken with somebody else, young man."

Then she saw the desperate look in his eyes, like he was going to reach over and grab it whether or not she offered. She handed the apple to him over her friend, and he took a bite equal to her huge dent. Without chewing the first portion in his mouth, he took another bite.

"You're like an alligator," she said, with more fascination than disgust.

"Just one more." He wasn't asking.

"You want some of my spaghetti?" the cobra-haired girl asked. Love turned his eyes toward her as she held out the plastic container, his mouth still fixed into the apple. She was definitely the less pretty of the two girls, he thought, now that his stomach had stopped panicking. Her offer, her desire to be liked, made her that much less attractive, though he was glad to take the food.

"Where are you coming from?" the one by the window asked.

He continued to chew and shovel spaghetti into his mouth. He pointed with his thumb. "The back of the bus."

"Well, where are you going?" the one on the aisle asked.

He paused to think about his answer. "Hell. One day."

"If you eat like that, I guess you sure will."

"What's your name?" he demanded.

"LaTanya," the one on the aisle blurted out immediately, as if she didn't know the rules of flirting at all.

"I didn't ask you," he said. He handed back her empty spaghetti container. "What's your name?" he asked the one by the window with the short red hair.

"Why should I tell you when you're treating us with such disrespect? You should apologize to LaTanya."

"I'm sorry," he said without taking his eyes off the girl by the window. "What's your name?" She pretended she might not answer, twisted her neck, and looked into the night.

"Whatever," he said, and feigned getting up to go.

"You give up awful easy," she said.

"So you gonna tell me your name?"

"Joyce."

He nodded and waited, but she didn't ask his.

"Love," he said, and patted his chest.

"Love? That's your name? Love? That's not a man's name."

"That's the only true man's name," he said.

"You're nothing more than just a little boy."

"Then you don't know what a real man is. They must not have real men where you come from." The sugar from the food was settling into his bloodstream and he yawned. Joyce stood up.

"Let me have that seat, LaTanya, in case I need to slap this boy."

"Don't you think you're in enough trouble already," LaTanya said.

"Shut up. Move over and let me sit there." Joyce remained standing as LaTanya squeezed beneath her. Joyce had a fine body and strong arms that seemed like they could fight off a truck. If there were two things Love liked in a girl, they were a spirit that would never get tired and low-down, and the feeling that, if she got to like you, no one would get past her to mess with you.

"How old are you, little boy?" she asked him.

"Sixteen."

"Yeah, and I'm a hundred and eight. You ain't no sixteen. You more like nine."

"You do look about a hundred an eight with your baldin head."

"You better go on back," she said. "Your baby-sitter probably waitin for you." She and LaTanya laughed and gave each other a high five.

Love stood. "I'm sorry to bother you, ma'am. You just reminded me of one of my grandmama's friends."

Love went back to his seat. There were still many hours left in the ride for the dance to continue. He closed his eyes and waited as Li'l Pit slept next to him.

It wasn't twenty minutes later that Love felt something flick his ear. He looked up to see Joyce brushing past him on the way to the bathroom.

When she came out, she turned in two rows behind Love and then threw a wadded-up paper towel that hit him in the head. He stood up, and she waved him back. Love took the seat by the aisle.

"I can't stay up there," Joyce said. "LaTanya snores when she sleeps. That your little brother?"

"Mmm-hmm." Love had his eyes closed, relaxed and cool, feeling he was in control of the situation since she had come to seek him out.

"What's your real name?" she asked.

"Love."

"Your parents named you Love?"

"Ronald's my first name."

"How'd you get to be called Love, then?"

"All the women call me that."

Joyce nudged him with her elbow, and he smiled.

"I guess you got a girlfriend, then," she said.

He considered this question for a moment. "I got lots of girlfriends."

"You a playah."

"You a playah-hater?"

"I guess I am." She relaxed into her seat. There was time for silence on the long ride, but Love started to feel the need to talk.

"Where you from?"

"Dallas. I just went to see LaTanya in El Paso, and now she's comin up to see me."

"They got Gs in Dallas?"

"Why, you a gangsta?" she asked, laughing.

"That's right."

"A gangsta named Love? Now that's a riot."

"I'm a G, which means a gentleman for the ladies."

"How old are you, for real?"

"Old enough."

"How come you won't tell me?"

"Same reason you want to know. You want to know if I'm down for the deed."

"What you talking about? I ain't doing no deed with you."

"Why not?"

"I don't even know you."

"So?"

Joyce laughed. "Boy, you too quick."

"I'm quick when I'm in love."

"What are you talkin about? You named 'Love,' but you don't even know what that is."

"I got the feelin you about to tell me."

"Love is you don't do anything to hurt each other on purpose. Didn't your mama teach you that?"

"I guess not." Love stared at the back of the seat straight in front of him. "Anyway, my mama's dead."

"For real?"

Love didn't answer. He felt Joyce being drawn to him.

"I'm sorry," she said.

"That's awright."

They sat in silence for a minute. Then Love asked: "So, what if you do something you can't help?"

"What do you mean?"

"I mean hurt them."

"Then it's not love."

"But sometimes people do things they can't help," Love said again.

"I know."

"What if someone couldn't help themself, they just got into something? Does that mean they didn't love you?"

She considered this for a minute and watched his face. She could see how seriously he was taking this, how important this was to him.

"I think it could still be love."

He looked back at her and nodded.

"You got nice hair," he said.

"I thought it was bald a-hundred-an-eight-year-old hair."

"Where you think I'm from?"

"Los Angeles."

"You think I'm a Blood from L.A.? I'm an Oaktown boy."

"Oklahoma?"

"Naw, dog. Oakland, California, like Hammer and Too Short."

"I don't listen to hip-hop."

"What kinda music you listen to, then?"

"Country."

"Country?" He sat up and looked at her. "Country?"

"That's right."

"Country?"

"Are you so closed-minded you only listen to hip-hop?"

"That's right. I don't let none of that funky White shit touch my ears."

"My daddy ain't White, and he likes country music."

"Man." Love shook his head. "You southern niggers all mixed up."

"You G-thang niggers the ones mixed up, singing 'bout shootin this and bitches that."

"That's how it is in Oaktown." Love tapped his chest with his fingers spread into the "W" for West Side Oakland. "You got to be down or you goin down."

"Yeah, right. Don't you know that's all just hype to sell you CDs?"

Love didn't answer and Joyce opened her mouth to repeat her assertion, but she saw Love looking straight forward again, as if he were thinking about something else entirely.

"How'd your mama die?" she asked.

"She just did," he said.

"You going to live with your dad?"

"He's dead too."

"Damn."

"So now you know." Love still looked straight ahead. Joyce studied his face, his high cheeks, dark red and smooth, and the strong but soft rim of his ear, open to her.

She leaned over and kissed him on the cheek, then moved back and looked at his face again. He turned toward her, holding his breath. She leaned in to him again and put her hands on his narrow face, pulling him toward her. They kissed for a minute, his hands down at his sides. Her lips were warm and wet, and for the first time in his life, he felt a tongue reach into his mouth. It was a strange invasion, a piece of another person inside him, and it seemed to demand a response. He stuck his tongue out too and, not knowing where to put it but remembering a scene from a movie, licked around the outside of her lips. Suddenly he felt like everything was disappearing around him—the bus, the trip, Li'l Pit—and that he was falling into her and into an open space in his chest at the same time. A sudden panic seized him; the open space closed, and he pulled back.

"What's up?" she said.

"Nothin." He pushed the recline button on the armrest and laid his seat back. "What about being too quick?"

"That's when I didn't know you. Now we know each other better."

"Aw, you scandalous."

"Mmm-hmmm." She nodded and, stretching her arm above his face, shut off the overhead light.

LI'L PIT WOKE up to an empty seat beside him. The daylight had just begun to stream in as the bus wove its way through the downtown streets of Dallas, past the Trinity River and the domes of the convention center, toward the Hyatt Regency with its giant ball on top. But Li'l Pit couldn't tell if they were just pulling in to Dallas or if they'd already made a stop and were now headed back on to the highway. He jumped out of his seat and ran up the aisle, but before asking the driver any questions, he realized that Love may have just wanted to sleep in a row all his own. So he ran through the bus and came upon Love sleeping in a window seat with Joyce beside him, her head resting on his arm.

"Rah!" Li'l Pit barked at them.

Joyce and Love woke up and blocked their eyes from the sun.

"Hey," Li'l Pit yelled. "Get off a my brother."

"Come on, dog." Love yawned slowly. "What you yellin at her for?"

"We got to make our rap so we can get some food." He turned to Joyce. "Sorry, you got to leave us alone now." Li'l Pit stared at her and breathed heavily through his nostrils.

"What's he talking about?" Joyce asked.

"Nothin. Go on back to your seat, bro."

"You tell her to get on back."

"You let your little brother talk to your friends like that?" Joyce asked Love.

"He ain't got no friends but me," Li'l Pit said. "I'm his best an only friend."

Joyce raised her eyebrow and looked at Love, but he didn't speak.

"All right, if that's how it is," she said. "Have a nice life." She stood up and headed to the bathroom in the back of the bus. Love felt like begging her to come back, but he knew Dallas was her stop, and soon he'd be alone with his brother again, so he let her go.

"Good. Now that bitch is gone, we can get to work," Li'l Pit said, jumping into the seat next to Love.

"What you gettin in my way for?"

"I'm just doin my job. You told me to watch your back. Who knows what kinda places she's been. We don't need no bitch gettin between us."

"Dog, you don't know a bitch from a basketball. Aw, you too young to understand."

"I am not."

"Whatever."

"Well, then you got to teach me."

"I don't got to teach you nothin."

"But that's what you're sposed to do."

"I'm sposed to get you to South Carolina. I ain't sposed to teach you about sex."

"I had sex."

"You ain't had sex." Love looked at his brother's face to see the truth. Li'l Pit looked into the pocket on the seat back and snapped the elastic, then looked straight into Love's eyes. "Yes, I have so."

"When did you have sex?"

"That's my business."

Joyce returned from the bathroom and went to her seat, throwing a long look at Love. The bus stopped and waited to turn left into the terminal parking lot. Both boys looked at the concrete structure and the downtown, with its glass buildings and traffic—in most ways, like any other downtown.

"You didn't have no sex," Love said.

"Well, I seen it."

The bus parked, and while everyone stood up to get off, Love watched Joyce and LaTanya get their belongings from overhead. Joyce put on a miniature pink leather backpack, then looked back at Love. She leaned over and said something into LaTanya's ear, at which they both giggled.

Love wanted to yell something crude at them, but instead, he waited until he and his brother were down the stairs onto the pavement where they waited for their baggage to change buses for Atlanta.

Love came up to Joyce and squinted at her angrily. He sucked through his nose and gathered saliva in his mouth to spit at her.

"You want to come to my place for breakfast?" she asked.

Li'l Pit's eyes opened wide, and although he was very hungry, he shook his head at his brother. Love turned and spit at the bus tire.

"You're disgusting," LaTanya said and turned to Joyce, who laughed. "You don't even know what you're getting into."

"So, you want to come or not? My daddy's out of town on business."

LaTanya shook her head at Joyce.

"What are you having?" Love asked.

"I ain't comin," Li'l Pit yelled. "We can earn our own breakfast."

"Well, I didn't invite *you*, now did I?" she said to him.

Love felt hot. He took off his black leather jacket and tried to fold it in two, but the arms got in the way and stuck out in either direction. He cracked his neck from one side to the other. Li'l Pit and Joyce both waited for his decision. LaTanya put her bag down and placed her hands on her hips.

"You got to invite my brother too," Love finally said.

Joyce looked at Li'l Pit, who smiled and stuck his tongue out at her.

"He doesn't want to come," she said.

Love opened his eyes wide and stared at her hard, in a way that Li'l Pit couldn't see.

"All right," she said. She turned to Li'l Pit again and got on one knee. "We would be honored if your grace would partake in some of our southern hospitality."

He turned and spit at the tire too, then looked back at her. "I don't eat no hospital food."

She laughed. "Well, fine. You can have cereal."

"But I don't want to go."

"How far from here do you live, anyway?" Love asked.

"I don't want to," Li'l Pit whined, but they ignored him.

"It's only a few minutes in a cab. Or we could walk."

"I don't care," Love said.

"Let's take a cab," Li'l Pit said. Love raised his eyebrows at Joyce and she smiled.

"Okay, then. Let's go." The bus for Atlanta left at noon, and Love had the driver move the trunk to the right baggage area.

JOYCE'S HOUSE WAS large with a lot of empty space, as if it were uninhabited much of the time. She lived in an upper-middle-class neighborhood on a block of large two-story houses with front lawns. Each home was different in shape or style, like they were trying to be better than the ones next to them by adding a marble column, a semi-circular terrace, Spanish roof tiles, or a brass fish spitting water. Joyce's home had a cactus garden running along the front of the lawn with a white stone path. She got out her keys and opened the front door, holding it for everyone to enter before her, like a guide to a haunted castle.

"Our housekeeper comes on Thursdays and my father won't be back until Saturday, so we have the whole place to ourselves. What do you think?" She threw her keys onto the center of the polished wooden table in the dining room.

"It's awright," Love said. He swaggered into the living room with his hand on his thigh near his crotch and threw himself on the couch. Li'l Pit joined him. The two girls went into the kitchen. "What's for breakfast, honey?" Love yelled, and gave Li'l Pit a tap on the fist. The house wasn't any larger than Ruby's on Cranston, but it was newer and more sterile. The hardwood floors were shiny, the Persian carpet perfectly placed, the tables bare. On the wall, there was only a single black-and-white photograph of a long-stemmed rose lying on a polished black grand piano, exactly like the actual piano below it. Li'l Pit went up to the big-screen TV and played with the remote until he got a music-video station.

LaTanya and Joyce came out of the kitchen every so often to put a bowl or box of cereal on the table. Love couldn't wait to eat, and he went to see what was sizzling on the stove, leaving Li'l Pit to explore on his own.

"Where's your daddy?" he asked Joyce.

"He's in Knoxville, looking at something they want him to build down there."

"Where's your mother at?"

"She lives in Tyler. It's about an hour and a half from here." Joyce stirred the eggs in the Teflon frying pan. LaTanya buttered toast on the kitchen counter, stealing quick glances at her friend.

"They divorced?"

"Yeah. She cheated on him with a photographer. She works on

makeup ads, and they'd do it in the bus waiting for the lights to get set up. Then he started with all his girlfriends."

"Damn. How you know all that?"

"I heard my parents fighting." The eggs started to burn, and she stirred them. The smell was potent and Joyce frowned, but she continued to speak, trying to inhale as little as possible.

"Now it's just me and him. Just me, really. He's never around. If he's not on some trip, he's with his girlfriend. It's kind of like I live alone." She picked up the spatula and scraped the eggs onto four plates. When she brought them to the table, Li'l Pit was banging on the piano in the living room.

"Get off a that, dog, and come get your breakfast," Love yelled. Li'l Pit ran over to the table.

"What do you want to drink? We have orange juice," Joyce said. "I could mix some up. I'll be right back. You go ahead and eat."

LaTanya and Love sat down and picked up the heavy silver forks. Li'l Pit poured Cap'n Crunch into a bowl and scooped it into his mouth.

"Aren't you going to use milk?" LaTanya asked. He just looked up at her and, still chewing and scooping, grabbed the milk carton with the other hand and poured it in.

"Your brother seems like he was raised in a zoo."

Li'l Pit spat wads of mushy yellow corn balls and milk at her, and she screamed. Joyce ran in from the kitchen holding a pitcher of orange juice and saw LaTanya out of her chair, wiping off her face and shirt while Li'l Pit laughed. LaTanya grabbed the juice from Joyce's hand and walked over and held it over Li'l Pit. Love shook his head.

"Don't do it, girl," Joyce said. LaTanya tipped the pitcher enough to splatter some on Li'l Pit. He just laughed even more. He reached across the table, grabbed a handful of eggs from Love's plate, and smashed them into LaTanya's chest.

"Boys against girls," Li'l Pit screamed. "Boys against girls."

LaTanya chased him into the living room. Love stayed in his seat. He shoveled the rest of his eggs into his mouth and swallowed. When he finished, Li'l Pit had a pillow in his hand and had climbed onto the top of the grand piano, swinging at the girls as they tried to pull him off.

Love went straight for Joyce. He grabbed her by the shoulders and threw her onto the couch so that she lay on her back. She didn't try to get up, but instead smiled at him and put her hands up in the air as if he were going to jump on her.

"Careful. Careful," she said. Empty-handed and unsure of what to do next, Love straddled her waist.

"Get off of me." She laughed.

He grabbed her wrists and held them firmly over her chest as she struggled.

Taking his cue from Love, Li'l Pit jumped off the piano with his pillow and chased LaTanya into the dining room, where he picked up a fork and brandished it at her. She ran screaming into the kitchen and tried to push the door shut, but Li'l Pit got his foot inside and she closed it on him.

He shrieked at the top of his lungs. "My foot. You're breaking my foot!"

LaTanya opened the door in fear, and he burst into the kitchen, laughing at her.

"So what are you going to do now?" Joyce asked Love. Her sweat smelled like musky wood.

He lay himself down onto her, his hands still holding her arms apart. He could feel the buttons of her pants pushing into his stomach. Her legs opened slightly, and he rested his cheek on her breasts.

"Now what?" she said. He felt himself getting excited, and he looked at her face. She was smiling.

"What you mean?"

She pressed into him and he hardened more. "Now that you got me, what you going to do?"

"Whatever I want."

"Oh yeah, big G? So let me see what you've got." She pushed up against him and he pushed into her a little. It felt good and he pushed into her again, but then it seemed that he wasn't in control of his own body.

"You a tease," he said.

"Maybe." She wrapped her legs around his butt and squeezed him into her. He didn't move for a second, then he pulled his pelvis away a little.

"Let go," he said. She smiled and squeezed him again. Without warning, he felt himself spasm. He was losing control and he hadn't even taken off his pants.

"Let go!" He pulled himself off her and ran to the door, facing away from her.

"Where you going?" She laughed. He turned his head toward her, his eyes wide, but she didn't seem to know. "What's the matter?"

"We got to go." He put his hands in his pockets.

"It's only ten."

"So?" He turned to the kitchen and yelled: "Come on, bro, we got to go!"

Joyce sat up and folded her arms. "What's wrong? I thought you were a man." She smiled at him, but he didn't smile back.

LaTanya came screaming through the living room with Li'l Pit in pursuit.

"Come on, blood," Love said. "We're leaving." Li'l Pit immediately stopped his chase and went to the door.

Joyce stood up. "Where are you going?"

"We got to get back to the bus."

"It's only ten. You still got an hour, at least." She approached him, but he grabbed the handle and opened the door. She took another step toward him and he walked outside. Li'l Pit followed.

"Thanks for the food," Love said without turning around.

"But you don't know how to get back."

"We'll figure it out."

"You can stay the night if you want," she said. But Love kept walking.

———

415

THEY CHECKED ON the bus to Atlanta and the driver said they still had about half an hour, so they rapped to get money for the next stop. They set up just inside the entrance to the lobby, a plastic cup in front of each of them. This time Love started by giving a back beat, covering his mouth with both hands like he was cradling a microphone. Li'l Pit rapped the opening lines about being the LeRoy Boys from Oaktown and then went into the new verses they'd written on the bus.

> Comin to you like prime time
> With the bomb of a land mine
> Playin words with a whack rhyme—

A smiling security guard came up to them and applauded, though they weren't done.

"Wonderful stuff, guys. Unfortunately, you're going to have to take it outside. And I don't mean in front of the doors. You've got to go down the block."

"But all the people are here," Li'l Pit said.

"Yes. That's true. That's true enough. And that's why you have to take it outside. You can't solicit. In case you don't know what that means it means 'so' 'lick' 'it.' "

"That ain't how it's spelled," Love whispered.

They picked up their cups and walked out on the street and down the block, the security guard looking after them. They stopped just at the corner by an alley and set down their cups again. The security guard nodded and waved, and Li'l Pit gave him the finger.

"Come on, dog," Love said. "Let's get us some change."

Li'l Pit danced while Love read the words from a sheet of paper.

> This is the story
> 'Bout Bigger and Minor
> Catchin the bus
> To South Caroliner

Got the Poh-Poh on their trail
Got the dope up for sale

Left it all behind
To try to free they mind
But don't mess with the Bigger
'Cause he's a crazy nigger
And Minor got the hands
Like lethal Jackie Chan's.

The few people who passed looked away quickly. The only time a man put his hand in his pocket was to grip his keys. A few younger girls walked by and laughed, and Love thought about Joyce. It had been going so well. He wished he had just run into her bathroom.

Two White kids came from the other direction and stopped to listen. They were older teenagers, one with a flattop and a flat face, like he'd been walking into walls, and the other with terrible acne. They both wore white undershirts with skulls and guns hand-drawn on them with red and black markers. They looked at each other and held back laughter as they listened to Love rap. When he was done, the two kids walked away.

"What's so funny?" Li'l Pit yelled at them.

"Nothing. We was just enjoying the show."

"Well then, pay us some money in our cup." He picked up the cup and held it out. The one with acne laughed again.

"What's so funny, volcano face?"

"I didn't know no nigger could read." His flat-faced friend burst out laughing and held out his fist for a tap, and they walked away.

A cab drove up and stopped in front of them. Joyce paid the driver, and he kept the car running as Joyce got out and approached them.

"Why are you outside?" she asked.

"None a your business!" Li'l Pit yelled.

"Whatever," she said. "I'm just glad you didn't get on the bus already. I called and they said that any ticket is good the whole week, till Saturday. So if you want, you can stay over."

Love didn't say anything, so Li'l Pit did. "We supposed to be in South Carolina."

Joyce shivered, crossed her arms over her chest, and held her hands over her bare shoulders. She ignored Li'l Pit and looked at Love. "I just thought it could be fun. We got the house to ourselves."

She wasn't afraid to meet Love's eyes, and he was frozen by how real she looked, how a separate person was looking back at him and showing that she wanted him, not dropping her eyes. It made him want to laugh. He wanted to turn around and see if she was maybe looking at someone behind him.

"He ain't got no time," Li'l Pit said.

Love looked at him. "We could stay just till Saturday."

"Naw. Naw." Li'l Pit stomped his foot. "I ain't goin back there."

"Let's go get some of your clothes and I'll go tell someone to put your trunk in storage," Joyce said, and walked toward the station.

"Naw!" Li'l Pit whined. "We got to get on the bus."

"We can stay just a few days," Love said.

"But we got a plan. Naw!" Li'l Pit took off running past Joyce, toward the terminal. Love ran after him and chased him through the lobby to the bus platform. Li'l Pit stepped up onto the bus.

"They ain't gonna let you on without your ticket," Love yelled.

"Well, give me my ticket. It's mine."

"We're stayin here."

"We got to get on the bus," he yelled from the steps.

Joyce walked onto the platform, and Li'l Pit spotted her.

"Come on, hurry up!" he yelled at Love. He ran down the stairs and grabbed his brother's hand. "Come on. Please." He pulled on Love's arm, but Love didn't move.

"We got a new plan," Love said.

"Naw. What do you mean? Naw. We got to get on the bus." He let go of Love's arm and ran to the door. "Gimme my ticket!"

"Just calm down, dog."

Joyce walked up to Love's side and smiled at Li'l Pit, who looked back and forth between the two of them. They stood next to each other, both of them facing him like they'd decided already, together.

He ran down the bus stairs and passed them, across the concrete platform and back toward the lobby. Love chased him and caught him just outside the front doors of the terminal.

"Let go of me." Li'l Pit squirmed in his brother's arms.

"Listen. Just listen to me."

"We suppose to be on it. We suppose to be leaving."

"I know. We're still gonna go to Norma. We're still gonna go. We're just gonna stay here a few more days, until Saturday. We'll have a good time, like a vacation before we start over."

"I don't want to."

"Just think about it. We're gonna have all that good food and maybe earn some money and we'll have everything so we can show up in South Carolina in style."

"You just want to be with that bitch ho."

"So what if I do? That ain't nothin to you. We still gonna hang together. We still brothers."

"But we suppose to be a team. Not a three-people."

"We is a team, bro. But a team player got to let his man have his bitches sometimes, right?" He shook Li'l Pit, who wasn't struggling any-more. "Right?"

"Yeah."

"Awright then."

Joyce came out of the terminal and stopped at a distance. She watched Love with his arms around his little brother and smiled. Li'l Pit saw her and barked loudly: "Rah, rah!"

He pulled free of Love and ran up the block. Love felt tired out already and just watched him go. He'd turn back any minute when he realized Love wasn't chasing him. Joyce came up and stood by his side.

"The cab is waiting," she said.

Love watched Li'l Pit run. He didn't stop. He crossed the street and then turned up another block.

"I've got to wait for him here," Love said.

"Let's follow in the cab." They got in and told the driver to turn where they'd seen Li'l Pit run.

The street was full of motels with unlit neon signs, each one run-down in its own fashion, parts of the names missing, some with boarded-up windows. There were a few people on the sidewalk, but Love didn't see his brother. Knowing Li'l Pit, he'd circle back to the station again.

They drove around the block but didn't see him outside the terminal either.

"Shit," Love yelled.

"Don't worry," Joyce said. "He's just going to wait here for you. He can't go anywhere without the tickets. Maybe he's on his way to my house already."

"I've got to wait," Love said.

The bus for Atlanta pulled out of the alley behind the station and turned.

"Well, now he's got nowhere to go," Joyce said. "Why don't you come back to my place and wait for him."

Love opened the door and got out of the cab. "We'll meet you there. You should just go on. I'm gonna wait. There's nothing else to do."

The cabdriver sighed. "You're racking up your time. You sure you got enough money?" he asked.

Love closed the door, and Joyce told the cabdriver to leave. Love saw her watching through the back window until they turned the corner.

Love waited by the entrance, scanning the street and crowds of people. He stood to the side of a newsstand next to a man who sat on the ground with a sign that read: SPARE CHANGE FOR BEER, GOD BLESS AND HAVE A SAFE JOURNEY.

"Have you seen a kid with a red sweater on?"

"There a lot of people with red sweaters on around here." The man lifted his cup.

"You a grown man. You ought to work for a living. At least do something."

"Well, I seen somebody like you're talking about."

"Never mind." Love looked back out to the street, where a convention of Japanese men dressed in suits with sunflower ties got off a city bus, and each in their turn thanked the bus driver by tipping his cowboy hat. He waited out in front of the terminal. An old woman carried her small black dog in a white cage, and it barked incessantly. She admonished it just as incessantly in a soft voice: "That's not the way I taught you to act in public, now is it? No, that's not how we say thank you. If you don't behave yourself, Mommy's going to give you a tranquilizer." One man at the newsstand looked at a *Playboy* magazine by putting it inside a *Time* magazine, and the lady selling the magazines saw him do it but didn't say anything to him.

By four o'clock, Li'l Pit still hadn't shown up. Love did one last check. He ran through the terminal looking for his brother, then out to the front of the station. When he didn't see him, he began to walk up the block. By the time he reached the cemetery, he was running, and the street blurred under him as he passed the statue of a bronze cowboy herding in his cattle.

LOVE WAITED FOR Li'l Pit at Joyce's house that night. He made spaghetti, the meal he'd always cooked at Los Aspirantes. They sat around the big table eating in silence, except for when LaTanya couldn't stand it anymore and began to slurp her food and giggle. Love knew Li'l Pit could handle himself on the streets of Oakland, but these were different, unknown streets, and now it was dark outside.

"I should have never taken him," he said.

"It's not your fault he ran away," Joyce said.

"It's my fault we even had to come out here."

They finished and Joyce convinced LaTanya to do the dishes while she and Love went into the living room. They sat at either end of the couch in silence, the room lit by the crystal chandelier above. Joyce took off her shoes and folded her feet under her legs.

"Don't worry," she said. "He probably went back to the station to sleep."

"I'm not worried."

"He might even be right outside in the bushes here."

Love turned to look out the giant, arching window but saw only his reflection against the darkness outside.

"I know what will help," Joyce said. She went to the piano and sat down on the bench. "Do you know 'Moonlight Sonata'?" she asked. He shook his head. Her naked foot pressed on one of the brass pedals, and she placed her hands gently on the keys. Straightening her back, she leaned her body forward into the first notes.

Love sat on the couch and watched her concentrate, her eyes focused at a spot just above the black surface of the piano. He could see her fingers gracefully caressing each key, sustaining the sweet, sad notes into the lulling repetition. The music reverberated off the wooden floor, into the high spaces of the living room and back around him. The deep, longing melody surrounded him and filled him with an ache for Li'l Pit. He knew something had changed, that Li'l Pit hadn't even looked to see if he was following. And now he was a thousand miles from home and from where he was supposed to end up. Love had an intense sense of being alone, of always having been on his own, even when he was at Ruby's, or at Los Aspirantes, or in Ace Trey. Even earlier, with his mother. The strongest memory he had of her was of being next to her but knowing that her mind was somewhere else.

The music rose suddenly in volume, and Love watched Joyce's fingers flowing across the keys, her hands moving together in an unconscious complexity that seemed to him a kind of magical power. It spread into her face as she anticipated the melody with a slight opening and closing of her eyes; it undulated through her chest and her strong arms. She hit the final notes and the room echoed with the ominous chords. As though a spirit were slowly draining from her, she stayed at the bench with her hands resting on the keys.

Love didn't speak.

"I had lessons since I was six," she said. "But I started seriously again in junior high, after we came back from France and I saw this one pianist that was really good."

A sort of anxiety was building inside Love, something he couldn't name, though he knew how to make it into anger. But that wasn't what he wanted to feel. He shook his head and stood up but felt unsure where he wanted to go.

"In France?" he said.

"Yeah, you know, in Europe."

"I know where France is. I'm not stupid." He turned away.

"I didn't say you were. Where are you going?"

He walked to the front door and stopped, his back still to her. She got up and followed him, put her hand out to touch his back.

"What's wrong?"

LaTanya came in from the kitchen, and to avoid facing her, he opened the door and stepped out. He stood there with his back to them, looking out into the quiet, dark suburban street, feeling utterly separate from everyone and everything.

"What's the matter with him?" LaTanya asked.

"Shut up." Joyce walked back to the hallway.

"Come see my room," she called to him. He didn't move.

"Come on. I want to show you my room."

"What am I going to do?" LaTanya asked.

Joyce stared at her hard, and she walked back into the kitchen. When the kitchen door shut, Love turned. Joyce was already down the bright hallway. She smiled at him and waved him in with her fingers, like a hypnotist drawing in her victim. Love smiled and went back into the house. The hallway walls had pictures of Joyce as she was growing up and her father, and in the middle a gold plaque hung in a glass frame. The gold was molded into the shape of a tall, rectangular building.

"This your daddy's?"

"He won it. Some engineering thing."

She walked into her room and flopped herself on her bed. It was a small bed, but high off the ground with a yellow cover on it. It had a white metal frame, and she grabbed the metal bars at the headboard, her arms stretched above her.

"You like my room?"

He'd never been allowed to be alone with a girl in her room at the girls' house at Los Aspirantes, and he hesitated at the threshold.

"Come on in."

He walked in but stayed away from the bed. He looked around at the pictures on the walls. There were magazine cutouts of frogs pasted all over: a little Day-Glo frog on the tip of a person's finger, a giant bumpy red frog, and a giant web-footed jumping frog.

"You sure is frog crazy," he said.

"They're cute."

"Frogs aren't cute, they're ugly and they eat insects."

"Well, I like them. Besides, they turn into princes if you kiss them."

"Don't come near me with your frog-kissin lips."

There was one cutout picture on the closet door of a black man in a cowboy hat, sitting on a fence and strumming a guitar.

"That's Charley Pride," she said.

He shrugged his shoulders and went to the other corner of the room where there was a giant gum-ball machine. Love twisted the knob.

"You need a penny," she said.

"Give me one."

She got up and went to a small wooden box with a dolphin carved into its side, took out a penny, and tossed it to him, then jumped back on her bed.

"Your daddy give you this?" he asked.

"Yes. It was going to be a present to one of his managers for when he first stopped smoking. But then he started again, I guess."

Love got a giant yellow gum ball and popped it into his mouth. His cheek bulged as he chewed and walked back to her closet.

"You sure got a lot of shoes."

"How come you don't come sit on the bed with me?"

Love shrugged.

"Why don't you close the door?"

He went to the door and closed it.

"And lock it," she said. He did.

She took off her sweater and her shirt lifted up over her stomach, which she let stay that way. She patted the bed, and he walked to her cautiously like he was approaching a wild animal.

"What's the matter?" she asked.

He folded his arms. "Nothing's the matter. I just ain't like one of your frogs, gonna hop in so quick." He lay down next to her on his back, crossed his legs, and propped his head up with a pillow.

"Are you going to take your jacket off?" she asked.

"When I'm ready."

She rolled over onto his thin body and kissed him. Then she pulled back, reached into his mouth with her fingers, and took out his gum. She tossed it into a wastebasket full of tissue, then went back to kissing him. He wanted to enjoy it, but he was trying to keep himself from getting too excited. They kissed again, and he began to rub his hand over her short hair.

There was a bang on the door.

"What you want, LaTanya?" Joyce yelled.

"What you doin in there?" It was Li'l Pit.

"Hey, dog, where you been?" Love said. He felt tears come to his eyes and he stood up.

"What you doin?" Li'l Pit yelled again.

"None a your business," Joyce said. "Go on and play."

"Let me in."

"See," Joyce said to Love. "I told you he'd come back." She went to the end of the bed and grabbed his arm.

"We got to go!" Li'l Pit said.

"Not right now, dog."

"When?"

Love let himself be pulled back onto the bed and Joyce kissed his cheek.

"What are you doin? What are you doin?" Li'l Pit cried.

"I'm busy now. The next bus don't leave until noon tomorrow." Li'l Pit hit the door again and then there was silence. Joyce rolled on top of Love, straddling his body.

"See," she said. "Now you can relax."

He was still looking at the door.

"You're a good kisser, you know that? You did have a lot of girl-friends." He didn't answer her. She took his hands and moved them down the sides of her body, over her T-shirt, and then up to her breasts. He kept his hands on them and she didn't say anything or move away at all. Instead, she reached down and unbuttoned her jeans. She wiggled out of them and threw them to the floor. Love looked down and saw her smooth legs and pink underwear. He undid his pants, but then stood up and got under the bedcover.

"Are you shy?" she asked.

"Naw. I'm just cold."

She smiled and got under the cover with him. They moved together again, their smooth skin sliding against each other, and then she took off her shirt. He stared at her erect nipples. She put his hand back on her and removed her underwear. Then she reached down and pulled off his underwear. She tossed it onto the floor and then touched him be-tween his legs. He could sense himself losing control again.

"Do you think I'm a tease now?"

He nodded.

"Do you want to go inside me?"

He nodded again.

"How much?" she asked with a smile.

He just nodded again, trying with all his might to hold back.

"Do you really want me? Tell me."

"Yes." He rolled onto her, and she began to push against him. It felt so good he thought it was over.

"Now," he said.

"Tell me that you love me," she said. The feeling overwhelmed him and he collapsed onto her, pushing frantically. "Say you love me."

"I love you," he whispered into her ear. "I love you."

"I love you too," she said, and caressed his head with the palm of her hand.

AFTER THEY HAD sex, they fell asleep against each other, Love's face on her breast. Then Joyce woke up and whispered, "Get off me now. I've got to pee." She got up, held her underwear between her legs, and went into her bathroom. He rolled over and covered his face with his arm. She came back in and lay close to him, her hand on his stomach.

"Did you like it?" she asked.

"Yeah."

"Was it the best you ever had?"

"D-e-f-i-n-i-t-e-l-y."

She laughed. He lifted his arm off his face and looked at her. "What about for you?"

"The best."

"Better than them frogs, I bet." Love got up and pulled on his underwear and pants.

"You are my frog prince, come to rescue me from this evil kingdom," she said.

"You crazy? You call this an evil kingdom? Man, I could tell you stories." He walked around the room looking at the magazine cutouts on the walls.

"You think you're so bad," she said.

"I am bad." He turned to her with a straight face. "I am bad, and you shouldn't get mixed up with me."

"I know, I know: you a G from Oaktown. A hard-ass G with a bad rap."

"That's right."

"You ain't all that."

"I killed someone once."

"You did not." She sat up in the bed, like she was about to hear a ghost story.

427

"You don't know." He walked around and put his fingers on the giant plastic bubble of the gum-ball machine.

"Then tell me."

"You don't want to know."

"You just don't have nothing to tell."

He shook his head and stared at the multicolored balls rising halfway up in the clear globe.

"You just talking," she added.

"I wish I was. But I ain't. I killed a boy named Snapple."

"Now I know you're lying."

"His name was Murrell, but he called himself Snapple. You know: 'made from the best stuff on earth,' like the commercial."

"Why'd you kill him?" She took the other pillow and held it in her lap.

"He was bugging me."

"So you killed him?" She shook her head and turned on her side.

"Ask my brother."

"Like he's going to deny anything you say."

"Whatever." Love went to the picture of Charley Pride, sitting on a fence in a wide-open expanse of grazing land. Joyce sat up again.

"How did you kill him then?" she asked.

"I thought you didn't believe me."

"Maybe I do and maybe I don't. That's why I'm asking."

"I pushed him off a building."

"High up?"

"No, I pushed him from the ground floor and he died."

"That's not what I meant. I mean off the roof?"

He turned to her. She was lying on her stomach, her chin in her hands, the blanket covering the lower half of her body.

He shook his head. "Why you smiling at me like I helped some old lady across the street or somethin?"

"I don't know. I guess it just seems funny to me."

"Well, it ain't funny. I'm probably going to hell for it."

"I didn't mean funny like ha-ha funny. I mean interesting."

"Well, you got a sick mind."

"I've got a sick mind? You said you killed a kid 'cause he bothered you, but I have a sick mind."

"That was a long time ago, and I didn't mean to do it."

"You killed him by mistake? That ain't no hard G."

"I pushed him on purpose. It's just that I didn't want to kill him."

"Then why'd you do it?"

"I just meant to hurt him. Never mind. You can't understand."

"Yes I can. Tell me. You didn't want to kill him, but you had to. Right? It was some G thang to get yo props."

Love shook his head.

There was a crash in the hallway, like a stack of china falling to the floor, and LaTanya screamed.

"What was that?" she said. She stood up, naked except for her underwear. She pulled a red robe out of her closet and ran to the door. Love opened it and almost stepped into the hallway, but Joyce pulled him back. Large pieces of glass lay on the carpet around the frame of the gold plaque. The front door was open, and LaTanya was standing in the middle of the street yelling: "You better come back here or I'm calling the police!" She ran back inside and shook her hands anxiously like she was drying nail polish. "He was chasing me with the fork," she said. "I locked myself in the bathroom and then I didn't hear him anymore, and when I came out, he took the frame and then smashed it against the wall and took the award and then he ran out of the house, and he's running down the block now, but I can't chase him. He ought to be locked up."

"Shut up," Love said. "Don't worry about the award. I'll get him." He went back into the room and put on his shoes.

"What are you doing?" Joyce asked.

"I'm getting the award back, what you think I'm doing? Then we'll be out of your hair. We're too much of a handful." He walked up the hall to the front door, but she came after him.

"Wait. You can get it tomorrow at the station."

"Don't you want me to get it now? He might not have it tomorrow. What if he loses it, or sells it or something?"

"Your daddy's gonna trip, Joyce," La Tanya yelled.

"Shit, shit," Joyce said. "What am I going to do?"

"I'll go get it," Love said.

"I don't want you to go. He'll probably just come back here tonight anyway, right? Where else is he going to sleep?"

"I don't know."

"You think he might sell it, really?" she asked.

"Why not?"

"Because it's not his."

Love raised his eyebrows and shook his head.

Joyce bit her thumbnail. "I bet he comes back. If not, we can check the station tomorrow."

Love took a step toward the open door, but Joyce put her hand on his back. He stopped, turned to her, and then they went back into the house.

LOVE AND JOYCE checked the station the next day before noon, but Li'l Pit never showed. They waited at her house that night and checked again on Friday, when LaTanya had to leave. There was still no sign of Li'l Pit when the bus took off to Atlanta.

"He thinks you're planning to leave Saturday," Joyce told Love. "That's when he'll show up."

Love nodded but didn't say anything. He stayed at the bus station until it got dark, then went back to Joyce's. That night, the night before her father was to come home, Love and Joyce talked until two in the morning. He told her about growing up in Oakland with his mother and Li'l Pit.

She lay on the bed as he paced the floor, and when he was done with his stories, she opened her arms to hold him. He made love to her as hard as he could, pushing her over onto her stomach, holding her arms down, but it was not enough to rid himself of the unpleasant feeling he felt after telling her the stories, and he thrust himself at her again and again. When they were done, he lay against her, exhausted, and she held him like a baby after a temper tantrum.

LATER THAT NIGHT, while Joyce slept, Love wandered into the living room. He didn't need to turn on the light, for the streetlamp illuminated the house through the front windows. He walked over to the piano and put his fingers on the keys. He petted them, feeling their cold smoothness, but he did not press down. Next he wandered over to the TV, picked up the remote, but then put it back.

There was a rustling out front, and he quickly ran to the window to look. There was movement in the bushes, but he realized it was just a soft drizzle starting to fall. He looked up the street but saw no one in the mist of rain under the yellow lights.

Love let out a breath and sat down on the couch, pulling his bare feet up under his knees. The ticking of the mounted clock grew steadily louder in the spacious and hollow room, so that it seemed to be crying out for him to jump off the couch and do somersaults in the air. He stood up again but didn't go anywhere. He had to do something. He felt himself sinking into the house as if it was quick-sand, like all of Dallas was quicksand. He wasn't sure he wanted to leave. He hoped Li'l Pit would be there on Saturday, but he also didn't want to leave Joyce now that he'd found someone who loved him. He might not find anyone like her again. But at least he now knew it was possible.

If he didn't leave, her father would come home and kick him out and he'd just be on the streets and everything would be bad again, even worse because it was a new city. And what if Li'l Pit didn't show up tomorrow?

He wanted to run out into the rain, to yell, to do something. He had promised Ruby he'd be a man, that he'd keep his promise, but now it didn't seem like anything was going right.

There was a phone on the table by the couch, and Love picked up the receiver. It would be earlier there. He dialed and let it ring.

"Who is this?" Ruby answered. He could tell she'd been sleeping.

"Nanna?"

"Love? Where you at?"

"Dallas."

"Honey, why you in Dallas?"

It was too complicated to explain.

"I thought you'd be in Norma by now," she added.

Love took a deep breath. "We was on our way."

"What happen?"

Love couldn't answer. He felt the tears rising up in him, and he didn't want her to hear him cry like a little boy.

"Where you callin from? You callin from jail?"

"Naw."

"Where you at, then?" He didn't answer immediately. The rain began to fall harder, and he heard it tapping against the window as it used to at Ruby's when he was younger.

"A friend's house."

"Hold on just a minute, let me get myself up." He heard her adjusting herself in bed.

"Okay now," she said. "Why you callin me so late? You in some kinda trouble?"

"No."

"Well, I've seen plenty of trouble come and go. You tell me what's the matter and I'll see how we can fix it."

"It's Paul."

"I knew it. What's he done?"

"I can't find him."

"What you mean?"

"I mean he's somewhere, but I don't know where."

"You mean you lost him, or he ran away?"

"Both."

He heard Ruby take a deep breath and let it out. "In Dallas?"

"Mm-hm."

"In the station? You think someone mighta took him?"

Love shook his head, but he couldn't answer. It was all his fault, and he'd promised her.

"How long he been gone?"

"Never mind," Love said. "I'll find him."

"How long he been gone?"

"A few days. And we've got to be on the bus tomorrow."

"Listen to me, Love."

"It's raining," he said.

"Listen, Ronal. Have you done everything you can to find him?"

"I don't know what else to do."

"Do what you can. Do everything you can, but you just make sure you get yourself to Norma. I'm going to tell you something. I know I said I sent you out there to save your brother, that's what I said, but it's you I been prayin for, Ronal—Love. I hoped you could both be safe out there, but if you have to, you got to let him go and save yourself."

"But I promised."

"I know what you promised, you promised it to me. But you got to listen now. Not everybody can hold up hisself and someone else too. If two people fall in a river, sometime the one that can swim get pulled down under by the one that can't. You understand. I don't know what kinda trouble Paul got into, but I'm sayin he ain't the reason I sent you out there. My mama's near ninety, and when she goes, all that lan and the house will be yours, you hear?"

"It's my fault," Love said.

"You're not hearing me. You're the last person I still got hope for in my life. Don't let me be disappointed, please Love."

Love felt the tears rise in him again and it choked him. There was a long silence while he tried to get control of his breath. Finally he spoke up.

"I'm going to keep my promise. I'll find him."

"I want you to make me a new promise."

"I got to get off. I'll call you when we get to your mama's."

"You hear me, Love? I want you to make me a new promise."

"We'll call you from Norma."

Ruby let out a long breath. "All right. You be sure to do that."

He hung up the phone and kept his hand on the receiver. He stood there in the dimly lit room, and he could hear his own breathing like someone who'd just been running from something and ducked into a corner. He stood there until his feet got too cold on the floor and he went back into Joyce's room to lie down again.

HE WOKE UP early the next morning to the sound of Joyce in the bathroom.

"You okay?" he asked.

Joyce didn't answer for a second. He heard the toilet flush and the water run, and then she came out.

"I'm fine." She got back in bed and lay close to him again.

They both closed their eyes, but Love was thinking of Li'l Pit waiting in the bus station. He was sure to be there this morning. He might even be waiting already. Love opened his eyes wide in panic now, realizing that Li'l Pit might not know the trunk was in storage, and if he showed up at the station, he'd believe he'd been left behind.

He sat up and pulled on his shirt while Joyce slept. He looked at her and thought of waking her to say good-bye. He wanted to at least put his hand on her hair, but he felt himself getting sad and decided he'd just better go before he thought about staying again. She didn't wake up when he closed the door and slipped out of the house.

It had rained all the previous night, and Love inhaled deeply the cleansed air as he walked away from Joyce's. He walked along the freshly washed streets beside the wet lawns and felt a slight intoxication, a sort of beginning again, but he knew that somewhere in the city, probably in an alley, in a box or even a Dumpster, Li'l Pit had been sleeping in the cold.

He hurried toward the station with his hands in his pockets. He hoped that his brother had perhaps spent the night in the lobby, but when he arrived, he remembered that the benches were divided with ridges so no one could sleep on them. The lobby swarmed with morning passengers holding their Styrofoam coffee cups at arm's length as they ran for their buses. The smell from the diner made Love wish he had eaten before he'd left, or at least gotten money from Joyce, but once he found Li'l Pit, they could rap for enough money to get food for the rest of the trip to Norma. They might get enough money to buy something at the gift shop to bring to Elise, like an Emmitt Smith T-shirt, but she might not even like the Cowboys.

Love hurried through the lobby toward the luggage depot. Then, as he stopped in line at the window, a calm settled over him. It was almost over. Soon Li'l Pit would show up and they'd be off together again, as if this detour had never even happened. He'd have kept his promise to Ruby to get his brother to Norma. And keeping a promise like that surely made you a man, although staying with the woman who you should maybe marry might make you a man too. He wished there was someone else he could ask, who would tell him he was doing the right thing; it seemed that most of the time, to be a man meant to pull yourself away when you felt like doing something easy and to force yourself to do the opposite.

The clerk at the storage window yawned as Love approached. Love handed him his ticket with the baggage tag.

"It's fifteen dollars," said the clerk.

"For what?"

"For the time it was stored."

Love's mind raced through all the options: the clerk was behind a wall, so he couldn't get to him, or to his luggage; there were fancy people in expensive suits with wallets and flashy watches to steal every-where; the store had easy-lift items; he could beg or rap the rest of the day, but fifteen dollars would be more than the food money he needed.

"I didn't know it cost anything."

"It's a storage fee."

"I don't got fifteen dollars." He wasn't going to say it, normally he wouldn't have said it, especially after feeling like such a man. Then he said it, couldn't help but feel it: "I'm just a kid and I didn't know. I'm traveling all by myself with my brother. Can't you let me send it to you or something?"

The clerk took a deep breath and got off his stool. "What's it look like?" Love watched him search through the luggage racks and find the trunk.

"I'm not taking this out myself," the clerk yelled. "You'll have to come back here and get it."

"All right. How do I get in?"

The clerk looked at Love for a moment. "Never mind. I'll do it. Where do you want it?"

"I'm going to South Carolina at noon. I mean, it's the bus to Atlanta, first."

"I'll put it out there later then."

"No, it's got to go out there now. My brother has to see that it's out there in case I'm out looking for him." The clerk shook his head and grabbed the dolly. After a minute of struggling to get the trunk on the lift, he wheeled it out to Love.

"Here. You can take it now yourself." He dumped it on the ground. "No need for a tip." He went back in and took his seat in the window again.

Love dragged his trunk through the station, stopping to rest every few feet. Finally, a man in a fancy suit asked him if he wanted a hand and helped Love carry it the rest of the way. When he got the trunk out by the bus gate, he positioned it behind the ropes but in plain sight. He sat down on it and waited, the sun coming up, reflecting a bright orange off the building across the alley behind the bus lot. He lay on the trunk, curled up in the fetal position, and fell asleep.

HE WOKE TO the blaring of a bus horn and sat up with a start. The corner of his lips stuck together, and his face felt pressed in from the side of his hand. His forehead was hot like he had the flu, and his stomach gnawed at him. He pulled himself off the trunk to find the bathroom, to wash his face and pee. But the trunk pulled him back like tar, and he had to struggle to stand up straight. As soon as he felt that he'd broken free, he realized that he was still lying on the trunk, asleep in a bad dream. He hadn't moved, and his eyes were still closed. He tried again to wake up fully, imagining that he was standing on his way to the bathroom, getting away, but suddenly the illusion broke again and he was trapped on the trunk. He couldn't leave the nightmare. Finally, he gave up the battle and went back to sleep fully; then, without any trouble, he sat up for real.

A line of people stood by the bus parked in front of him. A young man wearing a black "X" cap and holding a University of Pennsylvania bag waited at the end of the line.

"Hey," Love yelled out. "What time is it, man?"

"Time to go."

"No. For real, man."

With some trouble, the young man turned his wrist over. "Eleven-twenty."

"Where's that bus going?"

"Colorado."

"Right on."

"All right."

He definitely didn't want to leave his post at this point, when there was so little time left, but he couldn't ignore his bladder.

He was glad to see Joyce when she walked into the loading area.

"Stay here with my trunk just a second," he said, as if he'd been expecting her.

"Why?"

He didn't even turn back. He ran straight to the bathroom. But after he finished, his mind returned to the situation at hand. He couldn't leave her alone with his trunk too long. If Li'l Pit came by, she'd just scare him off, and she might even get the porter to load his trunk into a cab. He ran back to the loading area as quickly as he'd run from it.

Joyce sat on the trunk, waiting with a smile.

"So you came to say good-bye," he said.

"No. I want you to stay." She stood up and grabbed the handle on one side of the trunk.

"Naw. I told you, I'm not staying. I'm getting on the bus today with my brother."

"Let him go to Norma on his own," she said. "You can find him and give him the ticket and make sure he gets on the bus."

"He can't do nothing on his own." Love looked at her face. Her mouth was slightly open. Her shoulders were round and smooth and her breasts poked into her Tasmanian Devil T-shirt, which seemed a size too small for her.

"He'll make it to Norma," she said. She put her hand on his chest. "And you can stay. At least one more night. I'll buy you another ticket."

He looked her in the eye. "I want to, but I can't."

She turned and looked at the sky above the buses. "I thought you could do anything you wanted."

"I guess I don't want to, then."

She took out a sticky note in the shape of a frog, with her address already written on it in large round letters. "Here."

He took it and stuffed it into his pocket.

There was a high-pitched, sustained honk, but not from a bus this time, from a car in the alley behind the lot. A dark green Lexus, with its windows down, cruised by slowly and stopped with a skid. Love saw the driver look at him, and then a face in the passenger seat leaned forward. It was Li'l Pit. The car sped up again until it passed the driveway.

"Damn," Love said. He jumped off the trunk and jogged through the lot to the alley. Joyce followed.

Love turned left behind the wall and jogged toward the car. He saw three heads in the backseat, but low, without shoulders, the heads of children. He couldn't see Li'l Pit, but there was an older kid in the driver's seat. Love approached the back of the car on the passenger's side. Li'l Pit pushed the door open with his foot and got out.

"Hey, bro," Love said.

"Gimme my jacket," Li'l Pit said.

"Yeah, give him his jacket, motherfucker," a kid yelled from the backseat.

"Shut up," Li'l Pit yelled back into the car. "I can take care of my own business."

Love looked inside. The kid in the back had on a blue wool cap, a joint behind his ear. A girl sat on each side of him, and as Love looked in, the boy put his arms around their shoulders. The girls, like the boy, looked to be about twelve, but they were made up with braided extensions and wore tight satin shorts that outlined their crotches. The driver of the car, maybe Love's own age, didn't say anything. He wore sunglasses and stared straight ahead, chewing on a stick of cinnamon.

"You steal this car?" Love asked Li'l Pit.

"We didn't do no stealin, Officer," the boy in back said, and they all snickered. Li'l Pit left the door open and walked toward Love, but then passed him and kept going toward the lot. Joyce came from around the lot wall, and he knocked into her arm as he passed her.

"Hi, bitch."

"Bitch yourself, bitch," she said.

Li'l Pit stopped, turned to see if the people in the car had noticed, then waved her off and continued to the driveway.

Love slammed the door shut and walked after his brother. He followed him into the lot and caught up to him at the trunk, trying to pick the lock.

"Open this up for me. I got to get my stuff."

"We're leaving," Love said.

Li'l Pit looked up at his brother. "What about her, the ho?" He thrust his chin toward Joyce, who watched them with her hands on her hips.

"We're going to Norma now. It's almost time."

"I ain't goin nowhere no more. I'm down with these dudes now. So give me my jacket."

"You down with those punks? Those fools just got through sucking their mamas' chitas. What you want to be down with them for?"

"Give me the key or I'm gonna bust the trunk open." Li'l Pit stood up and kicked the case.

Joyce walked up behind Love and touched his shoulder. "Where's the award he took?" she asked.

"I sold it," Li'l Pit yelled at her. "It's gone forever, just like I wish you was."

"You better get it back!" she yelled.

Love walked up close to his brother. "You're gonna get on that bus, dog. We got to get you out of this place. It's the last day for the ticket. This is the whole reason we left Oaktown and now you're just back in this shit again."

"These dudes ain't small-time like Cranston. They got Uzis and shit. They got money and they got bitches and we hoo-ride all over town. They let me stay at they pad the last couple a nights, and I told them about South Carolina, and they say it's whack. I'm just gonna have to be out on some farm. They gonna give me a gold watch after we bring this car back. What you never gonna give me?"

"You got to think of your future, dog."

"I is."

"Naw, this ain't no kind of future."

"Whatever."

"You got to come outta here, bro."

Li'l Pit turned to Love suddenly. "I had to stay for you, now you got to stay for me. You got to come with us. I can get you in. They think we the shit, man, 'cause we from Oaktown."

"Naw, I ain't down with that no more. Come on, dog. We got to stick together. We brothers."

"If we got to stick together, how come you don't got to stick with me now? I been stickin with you."

"Naw," Love said. "We're done with all this shit, man."

"I guess you ain't my brother, then. These gonna be my real brothers. They ain't gonna take off on me like you always been doin since we was kids. Gimme my jacket."

"I ain't givin you shit."

"Then I'll just have to get my pahtnahs and we'll come back and jack you up." Li'l Pit walked out of the lot with a heavy side-to-side strut.

Love got his key out of his pocket and opened the trunk, then jammed his hands deep into the pile of clothes, blindly searching until he found the gun. Before bringing it out, he wrapped it up in a black T-shirt and then put it under his arm. The best game plan on the streets was to attack before being attacked. He looked back at Joyce.

"What's that?" she asked, but he could see in her eyes that she already knew.

"See how I am?" he said. "See how I am? You should just go."

"What are you doing?"

He jumped off the platform and headed for the alley with the gun gripped in one hand through the shirt. He rounded the parking-lot wall and saw Li'l Pit standing on the driver's side of the Lexus and the guy with the cinnamon stick listening to him with his head out the window.

"Stay the fuck outta this!" Love yelled to the driver. The boy in the blue cap gave Love the finger through the back window.

The driver opened his door and got out slowly, like he was an old man. He turned toward Love, shielding Li'l Pit, his sunglasses still on.

"What the fuck you want, nigger?" he said.

Love stopped at the back of the car. The boy in the blue cap pushed his way out of the backseat and stood on the passenger's side.

"Yeah, what the fuck you want?"

"This ain't your business," Love said. He held the gun knotted up in his shirt. "Come on, Li'l Pit. Our bus is leaving."

"Yeah, Li'l Pity," the boy in the cap yelled, "you got to get on the school bus."

Li'l Pit didn't move from behind the driver. Love could see the two girls laughing, staring through the window like they were watching a TV show.

"Give the brother his jacket," the driver said with indifference.

Love unwrapped his gun and held it down by his thigh.

"You need to shut up," Love said.

A bus pulled out of the lot behind him, but it turned the opposite direction.

"Let my brother go."

"I ain't stoppin him from goin." The driver spit out his cinnamon stick and reached in his pocket. Love raised the gun, aiming right at his chest.

"Be cool, man." The driver brought out another stick and put it in his mouth.

"Come on, Li'l Pit," Love said. "Elise is waitin."

"Yeah, Pit," the boy said from across the car, "you got to get to your great-grandmama's house before she keel over of a heart attack."

Joyce came into the alley but stopped when she saw Love aiming the gun.

"What are you doing?" she screamed. "Oh my God."

Love turned and saw the fear in her eyes. She ran back around the wall and disappeared into the lot.

"Come on, man," the driver said to Li'l Pit and got back into the car. The boy in the wool cap jumped into the backseat, and Li'l Pit ran around the front of the car to the passenger side, smiling like he was playing tag. The driver started the engine.

Love ran to him, the gun still in his hand. He got there before Li'l Pit could close the door.

"Get out," he yelled at Li'l Pit, aiming the gun at his head, then at the driver. "Turn it off." The driver turned off the car, and Love aimed the gun back at his brother, directly at his temple.

"Get outta the car. Get out."

"Ah, that's cold, blood," said the boy in the back. "Your own brother gonna cap you."

"You got to come with me. I promised Nanna. You got to come."

"Naw," Li'l Pit said. "You come with me."

"What you gonna do," the driver asked, "hold a gun to his head until he get on the bus?"

Love looked at the driver, who faced forward, indifferently, his sunglasses still on.

"You gonna hold a gun to his head the rest a his life?"

The only part of the driver moving was his jaw as he chewed on his cinnamon stick. Love looked at his brother again, who also stared forward, his head tilted slightly away from the gun.

"Stand up, dog," Love said. "Come on, bro. This ain't no game. This ain't funny." He grabbed Li'l Pit's shirt with his free hand and pulled him out of the car. Though Li'l Pit didn't struggle, he didn't go willingly either. He stepped out and stood where his brother held him, the gun at the side of his head.

The driver started the car again.

"Let me go," Li'l Pit yelled.

The driver pressed on the gas and the car began to move forward, slowly at first.

"Let me go," Li'l Pit yelled again. The car moved away with its door open, then stopped for the boy in the cap to jump out of the backseat, hop in the front, and close the door. "Peace out, muther fuckers," the boy yelled. Then the car sped off and turned the corner without stopping, the screech of the tires echoing off the high buildings.

Love and Li'l Pit stood alone in the alleyway, Love still aiming the gun at his brother's head. There were sirens a long way off in the distance. They might have been sirens for them or for a different reason—for a bank robbery, or a murder, or for a million other things going on somewhere in the city—but eventually they would be sirens for them.

Li'l Pit slowly turned his eyes toward Love, so the gun pointed directly at his forehead. Love studied Li'l Pit's face, the sickle part in his hair, his small ears and round head. He could see the muscles clenching and unclenching in Li'l Pit's jaw. But Li'l Pit's eyes were not angry or frightened. They were blank, almost empty, just waiting for the next thing to happen, for Love to make the next move.

Love shook his head. There didn't seem to be any other choice. He lowered the gun to his side. They stood a foot apart, looking directly into each other's eyes, their chests heaving, but neither of them spoke. Then Love turned, and he walked toward the bus lot, steadily, without looking back. He listened for Li'l Pit's footsteps. He listened with more of his mind behind him than in front. He kept walking until he reached the driveway and then stopped. He could see into the lot. The people were already in line for his bus, and there was no sign of Joyce or his trunk.

When he turned back to the alley, Li'l Pit was still standing in the same place he'd left him.

"I'm goin, bro," Love yelled. "For real." He tossed the gun into a patch of tall grass by the wall. Li'l Pit still didn't move. Love waited for a second. Li'l Pit's hands were down by his sides, not a muscle on him moving. Love turned and walked into the lot, closing his eyes briefly in the sun.

When he reached the bus, he checked underneath and made sure the trunk had been loaded. It was there, with the duffel bags and suitcases of the other passengers on top of it. He looked back toward the driveway, but it was empty. He took the first step up onto the bus. It was high off the ground, and he had to pull himself up by the metal handrails. He climbed each step slowly, his thighs straining as he pushed up to the next one. At the top of the stairs, he paused and looked down the aisle at the passengers and rows of seats. He slapped his hand along the top of each empty row until he reached the middle of the bus and swung into a window seat, from which he could see the lot and the platform where Joyce had been.

The driver stood outside smoking a cigarette, his hair flapping in the sudden bursts of wind that just as quickly disappeared. The cigarette was only half smoked when he tossed it onto the ground and stepped on it with the tip of his boot, pressing and twisting with the full weight of his body. He then walked to the door of the bus and adjusted his mirror, looked at himself, rolled his eyes, and stepped up almost as slowly as Love.

"Okay, folks. This bus stops in Longview, then heads into Louisiana, Shreveport, Monroe; Mississippi, Jackson, Meridian; up to Birmingham, Alabama, and to its final resting place in Atlanta, where you may catch another bus to many fine places along our eastern seaboard, to which I will not be driving. If you believe you are on the wrong bus, then this is the time for you to off-board, unload, exit, depart, and abandon ship.

I'll be coming around to take your tickets presently, but please know that you are responsible for getting off at the right stop. You will be charged for any extra mileage you incur. Thank you for traveling with us."

The driver walked to the back and checked passengers' tickets, marked them, and placed a small coupon on the luggage rack above. When he came to Love, he opened the ticket jacket and looked in.

"You've got somebody else traveling with you today?"

Love shrugged his shoulders.

"Well, you've got two tickets. Is your mother on board?"

Love shook his head.

"Your father?"

"No."

"Anyone?"

"My brother's sposed to come on."

"Well, he needs to hurry up. I'll mark his ticket for him now."

The driver returned the tickets to Love and finished with the rest of the passengers. He made a head count on his way back up and then sat down in his seat. He started the engine, but didn't close the doors. He looked back at Love with his eyebrows raised.

"He ain't comin," Love yelled up to him. "Let's just go."

"All right." The driver closed the door and reversed the bus out into the center of the lot. Love looked at the platform and half expected Joyce to come out of the building and run after the bus, but the platform was empty.

The driver turned the bus around and then headed for the exit. They stopped at the edge of the driveway, the wall of the station blocking Love's view of the alley. He got ready to look. The bus jerked into gear with a lurch forward, then a stop, and then forward again. Then it steadied and gained momentum into the turn. For an instant, Love pressed his face against the window, straining to see. But Li'l Pit was not in the alley anymore.

The bus finished its turn and moved slowly past the Dumpsters and fire escapes of the buildings. When it reached the corner, it stopped again. The turn signal slapped loudly within the passenger cabin. Love looked up the sidewalks on both sides of the street. He looked past the stoplights as far as he could see, and between parked cars. The engines revved and the bus moved forward again, slowly pushing out into the middle of the intersection. Love stood up in the space in front of his seat, his hand still on the window. He looked frantically at every person along the sidewalk, at every crevice and shadow, behind trash cans and into doorways, but he didn't see his brother. The river of cars in the street let up and the driver inched the bus forward.

Then Love saw something move behind a mailbox at the near corner. Li'l Pit's face stuck out above the curved blue top. Love knocked on the window. He couldn't be sure Li'l Pit saw him through the tinted glass, but he was staring at the middle of the bus as if he could. Love pushed on the window; he wanted to break through the glass and grab his brother and pull him up onto the bus. It seemed that Li'l Pit could see him, that their eyes met for a second.

"Hey, bro, what you doin?" Love said softly.

The bus moved forward again, farther into the street. Li'l Pit smiled. He lifted his hand, then waved to all the windows. The bus turned, and Love twisted to see behind him, stood on his toes, his face pressed against the window.

"Good luck, li'l man," he said. He remained standing as the bus drove up the street, past the convention center, the gas station to the highway entrance. The bus climbed the on-ramp, and Love slowly sat back down in his seat.

The bus's engines strained to gain enough speed to merge into the flow of traffic. The sun was now high above in the winter sky, illuminating the metal and glass buildings of Dallas with a dull glare. Love looked away from the window and faced forward. As the bus drove out of the city, he took his tape player out of his jacket pocket, pulled on his headphones, and pushed play.

SANTA RITA JAIL

WHO AM I to be standing up here pontificating and prognosticating? Who am I, up here every week before you with a book of history and a brown face? Who am I to tell you who you are and from where we came?

I'm not surprised you have to ask, though I have been telling you all along. I've been reading to you my arms, I've been shouting out my back, I've been crying to you my shoulders, and I've been laughing to you my eyes. I've been showing you the raft I stand on, and I've shown you the shore I want to reach, and I've shown you the River that surrounds us, that has brought me to this place downstream. I've been telling you all along. I've been telling me.

So is it clear? Can you see me? Don't you know me? Would it help if I told you my height, my weight, my crime, my name? Would it help if I told you I was a poet, a singer, a mythmaker, and a storyteller: if I rapped a line, sold a dime, slipped out of time?

It would still be unclear, as unclear as it has been to me all my life. I'm still as invisible to you and to myself as if I'd never looked into the mirror of that muddy River. And now I wish I could just forget it all, pretend that it never happened. I know you do too: you always tell me in the yard that you wish you could just forget that River and move on. You want to drown me in it and leave us behind. You want to forget us and just be. And I say: I want to forget it too! I swear, I wish I could forget it more than I wish anything in the world; but it rushes by my feet every day and sprays upon my face every morning.

I'm done reading to you, but I still have one more story to tell before I get out. It's not from one of these books in the library, but it begins where the books leave off. It's the last log of my raft, the one that didn't seem to fit until just now, until I'd finished laying the other ones down. It's a story my grandmother told me more than twenty years ago. It ends with me and passes to you, but it begins before I was born, before my older brother was born. It begins on June 19, 1959, when my grandmother, Ruby Washington, traveled through Texas on a bus from Norma, South Carolina, to Oakland, California, with her thirteen-year-old half brother, Love Easton Childers.

WORKS CITED

Brown, Claude, *Manchild in the Promised Land.* New York: Macmillan, 1990.

Craft, William and Ellen. "The Escape of William and Ellen Craft from Slavery." 1860. *Great Slave Narratives,* ed. Arna Bontemps. Boston: Beacon Press, 1969.

Drake, St. Clare, and Horace R. Cayton. *Black Metropolis: A Study of Negro Life in a Northern City.* New York: Fawcett Premier, 1968.

Equiano, Olaudah. "Life of Gustavus Vassa, the African." 1789. *Great Slave Narratives,* ed. Arna Bontemps. Boston: Beacon Press, 1969.

Grant, Joanne, ed. *Black Protest: History, Documents, and Analyses 1619 to the Present.* New York: Fawcett Premier, 1968.

————. "Mississippi Law of 1864." Rptd. in *Black Protest: History, Documents, and Analyses 1619 to the Present.* New York: Fawcett Premier, 1968.

Holt, Hamilton, ed. "Hell Itself." *The Life Stories of Undistinguished Americans as Told by Themselves.* 1906. Rptd. in *Black Americans: History in Their Own Words,* ed. Milton Meltzer. New York: HarperCollins, 1984.

Mannix, Daniel, and Malcolm Cowley. "The Middle Passage." *Black Cargoes: A History of the Atlantic Slave Trade.* 1962. Rptd. in *Justice Denied,* eds. William M. Chace and Peter Collier. New York: Harcourt, 1970.

Meier, August, and Elliot M. Rudwick. *From Plantation to Ghetto: An Interpretive History of American Negroes.* New York: Hill and Wang, 1966.

Parsons, C. G. *Inside View of Slavery.* 1853. "Day to Day Resistance to Slavery," *Journal of Negro History XXVII.* Raymond A. Bauer and Alice H. Bauer. 1942. Rptd. in *Black Protest: History, Documents, and Analyses 1619 to the Present,* ed. Joanne Grant. New York: Fawcett Premier, 1968.

Pennington, James W. C. "The Fugitive Blacksmith or Events in the History of

James W. C. Pennington." 1849. *Great Slave Narratives,* ed. Arna Bontemps. Boston: Beacon Press, 1969.

Phillips, Ulrich B. *American Negro Slavery.* Rptd. in "Day to Day Resistance to Slavery," *Journal of Negro History XXVII.* Raymond A. Bauer and Alice H. Bauer. 1942. Rptd. in *Black Protest: History, Documents, and Analyses 1619 to the Present,* ed. Joanne Grant. New York: Fawcett Premier, 1968.

Report of the National Advisory Commission on Civil Disorders. New York: Government Printing Office and The New York Times Company, 1968.

Stampp, Kenneth. "Troublesome Property." *The Peculiar Institution.* New York: Vintage, 1956. Rptd. in *Justice Denied,* eds. William M. Chace and Peter Collier. New York: Harcourt, 1970.

Washington, Booker T. *Up from Slavery.* New York: Doubleday, Page & Co., 1901.

ADDITIONAL SOURCES

Baldwin, James. *The Price of the Ticket.* New York: St. Martin's/Marek, 1985.

Bing, Léon. *Do or Die.* New York: Harper Perennial, 1992.

Blauner, Bob. *Black Lives, White Lives: Three Decades of Race Relations in America.* Berkeley: University of California Press, 1989.

Brown, Elaine. *A Taste of Power: A Black Woman's Story.* New York: Pantheon Books, 1992.

Ellison, Ralph. *Invisible Man.* New York: Vintage Books, 1995.

Frazier, E. Franklin. "Hagar and Her Children." Rptd. in *Justice Denied,* eds. William M. Chace and Peter Collier. New York: Harcourt, 1970.

Gaines, Ernest J. *A Gathering of Old Men.* New York: Knopf, 1983.

Hilliard, David, and Lewis Cole. *This Side of Glory: The Autobiography of David Hilliard and the Story of the Black Panther Party.* New York: Little, Brown, 1993.

Lacy, Dan. *The White Use of Blacks in America.* New York: Atheneum Books, 1972.

Lemann, Nicholas. *The Promised Land: The Great Black Migration and How It Changed America.* New York: Vintage, 1992.

Mfume, Kweisi, et al. *No Free Ride: From the Mean Streets to the Mainstream.* New York: Ballantine, 1997.

Praetzellis, Mary, ed. *West Oakland—A Place to Start From: Research Design and Treatment Plan Cypress I–880 Replacement Project. Vol. 1: Historical Archaeology.* Oakland: California Department of Transportation, 1994.

Spalding, Henry D., ed. *Encyclopedia of Black Folklore and Humor.* Middle Village, N.Y.: Jonathan David Publishers, 1990.

Wolters, Raymond. *Negroes and the Great Depression: The Problem of Economic Recovery.* Westport, Conn.: Greenwood Publishing Corporation, 1970.

Wright, Richard. *Black Boy.* New York: Harper & Row, 1966.

X, Malcolm, and Alex Haley. *The Autobiography of Malcolm X as Told to Alex Haley.* New York: Grove Press, 1964.

ACKNOWLEDGMENTS

I would like to thank all of the people who contributed their time and energy to helping me research, revise, and publish this work.

A special thank-you to Orson Bean and Alley Mills for your encouragement and support.

To Robert Loomis, David Blastband, Bill Henderson, and Theresa Parks: Thank you for helping me navigate the waters. Thank you to the family of Ruby Lott for opening your homes to me and giving me a taste of Saluda; to Dennis and Mary Johnson for your stories and your warmth; and to Phyllis Burke for believing in me and telling me so.

To Seneca Center and the Daraja Project, thank you for giving me the chance to contribute. My deep appreciation to Patty Lemele and Paul Guay, my first readers; to Mara Melandry at CalTrans; and to my friends in many parts of the country who helped fill in the details. Thank you, also, to those of you upon whose shoulders I stand, those who have written your stories for the rest of us.

Finally, I am greatly indebted to my agent, Victoria Sanders; my editor, George Witte; and the staff at St. Martin's Press. Thank you for your fine work and for your dedication to this project.